The Old Vicarage
A Novel

by

Catherine Anne Austen Hubback

Double 9
BOOKS

The Old Vicarage
A Novel
by Catherine Anne Austen Hubback

ISBN: 978-93-58592-85-6

Published by

DOUBLE 9 BOOKS

2/13-B, Ansari Road
Daryaganj, New Delhi – 110002
info@double9books.com
www.double9books.com
Tel. 011-40042856

ABOUT THE AUTHOR

Catherine Anne Hubback, the niece of renowned novelist Jane Austen, led a challenging life as an English novelist. After her husband's institutionalization, she turned to writing fiction to support herself and her three sons. Drawing inspiration from her aunt's unfinished works, she completed "The Younger Sister" in 1850, a continuation of Jane Austen's "The Watsons." Over the next thirteen years, Hubback wrote nine more novels. In 1870, she immigrated to California, settling in Oakland with her second son. However, her novels, which were once popular, have now fallen into obscurity and are difficult to find. Hubback's most notable work is "The Younger Sister." Sadly, she passed away in Gainesville, Virginia, in 1877 due to pneumonia. Although her novels are rarely read today, her contribution to the literary world and her connection to Jane Austen remain a part of her legacy.

CONTENTS

CHAPTER I. 7

CHAPTER II. 19

CHAPTER III. 32

CHAPTER IV. 43

CHAPTER V. 55

CHAPTER VI. 70

CHAPTER VII. 83

CHAPTER VIII. 96

CHAPTER IX. 112

CHAPTER X. 125

CHAPTER XI. 140

CHAPTER XII. 156

CHAPTER XIII. 170

CHAPTER XIV. 182

CHAPTER XV. 198

CHAPTER XVI. 214

CHAPTER XVII. 226

CHAPTER XVIII. 243

CHAPTER XIX. 256

CHAPTER XX. 269

CHAPTER XXI. 283

CHAPTER XXII. 298

CHAPTER XXIII. 313

CHAPTER XXIV. 328

CHAPTER XXV. 338

CHAPTER I.

"Children's voices should be dear
(Call once more) to a mother's ear;
Children's voices wild with pain,
Surely she will come again;
Call her once, and come away!"

The Forsaken Merman.

It was a summer's evening. The yellow sunshine streamed through the boles of the forest trees, tinting them with purple, vermilion, gold, or the richest brown. It gave a metallic luster to the tops of the giant oaks, and lighted up with a silvery gleam the long feathery sprays of the graceful beech-trees, waving gently and slowly as the soft breeze passed rustling among them. The same slanting sunbeams fell on the dark glossy foliage of the tall groups of holly, and twinkled like stars upon their stiff-pointed leaves.

Beneath these ancient and hoary trees, on a natural terrace clothed with soft mossy turf, and commanding, along the glade in the forest, a full view of the glowing west, there walked, with slow and lingering step, two persons, who seemed too deeply engrossed in conversation to heed the loveliness of the evening. One of these was a woman, who might perhaps be half way between thirty and forty, but still possessing a large share of personal beauty; tall, dark, glowing, with bright black eyes, and hair as black as jet, parted off her forehead in rich braids, and as she carried her bonnet in her hand, they caught the gleaming sunshine, and seemed to turn purple in its splendor. Her companion was a young girl, slender, fair, and rather pale, except that as she listened to the earnest discourse of the matron, the flitting color dyed her cheek for a moment, and then left it pale again. Her slim figure, and girlish proportions, gave a notion of extreme youth and delicacy, and yet her face was of that kind which brings a feeling of trust and repose as you gaze upon it; an idea that, young as she was, there was steadiness and principle to be read there.

"But, dear mamma," said the girl, "why do you talk in this way? You will soon be about again, and able to see all these things yourself."

And she gazed with earnest, anxious fondness at the face of her companion, unable to realize that danger could lurk near, or death invade a countenance so healthy, and so invariably cheerful.

"His will be done," said Mrs. Duncan, raising her eyes, and fixing them on the glowing west. "Life and death are in His hands; but, Hilary, it will neither increase my danger, nor my anxiety, if I give you such directions as may be your help and guide hereafter. It is a great charge, a heavy responsibility which will fall on you, should I be taken from you, but one which will not be laid on you, unless He sees good; and received from Him in a humble, trusting, loving spirit, the event will be blessed. In my weakness and want of faith, I shrink from the idea, sometimes; but I know that all is, all will be right, if you can but believe, and feel it so. Nothing He lays on us is too heavy to bear, if we do not add to it the burden of our own selfish repinings, mistrust, and impatience."

"Oh! mamma, it can not be best to be without you; such a trial can not be in store for us; for my father too—how could he bear it? and surely be so good, so heavenly-minded, so tender as he is—oh! he can not need affliction; do not talk so, mamma, do not fancy such things; you will do yourself harm by dwelling on it."

Mrs. Duncan's eyes filled, and her lip quivered for a minute; she was silent a little space, and then she spoke again, calmly, firmly, gravely.

"Hilary, ever since I have filled your mother's place, I have met with the duty and affection of a daughter from you. I came to you when you were too young to understand my claims, but I have never had to complain, so far as our relationship is concerned. Be ever the same! do not now, by giving way to your feelings, make it more difficult for me to control my own. Try to listen to what may be my last wishes."

Hilary clasped her step-mother's hand, struggled with her rising tears, swallowed down a sob or two, and then turning quietly round, said—"Go on, dear mother! I will attend, and endeavor to remember."

"Young as you are, Hilary, I do not fear to trust you, for I know that you have that within you which will lead you right. Experience, indeed, you can not have, and you may mistake sometimes; but with your earnest love of truth, your simplicity, candor, gentleness, and humility, you can not go very far wrong; and I would rather confide my girls to you, than to many an elder head. I know that you will lean on the true, unfailing Support—that you will not trust your own understanding."

"Dear mother, if I have any good principle or right habit, I owe it to you and papa; what should I have been, had you not led me so kindly and gently in childhood?" said Hilary, blushing at the praise which she could not believe she deserved.

"But my girls are not like you, Hilary," continued the mother, "and their characters have cost me many an anxious hour. Heaven knows how earnestly I have prayed sometimes, to be spared as their guide; but this is self-will, and self-conceit, perhaps; now my only prayer is, that, in whose hands soever they may fall, whatever troubles may come upon them, they may be brought home safe at last. We are so unbelieving, we would fain choose our own path, and the paths of our dear ones also; as if our narrow view could be better trusted than His, who has told us so plainly what we ought to seek, and what we may then hope for. All will be right at last, and now I trust them entirely to the Will which can not err: yet not the less would I warn you, Hilary, of the care and discipline they need. Sybil is tender, loving, feeble, clinging for support to those around her; do not act for her, my love; make her feel her own responsibility, or the realities and cares of life will fall with a crushing force on her. Look at the clematis which garlands this lime—such is she; take away her support, and the long wreaths will droop and sink to the earth, and may be trampled by every careless foot."

"But we can not change the nature of the clematis, mamma; we can only prop it up, and guard it carefully, and rejoice even in its clinging, graceful fragility, which gives a beauty to the bare and rugged stem, or the unpoetical wall and trellis."

"True, you can not change the clematis, Hilary; but therein a Christian differs from a soulless plant; her nature may be strengthened by attention and discipline, till she may be firm and yet flexible; yielding and yet self-supporting; regaining with elastic vigor the upward tendency, even after the hand has bent it down, or the breeze turned it aside. You can not make a clematis into a willow, but you may teach a feeble mind and drooping heart where to find strength of purpose and constancy of aim. Teach Sybil that the weakest may have strength sufficient to their need, but not in earthly things; earthly props break and crumble away, or are removed in kindness, lest we lean too much upon them. Trust to the One above. He never fails. Poor Sybil! she is very far from knowing this as yet!"

They were both silent for some time; then Mrs. Duncan seated herself, and continued, as Hilary nestled close to her side.

"As to Gwyneth, she is different; she has all the passionate and hasty nature of my country. Welsh blood runs in her veins, and along with this warmth she has much self-will and presumption; she doubts not her own opinion, and can not bear to have it questioned; yet she is so young that I have every reason to hope that attention may check what is wrong, and religion lead her to true strength and confidence. And then for my little Nest—the darling! who can tell what that little black-eyed, bewitching fairy may turn out? Heaven help me! but it is hard to think of leaving her."

Mrs. Duncan shuddered, and closed her eyes, as if struggling with some deep emotion.

"Why should you?" said Hilary, anxiously. "Dearest mother, do you feel ill now? It is so long since you have had one of your bad attacks of pain; not for months now; I am sure you need not be alarmed."

Mrs. Duncan smiled; a faint smile it was, as if she would rather put aside a subject of discussion than enter on it. Then, after a pause, she added, "I believe you will find all my papers and accounts quite clear, and for the rest, dear Hilary, you are well able to take my place in the parish now; and whatever may occur, you must do it for a month at least. But there are horses' feet upon the turf; your father and sisters are coming home. Say nothing at present of what I have told you, and let us go to meet them!"

They rose, and advanced toward the house; crossing a part of the garden, of which the terrace where they had been walking formed the eastern boundary. Dividing the lawn from an open green space which lay in front of the old rectory, was a line of wooden palings nearly covered by ivy, honeysuckle, roses, and many flowering shrubs, and over this they saw, approaching through a shadowy glade, three forest ponies; the tallest bore Mr. Duncan, an elderly man, whose figure was, however, active and upright, and his countenance marked with the glow of health and the look of peace; the other two riders were girls, the Sybil and Gwyneth already mentioned, whose black eyes, and long waving locks flowing from beneath their broad-brimmed straw hats, immediately reminded you of their mother. The children, for they were only girls of twelve and thirteen, sprung from their little ponies, and rushed up to the garden gate, just as Mrs. Duncan and Hilary reached it; and before their father had descended in his more leisurely way, and consigned the animals to the old gray-headed servant who came forward to receive them, they had advanced far in the history of their ride, its adventures, delights, and novelties. They had found a new path, had come to a beautiful stream; Gwyneth had leaped her horse across before papa came up; Sybil was afraid, and had hung back, even when encouraged by him; then they had seen such a lovely dell, all surrounded with trees—oh! such a place for a gipsey party; mamma must come there some day, and they would have tea out there, under the huge oaks and beech, beside that broken mossy bank, out of which such a bright tiny stream trickled from under a gray stone. Up came papa, and listened to the eager speaker, as Gwyneth, with her cheeks glowing, and her bright eyes glittering, dwelt with rather too much complacency, perhaps, upon the courage she had shown, until her father reminded her, with laughing but affectionate manner, how Gwyneth herself had shrunk and trembled when, as they were leading their ponies down a steep and precipitous path, a large toad had crossed the road, and hopped toward her; while Sybil's only care had been that the creature should not be hurt by foot or hoof; and after that, Gwyneth held her tongue for a while.

They sat in the large wide porch, which, with its projecting gable and curiously-carved roof, formed so conspicuous an ornament to the front of the Vicarage, and harmonized so well with the many angles, overhanging eaves, mullioned windows, and twisted chimneys of that quaint old house. It was a building well suited to the forest scenery on which it closely bordered, with its time-mellowed red-brick, and gray stone coignings, and huge oaken beams, whose ends were grotesquely carved. From that porch you could see the old church, half concealed in a grove of trees, principally lime and sycamore; and further off, the houses scattered on the village green, or retreating back amid the clumps of oak and holly; while to the south, through a long vista in the forest, you caught a view of distant hills, blue and shadowy, and a winding river, and a wide extended plain.

Here they sat and chatted gayly, while the young girls ate the fruit and cake, for which their ride had given them an appetite, and which Hilary brought out to them in an old-fashioned china basket, until the hour of bed-time arrived, and the children left them; and then the others returned to the cool parlor, where Hilary made tea, and smiled and chatted with her father; Mrs. Duncan meanwhile resting quietly on the sofa, nearly silent, and perhaps engrossed in thought.

Hilary's was the hopeful as well as the trustful temper of youth, unaccustomed to the vicissitudes of life; the storm of which she saw no symptoms could not alarm her; and although her step-mother's presentiments had at first raised a vague terror, she had recovered from this feeling, and was now tranquil.

The trust which she felt that all would be for the best, conspired to increase this peaceful state, for to her young mind, it seemed impossible that good could spring from such sorrow as the loss of the only mother she had known, would occasion her and her family; therefore this loss was not to be expected or feared. Hers was the youthful idea of divine protection, and fatherly care; years of experience alone can teach us that "His ways are not as ours," and that it is not exemption from suffering which is promised to His children, but such discipline as shall strengthen, and purify, and elevate their hearts.

It was a cheerful family party on which the bright summer moon peeped in through the old windows that evening; and Hilary, as she penned a few words at night, of the journal which she always kept for her only brother Maurice, recorded with a grateful heart, that hers was indeed a happy lot.

Yet scarce was the ink dry on the paper where she wrote these lines, than her pleasant dreams were suddenly dissipated, and the very sorrow which she had refused to consider as probable, was presented to her mind. Mrs. Duncan was ill—very ill—alarmingly so; and before that sun which had set in such glory, returned to their view, the eyes that had gazed on it so earnestly were closed in death, and the spirit which had looked out so clear and loving but twelve hours before, had fled to that land which needs no sun to lighten it, and which knows neither change, nor time, nor darkness.

The mother just now in all the prime of womanhood, in her glorious beauty, was cold, and white, and silent, and on her arm lay the tiny marble face of that little being, whose entrance to this world had cost his parents such a price, and whose stay had been so short, that you wondered why he came at all.

On Hilary devolved the task of making her young sisters acquainted with their loss; of communicating to them the sad change that one night had occasioned; for this, when all was over, and her father had withdrawn to the solitude of his own study, she crept softly to their sleeping apartment, and sitting down beside the bed, watched patiently and silently for their first awaking.

Her grief was very quiet, although very deep. In idea she tried to follow the departed, and to realize what she now was, so far as mortal fancy might paint it; and the glad, solemn, mysterious thought, that that dear one had felt her last grief, suffered her last pain, heaved her last sigh forever, made it seem even a profanation to indulge regret. It was when she permitted her thoughts to anticipate, that she shuddered and mourned; it was the future for herself, her sisters, her father, which made her tremble. How barren and blank it seemed; the sweet voice which had taught and soothed her, silent now; the bright smile vanished forever; the sunshine of the house gone; who would fill her place? Could it be that she so young, so simple, so inexperienced, that she should be called on to attempt this heavy duty? did it devolve on her to soothe, instruct, watch over her sisters, to think for the household, to comfort her bereaved father, assist in lightening his cares, or sharing his anxieties? *She* had told her such would be her duty—had bid her reflect on the responsibilities laid on her; had warned, encouraged, and comforted her—and as she had spoken so, Hilary had felt strong and trustful; but now—oh! how miserably weak, ignorant, helpless, and deficient she appeared to herself; the memory of all her own girlish faults, indolence, thoughtlessness, ignorance, selfish indulgences, idle ways, all the many failings for which she daily judged and condemned herself, rose up in her mind, and seemed to say, "impossible;" seemed to whisper to her that her task was harder than she could endure; that such a life of carefulness and watching, and thought for others, and denial of self, as her mother had depicted for her, *could* not be expected of one so young; it would wither her youth, and blight her spirit, and darken all the gay happiness which ought to be hers!

Nay, but it was her duty! it was *God's* will, and as such, it could not be too hard; her burden would not be greater than she could bear; more would not be expected of her than she would have power to perform; could she but fix her eyes aright, and draw strength from the Source of everlasting strength, she should not find it fail; weak, trembling, insufficient as she was, she need not fear, if she only trusted all to Him, and nothing to herself. And then a voice seemed to whisper to her heart,

"Child of my love, how have I wearied thee,
Why wilt thou err from me?"

and half unconsciously she repeated to herself the succeeding lines of the same hymn; there was soothing in the thought.

Yet ever and again, as she grew calmer, came rushing in the painful memory of her loss; and while she doubted not the wisdom and mercy which had ordered all, and accepted meekly the burden of care which seemed laid on her, her heart ached in bitterness when she remembered what had been, and what was.

That hour of watching and waiting was intensely trying. She had been occupied all the night, so eagerly and energetically, as to exclude thought or anticipation; now she could only sit in silence, and weary, worn out, sorrowful, and yet striving to be patient, remain quietly expecting the painful task before her.

She wished to keep awake, and opening her Bible, she tried to fix her eyes and thoughts upon it, and determined so to pass the time; but blessed sleep stole over her so softly, that she knew not of its approaches, and the tearful eyes closed, the heavy head dropped upon the pillow beside it, and a deep unconsciousness, a perfect dreamless repose wrapped all the past in oblivion, and brought the refreshment which that young, but willing spirit needed to fulfil her destined task. "He giveth His beloved sleep."

Gwyneth was astonished that morning, when, on unclosing her eyes, she discovered her eldest sister, half sitting, half lying on her pillow, dressed as last night, and yet sleeping profoundly, even though tears trembled on her eye-lashes, while her long and glossy brown hair lay unbound and unbraided over her neck and cheek.

With the thoughtless impulse of her nature, she at once woke her up, and eagerly inquired why she was there, what was the matter, what had made her cry.

That sudden waking bewildered Hilary; the vague, puzzled feeling which so often follows deep sleep, at an unusual time, or in an unaccustomed place, came over her, and for a minute she could remember nothing; not where she was, nor what had happened, nor why she found herself so strangely sleeping there. She pressed her hands over her eyes; the full tide of thought and memory came back, and she shrank from the pain she was about to give. But it must be done! yes, and done by her too, or the task would fall on her father, perhaps; and done at once, that the first wild agony of tears and grief might be stilled and composed in part before it came to add to that father's pain and desolation.

She drew the two rosy faces toward her, for Sybil was awake now, and pressing each in her arms, as they knelt or crouched upon the bed, she faltered out the words, through her tears,

"Mamma has been ill in the night!"

Gwyneth fixed her full dark eyes upon her sister's face with a gaze which seemed to ask for more, for some explanation. Sybil gave a frightened start, and said,

"Oh, Hilary, and how is she now?—has she been very ill?"

"Very," replied Hilary, forcing back her tears, and speaking gravely, calmly, but very sadly; "very ill indeed; but, Sybil, she is better now!"

Gwyneth still stared at Hilary. "Then why were you crying?" was her question.

"Let me go to her," said Sybil, struggling to release herself from her sister's clasp, which, however, now bound her the closer for her efforts to move. Sybil was quiet without a word, only glancing apprehensively at the face hanging over her, with brimming eyelids and quivering lips. Gwyneth exclaimed again impatiently,

"Speak, Hilary, or let me go;—nay, I *will* go to mamma."

"No, Gwyneth, you can not," said the elder sister, laying her forehead down on her sister's black curls.

"Who says so?—did she? she never refuses to see us! how unkind you are, Hilary."

"A higher hand than mine, dear Gwyneth—be quiet; you can not see mamma now, because—" and such a deep, heartfelt sob stopped her words, that Sybil saw it all in one moment, and quietly turning from them both, laid her head among the pillows, and, except for a slight convulsive shiver now and then, was still and silent.

"Why, why, where is mamma?" cried Gwyneth, fighting with the wild, incomprehensible terror which was overpowering her.

"In heaven, we trust," said Hilary, regaining her composure in a wonderful way; she pressed one hand upon her heart, made a strong physical effort to put away her grief, and then endeavored to draw Sybil toward her, hoping that the sight of her tears would touch Gwyneth's heart. For Gwyneth sat still now, with wide open, tearless eyes, and parted lips, and cheeks as colorless as her neck; and her breath came slowly and with difficulty, and in deep, sobbing inspirations, and yet there was no tear; it was not like childish grief, it was the stillness of despair—her face might have belonged to a woman of thirty, so old it looked at that moment.

Hilary felt helpless at first; then her whole heart was raised in prayer; words not her own came to her mind, to express her thoughts and wants, as she prayed that in all her troubles she might put her whole trust and confidence in that mercy which would not, could not fail.

Sense and feeling returned to Gwyneth, and with it the self-will, the passionate independence of her character. Hilary's arms had relaxed their hold: she seized the opportunity, escaped from the grasp, and springing from the bed, ran out of the room without so much as pausing to put her feet into her slippers. She crossed the broad passage, and rushing to the door of her mother's chamber, tried violently to force it open. It was locked. Hilary had followed the willful child, and now laid her hand upon her arm. But Gwyneth screamed, bursting into a furious passion, and uttering cries which resounded through the otherwise silent house. It was a mixture of feelings, terror undefined, and therefore the more oppressive, grief, vexation, anger—she could not well have told what it was; but the utterance of these wild screams for a moment relieved her, and appeared to throw off the weight on her heart.

In vain Hilary tried to soothe, to quiet, to command; her gentle voice was unheard, and Gwyneth, clinging to the handle of the door, and hiding her face on her arms, continued to scream with increasing energy. The old nurse appeared, and tried what she could do; but interjectory addresses, supplications, and entreaties, were unnoticed, and force made matters worse; when suddenly the door unclosed from the inside, and Gwyneth was only saved from falling on the floor by being caught in her father's arms.

The screams stopped instantly; she gave one glance at his pale, sad face, then hid her own upon his shoulder, and indulged in a copious and passionate burst of tears. He held her quietly and gravely, without a word. Hilary stood with the feelings of a culprit; it seemed to her as if in her very first endeavor, she had failed entirely of all she ought to have done; she blamed herself for her sister's willfulness, and changing color and trembling, waited for what might follow.

By degrees Gwyneth's sobs subsided, and she lay quiet in her father's arms.

"What is all this?" said he at length, glancing at his eldest daughter. She could not answer.

Gwyneth whispered, "Mamma—I want mamma." Hilary looked up hastily and fearfully at her father's face. A sadder shade swept over it, like the darkening gloom which precedes the heavy shower; then it passed away, and the quivering lip was still.

"Hilary, love, does she not know?" said he, gently, and drawing her close to him.

Hilary conquered the rising inclination to give way to tears; it was a hard struggle first, however, but she felt she must answer, and to her own surprise her voice came.

"I tried, papa, to tell her; but she would not believe—she can not understand—she is so young, and feels so acutely; oh, papa! it was my fault, I did not know how!"

"My poor child," said he, as he stooped and kissed her forehead, after anxiously scanning her pale cheeks and weary eyes; "you have had no rest; you have overtasked yourself: you should have gone to bed."

"Never mind me, papa dear! I shall do well enough, but let me take Gwyneth back, she will be cold. Come Gwyneth."

But the child rebelled again, clung to her father, and seemed about to renew her shrieks.

"Hush, hush! this will not do," said he, "this must not be. Be still, Gwyneth, and you shall see your mother once more."

He stepped into the darkened room, whose grave and solemn aspect hushed the mourner's emotion at once. He opened one shutter a little way;

the bright morning sun streamed in upon the white bed-curtains, and danced upon the toilet-glass. He brought his young daughter, clinging to his arms, to the bed, drew back the curtain, lifted the sheet, and Gwyneth's eyes fell on the cold, still face of her, for whom she had called in vain.

Words can not describe the feelings of a child thus brought face to face with death. The dead flower appears as a shriveled atom—the extinguished fire presents an uncouth heap of ashes—the setting sun vanishes from our sight—these speak for themselves, here the change is real, perceptible, obvious; but the soul departed leaves the body the same, and yet how different, how slight, yet how immense the alteration. Lost in wonder, unable to realize what is gone, the child gazes in unspeakable awe at what remains—death, is that death? it looks but too like a profound and happy sleep; for a moment the eye is deceived: but to the touch the truth is at once revealed, and the young finger shrinks, and never again forgets the strange, cold, unyielding, icy feeling of the dead. For years it will thrill through her frame.

Perhaps it was a hazardous experiment, to place that young and susceptible girl in such a presence. Mr. Duncan did not know what he was doing; he was one of those individuals who can not in the least understand childhood, its deep feelings, its mysterious impulses, its strange associations, its superstitions taught by Nature herself, its heavenly breathings, to which it can give neither form nor words. He believed the experiment was perfectly successful, for Gwyneth's tears and cries alike ceased in that solemn presence, and she gazed in quiet, awestruck, breathless surprise at the form before her.

Softly and gently her father talked to her, whispering of the absent spirit which had gone away for a time, but which might even now be near, how near to them they could not tell; and of that day when this spirit should return again, and that fair form, now motionless, cold, inanimate as marble itself, should arise once more to everlasting life. And then he knelt with Gwyneth in his arms, and prayed that they might all meet hereafter in that home of everlasting peace, where no partings come. She was very still and subdued as he carried her back from the room, and gave her to the nurse's charge, and they did not know the effect that sight had produced on her, for she could not speak of her feelings; but sleeping or waking, that face for weeks was before her eyes, and the coldness of death seemed over her lips and cheeks, such as she had felt it, when, at her father's bidding, she had pressed a last kiss on the corpse; and she would shrink into corners of the house or garden, to cry and shudder alone, when none saw her, and muse in silence upon what her mother was.

Sybil was different; she clung to Hilary, she hardly dared to be alone; but with a pallid face, and swimming eyes, and little trembling hands, she followed her sister all day long; and never wearied of talking of her mother; of her wishes, her tastes, her goodness; every action seemed referred to that object; and she spoke of her as one that was absent only for a short time, who would soon return to claim their obedience again.

Gwyneth would turn pale, shiver, and, if possible, quit the room at the slightest mention of her mother's name; nor could Hilary's utmost efforts win from her the feelings that oppressed her.

Of course, as time passed, it brought the usual mitigation of acute sorrow. Sybil learned to speak with dry eyes of the departed, Gwyneth taught herself to bear the thought without visible demonstration of feeling; but the effect remained upon their characters; Sybil was more soft and dependent, Gwyneth more reserved in her general demeanor, while the fire which burned below that outward crust of indifference and calmness was but the fiercer for its concealment.

CHAPTER II.

"Blowing between the stems, the forest air
Had loosened the brown curls of Vivian's hair,
Which played o'er her flushed cheeks; and her blue eyes
Sparkled with mocking glee and exercise."

Iseult of Brittany.

It was about two months after the death of Mrs. Duncan, when the cheering news arrived at the old Vicarage, that the ship in which Maurice Duncan was serving had reached Chatham, and was to be paid off immediately.

The letter was indeed a sunbeam thrown upon a gloomy path. Some change was greatly wanted at home. Mr. Duncan was a man of deep and true piety, but of little judgment in worldly matters. It would not be easy to find one less fitted to guide aright four girls like his daughters: he had no idea of what was good or hurtful to them. In education, indeed, both intellectual and religious, he could safely lead them; but of their physical natures he was quite ignorant. He had no quickness of perception. He did not see that Gwyneth was becoming daily more gloomy and abstracted, yielding to fanciful terrors, all the more powerful because she dared not speak of them. He did not discover that Sybil was giving way to indolence and repining, loving to indulge in visionary dreams of future happiness, or in retrospective pictures of past bliss, but shrinking from real, actual exertion, and the toils of every-day life. Still less did he perceive that Hilary was working beyond her strength, and sinking under a weight of responsibility which she felt too vividly to endure safely.

She was keenly sensible of her sisters' defects; she felt them with an acuteness and a self-condemnation almost morbid in its excess; it seemed to her as if they were entirely her own fault, and she saw that, however she might guard their health, minister to their comfort, and promote their pleasures, she was still failing in the more important part of her stepmother's charge, while these evils were allowed to increase and overshadow their characters. Yet she could do nothing to repress them by herself, and she was not seconded by her father. Not that he wished or intended to thwart her; he doted on her far too much for that; but he was quite ignorant of the best manner of training children, or of the importance due to the small points of which Hilary thought so much. He secretly attributed the stress she laid on such things to the over-anxiety of a new-made governess, precise about unnecessary particulars from the scruples of a young responsibility; and when Hilary had said as much as duty and respect permitted, and urged her opinions with the small degree of earnestness which diffidence and humility allowed her, he would reply with a kind smile and a kiss, "Very true, my love; you are a good girl to think so much about your sisters, and I hope they will be grateful. I do not know what I should do without you." But the things to which she objected, the indulgences which she reprehended, were continued just the same.

Theoretically, he would tell the children to obey Hilary; practically, he would encourage the contrary conduct. Not that there was any positive rebellion—there was no passion, ill-will, or disobedience apparent; these would have been instantly suppressed; but these were not necessary to gain her ends, Sybil found, and her nature was too soft to use them. So when she and Hilary differed about her occupations, her manner of employing her time, or her amusements, an appeal to her father, a smile and a kiss, always won him to her side of the argument, and gained for her the right of following her own taste, rather than submitting to the act of self-denial which her sister had proposed. Mr. Duncan only saw that both acts were alike innocent, why then should she not take her choice? Hilary saw further; for she not only reflected on the results of self-indulgence, but she felt keenly how her power was annihilated, and her actual authority annulled; all the more keenly because it was owing to an affection she could not bear to blame, even in thought.

One of Sybil's greatest indulgences was in drawing her father into long conversations respecting her deceased mother, recapitulating her virtues, and dwelling on their own loss. Had he possessed judgment enough to turn such recollections to good effect, to increase the child's desire of excellence by the memory of what her mother had been, to strengthen her faith and love by pointing out how these had been a support in trouble and a comfort in sickness or pain, and to incite her onward in the same course by the wish of meeting again, there might have been more reason in his conduct; but this was not the case, and every such discussion seemed only to soften and weaken her nerves, make her more indolently dreamy, and bring on floods of regretful tears, such as she ought to have checked as willful, not encouraged as amiable and affectionate.

Conversations such as these only drove Gwyneth more completely apart, and made her shudder in silence. If, when the girls were riding or walking with their father, as they did almost every day, Sybil fell into this strain, her sister would draw back, and endeavor to escape beyond hearing; or if this were impossible, her white cheeks, and firm-closed lips, and slightly knitted brows told plainly to Hilary how she was inwardly suffering.

It was too much for Hilary; the household cares, the anxiety for her sisters, the watchfulness and broken rest which Nest, the youngest, often caused her—for she had taken the little one to her room at night, and watched her as her mother had once done; and then the unwearied attention to her father, the arrangement of his books, papers, and accounts, all which she took up where Mrs. Duncan had laid them down; the superintendence of the village school; the parochial cares; all these fell heavily on her young head—on her willing but over-anxious mind. The discipline, however, was good for her, and taught her many things; she saw much was beyond her power, and that what she could not accomplish, she must be content to leave undone; she saw many things which should not be, and from clearly ascertaining the evil, knew better what was good to seek.

And then at length, when she had taught herself to submit with patience, and to bear what she could not remedy, and to ask and look for help for what she could not supply by her own power, help and comfort were sent to her.

Maurice came home: within ten days of their hearing of his arrival in England, his ship was paid off, and he was free; it was only for a limited period, however, for not having yet served his time as a midshipman, and being little more than eighteen, he had determined not to be idle, and had applied for immediate employment. Consequently he had but six weeks' leave to spend at home, after an absence of nearly four years.

The delight with which Hilary looked forward to the arrival of her brother, was a stimulus to every power of her mind; and the ecstasy with which she threw her arms around the tall, slight, graceful youth on his presenting himself, seemed at the moment a compensation for all past anxiety and wrong. Maurice was returned to her, and returned with the same loving smile, and dancing eyes, and cheerful voice which had dwelt in her memory for so large a portion of her life; he was the same! could she be thankful enough for this blessing, not only for her own, but still more for her father's sake?

How delighted she was to watch her father's eye brighten, and his voice assume a more lively tone, as Maurice laughed and talked, questioned and commented, with the gayety of youth at home and happy. For Maurice was always happy; his boyhood had been all joy and sunshine, so far as he could remember; his school-life had been cheerful and pleasant; and his ship! oh, that had been the happiest on the station; the captain the most considerate, the first lieutenant the best fellow in the world, and all his messmates, great and small, appeared to deserve the same character; and now, though for a short time, the blank in their home was felt and mourned by him, and he looked grave when he saw the empty chair and the disused work-table placed back in a corner: yet his joyous spirit soon rose again, and with so many blessings left, so much still unchanged, he said and felt it would be ungrateful to repine that one had been taken.

So, when, in company of Hilary, he had visited the spot where his step-mother was buried, and talked with his sister of her last hours, and heard what they had since discovered from her written papers, that she had been warned by a physician some months before, that, in all human probability, her days were numbered, and that she would not survive her next confinement, and when they had recounted her kindness and her virtues, and shed tears together at the memory of past times, and made a solemn engagement to return her affection for them as children, if possible, in double care and attention to the interests of her daughters, Maurice turned his thoughts to other objects, and endeavored to show his reverence for the dead by his consideration for the living. Cheerfulness was what was needed in his dear old home; cheerfulness to restore the tone of his father's spirits, to cheer Sybil, to excite Gwyneth, and, above all, to aid and comfort and sustain his darling Hilary.

Maurice Duncan had the happy, lively temper ascribed by common report to sailors; but he had not the wild *insouciance*, the careless, reckless, or coarse habits often attributed to them. He was delicately, exquisitely refined in all his feelings; his behavior to his father was perfect in the respectful attention, engaging confidence, and invariable consideration he showed him. It was a sight worth seeing, too, to view him playing with his little sisters; Nest perched in the back of the old large arm-chair, leaning over his shoulder, and bringing her bright dark eyes, and ebony curls, in such charming contrast with his genuine Saxon features; while two other elder ones each occupied a knee, and drew an arm close round their waists. Then he would pour out long tales of India, China, or some other distant land, of tornadoes and breakers, coral-reefs and palm-trees, of wild shooting excursions, and narrow escapes from danger—to all which the children listened with wonder and almost awe; and Hilary sat smiling by, with bright eyes dancing in joy and thankfulness, and Mr. Duncan paused over his book, and listened with feelings scarcely less moved and excited than his children.

But, above all, it was beautiful to see how he would wait on Hilary, attend to her least wish, accommodate himself to her habits and occupations, relieve her of every burden he could take upon himself, or share it with her by his sympathy when he could not. Without any verbal communication, he discovered in what respects she was overworked, and to some extent contrived to remedy the evil.

Without seeming to find fault, he contrived to arouse his father's attention to what was wrong, to what was unfair on her, or pressed too much on one so young. His devoted attention to her wishes, the importance he attached to instant obedience to her words, had a great effect on the younger ones; be the game ever so amusing, the romp ever so exciting, or the tale ever so deeply interesting, all was quitted the moment Hilary spoke; and this conduct in one older and much taller than Hilary herself, could not fail to produce most beneficial results on the children's habits and actions. Long after he was gone, his sister felt the good effects of his care and kindness.

No summer sea sparkling in the sunshine was ever more bright and buoyant than his spirit; and not even those same waves could exceed his determined energy of character, his steady perseverance in right, or the gradual but resistless force with which he won his way through impediments, and silently swept away obstructions and prejudices.

One Saturday afternoon, the young people all set out together for a long ramble through the forest, the two girls on their ponies, Hilary and Maurice arm-in-arm, an arrangement which suited them admirably, as affording pleasure to the young ones, and securing at the same time the luxury of confidential communication between the brother and sister. Thus they strolled along, the children choosing the way, and leading them down beautiful glades carpeted with mossy turf, and over-arched by the old elms, and beech, and oak, where thickets of holly, underwood, and fern made what Maurice called reefs, promontories, islands, or sheltering bays; winding about sometimes in one direction, sometimes in another, at length they were entirely beyond the knowledge of any of the party, and it suddenly became a matter of doubt which way they were to turn. Hilary had gone on, leaning, figuratively as well as actually, on her brother; and it had never occurred to her, that with all his experience, and knowledge, and learning, he might not be so well qualified to guide them as to deserve this implicit credit. They all came to a stand-still at last, and looked about them with different degrees of wonder and uneasiness. There was no track, no mark of foot-steps, no sound of man to guide them. Hilary sat down on a fallen tree, puzzled and yet amused, while Maurice and her sisters made little excursions in different directions, to endeavor to discover some leading indications. They had gone a little out of sight, and she was looking toward the point from which she expected them to return, when she heard footsteps approaching, and turning round, saw, through a thicket of thorn, hazel, and holly, a person whom at first she believed to be her brother.

"Maurice, have you found the path?" exclaimed she, eagerly; but the next moment she perceived it was a stranger who advanced, and who, springing over the intervening underwood of fern and bramble, presently stood by her side.

"I beg your pardon," said Hilary, as she looked at him; "I thought it was my brother when I spoke."

She addressed him with an easy grace and courtesy, which was very attractive; and the intruder replied, with as much eagerness as politeness permitted,

"I have not seen your brother; can I be of any service to you? may I infer from your question that you have lost your way?"

"Indeed we have," replied Hilary, frankly; "well as I know the forest generally, I am quite puzzled now, and my brother and sisters are gone a little way to try and find a path."

"If you will allow me to remain with you till their return," replied the stranger, "I shall be most happy to act as your guide. In which direction do you wish to proceed?"

"We belong to Hurstdene," replied Hilary; "I am the clergyman's daughter; perhaps you know the name of Mr. Duncan?"

"Perfectly; though I have not the pleasure of his acquaintance; but you are a long way from Hurstdene; five miles, I should think, at least."

"I have no idea where we are," replied Miss Duncan, looking round; "I never was so far on this side of the wood. Is there any hamlet or village near us?"

"I think my house must be the nearest inhabited spot," said the gentleman; "perhaps you may know that by the name, 'the Ferns,' and that may give you some idea where you are."

"Oh, yes, I know the gates and fences of 'the Ferns' very well," answered Hilary, looking with a sort of modified and restrained curiosity at her companion; "but I had no idea it was inhabited; I thought the owner was abroad still."

"I was abroad," said he, smiling, "until very lately; but just at present I am living on my own domain. Is this your brother approaching?"

Hilary looked round: Maurice and the children approached quickly, evidently surprised to find she had a companion.

"We can not see any path," cried Gwyneth; "what shall we do? we are quite lost." She looked exceedingly frightened.

"Maurice," said Hilary, stepping forward to meet him, "this is Mr. Huyton, of 'the Ferns.' I believe I am right," added she, looking with a sort of apologetic smile at the stranger.

"I am happy to make your acquaintance, Mr. Duncan," said he, frankly holding out his hand, "and still more happy to think that I can be of service to your party. I learn from Miss Duncan that you have lost your way, and I believe I can direct you to the road home. But do you know how far you are?"

"I am so great a stranger here," replied Maurice, "that it is easy for me to lose myself, and I have no bearings to direct me: so we shall be really obliged if you can set us right."

"But will Miss Duncan be able to walk back five or six miles?" inquired Mr. Huyton.

"Hilary, dear, you can not do that, I am sure," said Maurice, anxiously.

"Necessity knows no law," was Hilary's cheerful reply. "I am not so very tired; besides, I can ride a little to rest myself, you know; neither Sybil nor Gwyneth have walked at all!"

Both girls, who had been gazing most attentively at the stranger, now cried out that Hilary should ride when she liked; all the way, if she liked.

"Then your shortest way home," replied Mr. Huyton, "is through my park, and out into the road which skirts the side of it; that will lead you direct to Hurstdene."

The children looked delighted, and whispered, audibly enough, how they should like to go through the "the Ferns;" they had never been inside the gates.

This point was soon settled, and he led them along a green alley of the forest, until they came to the park palings. The fence was of the wildest description. Ivy, clematis, and woodbine, mixed in the utmost profusion with bryony, bind-weed, and other climbing plants, overshadowed by gigantic ferns and gorse, which might almost be classed among trees. Over these, huge forest trees swung their ancient branches, and made a sort of twilight of the spot. The children wondered what would come next; but Mr. Huyton, drawing a key from his pocket, and pushing aside a tangled screen of green boughs, soon threw open a little door, which at first had hardly been perceptible, and the party found themselves within the park.

A narrow path, which seemed but rarely trodden, leading between thickets of tall fern, picturesque old thorns, and ancient hollies, opened before them. Eager and amused, the girls pressed their ponies along at a quick pace; Hilary still leaned on her brother's arm, while Mr. Huyton walked by her side, and assisted Maurice to hold back the encroaching brambles, or overhanging prickly branches, which might have impeded her progress.

A turn in the path brought them suddenly in sight of the house, and then the owner, turning to Hilary, said,

"If you will trust yourself to the wild style of housekeeping which a bachelor hermit's establishment affords, you will come in and rest yourself, Miss Duncan?"

Hilary at first declined, but her companion would not be refused, and Maurice was so charmed with the manners of their new acquaintance, and with the style of his conversation, that he seconded his proposal, when, of course, Hilary yielded.

"Thank you, very much," exclaimed Mr. Huyton, warmly; "but I must tell you that to rest in my house is but a part of my plan. You must let me have the pleasure of taking you all home in my carriage, I am sure Miss Duncan is too fatigued for more exertion; and perhaps the young ladies would not mind exchanging their saddle for a seat in the britschka?"

"Oh, no; we can not think of giving such trouble," exclaimed Hilary quite shocked at the idea.

"Besides, there are the ponies!" suggested Maurice.

"Never mind them, the groom shall bring them home in the evening," replied Mr. Huyton; and without listening to any further objections, he called to a man who was standing by the gate of the stable-yard, close to which their path led them, and gave orders for the carriage to be got ready.

Their path now emerged into a beautiful triple avenue, which extended at least half a mile from the front of the house, along which Hilary's eye glanced with intense admiration, and a low exclamation of "beautiful!" escaped her.

"My ancestors must have loved trees," said Mr. Huyton; "there are avenues extending from each side of this huge, unwieldy house. I should like to show them to you some day."

"Is this the front?" inquired Maurice.

"Yes; I fancy this is; but the house is square, and either side looks like the front; each has an entrance in the same heavy, substantial style; but I like the south rooms, so I have chosen this part for my residence. Let me welcome you to my domicile," added he, smiling with captivating grace on Hilary, as he pushed open the door, and ushered her into a broad entrance passage. He then turned to assist the others from their ponies, and after directing a stable helper to lead off the animals, he took the hands of the girls and led them in.

"Oh, how charming!" cried both Sybil and Gwyneth, as they glanced along the passage which opened into a great hall, occupying the center of the house. They caught sight of a wide branching staircase with a heavy balustrade; of sundry trophies of the chase, and ancient arms and armor, of various unknown articles, and not a few packing-cases and great boxes, standing about in extraordinary confusion.

Mr. Huyton seemed amused at their wondering admiration. He opened a door on the right. "Here is my room," said he, "no other is quite habitable yet; I have not been home long enough to get another furnished."

"We never heard you were at home at all," said Sybil; "when did you come, sir?"

"About a month ago," replied he, as he pushed up a large easy chair, and made Hilary seat herself in it; "I will tell you all about it presently, but you must let me attend to your sister's comfort first, will you not?"

He rang the bell as he spoke, and then looked round to see what more he could do for her convenience, bringing her a foot-stool, and drawing down the blind, that the sun might not shine on her head; and showing, by his whole air and manner, how anxious he felt for her comfort.

"Bring some wine and biscuits, or bread and butter, or something," said he, as a servant presented himself at the door.

"Not for us, Mr. Huyton," exclaimed Hilary, eagerly; "pray do not take the trouble; we *never* touch wine, except Maurice, and I do not suppose *he* would either, now."

"Some ladies do not, I know," replied he, gently; "then bring coffee as soon as possible, and tell Leblanc to make it, that it may be good."

The servant disappeared, and Hilary found it vain to contend against such politeness and hospitality,

"Those are beautiful specimens of wood-carving, are they not?" said their host to Maurice, who was examining some book-shelves at one end of the room; "they are for my library—nothing is in its place about the house. Indeed I have hardly had time to get my things unpacked yet."

"You have always been abroad, Mr. Huyton?" said Sybil, coming up to his side.

"Yes," was his reply, with a smile, as he looked at her face of curiosity. "I have spent twenty-five years, my whole life indeed, abroad; but I mean to settle in England now, and make this my home. Look at these beautiful cameos, shall we show them to your sister? would she like to see them?"

"Oh, yes! Hilary has some of her own, which I know she likes very much," replied Sybil, eagerly.

"But she would like these best," said Gwyneth, decidedly; pointing to a book of drawings, between the leaves of which she had furtively peeped. It was a collection of drawings, copied from some of the most celebrated works of good artists, all done in a masterly style.

"She shall have her choice," replied their host, looking much pleased; "you bring the book, and I will carry the case of cameos."

Again Hilary begged him not to trouble himself, but without any effect: a small table was placed beside her, and one article after another produced for her amusement. Her admiration of the colored drawings was extreme, and evidently highly gratifying to her host.

"How much my father would enjoy these," said she to Maurice.

"If you think them worth the trouble of carrying home with you," said Mr. Huyton, "I shall be only too much flattered to lend them to you. I can see, by your careful handling of them, the book would be as safe with you as with me."

"They are exquisitely beautiful," said Hilary, gazing with intense admiration at a copy of one of Raphael's best works. "Who was the artist?"

"I made the copies myself," was his reply; an answer which brought Hilary's eyes on him with a look of reverence and admiration.

The coffee was soon brought in, most excellent of its kind; indeed, whatever they saw, belonging to Mr. Huyton, which could be supposed finished, appeared as perfect as possible. Although it was evident that as yet hardly any thing was in its place, and the whole house had the air of having been so long neglected, that Hilary could not wonder that its progress towards order and classification had gone on slowly.

"I shall get on by degrees," said he, in answer to some observation of hers relative to the labor before him. "By-and-by, when the library has been new floored and cleaned, we will have these carved book-frames put up, of which that is a specimen. But I like to superintend the whole. It doubles the value of a place to arrange it all oneself: unless one had the happiness of falling in with some second mind and fancy, which could sympathize with and enter into one's own peculiarities and wishes."

"And do you not find the noise and bustle of workmen disagreeable, Mr. Huyton?" asked Hilary.

"I do not mind it; and when I am tired I go out in the forest, or stroll about, and form plans for the ground and gardens."

"There used to be a famous garden here always," observed Maurice; "many a time have I bought peaches and nectarines at the Lodge gates in former years."

"These windows look up that beautiful avenue, I see," said Hilary; "what magnificent timber you have about here."

"Yes, and so quaintly planted," replied he; "one wonders at the taste. Straight rows seem the prevailing idea. Rows of oaks, rows of cedars, rows of larch trees, varied by quadrangles of enormous yews, or of double rows of limes, which must be delicious in summer. Miss Duncan, I do not wish to hurry you away, but whenever you please, the carriage is at your service."

Hilary rose to prepare for her departure. The children cast many a longing, lingering look towards the unexplored regions of the house, which Mr. Huyton observing, told them that they should come again some other day, and they would have a good game at hide-and-seek all over the house; a promise which they resolved not to allow him to forget.

The most unqualified admiration was excited by the beautiful horses and carriage which stood at the door, Sybil declaring they were just what he ought to have, and Gwyneth whispering to Maurice that the afternoon's adventure was quite like a fairy tale.

"Are you going to drive, Mr. Huyton?" asked Sybil, as he was preparing to hand Hilary in.

"Not if you can make room for me inside," was his answer; "do you think you two little girls could sit by your sister without squeezing her too much?"

"Easily, easily," cried Sybil, springing up and down on the elastic cushions of the carriage. "Oh, Hilary, is it not delicious? if we had but such a carriage as this for every day!"

Maurice preferred going on the box, when it came to the point, so that after all there was plenty of room; and Sybil and Gwyneth were able to change sides in the carriage every five minutes, a process which any one less patiently indulgent than Hilary would soon have stopped.

Mr. Huyton, however, sitting opposite to her, kept her in such pleasant conversation on really interesting subjects, that she had not much time to be worried by any restlessness of her sisters; and the half-hour's drive passed only too rapidly. He was as enthusiastic an admirer of scenery as she herself, and with an eye and taste cultivated by familiarity with the best examples; yet he did not despise or look down contemptuously on English scenery, or an English climate, because the one could not show the Alps, nor the other boast of the bright suns of Italy or Greece. The small specimen that he had seen was enough to give him most favorable impressions; and he was equally prepared to like the women of his country. His expectations were high, but he had not as yet met with a disappointment.

"I am so glad of that," replied Hilary, with a simplicity and candor which told how little she suspected that she was the first English lady he had conversed with since his return from abroad. The idea of his intending a compliment to her was as far as possible from her mind.

Mr. Duncan was naturally a good deal surprised when he perceived the style in which his children had returned home; but nothing could be more cordial and grateful than his thanks and his invitation to their new acquaintance to walk in and share their tea. Sybil and Gwyneth, too, seconded the invitation with all their might; but Hilary was engrossed with little Nest, and either did not or would not attend; he was not sure which was the case.

"I must say good evening," said he, approaching the end of the room, where she was sitting on the end of the sofa, with her arms around the little one. "Is this another of your sisters, Miss Duncan? I never saw more lovely children; and yet how unlike they are to you!"

Nest fixed her large black eyes on Mr. Huyton, with a perfect appreciation of his compliment. Her sister colored, looked grave, and then rising, held out her hand, only replying, "Good evening, then, and we are so much obliged to you!"

"The obligation is to me," replied he, gracefully; then stooping down to kiss the beautiful little face, which, half-shyly, half-coquettishly, rested against Hilary's shoulder, he added, "It has been a bright afternoon to me, and the acquaintance I have formed I shall not easily relinquish!"

No sooner was he gone, than the whole party joined in one unanimous chorus in praise of their new friend, his house, his trees, his manners, his carriage, and his coffee.

Maurice was as enthusiastic as the girls, and the whole of tea-time was spent in recapitulating the charms and virtues of Mr. Huyton. In short, the entire thing had so much the air of a romance, and they had so rarely met with any adventure before, that enough could not be said in praise, or delight.

After tea, Hilary produced the book of drawings, and they were thoroughly appreciated by Mr. Duncan, who had, in his youth, made a tour abroad, and taken the opportunity of cultivating a natural taste and love for painting.

In the middle of this occupation, a message was brought in, that Mr. Huyton's groom had brought home the ponies, and also a basket of peaches and grapes from "the Ferns;" sent specially directed to Mr. Maurice, to remind him of old times; an attention to her brother's pleasure which charmed Hilary more than all the rest of the transaction together.

CHAPTER III.

"Her 'haviour had the morning's fresh, clear grace,
The spirit of the woods was in her face,
She looked so witching fair——"

Iseult of Brittany.

Sybil's lessons, the next Monday morning, were much disturbed by sundry dreams and visions; she was possessed with the idea that Mr. Huyton would drive over in his beautiful carriage again to-day, and perhaps take them all back to the Ferns, for the promised game of hide and seek. She was listening every moment for the sound of wheels, and trying to catch a glimpse of the carriage driving over the green, toward the house.

After all, Mr. Huyton came, but so quietly, that Sybil was perfectly ignorant when he entered the house. He rode over, rather early for a morning visit, and met Maurice on the green, who put his horse in the stable, and took the visitor into the garden, to wait till lesson-time was over, as he knew Hilary did not like to be interrupted in her teaching. They were all much surprised, in consequence, when, just as the children were putting away their books, the two young men walked into the room. None of the party was sorry to see Mr. Huyton; he seemed to have such genuine pleasure in the intercourse, that it naturally communicated itself to the whole family.

Mr. Huyton, indeed, was delighted with the acquaintance. The simplicity, frankness, and refinement of the whole family enchanted him. Weary of the fashionable manners, and artificial style of living, prevalent among the circles in foreign capitals, which he had frequented, there was something bewitching in this little glimpse of nature and truth now presented to him. Of English society he knew nothing, save such as he had met abroad, seldom the best, or under the best aspects; and without troubling himself to discover in what the peculiar charm consisted, he resolved to cultivate the acquaintance of the Duncans, and make himself at home with them.

He was surprised to find in a girl of Hilary's age, and educated completely in retirement, such a degree of elegance, and what he called high-breeding. It was a wonder to him how she learned a style of courtesy, which is sometimes wanting under what he would have considered much more favorable circumstances. He had yet to learn that real Christianity is the best school of good manners; and that the rule of doing as we would be done by, secures that substance, of which politeness and refinement can only give the shadow or the reflection.

She was so unconsciously pretty too, with all her delightful simplicity; so unintentionally graceful, and quietly elegant, that he never discovered how plain her dress was, nor how slightly it conformed to the prevalent fashion. The black close-fitting gown, with the clean little white collar, seemed made precisely to show off her slender form and fair skin; and the pretty brown hair, with its long curl, just put back behind a small delicately-shaped ear, and the rich braid forming a Grecian knot, needed no coiffeur to make it look smoother, more glossy, or more becoming to the classic shape of her little head.

Without forming any definite ideas as to the ultimate results likely to ensue, he entered at once with youthful ardor upon an acquaintance so accidentally formed. It was not likely that a young man of large fortune and prepossessing person and manners, would long be left to the solitude of his own country house, nor obliged to pick up his acquaintance at random in the forest; but he was sufficiently peculiar and independent in his tastes and habits, to take his own line and adhere to it; and for the present his chosen line lay in associating almost exclusively with the Duncans. Prudent fathers of families, and speculating brothers, hoping for future *battues* or other delights, made visits at the Ferns, as soon as it was generally known that the owner was resident there; and, thanks to the necessity of eating and drinking, and the circulating nature of butchers and bakers, as well as gossip in a country place, that was pretty soon after his arrival.

No one had, however, as yet got further than the doorway, the answer being apparently stereotyped, that the house was in confusion, and Mr. Huyton did not receive company. The Duncans alone had been permitted to enter. They were perfectly unconscious of the superior privilege accorded them. They were out of the way of gossip, and had few visitors except the farmers' and cottagers' wives of their own village. Mr. Huyton himself was the only landed proprietor in the parish, and on that account might be considered as belonging to them. The lay-impropriator resided six or seven miles from them; he was a man generally well-spoken of, and the father of two daughters, but there had never been any intercourse between them.

In short, Mr. Huyton's appearance among them was like the discovery of a new and wonderful comet to an enthusiastic astronomer; and he could not be more ready for the acquaintance, than they were to admit and encourage it.

Had Mr. Duncan been really a prudent father, he might have hesitated, perhaps, to admit to such an intimacy a young man of whom they knew only the name and the residence; but his charity made him literally think no evil; and the young men proved so congenial to each other in general taste, that they speedily became as nearly inseparable as the five miles between their respective homes would permit.

Maurice would have been constantly at the Ferns, if the owner of that place had not been so often at Hurstdene; and the little girls never seemed to think of riding in any other direction, unless he was with them to guide them in a different path.

All his plans were brought over to the Vicarage to be discussed and re-arranged according to the tastes of his friends there; nominally of the whole family, actually of Hilary herself, in most cases, with the assistance of her father's opinion.

The number of nutting parties, whortle berry parties, and other rambling, scrambling expeditions in which he was engaged by the children, was wonderful. It was apparently all the same to him, whether their object was to pick berries or make sketches, he was an adept at either, and he soon constituted himself drawing-master to the whole party, and presented Sybil with a stock of materials for the work, which amply supplied, as it was perhaps intended it should, both her sisters also.

Then he was delighted to encourage Gwyneth's natural and native love of music, and finding their only instrument was such a piano as you might expect to find in an old-fashioned country vicarage, he transferred to her as a birth-day present, a small but beautiful instrument, which he had ordered for his own room at the Ferns, but which he succeeded in persuading Mr. Duncan, it would greatly oblige him if he could now get rid of. There were some scruples about accepting so valuable a present, but Mr. Huyton had his own way after all. If he expected Gwyneth to be able to play the music which accompanied the piano, he must have formed wonderful ideas of the capabilities of the child: but Hilary reveled in Beethoven and Mozart for months afterward, and it certainly was an advantage to Gwyneth herself, to *hear* such good music as was now placed within her reach.

So the weeks sped away, fast and bright, as the evening rainbow fades from the sky, until Maurice's leave was over, and the sad eve of parting arrived. It was a subject which had never been discussed in Mr. Huyton's presence, and one which had not occurred to his mind; so that it took him quite by surprise when, late one afternoon, on arriving at the Vicarage, after an accidental absence of nearly forty-eight hours, he found Sybil and Gwyneth with very sober faces, sitting in the porch, and was told by them, with tearful eyes, that Maurice was really to go early to-morrow, so Hilary was helping him to pack his trunk.

The door of the little room on one side of the hall was opened as they spoke, and Maurice called out, "Oh, Charles! is that you? I began to think I should have to leave without seeing you again!"

The visitor entered the door, and there he found Maurice sitting on a portmanteau, in the hope that his weight would bring the two sides into fair proximity to each other; while Hilary was half kneeling, half sitting on the floor, from which she made a sort of motion to rise as he entered, looking at him with very pale cheeks and mournful eyes. "I had no idea, my dear fellow! you were going so soon," said Charles Huyton, quietly placing himself beside his friend on the portmanteau. "Oh the misery of packing up," added he, taking a curious look round the room at the various litters it contained.

"Well, we have done for to-day," replied Maurice; "I never got through it so nicely before; but Hilary, dear, we will rest now. I say, Charles, where have you been?"

"I had to go to Hitchinboro' about some business, and could not come earlier. Miss Duncan, is it too late for a walk? I had hoped to be in time to finish that sketch of the old oak-tree."

"I don't know," said Hilary, trying to rouse herself. "What do you say, Maurice?"

"If my father will come," replied he. "I should not like to leave him for the whole evening; and he talked of wanting to visit those cottages by the tree."

Hilary said she would go and see; and rising, left the room.

"Poor dear girl!" said Maurice, looking after her; "do you know what it is to leave such dear ones, Charles?—I could cry just now with pleasure."

"Your sister will miss you immensely," replied Mr. Huyton; "but she has so uncommon a degree of self-control and firmness of character, that I have no doubt but she will bear up under it with vigor."

"Hilary is not the least like any other girl I ever saw," replied Maurice, thoughtfully, "and I have seen a good many, one way or another; she is just a hundred times better than any one I ever came across; you might live with her ten years, and never know her do a selfish or an unkind thing. I really do not believe she ever thinks of herself."

"It is certainly rare to see one so young so thoughtful and womanly in her mind," said Charles Huyton, earnestly. "I think you told me she is not yet eighteen?"

"Oh! no, only just turned seventeen; most girls are mere children at her age. To see how she teaches and manages the little ones, and cares for my father, and attends to all the old women and babies in the parish, knowing exactly who wants a flannel petticoat, or a pig, or a dose of rhubarb: it is really something wonderful! I do not believe she ever forgets any thing from one Sunday to another!"

"Except herself," replied the visitor.

"Ay, except herself, in the right sense. I say, Charles, though, I have seen many girls forget themselves when I could have wished them a little more memory, for their own sakes; and you never see Hilary do that."

"Never—I wonder you can make up your mind to leave your family," observed Charles Huyton, with the utter unconsciousness of the laws of necessity which young men of large fortunes, independent of guardians, sometimes feel.

"What would you have?" said Maurice. "I must work, and, indeed, I love my profession; and but for these leave-takings, have nothing to complain of. If I am only lucky enough to get promoted by-and-by, when I am older, Hilary and I will settle down together in some little cottage on the sea-shore, and live on my half-pay and her fortune together, and be a regular old cozy brother and sister. That's my notion of happiness. I don't think either Hilary or I shall ever want to marry!"

"Don't you?" observed his friend, with a somewhat incredulous smile.

"I only hope she will not over-work herself; she is too anxious about every thing; and with nobody to help her, the three children come heavily upon her. Charles, you will come and see them sometimes when I am gone?"

"Sometimes!" replied Mr. Huyton, quietly.

Maurice turned round abruptly. "I am selfish for her sake, perhaps; but you must excuse me; don't come if you do not like, however. I thought perhaps—but never mind; I daresay you have plenty to do much pleasanter than dawdling about here with such rustics as we all are."

"There is nothing I like better, upon my honor. My great fear has been, that your absence would make a difference—that perhaps I should not be admitted. Nothing would give me more pleasure than to think there need be no change."

"No change! well, I do not say that; but let Hilary settle the change for herself. I only wish you could help her teach the children a little," added he, laughing; "but I am afraid you can not quite take my place as tutor."

"We will see," was the reply, gravely given.

The little girls came running in, equipped for walking, and summoned the two young men to join Mr. Duncan and his daughter, who were out at the gate, settling Nest in the pannier of a pony, that being the way in which that young lady made her excursions with her sisters; and on this occasion she was not to be left behind.

There was a good deal of desultory conversation passed between the family, not the least connected with the subject which occupied their minds; *that* was too sorrowful to be dwelt on; and both Maurice and Hilary thought more of their father, and of amusing him, than of indulging their own low spirits at the moment.

When they came to the Great Oak, it was settled that Maurice should accompany Mr. Duncan as he went round to visit a few scattered huts and hovels, inhabited by a wild and somewhat lawless race of wood-cutters, brickmakers, and poachers, who had located themselves in this secluded spot, while Hilary and Sybil sat down, under Mr. Huyton's protection, to finish a sketch of the old tree.

"How well it looks this evening," observed he; "the tawney russet shade which has tinged the leaves, shows well against those orange-colored beech-trees which back it up. If you can but catch the effect of that slanting sunbeam falling on those bright leaves, and tinging the trunk with gold! It is made for a picture!"

Hilary laid down her pencil, and gazed abstractedly at the scene till the tears gathered in her eyes, and first blinded her sight, and then dropped on her sketch-book and blotted her drawing. Her companion saw it, and gently drew it away from under her hands, to which she passively submitted, hardly knowing what he did, and hoping to quiet her emotion more easily by keeping silence.

"The sunbeam may fade to-night," whispered he, "but it will come again to-morrow, Miss Duncan; and we can sleep away the hours of darkness, with the hope of a brighter dawn."

"I was thinking," said Hilary, after a pause, and carefully steadying her voice, "that that oak was like my father, how grand and venerable it looks; and that glowing, golden sunbeam was Maurice's visit to us, just slipping away; what a bright gleam it shed on us for a little time; and now it is over, and he will be left—as that tree will be—to the night-dews, and the cold light of the moon and stars, which may glimmer round him, and seem to make a show and brightness, but have no real warmth, or strength, or power, in their poor feeble beams."

"That is a comparison which does little justice to the bright light which shines on your father's home and household," replied Charles Huyton, warmly.

"I know it, Mr. Huyton," replied Hilary, understanding his words in a different sense from what he intended; "I know that he has that light within which makes external lights of little consequence. But yet, I can not help feeling that our home is not what it was once, and how sad, how desolate it must look to him. If I could but fill the place more effectually—but I am such a child—"

"Maurice says, your only fault is that you are too anxious," replied Charles Huyton, who found it much easier to praise Hilary than to answer her feelings.

"Ah, Maurice does not know—" was her only answer.

"You do not in general dispute his judgment," said Charles, smiling a little. "Do not take your responsibilities so to heart—do not fancy that you are called on to wear yourself out; the very fact of taking things easily yourself, will make them easy to others also. Nobody expects a woman's grave and severe prudence and consideration, from your youth. Give yourself more liberty, and take less trouble."

"Did Maurice tell you to say that to me?" inquired Hilary.

"No—I say it of myself; I can see that you are over-anxious."

"Perhaps I am—but can one really be too anxious to do one's duty, Mr. Huyton? Do I take uncalled-for tasks on myself—and if not, if, as I believe, what I do is merely what I ought to do, then, you know, it is what I have the power to do also. More is not required than is possible; ours is not a hard Master; but then the proper interest must be returned for the talents committed to us, or we are unfaithful as well as unprofitable servants."

He was silent, for she was talking in an unknown tongue to him, alluding to things as realities, whose existence he hardly recognized.

"I know the fault is mine when I fail; and the merit, if I ever succeed, is His from whom help cometh," added she, a little hesitatingly, as if in deprecation of his grave looks.

"Maurice has given me leave, as far as he can, to try and fill his place," said the young man; "and he referred me to you, as to the way in which I could be of use, and when I may come and see you."

"Will you really?" said Hilary, showing the most innocent pleasure at the prospect; "I thought when he was gone, you would not care much for coming here as you have done."

"Then you are mistaken. I have known no pleasanter hours than those I have spent at the Vicarage. Besides, how could I get on with my improvements? who would plan my walks, or choose my papers, or design my greenhouses?—no, I am not such an idiot as to throw away a valuable friendship when I have once made it."

Hilary laughed lightly, as her only reply.

"Gwyneth," added he, pulling the child toward him as he sat on the turf, "you know very well that I could not do without you and Sybil to help me, don't you?"

"We could not get on without you," replied Gwyneth; "Hilary wants to go on learning German, and I am sure nobody could teach her so well; and your French and English books, and your music and paintings are much better, and nicer, and prettier than any we have of our own."

"But then, Gwyneth," whispered he, "you have things which I have not—much better things, things that I can not buy."

"I thought you had money enough to buy every thing you wanted," said Gwyneth.

"Not every thing. I can not buy a father, or sisters, or a brother like Maurice—and you have all these, which I want; so who is best off?"

Gwyneth looked uncertain, or unwilling to speak.

"Suppose you were to give me back my sketch-book?" said Hilary, stretching out her hand for it; but he drew it back out of her reach, with a look which quieted Hilary, and prevented her saying any more, although she could not easily have told why.

The father and son returned, during the silence which ensued after Hilary's last speech; and Sybil, who had been very industriously working away at her sketch, now held it up for approbation, which it obtained, as it deserved. The party then prepared to return homeward, and little Nest, who had been wandering about under the charge of Gwyneth, was recalled, and once more lodged in her pannier.

Mr. Huyton was pressed to come in as usual; but thinking that on the last evening the family would be more comfortable without a stranger of the party, he declined, and mounting his horse, after very cordial farewells to Maurice, he rode slowly home, meditating on the charms of Hilary, and thinking what he should do with regard to her. To let things take their own course, and be decided hereafter by events, seemed to him the best thing to do.

In the mean time he carried away the sketch-book, with the intention of abstracting and appropriating the unfinished sketch on which her tears had fallen, and giving her a copy, of his own doing, of the scene she had attempted to delineate.

So things did take their course; and acting on impulse, with out any definite idea, or decided plan, Charles Huyton continued to come and go, between the Ferns and the Vicarage, all through the autumn and ensuing winter. He finished his house, and arranged his grounds, and returned his neighbors' visits, sometimes accepting invitations to dinner, sometimes even appearing at a ball, being exceedingly admired, and very much courted, and making himself universally agreeable when he did go into society; but withal preserving a sort of mystery about his usual pursuits and amusements, which rendered him *piquant* and interesting in the highest degree.

He never gave parties of any kind, not even to gentlemen; did not preserve his game, and did not either hunt or shoot; men were as much puzzled to account for his oddities as women. The neighborhood—that is, the part of the country inhabited by gentlemen's families—lay almost entirely in the opposite direction to Hurstdene, and so far removed from the vicinity of the Vicarage, that the length and frequency of his visits to the Duncans passed unheeded and unheard of.

All his leisure time was spent there, reading, drawing, teaching, gardening for them, and with them, and discussing his own plans and projects. Inspired by Hilary, and advised by her father, he did some very useful things: he built and endowed a school at the edge of his park, for some of the scattered population around; he improved the dwellings of the poor tenants, and, in short, fell in with all the usual schemes of benevolence patronized by a well-meaning landholder. But the hand that guided him was not at all apparent, and nobody could be more ignorant of her influence than Hilary herself: she really believed that all the right things Mr. Huyton did came from his own right feelings and good principles. Indeed this was one great secret of her power; he could see through the designs of the mammas who invited him to their houses, and their daughters who took such interest in his house, his park, his garden, or his school. He felt that they only cared for him because he was rich, and he believed that had he offered his hand and fortune to any of these elegant young women, it would have been unhesitatingly accepted on the shortest notice, and with the greatest triumph. With Hilary it was different; kind and obliging as she was, unreserved in many respects, frank and simple, he by no means felt sure that she loved him; on the contrary, as months rolled on, and the graceful girl grew and developed into a very handsome and elegant woman, while her mind matured in proportion as her person improved, he became more dubious on the question which he often asked himself, "Would she ever consent to become his wife?"

His own wishes took a most decisive shape before she had quite completed her eighteenth year; but his hopes stood on a very different ground: shifting in their appearance as if they rested on a quicksand, and varying with every interview. That such a notion had never entered her head he would have boldly maintained, had it been necessary; he would have staked his fortune fearlessly on her perfect innocence and simplicity; he had cautiously guarded against putting it there by any conduct of his own; for he had an intuitive conviction that the day his wishes were discovered would be the last of that pleasant, frank, comfortable intercourse which now existed; and he by no means felt convinced that it would be replaced by any thing more pleasant.

Every part of her conduct convinced him that she did not love him; Sybil and Gwyneth could not have appeared more unconscious and unsusceptible of this feeling. But he hoped that time would produce a change; there was no fear of a rival, so he could wait; and rather than risk all by a premature discovery, he did wait, and watch and guard his looks and manners, and lived in hopes of the future.

He was quite right; Hilary did not love him. He was very pleasant; a great comfort to her father; most kind to her sisters, and very good-natured to herself; but for some hidden reason, she never entertained for him the smallest approach to what could be called love; perhaps it was because she did not think about it: busy and useful, cheerful and yet thoughtful, she had adopted Maurice's notion that she should never marry, but should continue as she now was. To leave her father or desert her sisters, indeed, would have seemed a monstrous impossibility to her—a thing too much contrary to right even to be thought of with a negative. Nest, who was but just five years old, would want her care for fifteen years to come at least; and oh! what an age that seems to the girl who has herself only counted eighteen years of life.

But it was very kind and pleasant to have such a friend as Mr. Huyton, to lend them books, and bring them reviews and prints, and help them in the parish with money, and especially to be so fond of Maurice—write to him so often, and always show the letters he received from him to them. And so matters went on, and things took their course, and Hilary worked and read, and governed her household, her sisters, and herself, and, very unconsciously, the owner of the Ferns also; and months passed, and she saw her nineteenth birth-day arrive, and wondered to think how old she felt when she was yet so young, and questioned much with herself whether she had rightly fulfilled her task, and feared that could her step-mother revisit her children, she would find her best efforts had been fearfully imperfect, and that their characters were too much the result of chance and circumstance, and that the guiding hand had been too weak to be efficient.

No—she did not love Charles Huyton; no thought of him mingled with her reflections on her nineteenth birth-day.

CHAPTER IV.

"Far, far from each other
Our spirits have grown;
And what heart knows another?
Ah! who knows his own?"

Arnold.

Mr. Huyton, it may be presumed, did not know that Hilary gave him so small a part in her thoughts, or he probably would not have acted as he did on that very day. However, I will not venture positively to affirm this; for such are the inconsistencies and contradictions of human nature, that it is safer to calculate on resolutions being broken, and promises forfeited, than on the exact performance of either.

Charles Huyton's resolutions had not been communicated to others, and his promises were made only to himself, so there was no one who could charge him with inconsistency, or blame him for want of faith, when, after having firmly resolved to conceal his opinions and wishes with regard to Hilary, he betrayed them to her on her nineteenth birth-day.

She was standing in the church-yard, beside the graves of her own mother and her step-mother, recalling her past life, and renewing her resolutions to watch over, guard, and devote herself to her younger sisters, when Charles Huyton, directed by some extraordinary instinct, discovered and joined her there.

It was a very picturesque little spot. The east window, which was handsome in itself, formed the background; a beautiful spreading lime, with its pale tassels just then in full blossom, hung overhead, and sheltered it from the north; the graves were carefully preserved, and planted with myrtle, rosemary, and some other evergreens; and the wall of the church was richly decorated with large purple and white-flowered clematis, Virginia creeper, and climbing roses. Hilary was sitting on a bench under the lime-tree, plunged in profound meditation, when Mr. Huyton, whose footstep was inaudible on the short turf, presented himself before her.

"You have chosen rather a mournful place of retirement, Miss Duncan," said he, seating himself by her, after the first greeting; "may I venture to remain with you, or do you court solitude as well as gloom?"

"I do not feel either solitude or gloom in this spot, Mr. Huyton," said she, quietly; "but it seems to me a wholesome occupation for the mind sometimes to quit the brightness of life for the calm repose of such a scene as this."

He did not answer immediately—he was reading the inscription on the headstones before him; she, too, was silent. After some minutes, he turned to her.

"I should like to know the thoughts which occupy you so deeply," said he.

She colored a little, and replied, "They are sacred to the memory of the departed; but there are so many thoughts which come in such a place as this—I *could* not tell them if I would."

"The most prominent one, then—will you not trust me?"

"I was thinking how false our lives are to our professed principles."

"In what way?" questioned he, curious to learn the feelings of a girl like Hilary, although not in the least entering into them.

"I was thinking," replied she, "that all words spoken, and thoughts unuttered, too, exist somewhere—are recorded—not passed away into empty air—not perished like the flowers which fall to decay."

"Well, what then?" said he, not discovering any connection in the ideas.

"How many thousand times have those words been repeated here, in this church-yard, praying that the number of the elect may shortly be accomplished; and yet how little we realize our own meaning, or live in accordance with the words we use."

"You do not mean to say that we ought to be glad when our friends die?" inquired he.

"Partings for an indefinite time must always be painful, and those left behind to sorrow and struggle—to combat the waves of this troublesome world—must feel desolation and grief; but when we look at a quiet grave like this, where all is so calm and still, and think of the spirit away in some unknown but happy place, we ought not to feel gloom. Gloom might rest on the graves of those who call it 'Ultima Domus'—but for us, who daily repeat our belief in 'the resurrection of the dead,' gloom ought to be banished with despair."

"That is a very beautiful idea," said he, looking with admiration at her elevated expression of countenance.

"It should be more than an idea—it should be a guiding principle; I mean that our business here is so to live that we may think of lying down there without a shudder. Do you know, I have often wondered what I shall feel—with what kind of emotions I shall look down—when they lay *me* there—or rather what once was myself."

He looked at her with amazement. "Do you suppose you will be conscious at all?—but do not talk of it; *I* can not think of you in such a connection without more than a shudder. Did you train these creepers so gracefully round the church windows?"

"Partly; there have been other hands here besides mine, however; it has been the work of affection—the result of the very feelings of which I was speaking."

"Which is your favorite?" inquired Mr. Huyton, determined to change the subject.

"Of the shrubs?—that Virginian creeper, I believe."

"Why, it has no blossoms, and is not even an evergreen," replied he.

"I like it the better for that; it says the more to me."

"What does it say?" replied he, smiling.

"The fading of its leaves speaks of sympathy with us, which I never can fancy evergreens feel. And then they become more beautiful as they decay, glowing with richer colors lent by the frost which is about to strip them; just as those who have silently spent their strength in aspiring heavenward like that plant, often show, when touched by suffering, new and unexpected graces."

"You are fanciful—but I like to hear your imaginations."

"The Virginian creeper has another meaning to me," pursued Hilary; "it is an emblem of friendship, of which I am very fond."

"I thought ivy was the emblem of friendship," observed he.

"Not my emblem—at least, not of the friendship I mean. Did you ever notice the plants? ivy is a parasite, living on the substance which supports it; drawing its own existence from the life of another; and it is very persevering too, where any thing can be gained: it is difficult to check; tear it down, and it will send out new roots and fix itself afresh, until the prop is destroyed by the encroachment of the counterfeit friend; then it is so cold and apathetic, always green and unchanging in appearance, one can not love an ivy plant, or make a companion of it, however picturesque it may be."

"And your favorite, what character does it bear?"

"Examine it—do you see these little spreading hands with which it supports itself?—see how closely they adhere; if you tear it down, it can never be replaced, however; they will hold, while they have life, but forcibly detached, they can not fix themselves again. They ask nothing in return, but permission to be undisturbed; and once allowed to attach themselves, they soon cover their sustaining prop with their luxuriant foliage. But the prop must be *real* of its kind, stone, or brick, or wood; but not stucco for stone, nor whitewashed plaster; there they retain no hold; nor polished glass you see; to that they can not fix themselves, it is too hard. Is not that constant, true, devoted friendship?"

"And you think then friendship repulsed, or violently severed, can never be replaced?"

"Unkindly severed—no, I should think not; but mine is only theoretical friendship, Mr. Huyton; practically, I have no experience. You, perhaps, know better."

"I believe the only one I ever called a friend, was Maurice, your brother," was his answer.

"I had hoped," said she, looking up ingenuously, "that others of his family might have shared in that title."

"No," replied he, earnestly, and gazing at her clear, innocent eyes, "Mr. Duncan is too old. I respect him greatly, but we are too unequal for friendship, and your sisters, of course, are out of the question."

He paused—her eyes were bent down with a slight shade of disappointment in them: did he not think her worth caring for at all then? well, perhaps this was natural enough. She was startled by his hand being laid on hers, and his voice breaking the silence as he said,

"And for you, it is not *friendship* that I feel; that is not the name of the sentiment which just now fills my heart."

She looked up again, but her eyes fell under his once more, for she read there something which gave her no pleasure, although it occasioned her surprise. The idea for the first time flashed across her, that he loved her, and, quick as thought can go, her mind took in at once all the probable consequences of such a circumstance; the pain and disappointment to him, the interrupted intercourse, the loss to their society, which his absence would occasion, what Maurice would think, and whether he would wish it either one way or the other. The silence was not of more than a minute's duration, but her mind traveled far and fast during that interval. One idea did not occur to her; that was the possibility of marrying Mr. Huyton; she did not raise the question.

His thoughts had not gone so far, they were all concentrated round her, watching the changing color of her cheeks, and the long eye-lashes which rested on them. He was partly thinking how pretty she was, partly wondering what she was feeling. Of course he had to speak again.

"Hilary, I love you. Ever since the moment when I suddenly saw you standing alone in the forest, like some unearthly being, like one of those angels of whom you are so fond of talking, you, and you only, have filled my heart. I have lived for you, worked for you, thought of you all day, dreamed of you at night, watched your progress to perfection with an intenseness of admiration you little guessed; dwelt on your image when absent, loved your very shadow, doted on you with a heart which never, never loved before."

"Hush! Mr. Huyton," said she, gravely; "these are wild words, not language for one human creature to use to another; and to *me*, if I did not know you too well, I should think you meant to mock me; do not talk so!"

"Mock you! praise can not come near your merits; words are too cold; in that sense they may be unfit to be addressed to you; as any attempt to paint a rainbow is mockery. But my meaning is most sincere, earnest, true. I love you!"

He held her hand in both of his, and looked in her face with all the eloquence of which his very handsome eyes were capable; but she shook her head.

"I do not love you, Mr. Huyton—at least, not in that way;" ending her sentence abruptly, and with crimson cheeks, which made him think her mistaken.

"You do not *hate* me?" said he, perseveringly detaining the hand she endeavored to withdraw; "tell me, am I disagreeable to you?"

"Hate you! oh, no; you are so good and kind to me and mine; and Maurice loves you so, I could not *hate* you; but I am so sorry, so very sorry, that you can not think of me as I do of you; liking, wishing well to, esteeming one another, being friends and no more."

"Impossible! a man must be made of marble, who could see you as I have seen you, know you as I have known you, and not do more than like you. Are you sure—but no, I have no right to doubt, to expect, to fancy even, that you returned my passion; but I may hope for the future; perhaps now you know my heart, you will pity me. Let me try to make you love me; give me leave to devote myself to that; if I might look forward to one day making you my wife; oh, Hilary, it is for you I have worked at 'the Ferns,' in the dear hope of placing you there, where, surrounded by all that could reward your virtue, and enhance your charms, I might see my idol the center of worship, the admiration of the neighborhood—let me hope."

"I hardly know what to say to you in answer; you think of me a great deal too well, but yet I must thank you, and feel grateful to you for your good opinion and your kind wishes, and your love; and do not blame me, please, for not doing more, or not doing it rightly; I am very ignorant of what would be considered right to do or say; but indeed I only mean to be sincere and true, so if I speak too frankly, you must forgive me."

"You can not speak otherwise than rightly; like yourself, the very soul of innocence and modesty, and grace; be as frank as you please, I promise not to misunderstand you."

"Mr. Huyton, I can not be your wife, or the wife of any one, while my father and sisters require me with them. I believe the conviction of this was so strong in my mind, that I thought you must see it and know it too, and that was why I was so surprised at your talking as you do."

"But, Hilary, 'the Ferns' is not so far off, as to be called leaving them. If you give me no other objection, I need not despair; if your feeling for me would not prevent you giving me your hand, your feelings for them need not surely. I come here every day, so could you; the separation would be merely nominal, and how much more I could and would do for them, as *my* father and *my* sisters, than I could or might do now; what they lost in one way, might be more than compensated in another."

Hilary shook her head, and then, pointing to the grave before her, she said: "I promised her not to desert her children; I have since renewed the promise more than once, on this very spot; and for my father—oh, Mr. Huyton, what excuse could I have for leaving him? What selfishness to think of it?"

Mr. Huyton bit his lip, and then answered:

"If it is on their account you act, that need not prevent my hoping; if regard for them prevents your entertaining the thought of leaving them now, this reason will not always exist. In a very few years, Sybil will be able to take your place, and then—"

"But you mistake," said Hilary, drawing back, "if you think they are the *only* reason; I do not wish to give you pain, and I hope you will not think me proud, or any thing wrong, but, indeed I must tell you the truth—I do not feel for you what you would like; I hardly know what to say, but I mean, what you would wish your wife to do. I do not think I should make you happy, or that I could be happy with you, feeling as I do; and while I really am very much obliged to you for your good-will to my sisters, and all that you say, I do wish you to leave off thinking of any thing more. Find somebody more suited to be your wife, and the mistress of 'the Ferns,' somebody who could do you credit, and not a poor, ignorant country girl, like me, quite unused to society, and hardly knowing even how ignorant I am."

"I might search through all the world, and not meet one more thoroughly good, elegant, refined, and excellent than yourself, Hilary. It is no use to tell me not to hope and wish; it is no use to tell me to love another, after a two years' acquaintance with you. Only let me try to win you. I do not ask you to bind yourself—*you* shall be quite free and unfettered by promises of any kind; only do not send me away; suffer me in your sight, though I have had the presumption to love you!"

"I thought you would have wished to leave me of yourself, after what has passed," replied Hilary, in a little surprise.

"You did me injustice, then; while you are free, and therefore to be won by the man who can best deserve you, I will not leave you, unless you drive me away; and you will not do that, will you? I ask no more; only allow me to go on as I have done."

Poor Hilary! she was very young, very innocent, and very ignorant of the selfish pride of a man's nature, or she would not have yielded this point. She had no female friend to guide her—to warn her of the difficulties in which a promise which seemed so fair and simple might involve her, or to teach her how far the mere permission to try to win her might be interpreted in favor of her suitor's claims.

She felt how very disinterested it was of a rich man like Mr. Huyton—clever, fashionable, admired, no doubt, in the world—to ask for the hand of a simple country maiden like herself, whose future fortune bore no proportion to his, and whose family could add nothing to his honor or influence. He might represent the county if he chose; he had discussed the subject several times with Mr. Duncan; he might, no doubt, win a wife from any noble family in the land; and yet he loved her, and asked her to marry him. The wonder of her mind at his making such a choice, so unequal in every respect as her modesty made her think it, was only surpassed by her astonishment at finding that she could not love him in return. Why not?—why could not all his good qualities, his ardent affection, and his kindness to her family, influence her to wish to be his wife? Why did the idea seem incompatible with happiness? and why did the notion of reigning at 'the Ferns' make her cling the closer to her duties and responsibilities at the Vicarage?

Was it the mere idea of leaving those she loved? there was something in that; for she was not blinded by the fallacies of his arguments; she knew the separation would be more than nominal; she knew it must be real, because it ought to be so. Once mistress of 'the Ferns,' in how many new duties and cares should she not be involved, with which her old pursuits at Hurstdene would be incompatible; and once Mr. Huyton's wife, his claims on her time and society would be paramount; and would he yield them to others? She was convinced he would not. It was true, he was at Hurstdene every day *now*, but then it would be different; and every future plan on which he now dwelt would call him in an opposite direction.

She did not say to herself in words, or form a distinct idea in her mind, that he was innately selfish or self-willed; but it was this unexpressed thought and feeling which made her certain that his wife must make him her first and last object, if she would please him, and be at peace.

Hilary could not have told why she mistrusted one who talked so well and acted so fairly; she had unconsciously explained it by a symbol to him when she dwelt on the peculiarities of her favorite plant; but she did not know that she was the Virginian creeper, he the wall which bore the fair appearance of stone, and was in truth only stucco, and that, to one of her nature, the effort to attach herself to him must be utterly vain.

She really wished she could love him; I need not say not from any unworthy motives, but from gratitude for his kindness and his affection for herself; and although hardly believing that any change was possible, she yet engaged to allow him the opportunity to effect it which he desired. One other mistake she committed—one likewise resulting from delicacy and regard to his feelings: she promised to keep what had passed between them a profound secret, even from her father. She fancied she was doing right; a dislike to say what might seem to claim her father's thanks, a dread of appearing to boast of her attractions and the admiration she had inspired, had a little influence; she felt how unmaidenly it was to triumph in her conquests; but the chief reason for her silence was regard to Mr. Huyton's feelings, and a fear of mortifying him by making known his disappointment. It was the romantic delicacy of a young mind much accustomed to act and decide for itself—used to bear its own burdens in silence, and to endure rather than to indulge its feelings.

Her theory was right; secresy in such a case being, in general, honorable and just; but hers was one of the exceptions which prove a rule; and in her peculiar circumstances, it would have been her father's part to decide how their future intercourse should be arranged, as it was his due to know the footing on which they now stood.

Mr. Huyton was well aware of the advantage which he gained when he won from Hilary's gratitude and delicacy the promise that nothing should be said to others of this conversation. Conscious how unfair this requisition was, he quitted her, immediately she had given it, with many a word of gratitude, passionate affection, and intense admiration, and many an assurance of the changeless nature of the feelings he professed.

His love for her was very strong, as well as very sincere; he fully appreciated her character; he saw and admired her genuine truth and simplicity—her innocence and modesty—her humility and her loving nature. He had seen a good deal of women of the world—women of fashion—and could value pretty accurately their admiration of him; he understood his charms in their eyes, and despised them accordingly. He did not believe there was another woman besides Hilary who could have been constantly the object of his friendly attentions, and the companion of his pursuits and wishes, as she had been for the last two years, and yet have never understood his motives, or calculated on his probable intentions. He was aware that this was partly owing to her entire ignorance of the manners and habits of men in general, and the circumstance of having been long used to such devoted care and kindness from her brother as could hardly be exceeded by the attentions of a lover himself. But he saw also that it marked an entire disinterestedness of character, a total absence of selfish ambition, and a devotion to the plain, straight-forward duties of life, which, if her affections could but be turned into the channel he desired, would certainly secure his happiness.

He was not angry with her for refusing him; in his calmer moments he would have himself predicted such a result to any explanation between them; he had spoken on the impulse of the moment, and could not be surprised at the answer he received. He loved her the better, as well as admired her the more; emotion had given a more lovely hue to her face; and this proof of her purity of principles had added a brighter charm to her mental qualities. He was more thoroughly captivated than ever, and rode home, dreaming of Hilary the whole way; of the time when he could transport his beautiful flower, now blooming so fairly in retirement, and place it where all would admire his choice, and wonder at his good fortune, and honor his taste in the selection of a perfect wife. For as to failing eventually in the attempt, there was not a fear in his mind of that occurring. There was no rival, and no chance of one; nothing to interfere with his success; and he could exert all the powers of his mind and imagination to win her, undisturbed by jealous passions, unpleasant observations, or the cold interference of worldly customs and reserve. She had promised all should go on as usual, and reliance on her word was as unbounded as his love for her.

Scarcely had her lover left her, when Hilary, sinking on her knees beside the grave of her step-mother, and covering her face with her hands, renewed in a low but distinct voice the pledge she had already given, never to leave her sisters so long as they required her care, never to forsake them, unless she could see them under safer and tenderer guardianship than her own; but to devote her thoughts, her strength, her love, and her life to their and their father's service.

It was no sacrifice which she resolved on; she was not prompted by any enthusiastic impulse; she did not imagine herself acting a heroic part; she believed that it was simply her duty. The ties knit by Nature, the friends given her by Heaven, the charge imposed on her by God himself, these must surely have the first claim; and till she had discharged these faithfully, she felt she had no right to form others, or to engage in new and uncalled-for duties. Then she raised her head, and with the grateful emotions of a child relieved from danger or trouble by a tender parent, she thanked her Heavenly Father, that he made her duty so plain and so easy, that she had no counter-wishes to struggle against, no affection to subdue, no opposing feelings to torment and perplex her. She was glad, then, from the bottom of her heart, that she did not love Mr. Huyton, and wondered how she could ever have been tempted to wish it otherwise.

At that moment she felt that to love him was impossible, and that to allow him to hope or expect a change was unjust to him, as well as untrue to her own convictions; she repented that she had not spoken more clearly, regretted what she had promised, and resolved to take an early occasion to explain decidedly to him, that the sooner he resigned all his views on her hand, and allowed his love to cool into friendship and good-will, the pleasanter it would be for her, the better and happier for himself. She pitied him exceedingly; she thought it was so very generous and noble of him to love her so; she could not be insensible to such a compliment; and he had shown such forbearance and moderation after her refusal, had been so humble and gentle, so considerate of her feelings, as she fancied, that he deserved to meet with something better than disappointment. She would make no change toward him, she had promised she would not, she would keep his secret, and trust that her calmness and quiet indifference would soon dispel a love which could not live quite unreturned.

But it was much easier for Hilary to promise to make no difference toward him, than to keep her word, although she fully intended to do so; it was simply impossible. A conscious shyness took the place of her former open friendliness; she dreaded being alone with him, carefully avoided sitting near him, dropped her German lessons, gave up her drawing for the indispensable business of making frocks for the school-children, and was uncommonly silent in his company. He saw all this clearly enough, and he saw she could not help it; he did not blame her; he rather loved her the better for the bashfulness which made her shrink from him. It gave more interest to his pursuit; he no longer had the certainty of unchecked intercourse, but there was more excitement, more difficulty, and therefore more amusement as well as novelty. Sometimes he spent a whole afternoon at the Vicarage, without winning from her one open, straightforward smile; or obtaining even five minutes' conversation, unrestrained by her sisters' presence.

Any eyes less dim than her father's had lately become, or more awake than her young sisters, must have noticed the very great change in their mutual manners; the absolute and unreserved devotion on his part, the shrinking timidity and constraint on hers. Poor Hilary! she would have been very glad had her father noticed these circumstances; she wanted some one to counsel her, to teach her how to escape from the embarrassment in which she found herself; but she could not break her word, and her father saw nothing of what was passing.

However, things came to a crisis at last. Mr. Huyton took it into his head to add cloaks and bonnets to the set of new frocks which Hilary was getting ready for her little scholars. Of course he had a right to do so if he pleased, and Miss Duncan could not have objected, if he had not taken pains to let her know that it was done for her sake, and to please her. What could she do? he had mentioned it to her father, had received his cordial approval, and his ready promise that Hilary should co-operate, and assist his ignorance. She sat by in silence, until appealed to by Mr. Huyton, who suggested that she should take on herself all the active and responsible part of the distribution. Hilary felt that to do so would be giving a tacit encouragement to his wishes, such as she could not conscientiously bestow. If he had only *not* hinted that he did it for her, it would have been possible; but after that, she could not accept the office.

She replied, gravely, that she would furnish the necessary details, but that she thought Mr. Huyton's housekeeper would probably be far better able than herself to superintend the purchasing and making up of the articles of her master's bounty.

"I do not think so at all, Miss Duncan," replied he, smiling quietly; "my housekeeper, I am afraid, is a vast deal too fine a lady to enter into such schemes with the right spirit; it requires a certain degree of refined tact, the offspring only of a really elegant and generous mind, to do these things without hurting the feelings of those who receive the benefit. Mrs. Gainsborough, I feel sure, would put on a condescending and self-satisfied air, which would affront all the mothers, frighten the little girls, and probably bring on a quarrel with the school-mistress herself."

"Why do you keep so uncompromising a character, then?" demanded Mr. Duncan; "a bachelor like you, ought to have some one who can give away cloaks or any thing else, without fatal consequences to the recipients."

"I have been wishing to change for some time," replied Charles Huyton; "I know exactly the character which would suit me; can estimate to a nicety the advantages of truth, simplicity, steadiness, and gentleness, combined with benevolence, charity, humility, and a universal desire of making others happy."

Mr. Duncan laughed.

"Content yourself with those characters in a wife, Charles," said he; "do not expect romantic perfection in a housekeeper; lower your estimate, or you will go unsuited."

"I shall remain as I am till I do find them; but indeed it is only under one circumstance that I intend to change at all; the housekeeper I seek, my dear sir, will, as you suggest, be also my wife; till then, Mrs. Gainsborough may rule supreme."

"Except over cloaks and school-girls, it appears," replied Mr. Duncan; "and those Hilary is to undertake instead."

"If Miss Duncan will do me that favor," replied he; "but not if you do not like," he added in a lower voice, coming close to the table where she was working.

"Then I advise you, Hilary, to make your calculations of yards and quarters," said Mr. Duncan, rising as he spoke, and preparing to leave the room. "I am going to ride into the town to-day; and could order patterns sent out for you and Mr. Huyton to inspect and settle on, if you please."

He went out as he spoke, and Hilary was left alone with her lover.

CHAPTER V.

"For she was passing weary of his love."

Iseult of Brittany.

Hilary looked up from her needle-work with a trembling heart, but a face of calm determination. She had made up her mind to speak.

"Mr. Huyton, this will not do; this must not be."

"What, dear Miss Duncan?" sitting down close beside her as he spoke.

"I can not allow this; you must not suppose that if my father knew what has passed, he would act as he does now. He would see as plainly as I do, the impropriety of my undertaking what is done avowedly for such motives."

"Impropriety! nay, you must not put it so strongly; surely there is nothing improper in my assisting to clothe the same children as you do; or even in my caring for them because they are objects of interest to you!"

"That is not what I mean; and indeed, I am sure you will not press your request, when I tell you that after the motive you assigned, it would be unpleasant to me to grant it."

"I would not do what is unpleasant to you, not for the hundredth part of a minute; no, not if it were to procure me the greatest pleasure in the world. Say no more about these foolish cloaks, I entreat you."

"And tell my father the reason?" said Hilary, blushing very deeply.

"That is not necessary, surely," replied he, gravely; "there is no occasion to assign any other reason; make the business over to your school-mistress; I dare say she will be competent enough. But remember the *motive* is the same; I can not pretend to retract that; and whether you accept of it as a proof of devotion to you or not, there is no other plea to put it on."

Hilary was silent, and looked down.

"You did not suppose I *could* change?" continued he; "you are unjust alike to my constancy and your perfections. That indeed is the cause of my constancy; there is no merit in loving you unchangeably—nobody could help it."

"Mr. Huyton, I believe I was wrong," replied Hilary, with very crimson cheeks, and a rather unsteady voice; "when I promised to allow you to remain—to go on the same as ever—I can not—it is painful, embarrassing, most distressing to me. Am I asking too much in asking you to leave us for a time?—perhaps, too, absence might be good for you, might teach you how much you over-rate me; but, at least, it would do *me* good. After a time, I might learn to meet you unembarrassed, and look on you as I used to do: I can not now; I have tried in vain—your presence distresses, frightens me—makes me uncomfortable and unhappy."

Hilary ended her sentence in very great trepidation, and finally burst into tears, which both frightened and perplexed Mr. Huyton.

"Dear Miss Duncan, don't; dearest, sweetest Hilary; my beloved!—do not make yourself unhappy; I will not stay another day to distress you. Though to leave you is exile and banishment, and protracted pain, I will go; only don't cry. I would not cause you a tear if I could help it. I will make any sacrifice—there now, dry your eyes, take this glass of water! are you better? trust me, your happiness is dearer than my own. I will do any thing you ask."

Hilary dried her eyes, and quieted herself with an effort; then looking up, she said, "I beg your pardon for being so foolish; but—did I understand you rightly?—you said you would leave us!"

"I did, and I will."

"Thank you. You will tell my father, will you not?"

"I will explain all that is necessary. Compose yourself, and trust me."

She rose hastily, and left the room; dropping, as she did so, a carnation she had worn in her bosom, of which he took possession with a lover's enthusiasm. He did not, however, go away immediately; he could not, without saying good-by to her; but he sat down, and formed his plan for the future.

When Mr. Duncan returned, Hilary entered the room along with him, and glanced, with some confusion, at Charles, who, on catching her eye, said, half turning to the clergyman, "I propose to go with you, Mr. Duncan, and give these very important orders myself. I imagine my genius will be equal to that, if the shopman will only help me out a little; so if you will accept my society, I will order my horse round with yours, sir."

The offer of his company was readily accepted, and Hilary saw the two depart together, with much satisfaction, for more reasons than one; and having watched them off, and sighed to witness how uncertain her father's step had become, she turned again into the house, to attend to household duties.

Mr. Duncan's eyesight had lately been failing rapidly, and Hilary, who was aware of the circumstance, had become extremely unwilling to allow him to ride about alone; but it was not in her power to accompany him that day, as the girls were all poorly with bad colds, and she did not like to leave them. She was therefore as glad on her father's account that he should have a companion, as she was herself to get rid of Mr. Huyton's society.

She went to her sisters, and read or talked to them, to amuse and comfort them under the unpleasantness of their indisposition; and she continued with them until the sound of horses' hoofs warned her that her father had returned.

Charles Huyton was still with him, consequently Hilary went into the drawing-room to await his entrance, instead of running out into the porch. The two gentlemen entered together: the young man looking apologetically at Miss Duncan, as if to excuse his return.

"I made Charles come in and give an account of his purchases in the woolen-drapery line," observed Mr. Duncan, "that there might be no mistake in so important a transaction, Hilary; when you have arranged about quantities and other necessaries, he says he will turn the matter of making over to the village sempstress."

Hilary made no answer, busying herself with the tea equipage, which was on the table.

"How are the children?" inquired Charles, drawing near her; and then adding, as the vicar went out of the room, "do not be displeased with me for coming once more."

She colored, and answered, "I am very much obliged for your going with my father, Mr. Huyton, and also for the arrangements you have made about this business. The little ones are much the same, thank you, but they will be better to-morrow, I hope. Do you stay to tea this evening?"

"May I?—I should like—I have made up my mind during my ride; I will go abroad to-morrow; but I have not told your father, and it may seem unkind to leave abruptly, without any explanation. But I will do exactly as you please."

"I have made tea for you," replied Hilary, busying herself as she spoke, in putting water into the tea-pot, and thereby avoiding looking up.

While they three were sitting together round the tea-table, Charles Huyton said, rather to the surprise of Mr. Duncan,

"Do you know, sir, I am thinking of going abroad."

"Abroad!" exclaimed the vicar, with an expression of sorrow in his countenance; "I had hoped, Charles, you were going to settle here for life."

"So did I, at one time," replied Charles; "but circumstances have interfered, and I am proposing a visit to my mother's family at Dresden; they have asked me several times during the last two years, and now I mean to go."

"When? soon? not directly, I hope?" said Mr. Duncan, still looking much concerned.

"Yes, immediately; when a disagreeable thing has to be done, the sooner it is commenced the better. Unless Miss Duncan will give me leave to call to-morrow to say farewell to her sisters, I shall perform that painful ceremony to you both to-night." He fixed his eyes on Hilary with a look of meaning, which she had great difficulty in *not* seeing.

"Come to-morrow, by all means," replied Mr. Duncan. "Hilary, dear, the girls will be able to see him then, and they would break their hearts at missing him altogether. Are you going with any permanent views of settling in life, Charles? Excuse my curiosity, but do you mean to bring home a bride with you? Or, perhaps, you will marry and stay there."

"Most decidedly not," exclaimed he, eagerly and warmly; "there is not the smallest prospect of either one or the other. All my affections are centered in England, all my hopes of happiness are founded on a residence at 'the Ferns,' and every prospective plan of fancy, or retrospective glance of happy memory, will carry me at once to the parish of Hurstdene. You will see me here again as soon as it is in my power to come."

"I shall never see you here again, Charles," replied the vicar, with a gentle shake of his head, and a very patient smile.

"My dear sir, do not imagine such a thing; I trust to be with you at least in the spring."

"I trust you will, my dear Charles; but do you not understand what I mean? Before that time my old eyes will be quite worn out; at the rate in which they have lately failed me, they will be totally dark before the spring comes, and I shall not see your face, though you may look on mine when you return."

"I am shocked to hear you say so," exclaimed Charles, with a face of the deepest sympathy. His glance went from the father to the daughter; Hilary was very pale, and her brimming eyes and quivering lips warned him not to speak to her at that moment; he turned again to the vicar. "But can nothing be done, dear sir? have you had advice? *must* this sad fate befall you? Do not believe it inevitable till it is proved to be so."

"I do not imagine any advice can avail," replied the vicar, calmly; "I have looked forward for some time to this event; and having enjoyed my eyesight for sixty years, Charles, I have no reason to think it a very grievous hardship if I spend a few more in darkness. It will not last forever—light will come, I humbly trust, at length; a better, purer, brighter light than that on which my old eyes are so fast closing; the Light of everlasting day. There will be no darkness in heaven, Charles; and thinking of that, shall I complain?"

With a suppressed sob, Hilary started from the table, and ran out of the room.

"She is crying, is she not, Charles?" inquired the father, a little moved; "I can not see that dear face now as I used to do, to read all her emotions as in a book. Poor girl! she has not learned to think of it yet with composure; but she will find strength in her time of need. I mind it more, when I think of being a burden on the girls, than for any other reason; but *His* will be done—I will be as little troublesome as I can."

"Troublesome—a burden!" exclaimed Charles Huyton, extremely affected at the quiet resignation of the old man. You know *that* is impossible. A burden and a trouble implies something unwillingly carried; and Hilary, angel that she is, would bear any thing for you, or for others with pleasure. With such a daughter, your domestic happiness can never be entirely destroyed; I could almost envy you the blindness which will be waited on, and alleviated by her kindness."

"I am just going to take measures for inquiring for a curate. I can not trust my sight much longer, and some help I must have very soon," said Mr. Duncan.

Charles Huyton started. A curate settled at Hurstdene, and he away! images of a painful nature crossed his mind. He foresaw how much Hilary would be thrown with this curate; he knew the influence which religious enthusiasm exercises over the minds of women; he foresaw what he supposed would be the inevitable consequence—an attachment between them; the overthrow of his hopes. Should this be! what could he do to remedy or prevent it?

"I suppose you would wish for a *married* curate," suggested he, after a pause. "A lady resident in the village would be a comfort, perhaps, to Miss Duncan; it would be better in every respect to have the gentleman married."

"If we could lodge him; but how can that be done? Stair's farm would accommodate a single man, but there is no house in the village where a couple could live."

"True, perhaps; but I think, if you will give me time to arrange, it could be managed. You remember that cottage on the green, which is known as Primrose Bank, about a quarter of a mile beyond the church. Would not that do?"

"My dear Charles, are you dreaming? it is quite out of repair, and small besides."

"But that is easily altered; it is mine now; the lease fell in last Lady Day, and the tenants are gone. I must have it repaired, as you say, and a little addition, a couple of hundred pounds laid out on it, would make it just the thing."

"What a spirit you have, Charles; you never see difficulties."

"Not where there are none; but, my dear Mr. Duncan, I have a motive; it was only last week I heard from a sort of cousin of mine, saying, he wanted a curacy to marry on; and this would be the very thing. I do not know the lady, but I am sure you would like him; and as he is very well off, only wanting work, not pay, until a certain family living falls vacant, I am convinced it would suit exactly. I will put off my departure, until the whole matter is arranged to your liking."

"Can you do that?"

"My departure does not depend on myself, Mr. Duncan; but on one, who, for your sake, would, I am sure, endure me in her presence a little longer. I only wish to please one, for whom I would go or stay, work, beg, die, if needs were—your angel-daughter, Hilary!"

"Hilary!" exclaimed Mr. Duncan; "I do not understand! what has your going to do with her!"

"Dear Mr. Duncan, I love Hilary with a devotion which is beyond any words of mine to express; but she does not love me; and to please her, to prove my constancy, to relieve her from my society, to try if my absence will win a regard which my presence has failed to do, I have resolved to quit England for a time."

Still Mr. Duncan was puzzled; the idea of Charles wishing to marry Hilary was entirely new to him; and he trembled at the notion of losing her, even while he wished he could see her, as he supposed, so safely settled.

Charles explained all that had passed between them, dwelling much on Hilary's determination never to leave her father, with a sort of hope that his influence would be used to turn her wishes in favor of her lover. His eloquence was interrupted by the return of Miss Duncan, calm and composed, as usual; and on her resuming her seat, her father immediately entered on the discussion of Mr. Huyton's plan respecting his cousin, and the house at Primrose Bank, anxiously appealing to her for an opinion.

Hilary, who had been for some time aware that an assistant in the parish was every day becoming more necessary, and who saw at once the possible advantage of having that assistant a married man, admitted that the plan was a good one, and did not frown when Charles, with some anxiety and doubt, proposed delaying his departure from England for the purpose of superintending the necessary alterations. It was unpleasant to her, but she could not allow her own wishes or fancies to interfere with the advantage of others, or her father's comfort. To have this affair settled, was of great importance to him, as he had more than once hinted at the necessity of leaving the Vicarage for his successor, and retiring to some other home; but Hilary knew well that to leave the abode where he had spent nearly thirty years, to break off all the ties formed in a lifetime, to quit his people, his church, his schools, and all the interests accumulated around him, would be as painful to his mind and heart, as unknown rooms and paths, and people, would assuredly be trying to his bodily infirmities.

She could not refuse her acquiescence to these plans, although it increased her obligations to one from whom she was forced still to withhold the only return he asked for his kindness.

After a good deal of discussion, Charles decided that he would go the next morning to London to seek an interview with his cousin, Mr. Paine, and, if possible, bring him down to "the Ferns;" he further determined to engage some clever architect, who could give them the best plan for arranging Primrose Bank, and then the alterations could commence without the least delay; and having come to this determination, he took leave, and returned to his house, to think what more he could do to win Hilary's heart.

Left together, the father and daughter sat some time in silence; he broke it by saying,

"Hilary, my child, is it for my sake only that you will not listen to Charles Huyton's love?"

Hilary started, laid down her work, and going to him, she hid her face on the back of his chair, while she whispered—

"Dearest papa, I would not listen to any one's love, who proposed to take me away from you!"

"I could ill spare you just now; but yet, if it would make you happy, my child, I would give you to him," replied he, drawing down her face and kissing her.

"But it would *not*—it would make me miserable; I do not love Mr. Huyton well enough to marry him. To go and live with him would be wretchedness, and I am very, very happy, with you and my sisters—as happy as I can be!"

"I do not feel sure of that; I shall regret my blindness more than I ought, if it interferes with such a prospect for you."

"Don't say so, dear, dearest father; ah! how glad I am that I am not in any danger of being tempted away. Would I leave you in solitary darkness for any thing this world can offer; or, would I throw such a burden on my younger sisters, as to expect them to take the duties I deserted. I hope *nothing* would tempt me to such selfish wickedness. But, indeed, papa, I do *not* love Mr. Huyton in the least; I can not tell why, but the more I tried the less I found I could; so now I have given up trying, and mean to devote myself to one dearer, better, more precious than he, or twenty such;" kissing him over and over again as she spoke.

"Dear Hilary, I will not say a word to urge you to wed where you do not love; but be quite sure, before you decide for life. I should like to see you safely housed at 'the Ferns,' with such a guardian and husband as Charles Huyton."

"You never will, papa—do not talk of it; I will not leave you; I never mean to marry. I have made up my mind to be your single daughter for life, and to give away my sisters, as if I were an old maiden-aunt, or a lady-abbess, at least."

He smiled, and passed his hand over her forehead, putting back her hair, and looking lovingly at her face; then he added, in a sort of regretful tone,

"Charles Huyton loves you very much, Hilary."

"I believe he does now, papa; but I daresay it will not last; you do not think a man could go on loving a woman who did not care for him, do you? He will find some one else to marry; and when I am an old woman of thirty-five, he will be thankful that he has so much more charming a wife."

"You do not do yourself or him justice, my dear; I expect he will be constant!"

"Constant for a man, dear papa; but that is not constant to one woman, only to one idea—that of marrying somebody."

"What do you know of men, Hilary?" inquired her father, laughingly.

"A little from history and books; a little otherwise," said Hilary, smiling also.

However, Hilary coaxed her father into not minding her refusal of Charles Huyton, and not regretting her resolution of never quitting him; and the matter was dropped between them, although it could not be forgotten by either.

About four days after this conversation, as Hilary and her father were walking together in the garden, where the other girls, now quite recovered, were also amusing themselves, the sound of horses' feet upon the green drew their attention, and looking up, they saw Mr. Huyton advancing to the Vicarage, accompanied by three gentlemen who were strangers. He sprang off his horse, and came hastily into the garden, leaving his companions to occupy themselves by surveying the village.

After a hurried greeting, though a joyous one enough from all but Hilary, Charles told Mr. Duncan, not without some little embarrassment, that he had brought his cousin, Mr. Paine, to visit him; that one of his other companions was a Mr. Jeffries, a clever architect, who was to give them plans for improving Primrose Bank; and the other was a friend of his own, whose name he, for some reason, omitted just then to mention.

Mr. Duncan most courteously desired he would introduce any friends he wished; and the three gentlemen, leaving their horses to the groom, were ushered into the garden. Hilary had no difficulty in deciding which of the three strangers was the clergyman, during the short interval of their approach down the garden walk, and she as rapidly made up her mind that she liked his looks; his countenance conveyed the impression of benevolence, sense, and firmness: she hoped he would come to settle among them.

He, as might naturally be expected, gave his attention to the vicar, and they soon were deeply engaged in conversation. Mr. Jeffries, the architect, began talking to little Nest, to whom he speedily made himself very agreeable; Charles Huyton stood by Hilary in silence, while she made an effort to converse with the third stranger, a very clever, intelligent-looking man, who answered her remarks with a quick but pleasant manner, although with a slightly foreign accent, while his eyes followed Mr. Duncan's movements, and expressed great interest in him.

After a while, the whole party adjourned to see the church; Hilary then claiming her right of leading her father, Mr. Paine still by his side conversing on parish matters, the architect leading little Nest, and devoting himself to her prattle with astonishing pleasure, while the other two gentlemen followed behind, earnestly discussing some topic in under-tones.

Love of his profession, apparently, overcame his love of children in Mr. Jeffries, when in the church, for he examined the building minutely; but Hilary observed that the unknown placed himself beside Mr. Duncan, and seemed far more interested in watching his expression and countenance than in looking at windows, or deciphering brasses.

Her curiosity was excited; something more than curiosity, indeed, for whatever was connected with her father interested her deeply, and she determined, as soon as she was outside the church, to inquire of Mr. Huyton who this stranger was.

Meantime, the quick eyes and keen perception of Mr. Jeffries had revealed a circumstance which country church-wardens had not detected, and which Mr. Duncan's increasing blindness had prevented him from seeing. The chancel was exceedingly out of repair, and Mr. Paine suggested that immediate application should be made to the lay-impropriator to remedy that evil now first pointed out. Mr. Duncan promised to take measures to that effect, and they all left the church together.

Charles came up to Hilary's side as they did so, and rather detaining her behind the others, said, "Your eyes, Miss Duncan, have been questioning, ever since we arrived, who the individual now walking with your father is; he is an eminent French physician, a friend of mine, an oculist, I should rather say, whom I persuaded to come over here with me to-day, thinking that perhaps his advice might be of service to Mr. Duncan."

Hilary colored deeply; she saw, or thought she saw at once, that this was another obligation under which Mr. Huyton had laid them; possibly he had only invited M. de la Récaille to 'the Ferns' in order to see and consult about her father's sight. It was a positive pain to her to receive favors in their present relative situation; and while she felt she ought to be obliged for the kindness of the thought, she could not entirely suppress a feeling of repulsion toward one who would heap benefits on her which she would rather have avoided.

"Do you think Mr. Duncan would mind my friend looking at his eyes?" continued Charles, watching her countenance attentively; "I was afraid of doing any thing disagreeable, so did not like to mention it to him without your leave; but M. de la Récaille is such an enthusiast in his profession, that he declares I can not oblige him more than by bringing new cases under his notice; that is the reason he accompanied me here to-day!"

This speech in some measure quieted Hilary's mind; and after scolding herself in secret for being such a goose as to think that Mr. Huyton must be influenced by thoughts of her in all he did, she entered upon the subject more readily with him, and it was agreed that the suggestion should be made to Mr. Duncan.

"I am not afraid of hurting him," continued Hilary; "for his resignation to whatever happens, is too deep to be shaken by an observation, a hope, or a decision of any man. I have not learned to view it so calmly yet," her lip quivering as she spoke, "and can hardly discuss the subject—but, oh! if your friend could give us hopes—could tell us how to avert—" her voice was lost entirely, and Charles almost regretted that he had introduced the topic. However she recovered her composure again when M. de la Récaille spoke to her on the subject, inquiring particularly, methodically, and with great acuteness, all the symptoms of which she had ever been aware in her father's case; what advice he had taken, and what remedies had been used. His quick, business-like questions, the manner in which he caught the meaning and point of her answers, stopping her from entering on useless details, and arranging all the facts which he elicited during his searching interrogatory, compelled her to use her utmost endeavors to meet his inquiries, to banish feeling and agitation, and to look only at facts in the same light as that in which he viewed them.

It was too late in the day, when they returned from the church, to be favorable for an examination at that time; and it was finally settled that the gentlemen should proceed at once to Primrose Bank, conclude their investigations there, and return to Hurstdene the next morning; when Mr. Paine and the vicar could mutually make known their decisions concerning the curacy, and M. de la Récaille might carry out his wishes with regard to Mr. Duncan's eyesight.

It was an evening of great trial to Hilary; hope for her father had entered her heart, and she could not bid its gentle whispers be still: but she dared not impart her fancies, or allow him to see how much she dwelt on the idea. He was as calm as ever; the notion of approaching darkness had become familiar to him, and he was so firmly convinced of the incurable nature of his complaint, that he would hardly have been disturbed had all the oculists in the kingdom promised him sight. She would not distress him with her agitation; her feelings must be smothered under an assumed appearance of calmness, but she could not approach the topic; and while her sisters were chattering gayly about the gentlemen whom they had seen that day, and describing again and again the personal appearance of all three strangers, never agreeing in details, nor feeling sure whether any pair of eyes were blue, black, or brown, Hilary smiled, and answered, and gave her opinion with almost her ordinary cheerfulness and readiness, while her heart was palpitating with excitement, and her mind at every leisure moment putting up secret petitions for patience, strength, and submission, whatever the result might be.

The morrow came, and the visitors arrived punctually. After a brief interview between the clergymen in Mr. Duncan's study, he repaired to the drawing-room, and seating himself according to the oculist's directions, quietly submitted to his examination. His daughter stood beside him, her hand clasping his, her breath almost stopped from agitation, her very lips white with intense excitement, and yet her face calm, rigid, and pale as marble. Oh! the suspense of that moment: her eyes eagerly bent on the oculist's countenance, endeavored to read his decision in his face, before his lips pronounced it; and, unconscious of all beside, her whole mind and understanding was centred on that one object.

Charles was close to her, his eyes intently gazing on her, but she knew it not: had he been a hundred miles off she could hardly have been more indifferent about him.

It was over at last; that prolonged agony was ended; M. de la Récaille shook his head, sighed, and announced there was no hope, no human probability of any cure; perfect rest might delay the result, agitation might expedite the evil; but come it must; total blindness, sooner or later, was inevitably impending.

Mr. Duncan heard it unmoved; he only drew Hilary's hand closer to his heart, and said, in a cheerful voice,

"Then, my child, I must submit to be dependent on you for eyes; thank God, that I have still a daughter!"

She pressed his hand, words could not come, and she was too shy to caress him before strangers; but Charles saw that her feelings were wrought to the uttermost, that composure was on the point of giving way, and only anxious to release her, addressed Mr. Duncan, so as to call off his attention. Hilary had sufficient fortitude quietly to withdraw her hand, and then escaping from the room, rushed into her father's study, where, throwing herself on a chair, and burying her face in her hands, she gave way to sobs deep and agonizing, such as are the outpourings of suppressed feeling alone, the quivering of the spring long held in suspense.

She was not aware that Mr. Paine had continued in the study after her father left it; at the moment of her entrance he was sitting in a large chair, engrossed in reading, but startled from his occupation by her appearance, and the expressive agony she betrayed, he looked at her for a minute in silent commiseration, and then rising, and approaching close to her, he said, in a peculiarly gentle and sweet voice,

"Miss Duncan, I am grieved to see you so much distressed; has any thing occurred?"

She started at the sound of his voice, but her feelings were too strongly moved for ceremony, and the soft, kind tone went to her heart like the words of a friend.

"Oh, my father! my father!" she sobbed, "all hope is gone; he is, he must be—" then her voice was choked again in an agony of tears.

"M. de la Récaille gives no hope, then?" said he, very gently; "I am indeed grieved."

"Ah, if it had been to me," exclaimed Hilary, "I think I could have borne it better; but for my father, dear, dear father, that he should be helpless, dependent, dark—he who has such intense pleasure in beauty, who has been so active, so busy all his life—that he should be reduced to the state— oh, for submission, resignation, faith like his!"

"Is he much disappointed at the result?" inquired Mr. Paine.

"No, oh, no; he never hoped at all; and he is so good, so trustful!"

"Dear Miss Duncan," said Mr. Paine, drawing a chair close beside hers, "short as our acquaintance has been, it is impossible for me not to be interested in your father and family; and the future connection between us, the claim which I hope to have as your pastor, when I come to assist Mr. Duncan in his duties here, makes me feel that I have a right to speak to you. Will you let me address you as a friend, or shall I be intruding unpleasantly on a sorrow I would gladly assuage or mitigate?"

Hilary raised her head, and wiping away her tears, she said, with a sort of watery smile,

"Be our friend, Mr. Paine, and speak; I deserve reproof for my rebellion to the will of heaven!"

"I would rather give you comfort than reproof, Miss Duncan; and painful as the certainty you have just acquired must be, natural as grief is under such feelings, I think there is comfort to be found even here. The entire and beautiful resignation of your father shows so clearly that he has that blessed light within which is alone the source of true happiness, that I think you may repose in perfect confidence on this dispensation proving a blessing, not a scourge to him. 'He that formed the eye, shall not He see' the sorrow or the suffering of His servant? and can not that Arm guard him from evil during the rest of his life which has led him hitherto? He has not left him helpless, for He has given him daughters who, I am sure, will all make it their privilege to minister to his wants. There is the same home to shelter him, the same daily comforts to which he has been used, the same church, and the same loved services to cheer him. And best of all, beyond all," added Mr. Paine, looking upward, "the same hope of everlasting life in the brightness of light, when our poor, feeble bodies shall be changed into the likeness of the glorious body of our Adorable Redeemer, and when all sorrow, sighing, and darkness shall forever flee away."

Hilary could not answer, and he was silent, too, for a few minutes. Such thoughts as these make earthly trials and earthly pleasures seem small and poor indeed; and the young man just entering on life's serious duties and engagements felt he could readily have changed his own bright prospects for the fate of the elder Christian, whose active warfare must be nearly accomplished, and who must now retire from harassing duties to that quiet contemplation so suited to the last stages of our pilgrimage here.

Recollecting himself and his companion, who was sitting before him with downcast eyes, and composed though pale features, he added, in a more cheerful voice,

"And indeed, my dear Miss Duncan, if you have had any experience among blind people, you must know that there is far less trouble to the sufferer than to those who care for and watch over him. There are many alleviations mercifully sent in all trials; and I have often remarked that those deprived of sight are cheerful, and even joyous, under their affliction. To you, and to your sisters, the anxiety and responsibility may be great, but I feel convinced that, in such a cause, no labor will be a trouble."

"Trouble!" repeated Hilary, clasping her hands; "Mr. Paine, I can only consider it, as far as I am concerned, a privilege, a blessing, to be allowed to minister to such a father as mine. It is a thing to be thankful for for life."

"Fear not, then, you will not be deserted, or left without strength to fulfill your labor of love; services so rendered are indeed a blessing; and happy as I believe your father to be in having a daughter from whom he may receive attentions, I hold that daughter happier still who, from the truest, highest, holiest motives, can give her undivided affection to such an object. Miss Duncan, if you can view your position in the true light, you are not an object of pity; the line of your duty is so plainly marked out, you can have no hesitation in following it. Give yourself to it unreservedly, and your strength will not fail; or, if your cares should become too heavy, and your burden more than you can bear alone, then only believe, and help will be sent you in your need. Look above for aid, and you will find it come to you by earthly means, as you require it. Look below, fasten your hopes on temporal things, and they will wither in your grasp!"

"True, most true; at this moment I feel it true; just now, when, weak and fainting, you have been sent to strengthen me, Mr. Paine; thank you for your words. No, I am not to be pitied, indeed; for I can put my trust above, and even below I have blessings innumerable. You are right; my duty is plain, and with God's help I will not depart from it."

"I hope we shall always continue to be friends, Miss Duncan," added the clergyman; "looking forward as I do to a residence among you, I feel happy in the prospect of having such neighbors; and I trust to bring one among you, who, I am sure, will be desirous to be numbered also among your friends; one whose society will, I hope, be not disagreeable to you. I will not venture to say more, for perhaps you may not consider my evidence conclusive, but I hope we *shall* be friends.

"I am sure I shall be most happy to have a friend," replied Hilary, simply. "I have never had one of near my own age, and I shall look forward to the prospect of the acquaintance with very great pleasure. Now shall we go back to my father? perhaps he will want me; and," added she, with something between a sigh and a smile, "do not betray how weak I have been, and then my dear father need not know it."

CHAPTER VI.

"But in the world, I learnt, what there
Thou too wilt surely one day prove—
That will, that energy, though rare,
Are yet far, far less rare than love."

Arnold.

"I can not leave England, and quit for an indefinite time the spot which contains all that is dearest on earth to me, without one more attempt to avert the necessity of separation from you; one more endeavor to soften an indifference which occasions me so intense a regret. Dearest Miss Duncan, I fear, in my efforts for your father's benefit, I have increased your sorrow, have deepened and aggravated the wounds, from which your loving heart was already so acutely aching. Forgive me the deed for the intention; may I suggest that, however bitter was the pang of disappointment, it must be less severe than would hereafter be the misery of self-reproach, had you neglected any means which might have alleviated his affliction? Your pale face of suffering, self-command, and fortitude is ever before me; I longed intensely yesterday to speak words of sympathy and affection; my heart was yearning to pour out its passionate pity for your agony—but I might not—I whose love for you is, oh, so deep! so pure, so strong! I was forced to be silent, or to breathe only calm sentences of courteous regard, and polite, well-bred, decorous compassion. Do not be angry with me for putting on paper the feeling I can not hope to express otherwise; condescend to read and give some attention to what I say. Must I leave you now, with this sad destiny closing darkly round you! leave you to struggle alone, to toil beyond your strength, to sacrifice yourself in the melancholy fate that awaits you! Do you think I can contemplate such a conclusion with calmness? Oh, no! it is agony to me to dwell upon the idea, which haunts me night and day. Beloved, excellent, adorable Hilary, you have an angel's spirit in an angel form, but your strength, alas! is mortal, and well I know that rest and comfort for yourself will be your last thought, while your services of love are poured out on the helpless ones around you. May I tell you what is my dream, my vision of bliss? I fancy I see you all transported to 'the Ferns,' your younger sisters making joyous with their bright presence the dreary walls of the old house, and causing their empty chambers to echo to their merry voices; there I see them in idea, growing up under every advantage which can be procured by love and wealth united; proper attendants, masters, literature, enjoyments in doors and out, every taste developed, every talent cultivated to the utmost. I see your dear parent, too, enjoying under the same roof every blessing and comfort which perfect filial love and unbounded power could shower on him—every compensation for this new affliction which could assist to lighten the burden, and brighten the remainder of his path through life. And there I see, reigning supreme over all, with all the despotic power of love, and gentleness, and tender firmness combined, one whose presence is like a ray of sunshine, blessing and gladdening every thing within reach. I think I see you, ruling the family, governing the parish, protecting the weak, comforting the unhappy, delighting the gay; influencing all around by the imperceptible power of goodness, even as a delicate odor spreads itself unseen, and yet all-pervading, driving away what is bad, and purifying the surrounding atmosphere. Do you frown upon my dream? alas! that there should be that in *me*, which prevents its realization; that though to me it looks so fair and beautiful, my presence should cast the shadow on it, which alone makes it impossible. But is it so? let me ask, is there no change? may I have no hope? Have the three months which have elapsed since I first ventured to express my feelings passed, and left no trace behind? am I as far off as ever from the point, the only thing which can make me happy? If so, I go to exile and solitary misery to-morrow, for solitary I must ever be where you are not; solitary I shall continue until the weary months roll by, which you may consider necessary. But, tell me how long must it be? how long must my home duties be laid aside, my house be left untenanted, and myself a wanderer in foreign lands, away from all who have any claim on me? Hilary, you shall dictate; but remember you decide for more than yourself; look at the whole circumstances, and then tell me how long shall I be justified in absenting myself from what you have taught me to consider duties and responsibilities? Deign to give me an answer to this question. Must my dream continue nothing but an empty dream, while I go, and for how long—or may I remain and realize it?

"Charles Huyton."

Such was the letter which, on the ensuing day after the interview with the oculist, Charles Huyton's groom carried to the Vicarage; and to this Hilary was forced to reply, for the servant was waiting for an answer. Was it not a dazzling vision to place before a young girl's eyes, whose self-devotion to her family was her most prominent characteristic? Opulence and all its advantages for them, instead of a narrowing income, a humble home, and the wearing routine of close domestic economy; and the price was to give her hand to an amiable and agreeable man, passionately devoted to her, and a favorite with every member of her family. Ought selfish feelings to stand in the way, and prevent their enjoying benefits which she might so easily purchase?

For a moment she hesitated; she deliberated not for herself, but for those most dear to her. Then, too, there was his plea. Could it be necessary to insist on his leaving home and home duties, renouncing his occupations and pursuits, and all for her? Had she any right to require such a sacrifice? She pondered the question again and again: her head was bewildered, and she could decide on nothing. Time was flying quickly; the answer must be written. Oh! for a friend to guide and counsel her.

Nay, but she had a friend; One who would not leave her; One always accessible, always loving and patient. And there was a rule, too, a rule to guide her, if she could but discover it; she knew that she must not expect sudden illuminations, divine impulses to direct her; such were not the answers to her prayers for which she had been taught to look. Her line of duty was marked out, and she could see it, doubtless, clear and distinct, if she could but remove the intervening mists and shadows, which passion and prejudice, imaginations, mistrust, or too great anxiety for the future had thrown across it. She prayed to be guided aright, and then quietly set herself to review the case, trusting that she should eventually see what the right was.

The cloud passed from her eyes; she saw the snare laid before her; stepped aside, and thanked God that she had been saved from sin and danger.

"Thou shalt not do evil that good may come of it."

There was the rule; and plausible as the temptation had appeared, she saw now that it was *evil*. Yes, *evil* to give her hand without her heart, to sell herself for any earthly good, either to herself or others; to make the solemn vow to love, honor, and obey, one toward whom the two former seemed impossible, and the latter might be incompatible with other duties. What, if she shrank from the claims now existing on her, should she therefore form others more indissoluble, more exacting still? If she had not strength to act a daughter's part, should she take the responsibilities of a wife also? Would she have more time to attend to her father's wants, when she had added the cares of an extensive establishment, and a large dependent neighborhood? What madness to dream of such a change! And would the luxuries, the indulgences of wealth be a real blessing, a safe acquisition to those for whom she had been tempted to procure them. Whose words then were those who spake—"How hardly shall they that have riches enter into the kingdom of heaven?" Did not He know, or could He be mistaken?

She wept! not that she must resign the prospect, but that it should have proved a temptation to her; and seizing a sheet of paper, she hastily wrote the answer which should decide this point as she hoped forever.

"Again, and I trust for the last time, let me say, I thank you for your good wishes, but my plans, my intentions are unchanged. I deeply regret having been the cause of so much disappointment to you. Our duties henceforth must keep a separate path. Mine is too clear to be mistaken; nor am I making any sacrifice in my resolution; my wishes, my hopes of peace and happiness all point to remaining as I am, as clearly as my sense of right, and my convictions of duty. Now will you allow me, as the only return I can make for your attachment and kind wishes, to say one word to you about what your *duty* is? Is it right for you to throw on me the decision of what it should be? you know, whatever you may say, you can not really make me responsible for what I can not help.

"Must you renounce your country and your home, because you must renounce my society? I asked you *not* to come to the Vicarage; I did not bid you go to Dresden—neither do I tell you *not* to go there. If your mother's family have claims on you, of course you must attend to them; if the claims of others are pre-eminent, should you not give them their due place?

"Does it become any of us, poor, short-sighted, weak individuals to quarrel with our station in life, and because Providence denies us one thing we wish for, should we fret like a pettish child, and throw aside every other blessing in angry disgust? Pardon me for writing thus to you; I should not have presumed to do so, but for the part of your letter in which you call on me to decide. Mr. Huyton, when you have hereafter to answer for your conduct, will it be a good plea that you gave up the helm of your mind to another hand, one which could not guide you rightly?

"Now, farewell. I trust that we shall each be led right in our separate ways, and if I can give you nothing else, I will, at least, give you my poor prayers for a blessing on you, in return for the kind wishes you have expressed for my family, and the favors you have conferred on them.

"H. D."

This answer dispatched, of its results she knew nothing, except that Charles Huyton left the country with the intention of going abroad; and this information was conveyed by a servant, who brought over a little parcel, directed to Miss Sybil Duncan. There was the key of his library, and an order to his gardener to admit Mr. Duncan's family, when and where they pleased, in his grounds, a privilege accorded to no one else. Hilary was glad of this little proof of kindness, it shewed that he did not resent her answer; and she trusted that she was acting from right motives, whatever his course might be.

She was the only one of her family who did not either secretly or openly regret his absence; but to her the relief was unspeakable, and she knew that her father owned it was right, however much he might miss his society.

Charles Huyton gone, she was able to devote herself to other cares and occupations, and all disagreeable memories connected with him vanished gradually from her mind in the more pressing duties which surrounded her, and unexpected pleasures which opened upon her view.

Mr. Barham, the gentleman whose duty it was to keep the chancel in repair, answered the letter from the Vicar on the subject by a visit in person, accompanied by his steward, Mr. Edwards, and a surveyor, whose opinion was much relied on by his employer. Mr. Duncan's infirmities rendered Hilary's presence necessary during the interview; and the gentlemen really seemed much struck by the young lady's personal appearance, graceful manners, and quick yet clear powers of mind. Mr. Edwards paid her several compliments on her business-like habits and capacities; the surveyor admired her command over her pencil; and Mr. Barham, who was a courteous but calm-mannered person, and who was known generally as possessing a considerable degree of that pride of family and exclusiveness of habits which often develops itself in a lofty graciousness to all others supposed to be inferiors, intimated his wish to come again, and see how the building went on, and requested permission to bring over his daughters to visit a place which had so much to recommend it.

Hilary gave a ready acquiescence; and an early day next week was fixed on for a party from Drewhurst Abbey to come over and take luncheon at the Vicarage.

In the course of conversation, Mr. Duncan mentioned the circumstance of the expected arrival of the curate, who was to come down in a very short time, and take the duty on Sunday. Mr. Barham immediately began regretting that he had not known that Mr. Duncan was inquiring for a curate: there was a young man of good family and great talent whom he should have been glad to have seen settled there—one, in fact, who was about to marry a connection of his, a cousin of his daughters—it would have been pleasant to have had them in the neighborhood: Miss Duncan would have found the lady an acquisition to their society. He very much lamented that the arrangement had been made without his knowledge.

Mr. Duncan was privately a little amused at his visitor, who, having been contented for thirty years to have no intercourse with him, could hardly have reasonably expected to be consulted on the choice of an assistant in duties with which he had no concern.

However, he answered very mildly, "that the gentleman in question was, he believed, an excellent young man, which, so far as parochial matters were concerned, was of far more consequence than either high family or astonishing talents, and he hoped no one would find reason to complain that their Vicar had been hasty or injudicious in the selection of a pastor."

"No doubt that is very true, my dear sir," blandly observed Mr. Barham; "virtue in a clergyman undoubtedly ranks above all; nevertheless, the advantages of a cultivated genius and high family are not to be despised; and although there may be many men of low birth highly estimable in a moral point of view, yet it is desirable, for the sake of the character and standing of the clerical body, that there should be gentlemen also in the profession. They give a tone—an elevated tone to the whole!"

Mr. Duncan did not feel called on to reply; and after a pause, Mr. Barham added,

"I could have wished that your curate had been a man of good connections, and a certain fortune and position in society. Is he married?"

"Not yet, I understand," replied the Vicar; "but he has promised to bring a wife as soon as his new house is ready. And I believe I may venture to answer for his connections and fortune being both good. He is a relative of Mr. Huyton of 'the Ferns,' who assured me he was a man of independent income."

"Mr. Huyton of 'the Ferns!'—how strange! What may his name be?"

"Paine—the Reverend Edward Paine."

"My dear sir, this is most extraordinary! he is the very man I was thinking of. I am delighted to hear it; but it is strange that it should be settled without my knowing it; neither Mr. Huyton nor Miss Maxwell has informed us. I wonder she did not let her cousins, my daughters, know. I wonder Charles Huyton has not called to inform me."

"Mr. Huyton went abroad last week," observed Mr. Duncan, quietly.

"Abroad!—are you certain? I knew nothing about that, and I should have expected, from the sort of terms we were on, that he would have told me. I can hardly believe it."

Mr. Duncan made no observation.

"I shall call at 'the Ferns' to inquire as I go home. Perhaps you have been misinformed!" continued Mr. Barham.

"I have reason to think not," was the Vicar's quiet observation, conveying, however, no conviction to the mind of his visitor, who only thought he knew nothing about it.

"But about Edward Paine," continued Mr. Barham; "how came it settled without my hearing, I wonder? Whose arrangement, may I ask, was it?"

"It was so recently settled," answered Mr. Duncan, "that perhaps there has not been time to let you know; and in that case, I regret I have forestalled them in giving information, which would, no doubt, have come more gracefully from the parties in whom you are so much interested. Charles knew my wishes, and introduced his cousin here; and Mr. Paine, once introduced, is a person to make his own way; but almost nothing was said of the lady, so that I was entirely ignorant of her being a connection of yours. Charles did not even mention her name to us, did he, Hilary?"

"Excuse me," said Mr. Barham; "may I inquire who *Charles* is?"

"I really beg your pardon, Mr. Barham; I mean Mr. Huyton; but for the last two years I have been so completely in the habit of speaking *to* him by his Christian name, I sometimes forget and speak *of* him as such, too."

"I had no idea," said Mr. Barham, a little majestically, "that my young friend, Mr. Huyton, was so diffusive in his acquaintances. You were, then, on very intimate terms?"

"He has always been a kind neighbor to us, and being my principal parishioner, and owning most of the property about, we naturally were much interested in many of the same things. He has been very good to the schools, and, indeed, in many ways; the poor will miss him this winter, for we can hardly expect him to remember them at Dresden."

Mr. Barham's notions were quite discomposed by this speech. His amiable intentions of patronising and bringing into notice a family who had hitherto "blushed unseen" in the wilds of Hurstdene, seemed apparently quite thrown away; possibly they were not such entire representatives of modern Robinson Crusoes as he had imagined them. He saw, however, no reason for changing his views with regard to introducing his daughters, and, accordingly, he soon afterward took leave, with a renewed promise to come at the time talked of.

Isabel and Dora Barham were both younger than Hilary Duncan, but their friends had evidently done what they could to give them the advantages of age, or to deprive them as soon as possible of those peculiarities of youth which consist in simplicity, bashfulness, or diffidence. They had been early brought out into the world; early introduced into society; they had been taught to behave, talk, and dress as women, at an age when more fortunate girls are allowed still to feel themselves children. They were now, at sixteen and seventeen, extremely elegant young women, elegantly educated, elegantly dressed, elegantly mannered, surrounded from childhood by all the refinements and luxuries of life; accustomed to lavish indulgence of their fancies, and an unbounded command of money. Suffering was to them a fable; self-denial a mere myth. Had they not been naturally amiable, they would have been now detestable—but they were not. Isabel was a little proud, a little selfish, a little vain; but she had some very good qualities mixed with these vices, which, in good hands, might have turned out well. Dora had no particular character at all; she was merely a reflection of those she lived with; and as these were chiefly her father and sister, of course she generally fell in with their tastes, adopted their habits, and believed all they told her.

They were delighted with the introduction to Hilary; they both commenced a most enthusiastic girlish friendship with her. Isabel's was, perhaps, less sincere than Dora's—she had more of her father's patronising tone; and never, in the least, suspected how very far the vicar's daughter was really her superior in every essential particular.

Hilary was very simply sincere in her regard for the two girls. She admired them exceedingly, and their kindness, their caressing manners, and very amiable ways, engaged her affection. They soon became intimate, and the Miss Barhams would ride over of a morning, and gliding into the Vicarage drawing-room, would spend the whole afternoon hanging about Hilary, chatting, idling, or pretending to learn from her some of the many fancy works which she had acquired. They were continually trying to wile away Hilary to the Abbey; but this her home occupations forbade, and only twice, during the autumn and winter following, was she induced to spend an afternoon there, and then her father accompanied her.

The introduction of Mrs. Paine was another remarkable event in Hilary's quiet life, which gave her, perhaps, even more pleasure than the acquisition of her other friends. She was a very pleasing young woman indeed, and, although a cousin of the late Mrs. Barham, and having a good fortune, she was so earnest in her wishes to follow out her duty, so simple in her tastes, and indifferent to personal accommodation, that long before Primrose Bank was habitable, she was established with her husband in tiny lodgings at Stairs farm, and giving her time and attention as much to their new parish as to her future home.

The winter passed quietly, but far more cheerfully than Hilary could have ventured to hope; Mr. Duncan enjoyed Mr. Paine's society, and relied on his judgment in all parochial matters; he also liked the two young ladies who frequented his house, especially Dora, who, he once told Hilary, might be made any thing, either good or bad, as circumstances fell out.

Sybil and Gwyneth, meanwhile, were growing very tall; and whether it was from their intercourse with the young ladies from the Abbey, or their own nature, they had lately advanced so rapidly, that their appearance had got the start of their years, and no one would have guessed them to be less than sixteen and seventeen, instead of what was actually their respective ages.

The owner of 'the Ferns,' although absent in a foreign land, had by no means forgotten either his friends or his tenants. More than one extensive order on his banker was remitted to Mr. Duncan, for the relief of distress, and the encouragement of good conduct; and several letters were received from him, written to the same person. Hilary could neither quarrel with the act, nor the manner of performing it. Although Mr. Huyton was, of course, aware that she would necessarily be acquainted with the contents of the letters, there was nothing in the words which could in the least offend her; they breathed warm interest in his people, affectionate regard for the vicar, and kind remembrances to his family. No one could have suspected from these letters what had passed between them, and it seemed to Hilary's young and trustful imagination, that absence was effecting the desired cure; she hoped that when their friend returned, as he talked of doing in the spring, it would be to resume a pleasant and rational intercourse, such as it had been eighteen months ago.

One morning, about the first opening of spring, the two young ladies from the Abbey arrived earlier than usual; so early, indeed, as to break in upon the girls' school hours, which was a point Hilary had long begged them to attend to. She was looking graver than usual, which they attributed to this transgression; and Dora, putting her arms caressingly round her neck, exclaimed—

"Now, Hilary, dear, don't be angry, but give your sisters a holiday, and let us be happy for once; do you know we have come to say good-by for ages."

"Indeed! are you leaving home?" said Miss Duncan.

"Yes, we are going to martyrdom," replied Dora.

"We are going to town for the season," said Isabel, in answer to Hilary's look of inquiry. "We always do, of course; it is expected of people in our rank, you know; Dora pretends she does not like it, but she does really; and if she did not, one must make some sacrifices for duty."

"Going to London for the season—that means going to be very gay, does it not?" said Sybil.

"Oh, yes, Sybil," cried Dora, "it means turning night into day, and spending it in hot crowds, for whom one does not care the least portion of an atom; and employing all one's energies, faculties, and time in dressing, dancing, or sleeping—oh dear!"

"Don't be foolish, Dora; nobody likes company, or pretty clothes, better than you," said Isabel.

"That is the worst of it; I like them against my conscience, and every time I buy some extravagant ornament, I suffer from remorse; and yet am just as weak at the next temptation. I wish I could say I really hated it all. Do you know, Hilary, I envy you for staying here so quietly in the country, and being able to dress plainly and do good, while I am only able to wish to do either."

"I am afraid you would feel rather awkward, Dora, either with my wardrobe or my occupations. Our duties are so different; yours, you know, is to go with your father to London, to dress elegantly, and look pretty."

"That is just what I despise myself for, Hilary—my perfect uselessness, and life of gaudy show. I never leave you without wishing I were situated like you. Not too grand to be useful—living in a small house, instead of those fatiguing large rooms, which tire one to walk across; having a garden one could love and care for, instead of being merely allowed to look at papa's gardener's plants and shrubs; having to do things myself, instead of being always waited on; and oh, above all, having learned to despise the pomps and vanities of life, instead of all the time loving them in my heart, and feeling them necessary to my comfort."

"She is only talking nonsense, Hilary," interposed Isabel; "she is seized with these fits of despondency about her own rank in life, every now and then, and fancies we are all wrong, for living according to what is expected of us in society. I am happy to say, however, she acts on principles of common sense, and her democratic theories of equality and universal brotherhood are confined to theory entirely."

"It is not right," said Dora, thoughtfully shaking her head; "it can not be right; but I do not know what is wrong, and when I begin to think, I am involved in a labyrinth of doubt. To be admired, courted, and caressed, can not be the right aim of life, and yet I am sure it is mine. Now, is not that absolutely contemptible, Hilary, to live for such objects?"

"I rather suspect," replied Hilary, "you mistake your real motives. You know your father likes you to go into society, and is pleased when you are admired; and this, I have no doubt, is what makes you like it too. If nobody wished you to go out, I dare say you would be as quietly domestic as I am, Dora."

"I do not know; I believe if any body I cared for wished me to stay at home, I should yield to them with delight. One comfort is, I know the London dissipation will make me ill, and then I shall be forced to be quiet."

"That is an odd sort of comfort, Dora," said Hilary, smiling; "one I can not wish for you!"

"It is her nonsense," observed Isabel.

"Indeed, it is not. I was quite knocked up last year; and I am not so strong now. I mean, when I am ill, to ask Mrs. Paine to take me, for change of air, to Primrose Bank, and try how I like small rooms and a moderate establishment."

"Here come Mr. and Mrs. Paine," observed Gwyneth, who was sitting by a window; "you can settle with her at once, Dora; it would be so nice to have you at Primrose Bank."

Mr. Paine went to Mr. Duncan's study; his wife came to the drawing-room, bringing with her little Nest, who had been saying her lessons to her papa. There were some parish matters to be discussed first with Hilary; and then, before Dora had time to mention her plans for her expected illness, Mrs. Paine observed, looking earnestly at Hilary,

"What is the matter, dear?—have you had bad news of any kind to-day?"

"Not *bad*; at least, not necessarily so," replied Miss Duncan; "but we heard from abroad to-day."

"Your brother! nothing wrong about him, I hope."

Hilary's eyes filled, but she spoke calmly. Maurice had been ill, very ill, of a most dangerous fever; the danger was over now, they hoped, but, indeed, they believed it had been extreme, and he was not yet well enough to write himself. Their letter had been from his captain, who had most kindly written to his father, to assure him that danger was now over, and that they hoped, by care and attention, to restore this promising young officer to his family and his country; there was one to the same effect from the surgeon, also, who had written at the express desire of Captain Hepburn, to certify his being now in a state of convalescence.

"It was so kind, so very kind, of Captain Hepburn to write," pursued Hilary, with emotion; "and such a beautiful, feeling letter, speaking, oh, in such terms of Maurice, and so desirous to spare my father's feelings. I knew Maurice liked him very much, and now I do not wonder."

"What a wonderful girl you are, you dear thing!" said Dora, caressing her; "having all this on your mind, and yet teaching and talking, as if nothing had been the matter. How did you see, Fanny? for I never discovered any change in Hilary."

"Perhaps, Dora," said Mrs. Paine, "because you are more accustomed to attend to your own feelings than those of other people."

"Well, I am afraid I am; I want to know how to cure that. But do tell me something more about this brother of yours; how long has he been away? what is he, a captain, too? or what?"

"He is only a mate, Dora; but has served long enough to be promoted, only we have no interest. But the best part of Captain Hepburn's letter, Mrs. Paine, is, that he hopes to get him leave to come home for his health, and then we shall have him here again!" Hilary clasped her hands in a very unusual ecstacy.

"And what sort of interest does it need to make a young man a lieutenant?" inquired Dora, again. "Could papa do it for you?"

"interest at the Admiralty," replied Mrs. Paine. "I hardly think Mr. Barham would like to trouble himself about it, because he has a nephew at sea himself."

"Oh, yes! cousin Peter—I can not bear him, Hilary; I hope your brother Maurice is not like our cousin Peter."

"Absurd, Dora!" ejaculated Isabel; "Peter is a very good sort of young man."

However, Dora's inquiries were not to be stopped by Isabel's ejaculations; and before she took leave of the Vicarage, she had made herself mistress of the rank which Maurice now held, of the time he had served, and the wished-for promotion he deserved to attain.

Maurice's illness, and his expected return to England, so excited and engrossed the minds of the family at the Vicarage, that another piece of news, which reached them the same time, was comparatively insignificant; this was the projected return of Charles Huyton.

A letter to Mr. Duncan reached the Vicarage the week after the Barham family left the Abbey, intimating that he was proposing to be at "the Ferns" in about a fortnight. It was a calm and friendly letter; not one expression or sentiment betrayed any strong emotion, nor was there the smallest allusion to the motive which had taken him abroad. Hilary was much pleased; and when she had thoughts to spare for him at all, they were of a quiet and satisfactory nature.

CHAPTER VII.

"What lady is this, whose silken attire
Gleams so rich by the light of the fire?
The ringlets on her shoulder lying,
In their flitting luster vying
With the clasp of burnished gold
Which her heavy robe doth hold."

Tristram and Iseult.

The Barhams had been in town about a fortnight, when Hilary received a letter from Dora, inclosing another addressed to that young lady; Dora's epistle was written in the following words:

"Dearest Hilary—

"You see I have got it done at last; I have coaxed, and prayed, and begged; and not in vain. What would I not give to see your dear, beautiful face at this moment! I never forgot you, and I made up my mind at once. I said nothing to papa, because I thought my dear old friend, the earl (he is my godfather, you know) would do it for me; and I believe he only made me beg for the fun of the thing. I went down on my knees to him; we had such a laugh when he brought me the little note inside; I do not think it gave him any more trouble than just asking. Remember, I should not have begged for any body but *you*; and having never even seen your brother's face, my efforts must be acknowledged disinterested. Perhaps you had better not tell *him*; however, you may do as you please, for I am not ashamed. I am not ill yet, but, on my honor, I am not so well as I should be in the country; and though I have tried hard to be rational, I rather think I am as extravagant as ever. Tell dear Mr. Duncan I am so glad for you all, and I only wish I could have asked for a step or two more at the same time. The pleasure of making you happy is so great, that I think I am best off of the whole party, including your brother. Is that the reason you are so fond of doing good, Hilary? it is much better than jewels or balls; only now the excitement is over, what shall I do? Good-by, you dear darling! Mind, I expect a letter of thanks, of course. Your loving friend.

"Dora M. Barham."

Hilary read through her friend's letter in hopes of meeting with something explanatory of her meaning; failing that, however, she did not stop to puzzle over it, but opening the enclosure, found a little note addressed to the Earl, of whom Dora had been writing, informing him that a lieutenant's commission for Maurice Duncan had that morning been made out, and would be forwarded to the young officer by the next packet.

The delight of the whole family at this very unexpected news was quite as great as Dora could have anticipated; it was only a pity that she was not there to witness it.

Of course there was still considerable anxiety about Maurice's health; and until the next account arrived from abroad, they were in a state of too great and trembling uneasiness, to dwell very much on the prospect of seeing him again; the certainty of the issue checked their anticipations, and it required no small exercise of patience and trust, on Hilary's part, to go through her ordinary duties, at moments when her mind was tempted to wander off to the possible or the probable which might yet be in store for them. Mr. Paine's society was a great comfort to her; she could talk freely to him and his wife of her fears as well as her hopes; while to her father, owing to the relief she thus obtained, she was able to maintain the same cheerful demeanor as ever, and to speak with far more confidence of her brother's recovery, than she really felt.

Mr. Duncan and his daughters were all seated one day in the little summer-house at the end of the terrace walk; one of the girls was reading aloud, while the rest were busy with their needles, when a shadow crossed the window which made them look up, and the next moment Charles Huyton turned the corner of the building, and stood in front of them. Down went Sybil's book and Gwyneth's work in a moment; while Nest, slipping from her father's knee, made no scruple of throwing herself at once into the arms which were extended to take her.

"It is Mr. Huyton," said Hilary to her father, in explanation of the sudden cry of joy from her sisters; and Charles, putting aside the little one, advanced to the vicar, taking at the same time in his own, both the hand which was extended toward him, and that which guided and supported it. Excepting that one tender and prolonged pressure of her slight and trembling fingers, there was nothing in his greeting of Hilary which marked any peculiarity of feeling, and even at that moment he hardly looked at her; his attention was apparently given entirely to her father; his words, his looks, his smiles, half sad, half joyous, were devoted to him. He pressed *his* hand again and again, inquired most affectionately after his health, and then turning to the others, greeted Sybil and Gwyneth, with looks of open, undisguised pleasure, remarked on their wonderful growth, and paid some little compliments to their personal appearance, which brought a still richer glow into their cheeks, all the deeper because the admiration was but half expressed in words, and much more unequivocally in looks and smiles. Then sitting down among them, he exclaimed at his pleasure in being there once more, glancing from the one to the other of the party with happy eyes, taking Nest upon his knee, and bidding Gwyneth sit beside him, almost as if he had been Maurice himself; and all with such an easy, disengaged air, and so entirely devoid of any appearance of a nature to alarm Hilary, that after the first half hour her heart ceased to flutter, her cheeks to glow with consciousness or fear, and she was soon conversing with him as unreservedly, and almost as readily, as her sisters themselves. He entered into parish matters with Mr. Duncan, and his questions of, How do you like Mr. Paine? and How does he please in the parish? and many others of the same kind, were followed by an appeal to the girls as to how music and painting went on; and then a gentle questioning of Hilary herself as to the favorite scholars, the old women pensioners, the idle and mischievous boys who had formerly vexed her; and sundry other particulars, which proved that whatever else he had consigned to oblivion, he had not forgotten any thing connected with the welfare of his tenantry. Discussing the repairs of the church introduced the name of the Barham family, with whom he was already acquainted, and he seemed pleased to think that they had formed an intimacy with the Duncans, and amused at Sybil's somewhat enthusiastic friendship and admiration for Dora.

The relation of what she had done for Maurice might have justified this partiality, but Sybil did not know the particulars connected with that transaction; Hilary being rather shy of owning the influence through which the long-desired promotion had been procured.

"And oh! Mr. Huyton, Maurice is a lieutenant," was therefore the information which Gwyneth communicated, without any connection with Dora Barham's name.

"A lieutenant! I am glad indeed to hear that! I congratulate you, my dear sir," was Charles's exclamation, grasping Mr. Duncan's hand once more with warmth; "nay, I think I may do the same to you all," added he, taking the two girls' hands in his, and kissing little Nest very heartily. "Indeed I do congratulate you all—*you*, Miss Duncan, more especially."

He dropped her sisters' hands and advanced toward her, very gracefully, yet with a little hesitation, which bespoke doubt as to whether he were taking too great a liberty.

She could not help placing her hand in the one he extended, and she looked up with her clear innocent eyes to him, as he stood before her; there was nothing in his look to alarm her into shyness, and she met his gaze with quiet, comfortable confidence, as she said,

"Indeed it has been a pleasure, although it, like mortal affairs generally, has had a drawback, for Maurice has been ill."

"Indeed! I am sorry—not seriously, I trust!"

Hilary glanced at her father, and then replied, "We have only had a report from the captain and doctor as yet; we are expecting further news in a short time. I will show you the letter from Captain Hepburn."

She drew the letters from her work-basket, and gave them to him with another glance at her father, and a sort of beseeching look at him, as if deprecating any unnecessary alarm to Mr. Duncan. Charles Huyton understood her, and seating himself by her side, he quietly read through the two letters, and returned them; observing—"It was this, doubtless, that prevented his writing to me lately. I should not wonder if we were to see him here, before you hear again. He will, of course, return now."

She felt grateful to him for the cheerful tone in which he spoke, although she saw, by the anxious expression of his eyes, that he participated in her uneasiness on her brother's account.

"And what are your plans now, Charles?" inquired Mr. Duncan, kindly, laying his hand on his visitor's shoulder; "have you made up your mind to become a useful member of society, a good and hospitable neighbor, a justice of the peace, or to fill any of the other duties which country gentlemen ought to attend to?"

"I will place myself in your hands, my dear sir," replied he, with a sudden glow over his countenance, which Hilary did not see; "you shall dictate what my duties are. However, I have indeed made up my mind to renounce my hermit life at 'the Ferns;' and, as a preliminary step, have persuaded an aunt and cousin of mine to come over to England and pay me a visit."

"Indeed! who are they?" inquired Mr. Duncan, with interest.

"Mrs. Fielding was my mother's sister, and, like her, married an Englishman. Will you do me the great favor of visiting them, Miss Duncan?"

turning suddenly to Hilary. "I am anxious to give them, my cousin especially, a favorable impression of England."

Hilary replied she would be most happy; a sort of wondering feeling passing through her mind, as to *why* Mr. Huyton was so desirous to please his cousin. Perhaps he hoped to persuade her to settle for life at 'the Ferns,' and then how pleasant it would be to have a friend in his wife; her countenance brightened at the idea; and her manner became more easy and disengaged toward Charles from that moment.

He seemed readily to fall into his old ways, in every respect, except such as she might have objected to, and never thought of leaving them for the rest of the afternoon; taking it as much as a matter of course that he should remain to tea, as the younger girls did.

On their return to the house, while Hilary supported and guided her father's steps, he loitered behind with her sisters, strolling along the terrace, and laughing and chatting with them, telling Sybil he had found them out by the sound of her voice reading, which fortunately was not so much altered as her person was, or he should have run away, believing them to be a party of strangers. But when Mr. Duncan was safely past the window, by which he entered into his own room, and Hilary had turned away to take the path to the porch, he immediately joined her, and began, in a voice and words of sincerest sympathy, to inquire into the actual state of her father's sight. She could speak of it calmly at last; use, and the quiet submission and unvarying cheerfulness of Mr. Duncan, had reconciled her to the idea, and she was able to tell him with composure, or rather resignation, that all was quite dark to him now; but that she was thankful to say, that the affliction had been so softened and modified, as to be far less terrible than she had imagined it could be.

Then he alluded to Maurice; but here the chord of feeling vibrated too strongly; the tension had been too acute for it to harmonize entirely with faith and patience; and they sounded in a minor key, compared with the sharp tone that fear and suspense rang out.

It was with quivering lips and trembling eyelids that she spoke of her brother's danger, and it was with looks and tones of answering sympathy that Charles Huyton replied to her. Had not her eyes been at that moment blinded by her tears, she might have read how deep his feelings were.

"It is very wrong, I know," added she, dashing away the drops from her eye-lashes; "I ought to feel more resigned, knowing as I do he is in the same Hands still, and that nothing will happen but for the best. I still shrink and tremble inwardly as to what may be in store, although I ought to do better, considering the lessons of trust I have had."

He stepped into the porch, near which they were standing, and taking up a small basket from the bench, presented it to her.

"You told me once," said he, "that flowers preached to you, and taught you lessons of confidence and hope; may I trust that these will say something of the sort, and not be rejected?"

He lifted the lid, and showed her a bunch of lilies of the valley, carefully arranged, with their roots in wet moss.

"Oh! how exquisite!" she exclaimed, stooping over them to hide a little hesitating consciousness, and not venturing to take the basket from his hands; "these must be forced, Mr. Huyton!"

"Yes; I found them this morning in my conservatory, and brought them here, thinking you would all like them. Will you not take them?"

"It seems selfish when you have visitors coming to-morrow," replied Hilary, still looking at them.

"My aunt and cousin have nothing to do with these; the gardener raised them on purpose for you and your sisters, I know; I can claim no merit, except that of willingly bringing them; do take them, and put them in pots in the drawing-room; and let them speak of comfort."

"You have chosen your text well," replied Hilary, receiving the basket from his hands, and raising first one and then another of the delicate bells. "They do indeed preach eloquently. Thank you very much for so kindly reminding me of all these flowers bid me consider."

He gave her a quiet, rather grave smile; and then turned the conversation to some other topic, as they walked into the house together.

He seemed very happy afterward, assisting Gwyneth and Nest in preparing the flower-pots in which these lilies were to be planted, while Hilary sat with her father at the window, and gave her advice on the subject, but was not allowed by any of them to tire herself over the plants, as she had taken a long walk that morning, and was looking, they all agreed, both pale and fatigued.

Mr. Huyton did not come to the Vicarage again for two or three days; he was supposed to be occupied by his visitors, who, they heard from Mr. Paine, had arrived when expected.

To Hilary's great satisfaction, Mrs. Paine offered to accompany her to "the Ferns" to call on these visitors, a task which, for several reasons, was rather a formidable undertaking to her. They drove over together, in Mrs. Paine's little pony-carriage, and were received at the door of the large house with a degree of splendor and pomp such as she had never seen there before.

Hilary thought of her first visit to that place, and the quiet way in which she had then been introduced, as they followed the servants through the spacious vestibules and ante-chambers into the morning sitting-room, where Mrs. Fielding and her daughter were sitting. Happily for them, Charles entered as they did, and he introduced Mrs. Paine pointedly as his cousin; Miss Duncan was more slightly named, but it was evident, by the quick glance which Miss Fielding gave, that her visitor was an object of some interest to her. The elder lady was equally foreign in her look and her accent, both which betrayed her birth, although perfectly lady-like, and rather pleasing; the cousin, in whom Hilary felt more interest, was a handsome girl, more English than German in her air and voice, and looking so perfectly at home at "the Ferns," that Miss Duncan could not get the idea out of her head that she was consciously destined one day to be mistress there.

"Victoria has been wanting you so much, Charles," said Mrs. Fielding, turning to her nephew, who was standing by Mrs. Paine. "It was something about the drawing she was copying; I hope presently you will help her out of her difficulties."

Mr. Huyton said something about happy, and turned to his cousin with a smile; but Hilary, who unconsciously watched the expression of his face, was disappointed: it was not exactly the smile she wished to see there—not like the happy, frank look she had been used so often to receive, before she learned to know its meaning.

Victoria Fielding threw back a somewhat haughty head, and said, with a flashing, mocking look of her bright eyes,

"Mamma flatters you! do not fancy I wanted you in the least. I disdain help. My motto is, 'By my own hand.'"

"Very well," replied he, calmly, but with an expression of admiration in his face; indeed she was so handsome and graceful, that it was not easy to look at her without admiration.

Her conversation to him was all in the same style, to Hilary she hardly spoke at all; and when Miss Duncan tried to find subjects of conversation, she seemed little inclined to reply, unless Mr. Huyton joined; whatever she might affect of indifference toward him, Hilary was convinced, was simply affectation. The wish to attract him was obvious, although shown in a taunting and defying sort of way.

After about ten minutes' conversation of this uncomfortable and disjointed kind, Charles suddenly turned to Hilary, and said—

"Have you been into the conservatory lately, Miss Duncan? I should like you to see my camellias."

Hilary feeling that any change would be a relief at that moment, answered that she should like it very much indeed; and then he asked Victoria if she would come too.

"No, thank you," replied the young lady, carelessly, "I have walked round and about it, till I am more weary of that particular spot of ground, and those especial flowers, than of any thing else on earth; except myself," she added, in a sort of whisper.

He smiled again.

"Conservatories should be made like kaleidoscopes, to vary at every turn, or they grow intolerably dull," added she aloud; "don't you think so, Miss Duncan? Perhaps you don't know, however; you probably have not been so often in the one in question as I have."

"Perhaps not," said Hilary, very quietly; "but I always thought it very pretty when I did see it. However, it is many months now since I was in it."

"I can not fancy *you* tiring of flowers," said Charles, with more peculiarity of accent than he had used before; so much so, indeed, as to cause Victoria to raise her head, and turn a sharp look on the person thus addressed.

Mrs. Paine rose at this moment to go, and Hilary, glad to escape from the eyes bent on her, prepared with pleasure to take leave of the whole party. Charles, however, accompanied them out of the room, and then, as they were crossing the vestibule, repeated his request that they would come and look at his camellias; adding, with a quiet, grave courtesy, which he had assumed since his return, "I hope it was by your own choice that it is so long since you have entered the conservatory: for though it was optional with you and your sisters to visit it, it was not left so with the servants whether you should be admitted."

"I am afraid, from your saying that, Mr. Huyton," replied Hilary, "that Sybil omitted to thank you for your thoughtful kindness. I assure you, my sisters have paid several visits here during the winter, as Mrs. Paine can testify, having accompanied them every time."

"Yes, laying claim to relationship," said Mrs. Paine, smiling, "I ventured on that liberty."

"I am truly glad your sisters enjoyed it," was his answer; he saw at once the reason why Hilary herself had scrupulously avoided similar visits: he did not like her the less.

He cut huge branches of heliotrope, and the loveliest camellias he could find, "to send to her sisters," as he said. Most gardeners would have been in despair at the liberties he took; but Mr. Huyton was peculiar, and with his gardener, Mr. Allan, the Miss Duncans were great favorites; so perhaps the surveyor to the conservatory did not grumble very much.

"Your library has been a great resource to my father," said Hilary presently, wishing to say something which should show gratitude, and avoid misconstruction; "he has often expressed himself so much obliged to you for your liberality."

"Is not that a lovely bud?" said he, holding up a half-blown camellia, whose delicate white petals were just displaying the fringe which gives them such an air of lightness and refinement. "How I do love a pure, delicate, unostentatious flower, which seems unconscious of its own charms, and shrinks modestly from sight."

He placed it in her hand as he spoke; the only blossom he gave her; the rest he deposited in a basket to be carried to Hurstdene.

"I think you love flowers better than ever," was her observation, very innocently made.

"I do," replied he, gravely, with eyes turned away in another direction. "Take this little peeping red and white bud to Nest with my love, it is the very image of her dear little face. See how coquettishly it half looks out, half hides." He said this in a light and playful tone, and she made him a smiling answer, and then Mrs. Paine, having concluded a dialogue she had been holding with Mr. Allan, summoned Hilary to the carriage.

As he helped her in, he said, but without looking up at her—

"Was not I right in saying my cousin had nothing to do with lilies of the valley?"

"She would wear the crown imperial," said Mrs. Paine, laughingly; and then they drove off, while Hilary mused on the feeling he entertained for his cousin, and what she wished that feeling to be, now she had seen the lady.

She looked forward with a little anxiety to their visit being returned. It made her uncomfortable to think of it; there was something in the quick glance of those very bright eyes which discomposed her, and made her feel shy and shrinking. It was not, however, half so bad as she expected, when the visitors really arrived, which they did in the course of a week. Mrs. and Miss Fielding drove over, Mr. Huyton accompanied them on horseback. The ladies made themselves very pleasant; the mother conversing with Mr. Duncan, evidently and sincerely interested by the courteous manners, mild countenance, and quiet cheerfulness of the blind clergyman; Victoria devoting herself to Hilary with a sweetness, complaisance, and air of satisfaction, which, after her former reception, quite astonished Miss Duncan. She was delighted to meet her young acquaintance again; she was enraptured by the drive, enchanted with the dear, picturesque old parsonage, captivated by the charming antique room, with its old oak wainscotting, and fine rare china vases, bequests from Mr. Duncan's grandmother. She called Nest to her, and kissed and caressed the beautiful child, wanted to draw her portrait, begged to have her to spend the day with her, to all which requests Hilary replied with little more than a smile, considering them too entirely ideal to deserve a serious answer. But in the middle of one of her most complimentary speeches, Victoria was astonished to see Hilary suddenly start from her seat, stand one moment gazing through the window, with clasped hands and parted lips, and the next spring from the room, and disappear altogether.

Charles Huyton, who had been chatting with the other girls, rose and looked after her with an expression of anxiety and alarm, then approaching his cousin, asked if any thing was the matter with Miss Duncan.

"You, who know her so well," replied Victoria, with a peculiar smile, "ought to be aware if this is her usual manner to her guests. May be it is the perfection of English politeness!"

But little Nest ran after her sister, and throwing open the door, disclosed to their view, in the vestibule, Hilary clasped in the arms of her brother Maurice. It was a pretty thing to see; and the sister was too completely absorbed in her joy to be conscious there were spectators, as he bent over her glowing face, and kissed her again and again. The tall and manly figure, the bronzed complexion, and fine countenance of the sailor, forming a charming contrast to the elegant girl whose fair cheek rested on his bosom, while her eyes spoke the welcome she had not words to say.

Charles, however, cut short the amusement of the spectators by shutting the door, before the younger sisters had seen what was passing outside the room; and a few minutes passed in a sort of awkward silence between Victoria and Charles, although Mr. Duncan, ignorant of what had occurred, was comfortably talking to Mrs. Fielding.

All thoughts of the visitors at that moment in the drawing-room had gone from Hilary's head; she saw only her brother, and was conscious only of thankfulness to see him again, and a pang of sorrow for the one who could not see at all. After the first mute embraces, and then the whispered words of love and joy, Maurice pronounced his father's name, and Hilary, half angry with herself for having even during that short time engrossed all the delight of knowing him safe and well, placed her hand in his, and led him into the room.

Then she remembered who was there, and her color came and went: delight, shyness, pride, and embarrassment mingling in her feelings as she encountered the eyes within, and recalled how abruptly she had quitted them.

The visitors drew back, and the exclamations of the girls, the movement, the unusual step, and a whisper or two around him, warned Mr. Duncan something had occurred.

"What is it, Hilary?" said he, rising and stretching out his hand; "Maurice—my son!" as his fingers closed upon those which so warmly grasped his—"thank God!"

But Maurice could not speak. The sight of his father's helplessness, the closed eyes, the slow and cautious movement, and the increased appearance of age which the last three years had produced, overcame his fortitude, and the young man had to struggle hard with the emotions of tenderness and grief before he could control his voice to answer his father's greeting.

"Can we not go?" whispered Mrs. Fielding to Charles; "we are sadly in the way."

Victoria's eyes were fixed on the group with a thoughtful, longing expression; but she felt the propriety of her mother's proposal, and turned to quit the room.

Hilary recollected herself and them, and advanced to accompany them to the door, while Maurice still saw nothing and no one but those so dear to him.

"I am sorry you should be driven away," said she, gracefully, "though I can not pretend to be sorry for the cause. He is my only brother."

"Do not apologize, my charming young friend," replied Mrs. Fielding, with her gentle accents, "you must be glad to get rid of us, and I feel we have had a pleasure we do not deserve, in witnessing so captivating a family-picture. I congratulate you with my whole heart."

"If we have acquired knowledge we have no right to," said Victoria, pausing before stepping into the carriage, and warmly clasping Hilary's hand, "we have paid dear for the acquisition; at least, *I* have, for I have discovered my own poverty. I could envy you, Miss Duncan; and of all the charming things I have seen to-day, to love, and be beloved like you, appears to me, beyond all comparison, the best. What would I give for such a brother!"

She sprang into the carriage, not deigning to accept her cousin's proffered assistance, and turning on Hilary once more her bright eyes, brighter for the tears that filled them, she kissed her hand, and drove off.

"I will not stay now," said Charles, "to intrude on a happiness in which I can well sympathize; but let me come to-morrow, and welcome Maurice home—tell him how sincerely I congratulate him; he is not looking ill, although rather thin. Good-by!"

He released her hand which he had held in a long, lingering clasp, gave her one look of indescribable feeling, then mounting his horse, cantered quickly away; for when he turned to wave his hand to her, ere he had gone two paces, she was out of sight.

Hilary did not pause a moment indeed to watch his departure: she darted into the house, and was again beside her brother, ere Charles had looked round. And then, unrestrained, she could enjoy the full delight of seeing him once more. Oh! the kisses, the congratulations, the smiles, the tears, the silent rapture, and the joyous exclamations of that welcome. It was long before they were rational enough to ask how, or when he arrived in England, or to remember his increase of rank—they thought only of himself; while he could hardly find words to express his wonder and admiration at the change the three years had made in his sisters. Hilary so improved, and yet so little altered; the same darling girl, and yet more charming and dear than ever. And the others too! Sybil as tall as Hilary; Gwyneth not much behind; he could not believe they were the same. Oh! how glad he was to be here.

"And about your illness, Maurice?" inquired his father.

Then came the history of his fever, how it was increased by over-exertion, how suddenly it had come on, how bad it had been, and how, so far as human agents were concerned, he owed his life to the kindness of his commander.

"He is such a good fellow, father; I hope you will know him some day; I am sure you would like him, Hilary; he has nursed me like a brother; he gave me up his cabin; took care of me day and night; if it had not been for him, I must have died, I should have been stifled in my berth. How glad I am he is made; more glad than for my own promotion, which, by-the-by, I only heard yesterday at the Admiralty. Hepburn came home with me, you know: he was promoted from home, and had to return of course; and as I had leave for my health, we came in the same packet, and he promised to come down and see us here, when he has settled some business in town."

"God bless him!" said Mr. Duncan from his heart; "if a visit here could give him pleasure, how gladly we will welcome him: you must write to him in my name, Maurice, and repeat the invitation."

The girls were never weary of hearing Maurice talk, and the history of the last two months had to be gone over and over again; while every variation of praise which could be bestowed on Captain Hepburn was poured out by the grateful young lieutenant on his late commander. He was as true as steel, brave as a hero of romance, firm as a rock in duty, tender as a girl of others, where feeling only was concerned; indifferent to his own comfort, careful of his men's, devoted to his profession, a first-rate sailor, a pattern of an officer, a thorough gentleman in conduct, a true Christian in principle, and to crown all, in the imagination of the girls, he was tall, dark, good-looking, of an old historic family, and comparatively poor! This was the climax to the interest in his favor; for Maurice knew that Captain Hepburn's family had been unfortunate, had lost their property in a law-suit, and that he had, by much self-denial and economy, succeeded in paying debts left by his father, and honorably discharging every claim, far beyond what law alone required of him.

Allowances must, of course, be made in this bright picture for the favorable prejudice's of Maurice's feelings, seeing his senior officer's character through the beautiful vista of his three years of agreeable command, crowned eventually by the extreme personal kindness, which had largely contributed to save the young man's life; but if the brother, in his strong partiality, over-rated the worth and merits of his friend, it was not likely that the young sisters would curb their female fancy, and estimate him in their imaginations by a juster scale, or a cooler feeling for his virtues. Captain Hepburn was established as an indisputable hero, in the minds of Sybil and Gwyneth; and even Hilary gave more of her leisure moments to forming ideal pictures of him, than it was at all her custom to do, with regard to unknown individuals, or circumstances, which did not immediately connect themselves with her daily duties.

CHAPTER VIII.

"And women—things that live and move
Min'd by the fever of the soul—
They seek to find in those they love,
Stern strength and promise of control.

"They ask not kindness—gentle ways—
These they themselves have tried and known;
They ask a soul that never sways
With the blind gusts that shake their own."

Arnold.

Charles Huyton kept his word, and came over in the morning, as he had promised, to see Maurice. There was not much doing in the way of study, or regular employment, that day; even Hilary was unsettled by her joy, and after two or three vain attempts to promote reading, or to engage in their usual occupations, she had given it up, and the whole family were clustered together round Mr. Duncan's chair on the lawn, who, while enjoying the warmth of a spring morning, was also delighted to be surrounded by the happy voices, and caressed by the soft hands which seemed continually flitting about him.

The happiness of her feelings, and her conviction that Victoria Fielding was destined to be Charles's wife, made Hilary more than usually cheerful and disengaged in her manners to the visitor; and his looks and his words were in general so carefully guarded, that she had nothing to alarm her into coldness or reserve. Frank and friendly to Maurice, as usual, more so, perhaps, even than formerly, he was; but *he* must have been a very close observer, who could have detected from any thing which passed, that he regarded Hilary with a different feeling from her sisters. The only thing which could have indicated peculiar and strong attachment, indeed, was his extreme warmth and affection of manner to her father and brother; and this might also arise from other causes unconnected with her. So Hilary was happy and at ease; Maurice was with her, and Charles, as she supposed, grown so rational, as to be content to give up a woman who did not love him, and seek one who did, in her place.

While Mr. Huyton was there, Mr. and Mrs. Paine walked in, having just come up from the village school; that being one of the duties of which they had relieved Hilary, since her father's infirmity had required so much more of her time and attention. When pleasant people know one another well by name and report, they do not take long in becoming acquainted on meeting; so half an hour had scarcely gone by, before they were all on the most comfortable and easy terms imaginable.

"Only think, Hilary," said Mrs. Paine, "Dora Barham has carried her point, and is coming down here next week; let me see, this is Wednesday; yes, she is coming on Monday next, to stay with me, for change of air. I never thought Mr. Barham would have allowed her to give up the chances of a London season."

"The chances to her, I really believe, would have been a severe fit of illness," replied Hilary. "She is very delicate, and I have no doubt Primrose Bank will be more beneficial to her than Bryanstone-square in every respect."

"Who is going to be your visitor?" inquired Charles of his cousin's wife.

"Oh, Dorah Barham, my pretty little cousin; you remember her, I dare say, when you were in England last year. You used to visit at the Abbey, I know."

"I remember your cousins very well," replied he, expressively; "very agreeable women in society. Some of those girls who are reared entirely in a forcing-house, and brought out as fashionable ladies, when they ought to be only children. I used to think her rather idle and weak, but amiable enough if she were only allowed to be so. With such an education, one must not look for simplicity, or real refinement of mind, but be thankful for unaffected and elegant manners, when one can meet them."

"You are unjust, Mr. Huyton," exclaimed Hilary, with animation; "Dora Barham is much more than that; she has most genuine kindness of heart, and sweetness of disposition. No one must say a word against Dora Barham in my hearing, on pain of my intense displeasure. Maurice, I appeal to you—be her champion."

"I am convinced," replied Maurice; "I have been for some months convinced of her excellence; ever since she first formed your acquaintance I have been prejudiced in her favor; and though I have never seen her, there is no lady in the land to whom I am so perfectly ready to swear allegiance, and devote myself as her champion."

Mrs. Paine laughed.

"Well, you will have the opportunity soon, I believe; I shall be curious to know whether she will answer your expectations."

Mr. Huyton looked puzzled at the enthusiasm of Hilary and Maurice; he was not aware of the cause of his interest. The young lieutenant had learned his obligation from his sister, and although his pride might have been more gratified had promotion been the unsolicited reward of merit, his feelings were excited and warmed towards the girl, whose love for Hilary had chosen so judicious a way of exhibiting itself.

"I was charged with a commission from my aunt and cousin," said Charles, after a while, "which I hope to execute successfully, or the consequences will be, I can not venture to say what. Will you all come over and spend to-morrow at 'the Ferns?' Excuse the shortness of the invitation; it is not to be a formal visit, but a friendly one. Pray say yes!"

Some excuses were urged by Hilary, but Mr. Huyton would not accept them. He asked Mr. Duncan first; he appealed to every member of the family; and from each, especially from Nest, obtained a ready assurance that each would like very much to go to 'the Ferns' to spend the day. Hilary could not contend against such an overwhelming majority, and was forced to yield. Charles only urged Victoria's wishes to her; it was her invitation, her earnest desire; she wished to see more of them all; every thing should be arranged to suit the hours and the tastes of the various members of the family. There were plenty of amusements for little Nest, and another little girl, a very nice child, had been invited to meet her. The carriage should be sent to fetch them, and should take them back in the evening, and Mrs. Fielding hoped that she should be allowed the pleasure of devoting herself entirely to the entertainment and care of Mr. Duncan, who so strongly reminded her of her own father, now some years deceased, that she longed to see him again, and see more of him.

To resist such an invitation was impossible; and Hilary, mentally wondering why Victoria should be so anxious for her acquaintance, and yet gratified at seeing the kindness extended to her whole family, and not confined exclusively to herself, was, on the whole, much pleased at the idea.

The next morning proved as warm and bright as could have been desired by any of the party; and twelve had hardly struck from the church clock when the carriage drove up to the door. Nothing could exceed the warm welcome and the undisguised pleasure with which they were all received at 'the Ferns.' The ladies and Mr. Huyton were loitering on the lawn, in front of the conservatory, and Mrs. Fielding immediately proved her sincerity by gently taking possession of Mr. Duncan, to whom she devoted herself so unremittingly, that Hilary found nothing to do for him.

The luncheon and children's dinner occupied a considerable time, and after that, while Mr. Duncan was driven out round the park in a low garden chair, by his indefatigable companion, and amused by her lively and interesting conversation, the rest of the party adjourned to the bowling green. This, which was most beautifully kept, was surrounded by a double row of limes, whose long bare branches were already showing the bright crimson buds which precede the leaves, while they, as yet, afforded but a partial interruption to the sunshine, which, in April, in England, is not often too hot.

Charles, Maurice, Gwyneth, and Sybil entered into a spirited game at bowls, while Victoria and Hilary paced up and down on the broad walk under the trees, partly observing the game, partly engrossed in conversation. Miss Fielding seemed particularly interested in the details of her companion's daily life, about which she asked innumerable questions; she also admired Maurice very much and very openly to Hilary, who was as much pleased at this as she was amused and surprised at her companion's entire ignorance of English habits and domestic life.

"Yes, I know little enough about my father's country," replied Victoria, "but I want to understand it better; and I do not think my cousin's house or customs are at all a rule for real Englishmen; he is, like myself, half German."

"I do not think he would be a bad specimen," replied Hilary, "let his country be what it may, he is so very kind and considerate to every one about him."

"Charles! yes, he is a good sort of person," said Victoria, smiling; "lets me have quite my own way here; has given me *carte-blanche* to do as I please; a liberty I can not always expect, so I mean to make the most of it while it lasts."

"I dare say it will last," observed Hilary.

"Oh, I don't know; you English wives are so very domesticated and subdued; you seem to me to give up all will and way of your own; one's own identity is lost in the unity of the marriage state; one is merged into another's being; and so becomes nobody, in fact as well as deed."

"Perhaps it may be better where such is the case," said Hilary, "but it is not invariable."

"Well, I like to do things well," said Victoria; "and when I *am* an English wife I mean to behave as is expected of women of fortune and family. Upon the whole, I do not think it will be bad."

"You are going to marry, then?" said Hilary, a little hesitatingly, yet anxious for the answer.

"I am to be married in the autumn," replied Victoria; "meantime I intend to enjoy myself, and Charles lets me reign here *en princesse*. He certainly is good-nature itself with regard to me."

"He told me at first how anxious he was to make England pleasant to you," observed Hilary, recollecting the wonder she had felt when he had mentioned it to her.

"Now, I want to consult you," continued Victoria, "about some of my plans.—Ha! well bowled, Mr. Duncan; do you see, your brother plays well; I think we will weave a crown for the victor, shall we, or at least give him a sprig of myrtle to stick in his coat as a trophy? Charles, you will be beat entirely. I wonder you do not exert yourself more for the sake of your partner."

"I suspect Miss Gwyneth rejoices more in her brother's prowess than she would in mine," replied Charles, pausing before he sent off his bowl, which had been driven by Maurice's last stroke close to the edge where the ladies were standing. "My defeat excites no sympathy, and my victory would raise no exultation, so long as one of the family lost by what I gained."

He was gravely considering the bowl which he held in his hand as he spoke, and did not raise his eyes, although Victoria bent hers on him with a most expressive glance, as she answered in her native language; but what was the nature of her observation Hilary was not sufficiently mistress of German to understand; she only saw that the few words brought a deeper glow to his cheek, and a sort of suppressed smile to the corners of his mouth, both which spoke no ordinary sense of gratification. It was the first time she had observed any thing like emotion in his intercourse with his cousin, and she concluded that it was some expression of affection or encouragement which had called up that look of pleasure.

Victoria turned away, and drew her companion on also, resuming the topic which had interested her before this little interruption, namely, a party which she wished to give in her cousin's house. It was to be a sort of fête, uniting a daylight and an evening party—a déjeuné in a marquee on the lawn, and out-of-door amusements for the afternoon—a band of music in the gardens, flowers, fish-ponds, a boat on the lake, and any other diversions they could devise or invent. All the country should be asked, and no expense or trouble spared to make it delightful.

"But, Miss Fielding, consider the time of year," exclaimed Hilary; "we are but just at the end of April, and May is often so cold a month with us that we can not reckon on fine weather for an out-of-doors party."

"Stupid climate, then; what, not after the twelfth? I thought of the fifteenth, which would be a Wednesday; surely the weather by that time *must* be fine."

"*May* be," replied Hilary, laughing; "when you have been a little longer among us, you will find there is no *must* for an English climate at any time of year. Sometimes we have snow in May; but by the fifteenth, perhaps, there may be sunshine and green leaves."

"I shall trust to that, and plan accordingly," replied Victoria; "there is nothing like hope.—There goes your brother again; how he plays; ah, Charles is completely conquered."

The girls were tired, and the gentlemen, too, were willing to rest, so they all went into the conservatory, and seated themselves there, Victoria beginning a very lively conversation with Maurice, who was far too much of a sailor not to be ready to admire any handsome young woman, and quite able to make himself agreeable to her.

On the whole, the visit passed off most pleasantly; they dined rather early, and after coffee, were allowed to return home in sufficiently reasonable time to prevent Nest falling asleep before getting into the carriage. Hilary, whose mind was now quite easy regarding Mr. Huyton, for she never doubted but that Victoria was engaged to him, though she had not mentioned his name, was quite cheerful and happy; no longer afraid of addressing Charles, nor shrinking from his notice; and delighted to think that his future wife was so pleasant, and so well disposed toward herself and family.

From this time there was a great deal of intercourse between the two young ladies, sometimes carried on by notes, which Charles most frequently brought over, but more often by visits from the cousins to their friends at the Vicarage; for Hilary could not again be tempted to "the Ferns;" and therefore Victoria, who was always wanting her advice, had to seek her at home.

Often the elder lady accompanied them, and insisted on taking out the clergyman for a drive, while the young people settled their concerns together: half the notes of invitation, at least, were written by Hilary's hand, and plans for ornament or amusement suggested by her head.

The younger girls were wild at the prospect of such an unexpected pleasure; and as there were to be numbers of children of the party, Nest was included among the visitors.

Mr. and Mrs. Paine necessarily often came in for these conferences, although they did not intend to have any share in the grand fête, Mrs. Paine's health at the time affording her a rational excuse for avoiding excitement and fatigue.

Their domestic party at Primrose Bank was in due time reinforced by the promised visit of Dora Barham, who made her appearance at the Vicarage the next day; and whatever might have been the state of her health on leaving London, she certainly was glowing enough when introduced to her darling Hilary's tall brother.

The handsome young officer, with the frank gratitude natural to him, made a little advance toward shaking hands with the pretty young woman, to whom he was so essentially obliged; an advance which would have been instantly checked and cut short by recollections of what cold courtesy required, had she not perceived both the first motion and the subsequent impulse. More anxious to save him from awkward feelings than scrupulous about etiquette, she gave him her hand with a charming grace and a bewitching smile, from the powerful effect of which Maurice did not recover for the rest of the morning, at least.

Half an hour afterward, the party was scattered considerably; Mr. Duncan and Gwyneth out driving with Mrs. Fielding; Maurice, Sybil, and Dora, sauntering along the terrace in the garden; Mr. and Mrs. Paine, quietly at work in the school; and Hilary seated between Victoria and Charles, talking over plans, smoothing difficulties, and showing how impossibilities even might be conquered or set aside.

Several days slipped by, much in the same way. Dora was a heedless girl, and more than once left a bracelet or a handkerchief at the Vicarage, which made it indispensable that Maurice should go over to Primrose Bank, to return it, on those mornings when she did not intend to come to the Vicarage; and this intercourse was carried on to such an extent, that Mrs. Paine became seriously alarmed for the result. She knew Mr. Barham well, and was perfectly certain that any attachment to a poor lieutenant, on his daughter's part, must be as little to his taste as aloes to a child. To remonstrate with Dora, would infallibly make matters worse, if she had any inclination in his favor; and poor Mrs. Paine most heartily wished that she had never undertaken a charge of so delicate and difficult a nature, as the care of her young cousin.

To her great relief, however, before ten days had passed, Mr. Barham and Isabel came down for a few days to the Abbey, and Dora was summoned home immediately. Maurice regretted it much; but poor Dora, who had permitted her imagination to be most unwisely occupied by the charms of her new acquaintance, felt it a great deal more; and now looked forward to the grand fête at "the Ferns" as a day of possible felicity, because it would throw her once more into his society. She made some effort to go over to the Vicarage once or twice; but Isabel seemed backward to do it, observing, that now Hilary had her brother, it made a difference; and poor Dora, only too conscious that it did make a most important difference, dared not press a proposal of the kind, from this very consciousness. Whether Isabel knew of her frequent interviews with Maurice Duncan, she did not discover, and could not decidedly guess; the only motive avowed for the visit to the country, was to be present at Mr. Huyton's grand party; and as several friends accompanied Isabel from London, their abstaining from their former frequent visits at the Vicarage while engaged with visitors, appeared too natural to require an excuse.

As I said, Dora felt the separation more acutely than Maurice, partly because he knew his own admiration to be so very presumptuous that he could no more wonder at her being removed from his society, than he could at the setting of the sun or moon; and partly because he had another engagement, which necessarily engrossed his time and occupied his thoughts. This was a visit from Captain Hepburn, who came down in answer to the pressing invitations he had received both from Maurice and his father.

His arrival in itself was rather a disappointment to the younger girls; he came down in so very unheroic a style, as little accorded with their romantic fancies regarding him. In the first place, he did not take them by surprise, but having written to announce his intention, afterward came just when he had promised, and might have been expected. Then he drove up in a gig, and brought a portmanteau and hat-box; he wore a black coat, and an ordinary hat, and seemed to have met neither misfortunes nor adventures on his journey.

He certainly was tall and handsome, but he was also quiet and grave, with a complexion so bronzed by weather, and an expression so thoughtful and sedate, as to give him the appearance of six or eight years more than his actual age.

The two girls were awed into silence and fear, and even Hilary felt the regard she had already imbibed for him, deepen into a respect almost too strong to be compatible with ease, and which produced an appearance of timidity and reserve in her manners, not at all usual with her. This, however, was only at first; fear soon wore off with him, for he was as simple as he was quiet in his habits and manners, and as easily pleased as Maurice himself. He arrived in time for their early tea, and Maurice having once mentioned what their hours were, he appeared perfectly ready to conform to them. His friendly regard for Maurice was indisputable, and his pleasant and attentive manners to his father were very conciliatory. To the young ladies he was at first quietly civil, and Hilary learned to appreciate more correctly the anxious *empressement* and extreme attention once so naturally received from Charles Huyton, when she discovered that politeness alone did not dictate such devotion.

Captain Hepburn had not been twenty-four hours in the house, before all the young ladies learned to regard him with composure as well as respect. He was generally rather silent, and much given to reading, in which occupation he spent nearly his whole morning, in appearance so profoundly engrossed by the page before him, as to be unconscious of all else. This quiet habit made it perfectly possible even on the first morning, for the others to occupy themselves as usual; Sybil and Gwyneth read and wrote, worked, drew, or practiced on the piano, as comfortably as if Captain Hepburn had been a hundred miles off, instead of being seated at a table only three yards from themselves; and Hilary went in and out, and attended to her father's comforts, arranged her housekeeping, worked for Maurice, overlooked her sister's exercises, or taught little Nest her arithmetic, exactly as if there had been no visitor present, or as if he had been there all her life.

When she appeared with her bonnet on, and her youngest sister by her, and half-whispered to Sybil that she was going to take something to Mary Clay on the Common, Captain Hepburn roused himself from his studies, much to her surprise, and asked leave to go with her.

Leave was granted, and the trio set out together; Maurice was reading to his father, so he did not accompany them.

It was a very pleasant walk, after Hilary had conquered the first feeling of shyness which her companion excited. He conversed so pleasantly at first about the forest, and forest scenery in England and abroad, then about Maurice; and of him he spoke so kindly and cordially, that Hilary took courage to say what she had before been longing to express, their extreme and heartfelt gratitude for his kindness and attention to their brother during his perilous illness. Captain Hepburn would gladly at first have stopped her thanks; but she would not be stopped, and the earnest eloquence, the trembling tones of deep feeling, the glowing, grateful expressions, were of a nature to touch the heart of even a cold or selfish man, and on him, who was neither, produced a powerful effect. He looked at her eyes glittering with tears, at the color varying in her cheeks, at the lips trembling with emotion, and he thought he had never in his life seen so interesting a picture of affection and sensibility.

"You think a great deal too much of what I did, Miss Duncan," said he, when she paused; "I only wish I deserved your thanks. Maurice is as fine a fellow as ever lived, and one could not do too much for him; and now I see what his home is, and whose hearts and happiness were wrapped up in his welfare, I am doubly happy to have been of any use. There is no need of repaying me with thanks, it is more compensation than I deserve."

"We can not think so," replied Hilary, raising her eyes to his face.

"To see your brother with your father is perfectly beautiful," continued Captain Hepburn, well knowing how to return the pleasure which Hilary's thanks had given him.

"Oh, yes!" cried she, artlessly, "is it not? we are so happy when he is at home."

They walked on in silence for some time, and when he spoke again, it was to make some remark on the advancing spring.

From that time all remains of shyness had vanished from Hilary's manner to their guest, and she became as perfectly at her ease with him as with Maurice himself. The first week of his visit was a very quiet one; their visitors, except the Paines, had deserted them; Mr. Huyton had gone to London, and was not to return until the fourteenth, and Victoria and her mother had other engagements, which occupied them during the same time. This week of repose was very welcome to Hilary, it was a relief after the unusual bustle and occupation which had preceded it; she was able to resume her old domestic habits, and although the party in prospect must sometimes claim a thought, she was not obliged to give up all her leisure moments to its concerns.

She read, and worked, and walked as in old time, with one important exception, that she had a companion such as she had never had before. There is an affinity between some minds, which is inexplicable and incomprehensible to those who have it not. That week had not been passed away, before Hilary had learned to look with interest, and something more indefinable still, for the opinions of Captain Hepburn, as she gave her own; a glance told her how well she was understood, even before the words of agreement came, and then she felt she was right. She learned more, too; she saw how those dark eyes would fix themselves on her with an expression which sent a strange thrill of pleasure through her heart, even when it brought a bright color to her cheeks; she discovered how often when his head was bent over his book, his glance was following her as she moved about the room, and she was neither annoyed nor frightened at the discovery. It was so pleasant to find that this cultivated and intelligent man, as brave as he was good, and as clever as he was kind, could take such interest in her thoughts, her ways, her wishes. She looked up to him as something so immeasurably her superior, that his approbation seemed an honor; she felt she could trust him; that he would be one who would sacrifice all to right, and that no selfish consideration would induce him to forget her interests, or to endeavor to influence her to a questionable act.

There was some strange spell on her surely, which made her confide to him so many of her fancies and feelings; thoughts which were hard to put into words, but which he understood intuitively, or from a hint, a few hesitating sentences, or even an unfinished phrase. And then when he talked, it was so delightful to hear him, there was such a spirit of kindness, sincerity, uprightness, through all he said, that she unconsciously ranked him as the first of human beings, and his occasional words of half-uttered commendation as the most valuable praise she had ever received. Captain Hepburn, in that single week, had done what Charles Huyton, in two years, had failed to accomplish; he had, unknown to herself, touched Hilary's heart, and won a large share in her affections.

The day preceding the fête at "the Ferns," brought Victoria over to the Vicarage to make the final arrangements concerning Hilary and her sisters. Mr. Duncan entirely declining to be present, it had been settled that Mr. and Mrs. Paine should spend the day with him, while his daughters were all absent; an arrangement which Hilary was more than half inclined to contest, as hardly doing sufficient for his comfort. She and her sisters were to be under the especial care and chaperonage of Mrs. Fielding, who, since she could not persuade the father to come, said she should find some compensation in taking charge of his daughters. Victoria came on Tuesday to propose that the sisters should be fetched over rather early, that they might be comfortably established before the general assembly appeared; and, also, Miss Fielding said that Hilary might help her overlook the preparations, and see that all was complete and appropriate.

While she said this Victoria's eyes were glancing inquiringly at the tall, dark, handsome stranger who was seated, with a book in his hand, at the other end of the room, but who, she was sure, was listening attentively to her discourse. After a moment's consideration, Hilary asked leave for Maurice to bring a friend with him, and then named Captain Hepburn to Miss Fielding; but the introduction was not made without a slight blush, which Victoria's keen eyes perceived. She received this new acquaintance with equal grace and graciousness, gave him a cordial invitation to her fête, and was as pleasant as possible for a few minutes; then she turned again to Hilary, talked of Charles, who was to return that evening; his anxiety that all should be right, his confidence in Hilary's taste, and his wishes that it should be consulted, and some other remarks, of a kind which *she* passed by as mere compliments, from the woman who was engaged to Mr. Huyton;

but which there was another person whose ignorance of this fact made him view very differently.

When Victoria was gone, Captain Hepburn arose, and after walking once or twice from the window to the table, he suddenly asked Miss Duncan if she was not intending to exchange her thimble for her bonnet, and take some exercise that afternoon.

Maurice and his father had gone on a long expedition across the forest, the latter on a pony which his son led, and Hilary had intimated an intention of going to meet them on their return, which Captain Hepburn was evidently anxious she should fulfil. Her sisters were at Primrose Bank, and there was nothing to interrupt the perfection of their *tête-à-tête* except a slight and unusual shade of something in Captain Hepburn's eyes, which Hilary had never seen before, and did not quite understand now.

Whatever might be the source of this change, whether displeasure, anxiety, or weariness, it somewhat awed and chilled her; she looked up to him with such reverence, and thought so humbly of herself that she did not venture to seek an explanation. She fancied that either he was secretly tired of her society, or that she had said or done something which had appeared to him silly or wrong; and she felt ashamed of her imaginary fault, although quite unable to attach any definite name to her misdemeanor. She walked on silently, and so did he by her side, casting now and then a longing, sorrowful look at her face, which, had she ventured to meet it, would have told her it was neither anger nor contempt then occupying his mind.

At length he spoke.

"That Miss Fielding! what is she to the owner of 'the Ferns,' Miss Duncan?"

"Cousin," replied Hilary; she hesitated whether she should add more, but thought it best not to explain what she believed their relative position to be.

"And this Mr. Huyton, of whom she speaks so much; is he married?" said he, fixing an anxious look on her face as he spoke.

"No, not yet," said Hilary, almost unconsciously betraying a little of the amusement at the question, which she could not effectually suppress.

"And you know them all very well, I suppose?" was his next observation.

"I have not known Miss Fielding very long, but she is so kind and friendly, that I look forward with pleasure to—" she checked herself with a blush, that she was so nearly owning her expectations.

He saw it; and the momentary glow which colored his face gave way to a deeper shade and a paler hue than before.

"Mr. Huyton we have known nearly three years," added Hilary, looking up; "I think you will like him, perhaps; and yet I am not sure; there is a great difference between you."

"Very great," observed he, with assumed philosophy; "he has recommendations to which I can not aspire—wealth and station are great advantages; and three years allow time for all good qualities to become apparent; so lengthened a friendship is enough of itself to speak for him."

Hilary was silent for some minutes, and then raising her eyes timidly, she said—

"There is always a debtor and creditor side in all accounts, Captain Hepburn!"

"True, as a principle; to what do you refer, Miss Duncan?"

"To what you just said," blushing deeply as she spoke; "I only wish to remind you, that even Mr. Huyton may not have all the advantages of life within his reach; and there may be grievances to be endured even by him, of which we know nothing."

"True. I acknowledge we are more ready to reckon our troubles than our blessings," replied he, in a tone of self-correction; "and as we see the bright parts of our neighbors' life, and not those which are in shadow, we are apt to forget how much may be concealed."

"Yes," replied Hilary, "we gaze at our neighbors as we do at the moon, and often forget their existence altogether when they are not lighted by the rays of prosperity. It requires an effort of the reason to realize that our lot in life, like the face of our planet, may seem as bright to their view as theirs does to us; we are so intimately aware of the roughnesses and inequalities which surround our feet, and see so little of the light of Heaven on our own path."

He smiled, and answered,

"You are fond of picturesque analogy, Miss Duncan."

"Distance alone, I think, often prevents our judging with accuracy," continued Hilary; "what we take for an ornament, or a support, may be simply a chain or a burden; and what we fancy a halo of glory, is, perhaps, the torturing fire consuming its victim."

"You are exerting your fancy, I think, to make me view my lot in life with complacency."

"No, I was trying to convince you of the injustice of the charge you brought by implication against me just now," was Hilary's answer, half-shyly given.

"What charge?" inquired he, with some eagerness; "of what could you imagine I could accuse you, to require any justification?"

"By implying that the difference I alluded to, as apparent between you and Mr. Huyton, must necessarily be a comparison to the disadvantage of either. Or supposing that the possession of property had any influence on my likes or dislikes."

"Did I imply such injustice to you? And yet, though theoretically we know of how little importance wealth may be in attaining the great end of life, it is difficult always to regulate our wishes; wealth gives so much power of doing good and making others happy."

"But often, too often, takes away the wish to do so," returned Hilary. "But if the power to oblige can be obtained only by wealth, Captain Hepburn must have valuable hoards of available riches; for I know those who feel themselves unable to repay what they owe him, except by sentiments of gratitude which can never grow cold."

He turned his eyes upon her with a look of pleasure which was unseen, for her eyes were bent on the ground; but he made no answer.

"Mr. Huyton's wealth will oblige the whole neighborhood to-morrow," continued she; "but who will remember it as a favor three months hence? Oh, no, the obligations which wealth alone enables one to bestow can never be the most highly prized, or gratefully acknowledged."

"I admit it; at least by those whose gratitude is worth having," replied he, giving her one of those looks which she felt all over her, in every nerve; "the gratitude of the pure, unworldly, high-toned, tender heart, is very different in nature and quality from any which could count the cost of a favor by pounds and shillings. Our standard of worth is regulated, I suppose, by our favorite possessions, and the minds which value affection and truth the most, will often esteem services springing from these motives far beyond their intrinsic merit. They affix an imaginary importance to such acts, from certain properties which they perceive through the magnifying lens of a loving heart; while the ignorant and coarse-minded, seeing no token of what may be below the rough surface, naturally prefer a polished brilliant, even though it may be paste."

It was Hilary's turn to be silent now.

"It is La Bruyère, I think, who says that the way in which riches and honors are distributed in this world, shows of how little real value they are in the sight of Heaven," added Captain Hepburn, when they had walked on in silence a short time.

"That seems to me too much of a discontented sort of submission for poor people to comfort themselves by," said Hilary; "we know that riches and honors are great trials and temptations, but they may also be great blessings. Those who have them may view them in the light in which the satirist places them, and so learn to value them less; but I do not think it does for those who have them not to comfort themselves with thinking that they are bestowed because people are wicked. May be, it is their possession which has hardened the heart, or blinded the eyes, and so their owners are subjects for our pity, not our censure. Don't you think it is safer to view them as trials than as judgments?"

"You mean that we should be thankful, not self-complacent, for being poor: grateful, and also fearful, if we are rich," said he.

"Yes, and do not fancy, from what I said, that riches have spoiled Mr. Huyton. Papa thinks very well of him, and I have no doubt his wealth has hitherto proved a blessing to many."

The free and disengaged air with which she spoke would have carried the conviction of her calm feelings regarding the owner of "the Ferns" to any one but a lover, who felt his worldly circumstances formed a painful contrast to the individual in question.

After a little pause, Captain Hepburn began again.

"You have afforded me a striking example of your own theory, Miss Duncan, by showing that it does not require more than a wish to do right— to be able to confer favors. Your reproof for my discontented allusion to my worldly circumstances is an obligation, the value of which I hope I am not too dull to appreciate."

"A reproof!" said Hilary, with a look of alarm and crimson cheeks; "indeed I am not so presumptuous; I did not mean it."

"Then was the presumption mine, in supposing myself a sufficient object of interest to you to incur it," replied he, smiling. "I would rather be judged worthy of reproof than of contempt."

"I see you are laughing at me," replied Hilary, smiling also; "and it was stupid of me to believe you serious when you talked in that way; but you looked so grave, I thought you really meant it."

Whether Captain Hepburn might not have succeeded in convincing her that he did mean a great deal, and that his looks as well as his words could be depended on, can not be known, as just then Mr. Duncan and Maurice came in sight, and their conversation concluded as the others joined them.

CHAPTER IX.

"In the hall, with sconces blazing,
Ladies waiting round her seat,
Clothed in smiles beneath the dais,
Sat the Duchess Marguerite."

The Church of Beou.

Victoria was fortunate in her arrangements. The weather, that great object of interest, because of uncertainty, in our island, beginning with a little hesitation, settled into brilliancy and warmth; and the sun, after coquetting in the morning with the earth, through the clouds which it had called up round itself, finally dispersed them all, and smiled out graciously on the many anxious eyes turned toward it.

Pretty and elegant as Hilary looked when dressed for the fête, I do not believe that she gained any thing in Captain Hepburn's eyes by her more elaborate toilette; he would have preferred seeing her in her usual morning gown; although he blamed himself for selfishness, at the thought which would have deprived her, if possible, of so great a pleasure. However, he had an unexpected consolation, which more than made up for the pain of helping her into Mr. Huyton's carriage, when he perceived that the little bunch of double violets he had taken such pains to gather from under an exceedingly wild and overhanging sweet-briar bush, were now carefully arranged in a knot of white ribbon, and formed her only ornament as a *bouquet de corsage*. Hilary herself had no very overpowering expectations of pleasure from the party; her principal emotion was curiosity to witness a scene from the gay world, such as she little expected to find transported into their forest life. For herself, she was far too insignificant in her own opinion to form more than one of the many spectators of the festivity; she hoped that from behind Mrs. Fielding's chair she might look on quietly, and see how her friends were admired and courted. Victoria, of course, would be first and most prominent; perhaps the two sisters from the Abbey might come next in importance. She hoped Sybil and Gwyneth would enjoy themselves; she was sure Mr. Huyton would make it pleasant for them if he could, but he would probably be too busy to attend to them; but then, Maurice, too, would be there, and would certainly be kind and careful; and if Nest was happy and her sisters pleased, and if Captain Hepburn sometimes came and conversed with her, she should be very well off.

Such were her reflections as they drove along to "the Ferns;" and so she settled her expectations of amusement for the day.

Whatever other cares might have engrossed the master of the house, there was nothing to prevent his being ready to assist Hilary and her sisters from the carriage. He shook hands warmly with the young ladies, caught Nest in his arms, and kissed her affectionately, declaring it was an age since he had seen her, and then drawing Miss Duncan's arm under his, walked with her into the house, with an air of satisfaction and appropriation, which, perhaps, it was as well for Captain Hepburn's peace of mind that he did not see.

In the hall were a profusion of bouquets, prepared, as Charles told Hilary, that any lady might take one who liked. He picked out the two prettiest for her sisters himself, and gave them with pleasant speeches and open friendly looks; but in the ante-chamber he stopped again, and taking from a vase standing there a most exquisitely-arranged bunch of flowers, far more rare and beautiful than any of the others, he gave them to Hilary himself, without a word, but with a look, which made her feel as if the flowers had burnt her fingers, and raised an intense desire to dash them immediately on the ground.

The hot blood mounted to her cheeks, and her eyes were bent on the beautiful blossoms with an intentness which seemed to indicate a serious study of their botanical peculiarities; but she could not have told of what they consisted, nor have distinguished the moss-roses from the Peristerium, or the Deletria from the orange blossoms she held in her hand. She was thinking how much she preferred the scent of double violets; or, perhaps, comparing the glance which had accompanied each gift, and wondering why the one should recall the other, or why, if their expression was so much alike, the impression on her own mind should be so different. He led them on, without speaking, to the saloon where Mrs. Fielding was seated, and then, as that lady rose to welcome them, he said:

"I need not beg you to be kind to them, dear aunt; you know how much I trust to you when I place them under your care."

Hilary's cheeks were still glowing, as the elderly lady embraced her in foreign fashion, and expressed her extreme pleasure at seeing her there. Her manner to her sisters was hardly less cordial, and Nest received immediately the permission most valued by a child of her age, to run about and look at every thing before the company came.

A minute after, Victoria came in, and attaching Hilary immediately to herself, she said they would go round and take a survey of the decorations. Every thing was equally complete and beautiful, flowers and evergreens scattered about in profusion on the lawn, in the house, and in the pavilion in the garden where the feast was to be served. Victoria went about examining every thing, and explaining her plans to Hilary; how the band was to be stationed on such a terrace, and what music they were to play; how refreshments in any quantity, and of every description, would be procurable in the pavilion, between three and six o'clock, so that the most dainty young lady, or most hungry young gentleman might be perfectly satisfied. She pointed out the boats which had been brought from the boat-houses, and were now floating invitingly by the side of the sheet of water, the boatmen, in a picturesque costume, lounging by them; she showed the glen where she intended to produce a grand effect in the evening by a bugle, for she had discovered there a most enchanting echo; and with this she hoped to surprise the company while they were looking on at a grand exhibition of fire-works, to be displayed on the edge of the lake; then they might conclude with a magnificent supper in the banqueting-room, to be preceded, if they liked, by dancing, in the house; and singing from some professional performers, who had come from London for the occasion.

"In short," said Victoria, "I hope to illustrate my name in the country, and be remembered with gratitude for a half year at least."

She seemed in high spirits, and went about singing to herself, as she pointed out one ornament or another to Hilary—

"Voi che sapete
Che cosa él' amor."

Hilary did not feel very glad herself; for the sight of Victoria had reminded her of Mr. Huyton's supposed engagement, and she was shocked and ashamed of herself, to think that she had even for a moment imagined he had implied any degree of devotion to herself by his manner. She was angry at what she believed her own unpardonable vanity, and wondered what could make her so absurd. Then she began to meditate how it happened that she could have imagined any resemblance between the look of Charles and that of Captain Hepburn; could they really think alike? were they actuated by the same feelings, and if so, was the latter also engaged to another woman? why did such an idea give her pain? what right had she to turn so sick at heart as she contemplated it? what was it to her? Oh, shame, shame on herself, that she could have allowed such fancies to take possession of her heart; that she should be actually unhappy at the notion of his loving another; she, who had home duties which ought to exclude such feelings; she, who had so firmly resolved to devote herself to her father and sisters; she, who had never heard from him a word which could imply a similar preference for herself; could she have been indulging in such a weak and foolish partiality?

She could hardly attend to what her friend was saying; she was incapable of giving a rational answer, and her only wish was to be allowed to sit down in some remote corner, and hide her blushes and her emotion. Charles Huyton joined them as they stood on the lawn, to tell Victoria that some carriages were approaching down the avenue, and ask her whether she would not return to the house.

Hilary was most thankful for this relief; they went back to the saloon together, and she gladly retreated into a nook behind Mrs. Fielding's chair, where she hoped to be quiet and unobserved amid the expected crowds. The room soon began to fill with company, and after a while, Victoria, finding that although inconveniently crowded, nobody seemed to like to go out first, led the way herself to the lawn, and the band commencing at the same time to perform their part, every body was ready enough to follow her example; Hilary, who was still standing with her sisters in a recess of one of the windows, was, however, roused from her engrossing thoughts by the rapturous greeting of Dora Barham, whose party coming rather late, did not arrive until the first crowd had greatly dispersed.

Isabel, after speaking to the Duncans, and other of her acquaintance, wanted to draw Dora away, as their chaperon, Lady Margaret, had proposed going out on the terrace. But Dora would not leave Hilary, whom she had not seen for more than a week; so Isabel and her party passed on, only calling her a willful child as they went.

They had not been gone many minutes, when the one arrived for whom Dora's eyes had been anxiously searching, and whose appearance brought hot, quick, pretty blushes to her cheeks. It was impossible not to perceive her emotion, although the reason and object of it, amid such a varying assembly, might have been doubtful to those who had no clew to guide them. Maurice and Captain Hepburn entered together, and advancing at once toward Mrs. Fielding, to whom the latter had to be introduced, of course, came immediately afterward to join the little group in the window behind her.

Perhaps it would not have been easy to have found a more complete contrast than those young friends exhibited at that moment. Dora glowing, smiling, dimpling, with pleasure, and displaying, with a sincerity which her education had been intended to repress and contradict, the emotions which the sight of Maurice called out; and Hilary, pale and cold, struggling to conceal a degree of most unusual excitement, under a calmness which gave her an air almost approaching to haughtiness.

Captain Hepburn came up with an eagerness not often shown by him, although not to be compared with the glow of satisfaction which Maurice exhibited when he saw who was his sister's companion; and at the first tones of his voice, the first glance of his eye, Hilary's coldness vanished, her fears were removed, and all her happiness was restored to her; for she felt that his look and tone said openly alike that she was *first* with him, and that each look and tone was truth.

His conversation, after he had smilingly satisfied her anxiety as to her father's being comfortably settled with Mrs. Paine by his side, turned on the house and scenery. It was grand and beautiful; he had not been prepared for a mansion so fine, or a park so picturesque; she had never described it as so very charming; did she not think it so?

"Had she not? she thought she had mentioned how much she admired it; perhaps he had forgotten; descriptions of unknown places seldom made much impression."

That depended, he affirmed, on who gave the description; he did not think he had forgotten any thing she had ever said, any conversation they had ever held.

Hilary looked down at the bunch of exotics she held in her hand. They caught his eye also, and he remarked on their beauty, taking them from her hand to examine them.

"They are all foreigners," said he, "or raised in a hot-house!"

"Yes, I believe they came from Mr. Huyton's hot-houses, which are always beautiful."

"And what is that, and that, and that?" questioned he, still holding the flowers. He made her tell him the names of each blossom, and commented on them and their peculiarities.

He seemed very happy, and perhaps was rendered still more so, by an observation of Hilary's in reply to his remarks. As he returned her flowers, he said, with a sort of subdued smile,

"You should give me my violets back again, for they are quite put to shame by these grand specimens of floriculture. They did very well at the Vicarage, but here they seem out of place, and it would be a charity to hide them in their native obscurity again."

"Then they are exactly like their wearer," replied she, blushing a little, and smiling at the same time, "and sympathy forbids my throwing them away."

"I had no intention of doing that," was his answer; "the modest beauty and fragrance which may be eclipsed amid a crowd of gayer forms and brighter colors, are too dear to me, to be in danger of neglect. Should you consider it throwing them away then, to return them to me?"

Hilary hesitated.

"I do not wish to part with them," said she; and then afraid lest he should consider her refusal to do so, as the result of a regard for the donor, she added, "I love real English-grown violets better than the rarest exotics."

"At least, do not throw them away yourself," said he, earnestly; "give them to me when faded and withered; they will still be sweet."

Hilary was conscious that she had no intention whatever of throwing them away; but she did not wish to tell him so; she colored very much, and did not answer.

"Then you will not bestow on me even a faded bouquet?" said he, looking at her with smiling eyes, and not seeming much distressed at her conscious hesitation.

"If I give you two or three flowers now, will you leave me the rest in peace?" said she, playfully; "but I must say, I think it ungenerous to wish to take back from me what you bestowed unasked, unless you saw me neglecting or undervaluing the gift."

"Unsolicited gifts are sometimes not much prized," replied he, softly; "might I flatter myself that you fixed any value to *all* I have bestowed on you—"

"Miss Duncan," said Mr. Huyton, advancing to the corner where the little group stood, forming two distinct pairs, each too much engrossed to be conscious of aught beyond them, "Victoria has sent me to conduct you to her; I am not to return without you, on any account."

He offered his arm to Hilary, who started and colored exceedingly at the sudden interruption to a sentence, which from its tone and manner, she was particularly anxious to hear completed.

Mr. Huyton looked inquiringly at her companion, and then rousing Maurice from the whispered conversation with Dora, which had quite engrossed him, desired to be presented to his friend.

Hilary's hand was under his arm, as he made polite speeches to Captain Hepburn, and he looked so very much as if he thought she belonged to him, that the other could not forbear noticing it; and a doubt shot through his mind, whether the conjectures of Maurice relative to his engagement to Miss Fielding, could have the slightest foundation.

It had been this very announcement which had raised his spirits, and made him bolder in his own advances; and the contradiction of all his hopes which his fancy drew from Charles Huyton's manner, was such as immediately to depress and silence him.

"Where are my sisters?" inquired Hilary, looking round, now first aware that they had left her.

Charles told her they had gone out on the lawn with Mrs. Fielding some time before—had she not missed them? he hoped, then, she had been pleasantly engaged. It was said in a simple and friendly tone; but the thought of betraying such absence of mind, deepened the color in her cheeks, and she glanced apprehensively at Captain Hepburn, to see if he had noticed it.

Perhaps he had, for his eyes met hers, and she hastily looked away.

"Are you going, Hilary?" said Dora, now perceiving the movement around her; "oh! don't leave me! I have not the least notion where my sister and Lady Margaret are."

"You must come with us then, Miss Barham," replied their host; "for Miss Duncan must go—Victoria wants her."

"*Must* is for the king, Mr. Huyton," said Dora, in pretended indignation. "Please, Hilary, do not let him dictate to you! I would not submit to such assumption of authority."

Maurice offered to conduct her to her party, wherever they might be; and Dora, caring more for the present pleasure than prudence, took his arm, and walked happily after her friend.

Hilary did not mind the interruption so much, when she found Captain Hepburn still accompanied them; she hoped for other opportunities of conversing with him.

Victoria was standing amid the grandest and most important of the guests, receiving and returning courteous speeches, taking admiration as her due, and flattery as the air she breathed; but she welcomed her friend with a smile, shook hands cordially with Maurice, and advanced with alacrity to greet Captain Hepburn. Her attention to a party almost unknown to the whole of the surrounding circle, and the position Hilary occupied on Mr. Huyton's arm, roused a good deal of observation, and many eyes and eye-glasses were turned on them, and not a few whispered commentaries and inquiries passed round, as to who they were.

Criticism and satire were, however, unable to find any thing for observation in the quiet grace and refined simplicity of Miss Duncan, who was much too unconscious of the observation drawn on her, and too little engrossed by thoughts of herself, to be shy, although she was too humble not to be retiring in such a group. If she noticed that people looked toward her, she naturally concluded that they were attracted by the appearance of their host; and if she had been observing enough to discover traces of admiration, she would still have attributed it to his claims, or those of Dora, who was close to her.

"You belong to us, Hilary," said Victoria, quite loud enough to be heard by those near, although in a sort of stage-aside; "you are part of our *home* circle, and must not get away. I can not do without you."

She then turned and drew Captain Hepburn into conversation; Maurice and Dora joined his sisters who were a little behind, and although Hilary would gladly have disengaged herself from Charles, she could not do so immediately, without an appearance of awkwardness, which she wished to avoid.

The grand luncheon, or breakfast, or whatever name the meal deserved, obliged him to quit her, for there were Countesses' and Earls' daughters present, whose claims could not be disregarded; and when they were all seated at table, Hilary found herself, much to her relief, with her own family, and Captain Hepburn beside her. They were, however, close to Victoria, and, in spite of all the Lord Williams and Honorable Johns who courted her notice, when they rose, she still seemed inclined to pay more attention to the naval captain than to any of the other gentlemen.

He had been admiring her in a low tone to Hilary, during the repast, and she, with a sort of satisfaction for which she was afterward ashamed of herself, informed him she was going to be married and settled in England, in the autumn, but without adding her own idea as to who her future husband was. Although, therefore, Hilary would rather he should have stayed near her, she was not much disturbed at Victoria's preference for his society; and when she saw them slowly walking together, gradually disengaging themselves from the company, and finally disappearing behind a thicket of evergreens, she felt no jealousy, although she did wish to join them. The company then gradually scattered themselves about; some went to the lake, and entered the boats; some strolled through the conservatories and forcing-houses; some visited the stables; some wandered amid the wild scenery of the park; there was a game of bowls going on between some lively parties, while others were content to remain still and listen to the music. An air of general content and satisfaction appeared; every body was determined to be pleased, and a great many actually were so. The party of a wealthy and single man, would naturally be popular; and as he took great pains to go about and diffuse his civilities among all the young ladies, introduce those who wished it to each other, recommend amusements, suggest variety to the dull, and encourage every kind of hilarity, there was no outward symptom of discontent or ennui; all was as lively and harmonious as the music on the lawn.

Victoria had carried off Captain Hepburn, to show him what she considered the most curious part of the park. Such was her excuse.

This was an avenue of very ancient yews, whose large stems and branches, intertwined over head, formed a gloomy aisle, which reminded one of a cathedral crypt. It led to a circle of still older trees of the same species, surrounding a mound of earth; the trunks were hollowed by time, the over-hanging boughs were, many of them, blanched and bare, and sprung out like huge skeleton arms, which produced a ghastly spectral effect; beyond, and inclosing them, was a double row of gigantic oaks, just now in all the glory of young spring foliage; but even their bright green was unable to give a liveliness to a scene in which such heavy and dark hues predominated. The ground beneath their feet was dry and brown, a thick carpet of the needle-shaped leaves of the yews making it soft and slippery; no green plant could spring under their poisonous shade; there was neither leaf nor flower to be seen; all was gloomy and somber as a neglected church-yard.

"Now, is not this wild and strange, Captain Hepburn?" said the young lady. "I brought you here alone, that you might enjoy the full effect of contrast; we left light and music, company and mirth—here we have gloom and silence, solitude and somber thoughts. Tell me, do you think this is the work of those ancient Druids, who ruled your country before history begins, or do you suppose the Saxons, my countrymen, worshiped here their Thor and Friga?"

"It is very strange and wild, truly, Miss Fielding; do you delight in such violent contrasts? Old as they are, however, I think these trees are hardly old enough to be planted by Druid hands: remember the lengthened period— nineteen hundred years at least."

"Horrid, to destroy my pleasant illusions; I had hoped to awe you into immediate acquiescence with my fancies."

"And pass for Friga with the golden hair, yourself, for you are more like a Saxon than a British divinity of old?" said he, with smiling gallantry.

"I am Saxon on my mother's side," replied she, "as you doubtless know; so is my cousin Charles; but I believe we both intend to turn English in our habits and homes for the future."

She colored a little as she said this, and, after a moment's pause, she added—

"Do you know the county of Cheshire, Captain Hepburn?"

"Not at all—do you?"

"Not yet, but I expect hereafter to get pretty well acquainted with it. It is there my future home is situated, and, of course, the place excites some curiosity in my mind."

"Your future home!" repeated he, a little surprised.

"Yes, did you not know? I thought Hilary might have told you," replied she.

"I had heard that Miss Fielding had done one of my countrymen the honor of promising to take his name and adopt his nation!" he answered, in a sort of tone which, however, implied a dissatisfied or uncertain mind.

"Then why are you surprised at my mentioning it? perhaps that shocks British prejudices; but with us a betrothal is not a secret! Was that what astonished you?"

"No, to say the truth, it was at discovering a mistake of mine. I had fancied 'the Ferns' had been the future home which you had selected," was his reply.

"Oh!" said Victoria, coloring and laughing, "that was your guess, was it? I wonder at your want of penetration. If this had been my future home, I should not have been visiting here now, and you must have seen—oh, by the way, Charles was not here before, so you have *not* seen any thing. But Hilary did not tell you that, did she?"

"Miss Duncan mentioned no names to me," said he; "she only informed me to-day, that you were to be united to a countryman of ours."

"Oh, Hilary, of all people, has reason to know better; for though I never mentioned Mr. Legh by name to her, she knew Charles was not my *futur*. Perhaps if you had seen them together, you would have known it too."

"Seen who together?" asked Captain Hepburn, with a countenance of extreme self-command, which baffled, by its quietness, the scrutiny of Victoria's bright eyes.

"My cousin and Miss Duncan! She will not engage herself at present, because of her father and sisters; she devotes herself to them; but that kind of thing will not last forever; and though one has no right to speculate on a young lady's feelings, in spite of her saying *no*, I suspect Charles's constancy is making way with her, and will meet with its reward in time. Meantime, I say nothing to her on the topic."

Captain Hepburn was a brave man, one who had met peril unflinchingly, and dared death in a good cause. His nerves were under perfect control; and one reason, probably, of the influence he exercised over those about him, was that he had learned, before commanding others, to command himself. Whatever his feelings were on hearing this declaration from his companion, he betrayed none of them; and after a little pause, he asked, in a quiet tone, devoid of all trace of emotion,

"Do you mean that Miss Duncan refused your cousin, when he offered his hand?"

"Yes; but that was nearly a year ago, and there has been, I suspect and hope, a gradual change working since that. She was very young then, and had never thought of marrying, and her father's blindness was just ascertained, and was a great shock to her, so she thought she should never leave him, and would not listen to Charles; but he is very persevering and patient—quite a model of a lover; and as her sisters get old enough to take her place, and other feelings for other people arise, she will retract. As to my cousin, he, I am sure, will never change."

Victoria did not intend to do any harm by what she had said: she really believed that, in promoting a union between her cousin and Hilary, she was acting as kindly by one as the other, and her assertions were strictly true. She thought he was gaining ground, and fancied that if she could only keep away rivals, his interests would be safe; time and constancy, a better knowledge of his value, and a more thorough appreciation of the honor his love did its object, would alter her opinions, and change her tone.

His value she hoped to assist in demonstrating by showing him to Hilary as the center of attraction, the admired, courted, popular master of "the Ferns;" and the distinction which his notice conferred on her in that party would perhaps induce her to consider that it would be worth while to become his wife. It was very natural that she should imagine this; she judged, as all must do, by her own feelings, and set before her friend the temptations which would have had most influence with herself.

She had, on first arriving at "the Ferns," been a little vexed that she could not awaken any visible partiality in her cousin's mind; for though betrothed, she had a strong taste for admiration and flattery; but she had soon penetrated his secret, then gained his confidence, and warmly taken up his cause. The appearance of Captain Hepburn, his manner to Hilary, and her glances at him had alarmed her; and desirous to prevent her young friend from throwing away what she conceived to be the substance, in grasping at a shadow, she determined to give him such information on the subject as would probably occasion him to draw back, and leave the ground open.

She did not know her companion's character, and was quite mistaken in Hilary's also; she was, moreover, too late in her interference to do any good. Captain Hepburn felt, as he heard Victoria's suggestions, that he loved Hilary, and he believed that he had made his partiality evident to her and others. To draw back, therefore, because he had a rival was not to be thought of; it would compromise his own character for truth and honor. She might refuse him; of course, if she preferred Charles Huyton, she would; and he had as little taste for a refusal as any other man in England; but his character required that he should take his chance; and his feelings of honor, nay, his principles of integrity, were stronger than his vanity and self-love. He had given her reason to believe in his preference, he must give her the opportunity of answering it, not so much for her own sake, for she might not care, but for his! Then came fancy, whispering, would she not care? was there no soft glance in her ingenuous eyes, no thrilling tone in her voice, which might give him ground of hope? He was poor, compared to his rival; but she did not value riches; he thought, if she would not accept a man because he had them, neither would she refuse another because he had them not. His profession would probably soon call him away, and perhaps he could not offer her immediate marriage; but then she herself considered that incompatible with her family bonds; when these were lighter, would she not consent to become his? It seemed as if the very circumstances which, in most cases, would have been evils and drawbacks, were now advantages to support his claim. His own freedom from family ties, his having no settled home, no landed property which bound him to one spot; all these would be no objection in her case, whereas the reverse might have formed impediments to his wishes.

It did not take very long to think all these thoughts; and the consequence of these ideas was, that, instead of exhibiting depression and uneasiness at Victoria's observations, he showed a calm face and a self-possessed manner, which induced her to believe he, at least, was indifferent on the subject.

"Where does this path lead?" inquired he, ascending a slope on one side of the circle of yews, and looking round him.

"We are just above the lake, and I thought of going down that way," replied Victoria. "Come along this winding path, and we shall reach some of the company. I hear voices down below. You are a sailor, will you not take me out in a boat for a sail? we will ask Hilary, or one or two other ladies, to go with us."

"I am afraid you will think me a very ungallant and disobliging sailor, Miss Fielding; but I must say, of all things in the world, I dread a water-party of ladies, and never, if I can help it, embark in one."

"Ah! it has no charms for you—no novelty. 'Too much water hast thou,' as the Queen says to Ophelia. I daresay it is stupid."

"I may be stupid, perhaps, but I think it dangerous, and willingly avoid the responsibility. So few men understand how to sail a boat. Unless you had heard as much as I have, you could not imagine how often they upset; and when women are on board, what can be the consequence but mischief?"

"Some people are not so cautious, for I see a boat on the lake; and if I do not mistake, Maurice Duncan and the two Barhams are in it."

"Yes; but they are only sculling along, and a girl might do that. I really do not suppose we could sail if we tried; there is scarcely a breath of wind, or only a puff at intervals."

The path down which they were descending was so screened by shrubs, that although they could catch a glimpse of the lake and its borders here and there, they were unseen themselves by those below.

There were a good many people on the bank; at a little distance, a group of children were merrily dancing to a violin which one of the woodmen had produced; near them were some mammas and elder sisters, looking on, and admiring. Victoria was close enough to recognize some individuals; they saw Charles Huyton, encouraging the frolics of the children; Mrs. Fielding and Hilary were standing under a tree at the edge of the lake, where a steep bank formed a promontory above the water, apparently watching Maurice's boat, which was slowly approaching them.

When they had descended a few yards further, they entirely lost sight of the loiterers by the lake, and, although so near as to catch voices and laughter, were unable to discover what was passing. They heard a child's voice cry, "Hilary! Hilary!" and recognized the merry tones of little Nest; then some one, in an accent of alarm, cried, "Take care!" and then there was a shriek, an exclamation of terror from many voices, a plunge in the water, and a silence.

Captain Hepburn sprang forward, and in a moment had cleared the underwood, and obtained sight of the bank and the water. Mrs. Fielding stood where she had been, and many had rushed to the water's edge, and were gazing in. Hilary and Nest were both out of sight.

CHAPTER X.

"What! thou think'st men speak in courtly chambers,
Words by which the wretched are consoled?
What! thou think'st this aching brow was cooler,
Circled, Tristram, by a crown of gold?"

Iseult.

The cry of alarm had brought Charles Huyton also to the spot where the accident had happened; for one brief moment the rivals stood side by side and gazed upon the scene. Under the steep, shelving bank, nearly submerged in the water, but clinging with her left arm to a long, pendant root, hung Hilary, and with her right hand she grasped, with all the energy of terrified love, the skirt of her sister's dress, thereby but little supporting the child, and risking herself to be drawn from her precarious hold, and plunged in deep water by her struggles.

Captain Hepburn and Charles Huyton simultaneously flung off their coats.

"Save Hilary—I will secure the child," said the sailor, in a tone of decision which seemed to command obedience, and without an instant of unnecessary delay, sprang from the steep bank head-foremost into the water. Mr. Huyton followed his example, and almost before she was conscious of help being at hand, Hilary felt an arm supporting her, and heard a well-known voice saying—

"Trust to me, dearest, and you will be safe."

She was too exhausted to understand exactly what was passing. She felt her sister was raised, released her grasp on her dress, and had just sense and energy enough left to remain quite passive, as she was borne to a more practical part of the bank. She turned her head, saw Nest was safe in Captain Hepburn's care—his strong arms had drawn the child quickly out of danger—and then, perfectly overpowered, she fainted away. Landing her was by no means an easy task, the ground was soft, crumbling, and treacherous; but for the ready help at hand, Charles could not have done it; and he was so much exhausted by his efforts, that when he was assisted from the water, he was not only unable to support his burden, but had himself to sit down on the grass, to rest and breathe.

Captain Hepburn hastily placed the dripping child in some of the many arms stretched out to take her, and turned with an eager bound to Hilary, who seemed as lifeless as her sister. But Maurice reached her at the same time; he had seen the accident, and with rapid strokes had brought the boat to the nearest land, where, utterly forgetful even of Dora Barham, he had thrown the chain, by which the skiff was moored, into the boatman's hands, and sprung ashore to assist Hilary.

He clasped his sister in his arms, exclaiming, as he did so, "Darling, dearest Hilary!" in the tones of the fondest endearment; then added, with agonized doubt,

"Oh, Hepburn, is she dead?"

Her pale cheeks, closed eyes, and inanimate form terrified him, and he looked to his friend for advice, assistance, or at least for comfort.

"Heaven forbid!" cried the other, eagerly catching her hand, and endeavoring to feel her pulse, "she has only fainted from alarm. She must be taken to the house."

"Carry your sister to the house this moment," cried Victoria; "I have dispatched little Nest there already, and will send some one to make preparations, and give orders."

A gentleman present, a relative of the Barhams, offered to run on and carry a message, but Sybil sprang forward—

"Let me go, Miss Fielding, give me the necessary directions."

Victoria gave a hasty message to the housekeeper, and Sybil was off with a fleetness, and a knowledge of the shortest road, which distanced Mr. Farrington completely.

Some of the many shawls which were proffered for the use of the sufferers, were hastily wrapped around Hilary, and, raising her in his arms, her brother walked off with steady steps toward the house.

Charles and Captain Hepburn accompanied him, each entirely occupied by thoughts of her, and neither at that moment caring to conceal it.

Either the fresh air, or the warmth, or the motion, revived Hilary; she sighed, opened her eyes, looked up for a moment, in doubt where she was, and what had happened, then recollecting every thing, she started up, and cried—

"Nest—oh, Maurice, is she safe?"

"Be still, darling," replied he, and it was echoed by the other two; but she only repeated the question in greater alarm.

"Yes, yes, she is safe; she is just on in front. Some one is carrying her to the house. Hepburn saved her."

The look which Hilary gave the sailor at that moment, was one which he never forgot.

"I could walk, Maurice, I could walk quicker, if you would set me down," said she, eagerly. "I am quite well, do let me try."

"Patience, we are just there!" and he would not let her go, until they reached the door.

Several female attendants, and Sybil herself, were waiting there; they were carrying the little one up to be placed in Victoria's own bed; and, a moment after, Miss Fielding herself joined them, having hurried on to summon a physician, who, as Isabel reminded her, was happily one of the party. Dr. Pilgrim was found, and at once took the lead in ordering and advising; gave the necessary directions for restoring animation to Nest, who still continued insensible, sent Victoria instantly to superintend the proper precautions for Hilary's safety, and insisted on both the gentlemen retiring to procure dry clothes, declaring that they could do no good to any one, until they had first taken care of themselves.

Happily, by the time Hilary was allowed by her active and judicious attendants to be well enough to seek her sister, Nest was not only perfectly restored to consciousness, but had dropped off into a quiet sleep, and Miss Duncan, at her own urgent request, was permitted to watch by her, on condition, as Dr. Pilgrim insisted, that nothing should be allowed to disturb the little one's slumber, on which he declared her entire recovery to depend. By this means, as he communicated to Mrs. Gainsborough, the housekeeper, they should compel Miss Duncan to keep quiet also, and he was really more alarmed on her account than her sister's, if the evident excitement under which she was laboring was not checked by some decisive measures. She ought to have gone to bed also.

In the darkened room, reclining on an easy chair, beside the bed where the child peacefully slept, Hilary passed the rest of the afternoon, putting up mental thanksgivings for the safety of her darling, and for the preservation of her own life; grateful for the kindness and care she met with, and more grateful still that *he*, the one to whom her heart had turned for help in the moment of horror and alarm, had been near enough to hear her cry, and rescue her sister.

She was hardly aware who had saved herself; the absorbing idea of Nest's danger and Nest's safety, had prevented her making other inquiries, and her head still felt too weak and confused to think with accuracy, or recollect with precision. It all seemed a cloud of fear and agony, from the time when she saw her sister was running into danger, by so rapidly descending the steep bank, and when, in her effort to arrest her, she too had lost her footing on the short, slippery turf, and crumbling, sandy edge, until she had once more recovered herself in her brother's arms, and had heard the delicious assurance that Nest was safe.

At intervals, Sybil or Gwyneth would softly creep into the room, kiss her, look at Nest, till the tears sprung, and then glide away without a word; or Victoria would come with some refreshment, which she urged on Hilary with whispered eagerness; or Dr. Pilgrim would steal in with a stealthy, noiseless tread, glance at the child, feel Hilary's pulse, and in low, positive tones, renew his orders for perfect quiet repose.

The watchful housekeeper, too, was frequent in her silent visits, and the German maid, who sat in her mistress's dressing-room, knowing no tongue saving her own, was deaf to entreaties for admission from all others, according to the express injunctions of Fraulein Victoria.

Meanwhile, beyond that silent room, away even from sight as well as hearing of its inmates, all was excitement, bustle, interest, and gossip. Seeing that the accident had not been attended by fatal consequences, and that after the first lively alarm there was nothing which need disturb the festal party, the visitors listened to the earnest entreaties of Miss Fielding, and remained as if nothing had happened. Of course, there was much to be said about this interesting circumstance; all who had seen it had to tell their own story, each version differing considerably from the other; all who had not enjoyed the advantage of being spectators were naturally eager to inquire the needful information; and every lady there was loud in praise of the heroism of Mr. Huyton in saving Hilary at the risk of his own life.

It was remarkable how much was said of him, how enthusiastic were the encomiums bestowed on his courage and presence of mind, while the equal devotion of his companion was passed over in silence. Every one could tell that Mr. Huyton, without a moment's hesitation, had sprung from the bank to rescue the sufferers; none but himself and one other seemed aware that he was second in the attempt, and that it was the prompt decision of another mind which had influenced his conduct. Charles was brave, perhaps, but the total disregard of danger, the self-devotion which could calmly risk death itself in the cause of humanity, the quiet trust in a higher power which true Christianity alone can give, these were not his. Neither had he the quick eye to see the best means of help, the rapid decision to carry it out, nor the unselfish prudence which could resign the efforts love would have prompted, rather than fail of doing all that was required; to these he had no claim. No human eye could see that jealousy and rivalry had prompted what others call heroism and self-devotion; that but for the example of another, he would have shrunk from the attempt; or that had not his companion been more generous than himself, they might have clashed in their efforts to rescue Hilary, while Nest might have been lost by delay.

When Mr. Huyton returned to his guests, having changed his own clothes, and taken care that Captain Hepburn was properly accommodated, he was received as a hero. Every one crowded round him to congratulate and admire; one enthusiastic lady (she had two grown-up daughters) insisted on his being crowned with laurel; and the professional singer, Madame G— —, came forward, and volunteered a grand *bravura* in his honor. In short, such was the crowd about him, that Maurice could hardly pierce through to shake his hands in both of his, and thank him, with grateful emotion, for the safety of his sister. Charles bore it very well, he put aside the plaudits, escaped from the ovation, gracefully denied all merit, and seizing Maurice by the arm eagerly drew him aside to pour out his rapturous delight at having been of use to Hilary. No one was near, for he had retreated quite away from his guests; and they had the consideration not to intrude on the gratitude and thanks of the brother, whatever they might have wished to do. In this moment of feeling and excitement, Maurice learned, with surprise, what Hilary had hitherto carefully concealed even from him—the ardent, constant, unchanging devotion of his friend for his sister. Charles gave vent to his feelings, told of his love, his disappointment, his hopes, his fears; Hilary was dearer to him than ever, dearer far than life (he really thought so, now there was no danger); had he any chance, could Maurice give him any encouragement; at least, would he give him his good wishes?

Surprise was the brother's principal feeling; not surprise that Hilary was loved, but that he had never discovered what was passing close to him. As to his sister's feelings, could he have guessed them, he would not have betrayed his guesses, nor breathed a word which could make her blush. He was saved from further solicitation by a summons to Charles, who was wanted by his cousin immediately.

Maurice at that moment was in no humor for making love himself—his thoughts were absorbed by his sisters' peril, and their escape; the crowd was irksome to him; his feelings wanted a higher and better outlet than the idle gossip and careless chatter around; he could not hear the subject lightly discussed, with even outward calmness; and now, reassured by a recent report from Dr. Pilgrim, that both patients were doing as well as possible, he quietly stole away into the shrubbery, and then retraced, with thoughtful step and swelling heart, the path along which he had borne his sister's inanimate form.

He reached the spot where the accident had occurred, he saw the marks on the bank, he gazed at the dark, still, sullen-looking water, whose black depth had so nearly been the grave of those two loved ones; and lifting his hat from his head, he raised his whole heart in grateful praise, that she, the light, the support, the comfort of their home, and that little one, whose merry voice always spoke of mirth and love, had been spared to bless them still.

He was roused by a footstep; his hands were grasped by Captain Hepburn; and warm, earnest, deeply heart-felt congratulations were poured out to him on his sister's safety.

"My dear fellow! I can not speak my joy—they say she is doing well! have you seen her yet?" continued he, eagerly.

Maurice answered he had not.

"They insist on perfect quiet at present, and then, Dr. Pilgrim says, all will be well; but, Hepburn, how can I thank *you* enough for this additional benefit—dearer, more precious far than my own life? I wish I could speak—"

Maurice could not quite control his voice, and was obliged to break off abruptly.

"I did not save Hilary," replied he; "thank Mr. Huyton for that!"

"You did what I am certain Hilary will thank you for more than for her own life—you saved Nest; and I think she will feel as I do; although she may not have so entire an appreciation of your motives as I have."

"My motives were simple enough," said Captain Hepburn, after a little pause; "I felt I might trust her to the exertions of Mr. Huyton, at least, till I had placed the child in safety; and Nest's struggles made it difficult to do any thing for either while Hilary retained her grasp on her clothes."

"I knew it! I was convinced that it was your doing—your judgment, decision, prudence, and promptness by which either was rescued! Others may give Huyton the credit—they are making a hero of him out there—but *I* know, and Hilary, too, shall know, to whom we are truly indebted. What can I say! how poor words are! what can I do to show our gratitude?"

"Nothing—nothing more, my dear fellow! it was nothing to speak of, although the result was so important. If Hilary will only believe that I acted as I thought *she* would wish—that for her dear sake I did what I did—would have done any thing possible—would have dared a thousand times more, had it been necessary—then I shall be amply repaid!"

Maurice looked at him earnestly and inquiringly. Captain Hepburn went on after a moment.

"I should have acted as I did, Maurice, even though I had known that in resigning the charge of her to Mr. Huyton I was resigning all claim on her forever. Her safety was more to me than my life, as her happiness is more important than my own. May be, she may never know this; be it so! if she is happy, I will try to be content."

"I hardly understand you," replied Maurice, "at least, I am not sure; but if your wishes are what I suppose, I can only say that mine will go with them; more, infinitely more cordially than with Charles Huyton."

"I did not mean to have said so much," replied Captain Hepburn; "it was a momentary excitement; we will not discuss it now. I want to know about going back to the Vicarage. Hilary and Nest must remain here, and will require something in the way of wardrobe, certainly; and you must remember, the little one was to have returned about seven, and one of her sisters with her. I think these were the first arrangements. Your father will be expecting them, and the Paines will wish to go home."

"True; what is to be done? Hilary *must* remain here, of course."

"I could go home with your sister Gwyneth, if you like; perhaps you would wish to remain as late as possible, to hear the last account; and probably Miss Sybil had better, if she can, stay with her sisters altogether. What do you think?"

"That you have the clearest head for arranging in the world."

"Well, you may propose it, I can only suggest privately to you, and have no wish to put myself forward. If they will send us home, I shall be ready whenever Gwyneth likes, and the carriage can take back the clothes."

They turned to walk toward the house, Maurice anxious to find his sisters, and settle with them what they would wish to have done.

It was soon arranged, and just as Captain Hepburn had suggested. The invitation to the younger Miss Duncans to remain with their sisters, had already been given, through the thoughtful kindness of Charles, and although it was impossible both should accept it, it was gratefully taken advantage of by Sybil, who shrank from the idea of being the one to break the intelligence to Mr. Duncan, and gladly persuaded herself that she could be more use at "the Ferns" to Hilary herself, while Gwyneth would certainly be much the best able to act for her father alone.

The carriage was ordered immediately, and Gwyneth stealing up stairs to take one more look at the invalids, found Hilary had just been positively ordered by Dr. Pilgrim to go to bed, where he hoped a composing draught would procure necessary sleep, and avert the symptoms of fever which he reluctantly admitted were becoming stronger.

Gwyneth, however, was not informed of this alarm; she stayed to see Hilary comfortably settled for the night, and as her heavy eyelids closed almost as soon as her head touched the pillow, it was hoped by all her nurses that a good night's rest would cure every thing that was wrong. Sybil wished to remain with her, but there was really nothing to be done, and both patients appearing to be quietly asleep. Victoria persuaded her to trust them to the watchfulness of Mrs. Gainsborough, and return with her to the company for the present; and her entreaties being enforced by a threat, that if she did not come down, Miss Fielding would remain with her upstairs, Sybil was obliged, though somewhat reluctantly, to yield the point.

As they were issuing from the house, they met Mr. Farrington strolling about near the door; he joined them immediately, and after inquiring earnestly for the sufferers up stairs, he turned to Sybil, and expressed, in very gentlemanlike and pleasant words, his strong admiration of her promptness in action and swiftness of foot.

Sybil, of course, like a great many other people when undergoing a compliment, or accused of a virtue, took refuge in denying the facts, declaring herself peculiarly slow in action, and undecided in thought, and hardly even allowing that she could run faster than other people; although, to say the truth, her forest-life, and habits independent of governess and dancing-master, had given, or at least had not taken away, a power and ease of motion not common to many young ladies.

Mr. Farrington did not persist in compliments which were evidently received with as much shy reluctance as conscious pleasure; but changing the conversation, first discussed with her the details of the accident, listening with extreme interest to Sybil's enthusiastic gratitude to Captain Hepburn and Mr. Huyton, and then led her on, how she hardly knew, to give a long detail of their usual mode of life; their quiet habits, their father's state of health; followed by glowing descriptions of the lovely forest scenery, through which they were wont to roam, the quaint manners of the woodmen, the vagrant ways of the gipsies, and a hundred other particulars, which Sybil detailed with a poetic feeling for the romance of their situation peculiarly attractive to him.

Her ardent affection and admiration for her half-sister, convinced Mr. Farrington that Sybil herself must be equally amiable, and perhaps equally clever to appreciate her so entirely; and altogether he was so much interested in his companion, as to feel disinclined to quit her again during the rest of the evening.

Sybil was too tired, from excitement and exertion, to be disposed to do any thing but sit still beside Mrs. Fielding, except at the intervals when she stole up stairs to learn how Hilary slept; and her spirits being naturally depressed by what had already passed, and anxiety for the future, she was just in that state of mind which made her communicative of her hopes and fears, inclined to take retrospective views of bygone happiness, and thankful to hear cheerful anticipations for the morrow.

As to Maurice, after he had made the arrangements before recorded, feeling easier for his sisters at "the Ferns," and depending entirely on his friend's direction to give as little pain as possible to his father in making known the accident, he suddenly returned to thoughts of his own affairs, that is to say, to recollections of Dora, whom he had left with her sister, and wonder what they had done, as well as what they would think of his conduct.

Isabel he saw was with her aunt, Lady Margaret, and her party, which was tolerably numerous, but Dora herself was invisible. He went up to Miss Barham, and apologized for his conduct, in quitting them so abruptly in the boat; an apology which she declared totally unnecessary, as of course Hilary must be his first object; but in answer to his inquiries after her sister, she could only tell him, that Dora had gone in doors to rest, as she said she had a head-ache, and the band made it worse. As soon as he could, Maurice went to the house to look for her, but was unsuccessful in his search through all the public rooms. Vexed and disappointed, he strolled out again, but on the opposite side to that on which the pavilion stood, and wandered away by himself, into a small thicket of laurel and other evergreens, overhung by some remarkably fine old hawthorns, whose long sprays, wreathed with snowy blossoms, shed around their rich and enervating perfume.

A sudden turn in the walk brought him to a small alcove, and there, reclining on a bank of turf, her face concealed partly by her arm and partly by her handkerchief, was Dora Barham, sobbing as if her heart was broken, and so engrossed by the cause of her agitation, as to be quite unconscious of his approach.

He hesitated a moment, for he could not leave her in such grief, and yet he did not dare to intrude upon it; he stopped, looked at her, waited, and was then resolved to go back, when accidentally treading on a broken stick in the path, the sharp crack it gave under his foot, startled Dora, and made her instantly raise her head.

"Mr. Duncan!" exclaimed she, trying to brush away her tears in a great hurry, as she saw him, but not looking at all sorry at the interruption.

"I hope I do not disturb you," said he, apologetically. "I had no idea of finding you here."

"Not in the least," looking at the bank beside her (she was now sitting upright), as if she longed to ask him to sit down. "How is Hilary?"

"Doing quite well, they tell me; she is going to bed; I hope she will sleep well, and be all right to-morrow." He ventured to sit down as he spoke.

"Oh, I am so glad! dear Hilary—it was horrid, dreadful—I can not get the idea out of my head; oh, Mr. Duncan! if they had not been there to save her!" Dora shuddered again, and again tears filled her eyes and rolled down her cheeks.

"Do not agitate yourself so," exclaimed her companion, "do not think of it; can I do nothing for you; get you nothing?"

"No, thank you! I shall be better presently." She sobbed a little, and then was quiet.

"And your head-ache? Miss Barham told me it was bad."

"I believe it was my heart, more than my head, Mr. Duncan," replied Dora, with a smile. "I can not bear things as Isabel does, and I was so frightened; and people seemed so thoughtless and indifferent, and so ready to forget—so little thankful. Oh, dear! what a set I live with; it made my heart full, and my head ache; so at last I crept away here, to be happy and grateful my own way."

He looked at her with a smile, half-admiring, half arch, but said—

"I had no idea I found you in a state of *happiness*."

She crimsoned, laughed, and then said—

"It is, nevertheless, very pleasant to cry sometimes."

"I have heard so before," was his answer.

"And one can not do it in company, you know; it would look absurd, and be considered bad manners, which is worse; and besides, people do not ever understand one; I believe *you* are rather shocked at me."

"Do you? then I am afraid my looks are deceitful."

"Don't you think me foolish then?" coloring again, and looking down.

"Foolish for feeling for my sister's danger! foolish for caring for her safety! if affection, sympathy, friendship, sensibility, gratitude to Heaven, sincerity, simple truth of feeling, if these are folly, or if you suppose I consider them so, then accuse me of thinking you foolish."

She was silent, but was visibly gratified by his warmth of manner.

"What have I ever done or said, Miss Barham, which can justify your suspecting me of such hard-hearted, cynical want of feeling? Tears, which do honor to my sister's worth; tears, which prove your disinterested regard for the dearest objects of my heart; tears, which show how nearly we sympathize in some of *our* feelings and affections; if I do not honor and respect such—if I do not feel intensely and most humbly grateful for them, I do not deserve to be admitted into civilized society, far less into yours, Miss Barham."

"Please don't talk in that way; I did not mean to imply you were any thing bad; how could I, when I know you love Hilary so?—but I am sure you give me credit for a great deal more good than I deserve."

"I do not think that possible."

"Amiable people always do give the sunshine of their own virtues to their companion's character," said Dora, somewhat thoughtfully.

Maurice kept his gratification to himself, and wisely changing the subject to one less personal, began relating to Dora all the arrangements which had been made by Charles Huyton and Victoria for the accommodation of his sisters.

This was followed by a warm eulogium from Dora of the virtues and amiability of Mr. Huyton, in which, as on most other subjects, there was a wonderful similarity in their opinions; and after lingering together in that pleasant retreat a longer time than it was at all prudent for a poor lieutenant to spend in the bewitching society of the co-heiress of the Abbey, they at length remembered that they might as well return to the world, unsympathizing and hard-hearted as Dora had just discovered it to be.

On the whole, in spite of her tears and agitation, Dora felt, as she considered the circumstances of the afternoon, that the party had produced quite as much pleasure as she had anticipated; by no means a common occurrence. This was her conclusion, as she stationed herself by Sybil's side, on the quiet sofa where she and Mr. Farrington were composedly conversing; and as Maurice had nothing to do more perfectly natural and justifiable than to seat himself close to his sister, and remain there to take care of her, Dora seemed likely to have a good deal more enjoyment.

The shades of evening came down; and though dancing in the house had been given up, as the fireworks had not, in due time the company betook themselves once more to the park, where, under the shelter of the trees, they could conveniently view the display of cascades, bouquets, stars, serpents, and initial devices, with which the pyrotechnist was to delight them; the whole effect being doubled by the reflection in the waters.

"I really can not go out again," said Mrs. Fielding to Sybil; "perhaps, if you wish it, your brother will go with you to see these fireworks."

Sybil hesitated; she would rather have gone to Hilary.

"Do come," said Dora, coaxingly, and foolishly anxious to enjoy the walk with Maurice. "I want so to see them, Sybil dear, do come."

Sybil consented; Mr. Farrington gave her his arm; Mrs. Fielding insisted on her wrapping an additional shawl over her shoulders, to guard her from the night air. Dora said she would like one also, and sent Maurice to find a cashmere she had left in the cloak room. At that moment, Lady Margaret called Dora, who explained that she was waiting for her shawl, and would follow with Sybil and Mr. Farrington; she begged the others not to wait; and Lady Margaret, satisfied that Mr. Farrington, who belonged to their party, should be Dora's escort, went on; but as Maurice was some minutes finding the proper article, her aunt was quite out of sight before Dora, with Sybil, went after them.

Dora was only too happy; the fireworks were nothing to her; but the gentle grace with which she was guarded, and the quiet strength of the arm on which she leaned, were pretty nearly all she cared for in the world at the moment; she would not think of results, or calculate consequences; all she wished was to prolong the pleasant intercourse, dangerous as it might be to future peace.

Something was said about his profession, and Maurice expressed his hopes of very soon being employed afloat. Dora started, and inquired, in a faltering voice, if he wanted to go?

"Of course I do, in one sense," was his answer; and even as he spoke he could feel the nervous, tremulous movement of the little hand which rested on his arm. "My first wish is to distinguish myself—to obtain promotion—to rise. One can not do that without serving."

"I suppose honor and glory *ought* to be a sailor's first wish?" said Dora, in a slightly disconcerted tone, as if she did not like the thought.

"The honor leads to promotion; and on promotion all one's hopes of domestic happiness, the power of settling in life, making a home of one's own, and living in it, depend. One must work, deny oneself now, to rest and enjoy hereafter," was his answer.

"Then you will not always be going to sea?" continued she.

"I don't know. Perhaps not."

"Or wishing it? I suppose, then, you would be really glad to get an appointment now—to-morrow—any day?"

"Not quite to-morrow, unless Hilary is well first; and come when it will, it is a desperate struggle, Miss Barham, to leave all that is dearest and sweetest on earth for the chances of being tossed about, living among wild and careless companions, exposed to all manner of little trials and vexations, and no woman near to soothe one; no sweet sister to smile one into patience; no sister's sweeter friend to bewitch one into forgetfulness. Don't think we are all stones or blocks, because we do our best to put on the look of unconcern, Miss Barham. It often hides a very heavy heart."

"And how soon can you be promoted?" inquired Dora, after a little pause, not feeling herself exactly equal to pursuing the conversation on the same topic.

He told how long he must serve before he had the claim; how much longer, probably, before he could have the chance to be promoted. Then, as she continued silent, he went on, emboldened by the darkness and the solitude, for they were a little apart from the others, and no one could see any thing distinctly.

"I am not sure whether I ought to say it, but I have so longed to express—do not be angry with me for mentioning the subject—to express my gratitude to you for the trouble you took for my benefit. I have never dared speak of it before. Perhaps I may not have another opportunity."

"I was very glad to do it," said Dora, hurriedly; "but *you* owe me no thanks, it was for Hilary I asked; you know I had never seen you then!"

"I am perfectly aware of that; I never flattered myself it was personal regard for me; the kindness, I know, was to Hilary; but the benefit was to myself. Whatever I felt at the time, I can only say now, the rank is dearer to me, when I remember from whose hand I received it; and my earnest wish not to disgrace my name, my profession, and my country, is changed into a longing, ardent desire, to show that I am sensible of the honor done me, and will do any thing, lay down my life, were it necessary, to try and deserve it."

"Heaven forbid!" murmured Dora; "don't say such dreadful words; you make me feel as if I should be a murderess. Please don't be too anxious to distinguish yourself."

"I hope you will never have to blush for your kindness, Miss Barham. There is little danger in these times of peace of any thing leading me to too great distinction."

"And I—oh, Mr. Duncan! if your promotion should lead to any misfortune, I should never forgive myself for having interfered; I could never look at Hilary again." Dora spoke with great emotion.

"Nay, do not distress yourself, dear Miss Barham; events and their results are not in our own hands, and we are not responsible for them. We have but to do and dare; you in small things at home, perhaps; I in more distant, but may be, not more trying scenes abroad; to go forward bravely, trusting heartily in Providence, do our duty firmly, and leave the rest to heaven, that is our best as well as our wisest course; and if the end should be stormy, let us still trust and be strong."

"I never was strong; I never can be brave. I am afraid of storms, and whenever some people tell me one thing is right, and others declare the contrary, as so often happens to me, then I become so puzzled, that I can do nothing at all. You do not know the misery of indecision."

"No; but we all have the compass and chart to guide us, and mostly find a pilot, if the passage is very shoal, and the rocks are intricate, and the navigation too puzzling for us; and there are light-houses, and buoys too, to direct us right. Do you understand me?"

"I think I do; but although I hear of rules, and discipline, and self-control, when I go to church, and have been taught to reverence the Holy Word, and believe in the existence of conscience, theoretically, practically it is all nothing to me. I do not understand it. I dare say I ought not to say this to you. It seems strange to confess all this; only you led to the subject, and I can see that what is all a mist and unsubstantial phantasmagoria to me, is a light and comfort, and real guiding force, and existing present support, to such as you and Hilary."

"And to you also, if you choose, Miss Barham."

"Oh, no! never to me; I am too weak to lay hold of them, too foolish to understand them. Life in itself frightens me. It has claims to which I ought to attend; but if I try, a whole host of ceremonies, fashions, customs, prejudices, follies, rise up between me and my duties; I stretch out my hand, and can not reach it, and spend my time in sighing and idle wishes."

"And I am not theologian or philosopher enough to know what advice to give you. I think, however, I understand your feeling. I wish I could help you."

"I was brought up," continued Dora, "to value nothing but what contributed to outward show; to consider only appearances; to act only for effect; I feel the whole root and source of my actions is false; I despise myself, but I do not know how to mend it. I have waked up to a sense that there ought to be reality in life, but know not how to find or make it."

"Take one duty at a time, and conquer that; give yourself one good rule, and act upon it; do not look at every thing at once, or you are bewildered by what is before you. One takes the problems of Euclid, one by one, and learns them all; without a gradual advance, or beginning at the simplest, how could we get on?"

"If I only had some one to guide and teach me always; some one like Hilary, who could keep me right," sighed Dora. Sybil just then joined them, and their conversation was ended for the time; but Dora, when Maurice wished her good-night at parting, whispered: "I shall try to remember;" and his answer was an enthusiastic "*I* shall never forget."

CHAPTER XI.

$------$"Let their hands
Tremble, and their cheeks be flame
As they feel the fatal bands
Of love they dare not name,
With a wild delicious pain,
Twine about their hearts."

Tristram and Iseult.

Gwyneth and Captain Hepburn drove home through the beautiful twilight together.

"I do not think we need alarm your father very much," said he, after a considerable silence: "there is every hope that she will be better to-morrow."

"Oh, yes! I have no doubt of that," said Gwyneth; "I am not afraid about my father, he is too reasonable to entertain foolish fears; and now that all risk and danger are over, there can be no real ground for alarm."

"We must be careful in telling it," continued he; "you will be able to break the news to him, perhaps; a woman's tact is best: you will undertake it."

"I have no doubt but that I can do it—I am not at all afraid. There is every probability that Hilary will be home to-morrow," repeated she.

Gwyneth's sanguine anticipations rather surprised Captain Hepburn; he had seen Dr. Pilgrim himself, just before quitting "the Ferns," and had learned that the danger of fever was very far from passed away: the doctor had spoken openly to him, considering him a friend of the family, who had a right to know, and had told him that the result must be a matter of great anxiety, while the symptoms were so alarming. As, however, there was room to hope that to-morrow might bring a better report, and relieve all apprehension, he considered that there was no reason for exciting unnecessary fears; and also that if Gwyneth did not know how much there was still to dread, she would be quite secure from giving alarms which might eventually prove unfounded.

She really managed it very well; and though Mr. Duncan heard the intelligence with emotion, he bore it with the firmness and resignation of a Christian. It was quite evident, however, to the keen perception of his guest, that he did not share in the hopeful anticipations of his daughter. He did not check her, it was true, but allowed her to reckon with confidence on the safe return of the other three to the Vicarage the next day; but when she was out of the room, forgetful of Captain Hepburn's presence, who had been sitting some time in silence, the blind old man clasped his hands together, and breathed out in deep, heartfelt tones of patient resignation, his fears, and his aspirations for submission, if the stroke he dreaded should be really impending.

Captain Hepburn was deeply affected. The thoughts of what Hilary was in that home, of her importance to her sisters, her indispensability to her father; of what it would be for them to lose the music of her voice, the sunshine of her smile; for that parent no more to feel the touch of those gentle hands, tending his infirmities with such indefatigable zeal; or to hear the light echo of her busy feet, as she passed by in her accustomed household duties: for all, to miss her in her usual seat, in her daily walks, from her place at church; these thoughts were so replete with sadness, so full of heart-sinking desolation, that his whole soul was moved at the idea.

He crossed the room, and laying his hand gently on that of his host, said in a voice which, in spite of his utmost efforts, was unsteady with deep feeling —

"Dear sir, if your fears should be realized, may your prayers be granted too! but, from my soul, I trust they may prove groundless, and that Heaven may long, long bless you with such a treasure as your daughter must be to you."

"Thank you, Captain Hepburn; I believe you are a true friend to me and mine, and I owe you much, much more than I can speak. If you could save Hilary for us, I believe you would, although you do not know half her worth. But when one has an angel-visitant on earth, one feels her stay must be precarious, and may be short."

"Perhaps so; but surely Heaven will hear your prayers, and she will be restored."

"Captain Hepburn, when you have twice mourned, as I have done, over the heart's dearest treasure, you will learn perhaps, better I hope than I have learned the lesson, not to make a mortal's life your idol; and to know that the Love which is above all other love, sees not as we see, judges not as we judge, but works always for our best and surest interests, even when it thwarts our weak and passionate desires here. We never know what is unfortunate or what is good for us, except the one thing, submissive trust. I have no other wish, but that, come what may, I may be patient and resigned."

Captain Hepburn was silent. What was his short-lived affection, true and warm as it was, compared with the fond love of a father for his eldest daughter? His heart smote him for his selfish wishes, as he thought that he had even for a moment contemplated taking her away himself; that he had hoped to tempt her to another home.

"No, never," said he to himself, "never will I rob their household of its dearest treasure; never shall this fond and trusting father charge me with stealing away the daughter in whom he delights. Every selfish desire of my own shall yield to his happiness, and unless I can really fill the place of a son to him, I will not deprive him of the child on whom his comfort depends. If my love can add to their happiness, it will be well for me; if not, it must be crushed and extinguished in the performance of higher duties."

As it would probably be late before Maurice returned from "the Ferns," they persuaded the vicar not to sit up, promising that he should immediately hear the report which his son would bring; and more for Gwyneth's sake than his own, he yielded to their wishes; so the visitor remained alone to wait his friend's arrival, and wile away the long minutes as best he could. He had plenty of time for reflection and consideration then; time to recall all that Victoria had told him, to weigh her words, and guess what her motives were: time to remember Hilary's smile and blush, as she talked of the violets with him; time to take from his bosom that little bunch of flowers with its soiled and dabbed white bands, and to smooth and dry the valued memorial of her peril and his exertions, which he had picked from the grass where it had dropped as Maurice raised her in his arms; time, too, to put up ardent prayers for her safety and petitions for her happiness; and to endeavor to judge how far that happiness was likely to be affected by his continuing there, persevering in an attempt to win her heart, and obtain a promise of her love and faith.

The report which Maurice brought, did not materially differ from the opinion Dr. Pilgrim had given to Captain Hepburn; she was sleeping, but not quietly; there was still a threatening of fever, which might subside in the night, or might increase toward morning. Mr. Huyton had persuaded the doctor to remain all night at "the Ferns," and Maurice intended to ride over before breakfast the next morning, to ascertain, as early as possible, how she had passed the night. Not that the brother was much alarmed; his sanguine temper and cheerful disposition made him take a happier view of probabilities than the father or the lover could do, and he anticipated with tolerable steadiness a much better report in the morning; or even should there be a little fever for a day or two, it need be nothing to alarm them; she was always well, and he did not think her delicate; surely there could be little serious fear, although there was room perhaps for some anxiety.

So thought and argued Maurice, and apparently Captain Hepburn agreed with him; he was, however, found anxiously pacing up and down the green, the next morning, when Maurice returned from his early ride; and the eagerness with which he asked for intelligence, rather by look than word, did not indicate calm indifference, or careless certainty.

Not so well—feverish and restless; still Dr. Pilgrim hopes the best, and thinks it will soon pass off; however, she must see no one but her nurses, and is to be kept quiet. Nest was sleeping soundly, and to guess from appearances, would wake quite well.

Such was the report. Charles had promised to come over rather late in the forenoon, to bring word how she was going on, as the doctor had recommended some new mode of treatment, from which he expected much benefit.

Just as they were sitting down to breakfast, the letters arrived. Among those for Captain Hepburn, there was one large, business-like, official-looking letter, with "On her Majesty's Service," in the corner, which was not to be seen and opened without some excitement.

It was too truly a summons away from Hurstdene; a notification that his presence was greatly desired at the Admiralty, to receive his appointment to the command of a vessel fitting out at Sheerness. There was time neither for delay nor hesitation—go he must that very day; though to leave Hilary without seeing her again, ill, in his rival's house, and utterly ignorant of his hopes, his love, his sincere love for her, was a trial which required no small amount of self-command and resolution to bear calmly.

Long he sat, with his eyes bent upon the letter, with lips compressed and brows slightly knit, and cheeks glowing even through that bronzed complexion, before he could force from his tongue the words which must announce his departure, or trust his voice to speak without betraying more than he desired. How he craved a little delay; could he but have waited a week, oh, how precious the days would have been! Or had the appointment come before he had known and loved, how welcome, would then have been the announcement.

But it must be done—the words must be spoken; was he turning craven then, to shrink from the duties he had undertaken, from the sacrifice required of him! Would Hilary esteem one who valued inglorious sloth and pleasure, beyond exertion and honor, and self-denial and courage!

He tossed the letter across to Maurice.

"There," said he, with a smile, "see there; read it aloud, Maurice, and let your father hear!"

Maurice did so.

"Oh, Captain Hepburn," exclaimed Gwyneth, starting up, and looking over her brother's shoulder, as he read; "it is an appointment! it will take you away! how sorry, how very sorry I am!"

"Thank you, Miss Gwyneth; your sorrow is more than I deserve; *your* congratulations will be different, Duncan, I expect; shall I apply for you?"

"Do, sir, I shall be delighted," exclaimed Maurice, professional zeal and enthusiasm for the moment overpowering, with their warm glow, the cooler calculations of love, or home affections. "I should be happy indeed to serve with you again."

"And *I* must go to-day," observed Captain Hepburn, struggling with his own feelings in the wish to appear cheerful.

"To-day!" again exclaimed Gwyneth, "and Hilary away, and not able to say good-by, nor Sybil either; oh, do stay at least till to-morrow, and see Sybil again!"

"You are inconsiderate, my dear Gwyneth," said her father; "you ought to know that duty admits of no delay, and that his profession has claims on Captain Hepburn beyond and above all private ties or inclinations."

"True, my dear sir, it leaves me no choice, no room for hesitation, which, perhaps, is a blessing. Could I consult my feelings, Miss Gwyneth, thus abruptly, and under such circumstances, to quit your father's roof, would be the last thing I should wish; nothing would be more precious to me than delay might I indulge in it. Maurice, will you help me to make arrangements as to the means of going?"

In a couple of hours more every thing was ready for starting, and Captain Hepburn had nothing to do but to say farewell to his host and Gwyneth.

"If it is in your power," said Mr. Duncan, as he grasped the sailor's hand, "we shall be happy to see you here again before leaving England; do let us hear from you, at least."

"If possible, I will run down and see you again," said the other, warmly; "it will not be want of will that can stop me, my dear sir; I shall be very, very busy, I know; but my memory and my heart will be here with you; and my first wish will be that you may have improving tidings of your daughter to communicate. Maurice has promised to write."

"You shall hear regularly, if you are so kind as to wish it," replied the clergyman; "but, Captain Hepburn, take your heart to your work, or I fear it will be but ill performed, and we shall have spoiled a good officer."

"My professional heart, sir, may go with me, but when memory wishes to conjure up an image of domestic happiness, purity, piety, affection, truth, and all lovely virtues, it will certainly go back mechanically to the Vicar of Hurstdene and his charming daughters."

"God bless you," replied the other, shaking his hand again and again; "you have been a blessing to me and mine; I owe you, under Providence, the lives of one, two, perhaps three of my children; and if a father's warmest prayers and most heartfelt benediction can call down aught of blessing or well-being for you, then may you be sure of happiness, lasting, satisfying happiness, wherever you may go. Farewell!"

To such words, at such a moment, the only answer was the low, earnest "Thank you!" of subdued feeling, and the close-pressed hand lingering long in a friendly grasp.

Both Gwyneth's hands, taken and clasped in silence for a moment, and then a softly-whispered "Farewell!" which the quivering lip could hardly utter, was all he had firmness for, as he turned away.

"Have you no message for the absent ones?" inquired she, half-reproachfully, as she accompanied him to the porch.

"I pass 'the Ferns' on my road. I shall call there to hear the latest news, and at least, see your sisters, Sybil and Nest," was his justification, which amply satisfied Gwyneth.

He reached "the Ferns" just as Charles Huyton was on the point of stepping into his carriage to drive over to the Vicarage. He turned back, however, and accompanied his guest into the house, who explained his errand as they crossed the hall.

"I congratulate you on your appointment," exclaimed Charles, with much sincerity; "I am truly rejoiced to hear it. I have learned enough of a sailor's feelings, during my acquaintance with Maurice, to know how, beyond all other things, they value professional employment, and covet professional distinction. I will call my cousin to you, and, perhaps, as you are going, you will like to say good-by to Miss Sybil Duncan, and little Nest."

"It was the particular object of my stopping here. If you will let Miss Sybil know I am here I dare say she will see me; but do not disturb Miss Fielding on my account if she is engaged."

Mr. Huyton sent a message to Sybil to inform her who waited for her in the saloon. In a moment she came running down.

"How good of you to call, Captain Hepburn! I saw Maurice this morning; did he tell you?" Her eyes filled with tears as she spoke.

"Could you come out with me for five minutes on the lawn?" said he, determined to speak to her without Mr. Huyton's presence; and almost without waiting for her acquiescence, he drew the hand which he had been holding under his arm, and led her through the open window.

"Tell me truly, how is your sister now?" was his first question.

"Restless and feverish, but not worse—rather better if any thing; but to be kept quite quiet."

"Thank Heaven! I am come to say good-by to you," he added, in a changed voice.

She started, and exclaimed—

"Why, *must* you just now?"

He explained; and Sybil knew enough of the service to be aware that there was no choice in such a case. She listened quietly, but her eyes filled with tears as he spoke.

"You must go then," said she, sorrowfully; "how we shall miss you. I suppose I ought to be glad that you are employed, but I am so selfish as to feel very, very sorry to part. We owe you so much; and when you are gone, how can we show our gratitude to you, or make you feel how we thank you every day? What can we do for you?"

"Remember me, dear Sybil; and help others, your sister above all, to remember me too. Do not let absence or time make you forget me," said he, formality giving way before warmly excited feeling.

"Forget you! oh, Captain Hepburn, never! we none of us *can* do that. Hilary, when she knows what has happened to you, will grieve that she has not thanked you with her own lips; but will she ever *forget* the preserver of Nest? One of the few things she has said has been to express her gratitude, and to charge me, when I saw you, to say how infinitely she felt your courage, and how much more she thanked you for that action than she would have done for her own life alone. I hoped in a few days you would have heard it from herself; but since that can not be, you must try to be satisfied with her gratitude second-hand. What shall I say to her from you, in answer, when I can talk to her again."

"Tell her that nothing dearer than duty would have taken me away from Hurstdene at the present moment; and that so soon as duty permits, I pledge myself to be here again. Meantime, I shall write to Maurice." His tone gave additional force to his words.

"Write often, do," said Sybil, earnestly looking at him, with an appreciation of his meaning dawning on her.

"As often as I can. I must not linger now." He felt that he was understood, but dared not say more.

They turned toward the house.

"Mr. Huyton wants my father and Gwyneth to come over here to remain," said Sybil, as they retraced their steps; "he is going to fetch them, if he can."

"That is very kind; it will be more comfortable for you."

They entered the saloon, and found Victoria there; Mr. Huyton was looking slightly impatient.

Miss Fielding's greetings and adieux were, like herself, lively, gracious, and emphatic. The traveler did not linger a minute more, and as soon as he was gone, Charles Huyton drove off to the Vicarage, for the purpose Sybil had named. The latter went out again for a short stroll. Hilary was sleeping, and her sister, fearful of disturbing her, resolved not to return until summoned on her awakening.

Nest, though pretty well, had enjoyed so prolonged a slumber, that she was not yet dressed; so Sybil resolved to refresh herself by a solitary walk under the beautiful avenue in front of the house. The sound of a horse approaching roused her from her reverie, and looking up, she saw Mr. Farrington, who, immediately on perceiving her, alighted, and giving his horse to the groom, joined her in her walk. His object was to inquire for Miss Duncan; he had been deputed by the party at the Abbey to come over early for news; and the sisters themselves, or some of them, were intending to drive to "the Ferns" later in the day to see Sybil, and hear the bulletin in person.

This was his account of himself; perhaps it would have been more strictly accurate, had he said that he had volunteered the service, which otherwise the groom would have performed alone; and that, though feeling a natural interest in the welfare of a young lady in such circumstances as Hilary, he yet thought and cared a great deal more about her sister. His fancy had been strangely captivated by the tall, handsome girl, whose appearance and manners had haunted his memory, and formed the principal subject of his conversation with Doro Barham all the morning.

Sybil turned when he joined her, and walked toward the house, from which they were distant about a quarter of a mile; giving him, as they went along, first, an answer to his inquiries after her sister; and then a voluntary detail of her regret at parting with Captain Hepburn, whom they all valued so highly.

Mr. Farrington listened with real interest to the account of the family obligations to the gallant officer, and readily conceded that they owed him great gratitude for an amount of benefit not often bestowed by one person. He would have admired and applauded kindness and courage under any circumstances; but when the narrative was enforced by the bright flash of those dark eyes, and the peculiarly sweet tones of the voice which recounted it, his enthusiastic appreciation of Captain Hepburn's merits was quite equal to what even Sybil considered right and becoming.

Her energetic eloquence was interrupted by a slight incident: glancing upward as she spoke, and quite forgetting all minor considerations, she hit her foot against a projecting root, and was very nearly thrown down on her face: she was not hurt, only a little confused at her awkwardness, as she called it; but the gentleman persuaded her to take his arm after that, and the abrupt pause which ensued was broken by his starting another topic, namely, that he had to return to London the next morning, having only come down to the Abbey for a couple of days, for the sake of Mr. Huyton's party.

This information by no means disturbed Sybil in the way in which Captain Hepburn's departure had affected her. She had found Mr. Farrington a pleasant companion, but she had not expected even to see him a second time, and there was neither any surprise or regret visible, when he talked of going. It seemed to her simply natural. He talked of regret, and said a good deal about his memory lingering amid the green shades of "the Ferns," and his wish to visit this country again; to which Sybil listened quietly, and presently observed, "If he liked it so much, what would prevent his coming?" He could not construe her remark into any thing approaching to conscious encouragement; she did not seem to have an idea that she had the least to do with his coming or wishing to come: he found this natural simplicity particularly captivating, and his admiration for her mind increased as much as his conviction for her uncommon beauty did. He thought her more lovely by day-light, in a simple morning dress, than he had done the evening before, in her more elaborate toilette.

In spite of all his efforts to lengthen out the walk, by stopping to admire glens in the park, or remarkably fine trees, or to conjecture the date of the mansion, she yet proceeded so decidedly onward, with so evident a resolution to reach the house, that he was compelled to suppose her quite indifferent to any peculiar charm in his society, or very strictly correct in her notions of propriety and etiquette. He tried to flatter himself rather it was the latter, as she was evidently very young, and young girls, he believed, are always either rigidly prudent, or immensely careless about decorum; but he could not quite convince himself that this was the fact; he was too diffident, indeed, to be very certain on this point.

On she walked, at least, straight into the house, and never lingered till they reached the saloon where Mrs. Fielding and her daughter were sitting. Then she quietly said that she would go up and learn the very latest tidings of Hilary, for Isabel and Dora's benefit, seeming to expect he would instantly start off to the Abbey with the report. The interval was employed by him in learning from Victoria all the particulars relative to the expected visit of Mr. Duncan, whom Charles hoped to bring back with him; an announcement which excited so strong a wish in Mr. Farrington to see the clergyman, that the ladies proposed at once that he should stay and lunch at "the Ferns," sending the groom back to the Abbey with the report he had come to fetch.

No pressing was needed to elicit a very ready acceptance of this proposition; and, to say the truth, Victoria was as glad of the company of a pleasant and gentlemanlike young man, as he could be to stay. The morning after a fête is generally flat and dull; and if a gentleman desires to make his presence thoroughly appreciated, he should contrive to drop in on such an occasion, among a family party in the country.

On Sybil's return, she seemed rather surprised to find that the message was to be intrusted to the groom; and apparently doubtful whether he could convey safely so important a verbal communication as that Miss Duncan was asleep, but seemed much the same, she indited a little note to Dora Barham; and by this means that young lady became possessed of the interesting fact, that the whole family from the Vicarage were expected at "the Ferns," to remain there as long as Hilary's health required it.

Nest, who was now quite well, had entered the room with Sybil, and the gentleman soon coaxed her on to his knee, and began conversing with her about her home, her father, and her sisters: they were excellent friends before Sybil's note was finished.

"How wonderfully the sisters are alike," said he to Victoria, as he gazed admiringly at the little one's large black eyes and raven hair; "I should like a sketch of this child."

"I believe I can show you some, although I can not give them to you," replied Victoria, going to a large portfolio which was standing near. She opened the boards, and began to turn over the sketches it contained. He put down Nest, and went to examine it with great interest; there were many views in the forest, at the sight of which Nest frequently exclaimed she knew that spot, or she had seen this in Hilary's sketch-book; and when Sybil joined them, she seemed to know every view, and owned that they had all been together, when such or such was done. At last they came to some groups of figures; the sisters again and again, Hilary always principal; and then single drawings, Sybil, Gwyneth, and Nest, evidently younger and more childish, but still very like. There was no finished drawing of Hilary alone; and Sybil owned that her sister never had sat to Mr. Huyton, as they had, again and again; she did not know why, perhaps he had never asked her: the views there were of her, were taken by stealth, or done from memory, perhaps.

"It is hardly fair to show drawings which so plainly tell a tale," whispered Mr. Farrington to Victoria, when Sybil had turned away to listen to Mrs. Fielding's questions. "If these were mine, I would not allow them to be carelessly examined and investigated."

"Oh! I am breaking no confidence," replied Victoria, in a laughing whisper; "Charles makes no secret of his object; the whole plan and intention of yesterday's fête, was to distinguish one person above all others; and though we did not propose to risk drowning her, yet, I believe, he will by no means regret the accident, if all ends well. At any rate, it has secured him some important advantages."

Mr. Farrington looked excessively surprised at this communication, and made a mental determination to keep his own counsel, so far as Victoria was concerned, unless he wanted all the world to know his affairs.

Sybil disappeared again just after this, much to Mr. Farrington's disappointment; the only amusement left for him was what Victoria supplied; and although she was very entertaining and agreeable, as he was wishing all the time for something else, her powers of pleasing were lost upon him.

"Where have you been?" was Victoria's question, when Sybil joined them at the luncheon table; to which she replied, "she had gone out to finish her walk, as Hilary was still sleeping soundly; and she wished when her father arrived, to be quite fresh and ready to attend him."

Very fresh, and very handsome, too, she looked, with the bright color which exercise had brought into her cheeks, and the happy expression which a conviction that her sister was now doing very well, produced; and her perfect unconsciousness that Mr. Farrington's visit was made for her sake, or that his eyes were incessantly attracted to her in admiration, greatly heightened her charms in his opinion. He tried to detain her in conversation; but no sooner was the luncheon finished, than she again withdrew, and remained invisible for the next hour.

It was not Mr. Farrington's conversational powers which brought her down at last, but the arrival of her own family, with Charles Huyton. No sooner did she see the carriage at a little distance, than she ran hastily down stairs, and was on the steps to receive her father when it drew up, quite regardless of all the state formalities of porter, butler, or footman, who had to stand off to make way for her.

Charles sprang out first, and his inquiries of "How is she now? How is Hilary?" were hardly less earnest and eager than those of Gwyneth and Maurice. But Sybil had scarcely words to answer them: it was to her father she looked, of him she thought; and when, by the assistance of his son and host, the clergyman had been safely placed upon the broad steps, she threw herself into his arms, and in accents choking from delight, she whispered that Hilary was better, Dr. Pilgrim had just seen her, and said she was out of danger.

Mr. Farrington, who was standing near enough to see the meeting, thought he had never witnessed a more touching sight, than the glad thankfulness of the young people, and the deep, reverend gratitude of the father, as he raised his hat from his head, and uttered audible thanks for this joyful tidings. Mr. Huyton himself was in a state of excitement most visible to a calm looker-on; he shook hands ardently with Mr. Duncan, kissed the hands of Sybil and Gwyneth with most un-English grace, and as to Nest, he caught her up in his arms and almost smothered her with caresses, the overflowings of a full-hearted happiness.

They became rational at last, and moved into the house. It was necessary that Miss Duncan should still be kept quiet; but, under promise of silence and discretion, Gwyneth was permitted to take her sister's place in watching the invalid, and Sybil was able to devote herself to her father.

Mr. Farrington's wish of being introduced to the clergyman was gratified, and he found the next hour spent in conversing with him, and looking at Sybil, so very pleasant, that he heard with great regret the announcement of the arrival of Mr. Barham and his daughter. This brought back Charles Huyton and Maurice into the saloon, they having been pacing on the terrace, and discussing the wishes of the latter to sail with Captain Hepburn, in which Mr. Huyton very cordially joined.

Dora's vail and bonnet hid her face from her father when she spoke to Maurice, and after a few fluttered sentences, she turned to Sybil, and asked if she might not go up stairs and see Gwyneth for a minute; so the two girls left the room together, with a word of apology to Victoria. Then Mr. Barham expressed a strong wish to see some alterations Mr. Huyton was making in his hot-houses, and Isabel said she should like to accompany them; Victoria politely offered to go with her, and as Charles seemed to regret leaving Mr. Duncan, both Maurice and Mr. Farrington volunteered to remain with him; while Mrs. Fielding, just then entering the room, declared it was her peculiar right to wait on and attend to him, when he was at "the Ferns."

Had Mr. Barham and Isabel intended to do what was most pleasant, but least profitable, to Dora and Maurice, they could hardly have arranged better. Sybil and her friend returned to the saloon, to find the party very much reduced; and as Mrs. Fielding was as good as her word, and entirely engrossed Mr. Duncan, Mr. Farrington enticed Sybil to sit down with him by the portfolio before alluded to, to tell him more about the beautiful sketches it contained; and she, quite unaware how little he had cared for them when only Victoria had turned them over, very good-naturedly complied with his request, and discussed the times and places where the sketches had been drawn, with such amusing vivacity, and in such graphic language, that he did not discover how time slipped by while so employed.

Why Dora and Maurice chose at the same time to go out of the window, and continued for the next hour to walk slowly up and down a long green alley beside the flower garden, or to stand in deep talk, leaning over a pedestal, was best known to themselves. Mr. Barham was so very well satisfied to see his eldest daughter attended through his gardens by Mr. Huyton, and leaning on his arm, that he quite forgot to think about how little Dora was employed; he could not on any account hurry a stroll which afforded Isabel so good an opportunity of displaying her interest in science, and her peculiarly sensible opinions relative to the regulation of hot-houses, gardeners, village schools, farmers' prejudices, and the poor-law; on all which subjects she spoke with much earnestness and grace. Mr. Huyton being much too well-bred to show how excessively he was bored, or in the slightest degree to hurry Miss Barham, although longing to return to the house, the elder gentleman was quite persuaded that he was delighted with their society, and fully appreciated the honor done to him by the owner of Drewhurst Abbey, and his eldest daughter. He judged Charles by himself; and conscious that no claims of civility would have made *him* submit to a *gêne* of any kind, and that the use he made of politeness and courtesy, was, not to please others at his own expense, but to gratify himself on all occasions without actually giving, offense, he conjectured that what was so gracefully borne, must be a pleasure in itself; and lingered long on purpose ere he brought his visit to a close.

And all this time Maurice and Dora were together, on a warm, sunshiny May afternoon, straying in a beautiful garden, where early roses, lilacs, and hawthorns, mingled their scent with the rich rhododendrons, daphnes, and still rarer exotics with which the flower-beds were glowing, and talking as young people will talk, when, in the warm glow of true first-love, they forget the cold calculations of worldly prudence, and ambitious hopes.

He told her how suddenly Captain Hepburn had been called away, and she turned pale, and her voice faltered, as she suggested that the same thing might occur to him; and when she heard that his friend had promised to apply for him, and that his interest was such that there was little doubt the application would be successful, she was quite unable to conceal how much she was pained at the idea. In vain she tried to say she wished him honor and success in his profession; she was too sincere to deceive, and too thoughtless to remember any thing but her own emotions. And what could be the result, but that Maurice made a rash avowal of his passionate admiration and love, his presumptuous affection, his hopeless attachment, and received in return a still more rash acknowledgment, that her feelings were but too much in agreement with his own, and that the certainty of his devotion to her was the only thing which could console her for his departure, if he must go.

It was a moment of wild intoxication; the delight of knowing each other's hearts, was dearly purchased, and yet it was a delight. Their whole acquaintance had been a series of imprudencies, and this conversation was but the crowning imprudence of all. For as to hope, they really, hardly dared entertain an idea of it; Dora felt, and Maurice feared, that there was small chance of her father's consent to an engagement, and without Mr. Barham's consent, Maurice would not even ask her to make him the smallest promise of constancy or faith.

He indeed, would have gone straight to Mr. Barham, owned his affection, and asked to be allowed to win her hand by gallant deeds, or constant devotion; but Dora dared do no such thing; she shrank from cold looks, and harsh, stern words, and contempt and censure. She could not encounter Isabel's surprise, or her father's frown; she would have gladly plighted her hand to Maurice, and would have trusted, with the coward's trusts, to time or chance, to circumstances, to accident, to any thing in fact, rather than to bold, straightforward measures. It was his sense of honor, and his rectitude of feeling alone, which saved her from the misery of a clandestine engagement; she would have ventured that for him; she dared not be open, but she thought she could be true. His, too, was all the regret, the remorse, indeed, for what he had done. When the first violent emotion had passed away, and he saw how he had won her heart, and yet must not avow their mutual affection, he became aware how great an injury he had done her; what a cloud he should have thrown upon her young life, what a constant, fretting, wearing anxiety he had brought upon her. Then, in his true and honorable love, he prayed her to forget him; not to let the thought, the memory of him, darken her days, or interfere with her future prospects. His love saw no shadow, no fault in her; it was too warm to permit the thought that she was a coward at heart, and shrank from the only right step; he called her weakness, gentleness, docility, feminine tenderness; and while he would have braved all and any thing for her, he almost trembled at the idea of entailing on her a moment's care or mental suffering.

"No, I do not deserve your love; do not make yourself unhappy for a fellow like me, dearest, sweetest Dora! it is too good of you; I can never, never forget *you*! but think of me only as of a brother, as of one who would bring you nothing but good, not sorrow; think of me with kindness always, but not with sorrowful regret; think of me as one who loves you devotedly, passionately; I shall treasure your image in my heart, and dote upon it in my fancy, and in the lonely nightwatch, dwell on the recollection of your smile; and perhaps in moments of danger, in storm, and peril, and difficulty, your dear, bright eyes will shine on my memory, and nerve me for daring deeds; but do not think of me. It is enough for me to know that had there been no obstacle you would have loved me; that had my birth and fortune entitled me to ask your hand, I might have won you; that your heart should have been mine, had Heaven so willed it. But do not grieve that we must part; nay, do not shed those tears; dearest Dora! I do not deserve so very great an honor."

As if such words would make her care less, or quiet the heart-broken sobs with which she listened to his protestations!

"But you are not going yet?" she murmured.

"Heaven knows how soon; but, Dora, after this, even if I do not, we must not meet again."

"Oh! Maurice," ejaculated she, in overwhelming distress.

"Not purposely, not alone; no, Dora, it has been madness, wickedness almost, to love you and make you unhappy; but we will not add to that unintentional error the real, downright crime of carrying on a secret understanding, a clandestine intercourse. If I may not ask you of your father now, at least he shall not, when I do, throw back on me the imputation that I have meanly, basely encouraged you in defying his wishes or thwarting his hopes. If that blessed time should ever come when I may seek you openly—if—oh! Dora,—if you still love me in some happier future, then let us, at least, have the power of saying and feeling we were rash, imprudent, thoughtless, but we were not deceitful."

The little hand he held tremblingly pressed his fingers with a convulsive clasp, and then she murmured again—

"Oh! Maurice, I will be true to you for life; I will never, no, never, be the bride of another; you have my heart, and shall have my faith for life."

"No, no, Dora, you must not say so, I will not hold you bound; dear as your words are, sweetest! you must take them back; no promise must be given or accepted which truth and honor do not sanction. Time alters all, every thing; and when I am gone, and you learn to see my character as it deserves, unblinded by your own sweet fancies, and that delightful kindness which has moved you to pity a poor sailor like me, then you must still think of me as of one who would not, even for his dearest hopes, allow you to fetter yourself with a bond you might regret, with a promise which, being wrong, could bring no happiness with it. Dora, your peace of mind is dearer than my own!"

"Good, kind, generous," was all she could say.

"Give me that ribbon from your wrist," added he.

She hurriedly undid the blue ribbon that she wore round her left arm, put it for one moment to her lips, then tossed it to him, and turned with hasty steps toward the house. He followed her quietly until he saw her enter the saloon, and turning off by another path, he escaped, to consider what had passed, and console himself with the blue ribbon as he could.

CHAPTER XII.

"Ah, on which, if both our lots were balanced,
Was, indeed, the heaviest burthen thrown?
Thou a weeping exile in thy forest,
I a smiling queen upon my throne."

Iseult.

The amendment in Hilary's health continued to advance so favorably that the next day she was considered well enough to see her father without risk from excitement, and then she began clearly to understand the fact that her whole family were at "the Ferns." She did not at first make any audible comments on the circumstance, but toward evening she took the opportunity of no one but Sybil being present, to make her tell her who had proposed this arrangement, and what had been said on the subject.

Sybil said it had been entirely Charles Huyton's own idea; and nothing could be kinder or more hospitable than he was, making it most pleasant for them all, and avowing that, were it not for Hilary's illness, he should be the happiest man possible, with such a family round him.

Miss Duncan lay silent for some minutes, then observed —

"Were it not that my illness makes it inevitable we should not be here at all."

"So Nest proved to him," remarked Sybil; "and she added, somewhat uncourteously, she would rather have you well, and be at home."

"Nest must not be rude, but it is well she thinks so. I must get well as fast as possible. I shall leave this room to-morrow, I hope, Sybil."

"How glad we shall be to have you down stairs," said her sister.

"I shall not go down till I am well enough to go home," replied Hilary, decidedly; "I hope to get into the dressing-room to-morrow, and on Monday, if Mr. Huyton will lend us his carriage, we can all go back to the Vicarage."

"I am sure I shall be glad if we can," was Sybil's answer. She partly understood the motives of Hilary's conduct.

"Where is Captain Hepburn?" added Hilary, after a pause, turning her head on the pillow of the sofa where she was lying. "Is he gone?"

"He went away yesterday morning, and hopes to come back again soon. He promised he would return as soon as he could."

There was another pause; then Hilary asked —

"Did you see him yesterday?"

"He called here to say good-by, and hear the last account of you!"

"Why did he go, did he tell you?"

"Business, indispensable business," said Sybil, fearful of distressing her sister by announcing his appointment, and the expected consequences to Maurice, who, Hilary well knew, had always reckoned on going with him.

"Business!" repeated Hilary, looking anxiously at her sister, "that is a vague term; however, I suppose I have no right to question about it. Gone without my being able to thank him! I should have liked to do that!"

"I gave him your message, dear Hilary; do you remember what you told me to say?"

"Yes, and he—what did he say, Sybil?" said her sister, eager to hear something, she hardly knew what. Sybil repeated Captain Hepburn's message verbatim, and with emphasis.

It was listened to with silence, but after a long pause she repeated — "Duty."

"The fact is," added Sybil, seeing she was perplexing herself about his departure, "he has been appointed to the command of the *Pandanus*, a fine new screw steamer, one of the finest in the service, he says; and he has gone down to Woolwich, where she is fitting out."

"Will he take Maurice?" exclaimed Hilary, eagerly. "Oh, I hope he will!"

"They both expect it, but there has not been time yet; he only went yesterday; now do lie still, dear, or you will bring on your fever again, and we shall not go home on Monday."

Hilary laid her head back on her pillows, and remained perfectly quiet for the rest of the evening. She resolved not to think of Captain Hepburn, or to bewilder herself in conjectures relative to any thing uncertain or unpleasant; she resolutely quieted her mind, banishing doubt and conjecture, which are worse and more irritating to the weak, than certainty of evil, and dwelling only on soothing subjects.

Her self-discipline and mental government were successful, and were rewarded by finding her strength as much improved the next day as she could have expected. She was able to resume her usual dress, and sit up in the adjoining room, where the balmy air of a sweet summer Sunday morning seemed every minute to add to her strength. She kept her resolution, however, of not going down stairs, or joining the family party, in spite of Victoria's urgent entreaties. It was quite true, that her head would not as yet bear much noise, and she had no intention of risking a relapse, by taking liberties too early.

She must, of course, have an interview with Charles eventually, and thank him for his share in saving her life, but she rather shrank from the thought; she hoped it was not ingratitude, she really did feel thankful to him; and had there been no recollections of former conversations and past professions to trouble her, she would have been ready and anxious to express her gratitude. But now she feared to say either too little or too much; she dreaded to raise hopes which she had once trusted were extinguished, and she had a vague foreboding that any sort of emotion would inevitably lead to painful and perplexing discoveries.

As memory had resumed its power, a distinct impression of his words and tone when he reached her in the water, impressed itself on her mind with unaccountable accuracy and vividness; and though it was not usually her way to shrink from duty, even if painful, or to put off the evil day, with that weak procrastination which often trebles the suffering by unnecessary and prolonged anticipation, she determined to delay this interview to the very last, that escape to her own home might immediately follow.

Her resolutions, however, were over-ruled, and her wishes set aside, by the stronger will, and less scrupulous determinations of others. Charles and Victoria were alike decided, that she should see him; and Hilary found herself actually without a choice, although nominally consulted on the occasion.

It was in the afternoon; the family had returned from church, and Gwyneth, who had remained at home to read to Hilary, was persuaded by her to go down stairs, and if Maurice was at leisure, to ask him to come and sit with her. A knock at the door a few minutes afterward, made her suppose he was there; but in answer to her invitation, Victoria entered, inquired how she did, whether she was equal to conversation: and on Hilary's cheerfully assuring her that she was going on nicely, Miss Fielding added, in a manner which left her almost without choice —

"You will not mind, then, seeing Charles for a moment, who is dying of impatience to kiss your hand."

As she said this, she admitted Mr. Huyton into the room, and then turned toward the toilette table, where she busied herself with her back to Hilary, in searching among caskets and drawers for unknown articles, with an evident determination not to see or hear any thing else; which was extremely distressing to her friend, however pleasant it might be to her cousin.

Surprised and flurried by an intrusion so unexpected and unwelcome, Hilary's pale cheeks flushed, and her hand trembled, as she endeavored to rise from her easy chair to meet her host. Somehow she hardly understood how, she was gently put back into it, and in another moment she found Charles, placing one knee on the ground, was really and very warmly kissing the hand she had held out, as he pressed it in both of his. She endeavored to draw it away; she tried to express by a glance, that whatever gratitude might inspire, love for him did not exist; but although words may define differences, and draw lines of distinction, it is often difficult for looks to express nice shades of feeling, and to mark accurately all the gazer would wish. At least, she feared her looks were incomprehensible; for though Charles's tongue was mute, his eyes declared so plainly and unequivocally the ruling passion of his life at that time, that it was perfectly impossible for her actually to misunderstand him. She saw that Victoria was nothing, and that she was all to him.

The color flitted from her cheeks, and they became white, whiter than her illness had left them—deadly pale; her hand turned cold in his grasp, and after feebly trying to draw it away, she sank back against the pillows behind her, and, for the second time in her life, she fainted.

When she recovered, she found herself lying on the sofa; and as sense and perception gradually returned, she discovered that Charles was supporting her head on his arm, while Victoria was plentifully bedewing her face with eau-de-Cologne. She moved her head, and whispered, "I should like to lie down," which compelled Mr. Huyton to resign her to the pillows, where common sense would have taught him, she had better have been all the time.

"Are you better?" said he, softly and anxiously.

"Yes, thank you; please leave me, and send Sybil;" and she fixed her eyes for one moment on him so decidedly, that disobedience was out of his power. He was forced to withdraw, and went to find Sybil, with no other advantage from his visit, than the idea that if she was so very weak, it would be impossible for her to leave "the Ferns" next day.

But half an hour's quiet restored her strength; and reflection on what had passed, made Hilary more than ever certain of the propriety of leaving the house the next day, even should the effort be attended with fatigue to herself. It had been a transitory emotion which had made her faint; she was not at all accustomed to such attacks; but her physical weakness had perhaps made her feelings more than usually acute, and herself less able than in general to govern them. It was the expression of Charles Huyton's eyes which had overpowered her: she had read, or seemed to read in them, such a world of strong concentrated passion, such selfish self-will, such deep determination to carry out a point which he had never for one moment abandoned; so much of human pride, and of stern resolution not to submit passively or unresistingly to what thwarted his wishes, as opened up to her mind a new view of his character, and made her almost regret that he had not left her to sink under the black waters in that shady pool, rather than live to enter into a contest with one who seemed so well fitted to trample down and overpower her, when their happiness or their desires crossed. Calm reflection recalled her courage and her firmness. Let her but walk straight on, he could not hurt her. The spirit of evil itself was powerless to harm those who trusted in "the shadow of those Almighty wings," which she believed stretched out over her and hers: and should she then fear one who was but man? No; he might pain, but he could not injure her, unless he enticed her feet from that narrow path of duty, within which she was safe.

And as her evening prayer arose, that she might "have understanding in the way of godliness," she felt more strongly than ever that *that* way did not point to becoming Charles Huyton's wife.

When the family met at breakfast the next morning, Mr. Duncan announced, that Hilary was quite well enough to go home that day, and therefore, if Mr. Huyton would be so kind as to lend them his carriage, he would no longer trespass on his hospitality.

In vain his host and Miss Fielding urged her supposed weakness, and their desires to detain them all, by every argument which love and policy could devise. Mr. Duncan was calmly immovable, and they were obliged to yield the point at last. The younger girls, naturally enough, had enjoyed the change, and were extremely sorry to quit "the Ferns;" but Maurice, whose spirits and gayety seemed at times entirely to fail him, and who, except when with his father, appeared wrapped in a cloud of impenetrable gloom, was entirely on his father's side, and expressed, as warmly as politeness permitted, a strong desire to return home before his being obliged to quit Hurstdene, an event he now daily expected.

The carriage accordingly was ordered directly after luncheon; and meantime, Maurice walked home, to give notice that they were coming, taking Gwyneth with him, that all might be ready for the reception of Hilary.

"So you are determined to leave us," said Victoria, as she entered the dressing-room, where Hilary had breakfasted; "however, if you are so well, you will, I trust, come down stairs before quitting the house; you could surely give us your company in the saloon."

"I shall be better at home," replied Miss Duncan; "I am very anxious to be there on Maurice's account, for he will want a hundred things done and arranged, and it would be much less anxiety to me to see to it all, than to remain absent, and trust to the chance of others doing right. I can keep quiet at home, you know."

"Yes; I can understand how quiet you will be, from what I know of your usual habits; you will only wait on your father incessantly, see to your brother's having every comfort, teach Nest, look after your servants, attend to the housekeeping, and listen to every old man, sick woman, or unhappy child, who may choose to come and drawl out their long story to you. That is your quiet."

Hilary laughed.

"Well, if all that is to be done, the sooner I get about it the better."

"Meantime," said Victoria, "come down stairs."

Hilary seemed inclined to demur.

"You must," continued Miss Fielding, urgently, "or I shall conclude it is want of will, not want of power, prevents you."

"I will come down by-and-by," said Hilary, gently, "but I dare not exhaust myself before I take this little journey; and if you would be so very kind as to let me, I should like to lie down and rest now."

Victoria really could not find in her heart to oppose Hilary's meek petition, or to say any more at present about her own wishes; so giving her friend a kiss, she settled her comfortably on the sofa, and then left her to peace and solitude.

"Will she not come down, Victoria?" asked Charles, eagerly, as he met her on the stairs.

Victoria told him what had passed, and strongly recommended, under present circumstances, patience and caution on his part. His rival, if Captain Hepburn was his rival, was gone, and had left without an explanation; but although the field was thus open to him, it by no means followed, that he should rush forward hastily and unadvisedly. She was not in a state to bear it, and he might lose all, by hazarding too much.

It was about half an hour before luncheon, when Hilary, leaning on Victoria's arm, eventually entered the saloon, where Mr. Huyton had been passing the morning, in an uncontrollable state of restless impatience. How he sprang forward to meet her at the door, and how carefully he provided the easiest chair in the pleasantest corner of the room for her accommodation, may be imagined. His manners seemed scarcely to allow that any other person could have the least claim upon her; and his whole wish seemed to be to engross her himself. But Hilary would sit near her father, would give her principal attention to him, and would at first, when she spoke, whisper in her soft voice, words which marked her regard and consideration for him as her principal object.

Presently, however, gathering courage and firmness, she turned to her host, and said:

"I have no doubt that my father has conveyed the thanks I sent by him, Mr. Huyton; but let me now for myself, thank you again for your share in the exertions which saved my life. I was too weak to say so yesterday. I hope you believe that I am grateful."

"If ever an action brought its own reward," said he, in a low voice, and placing his hand on the fingers which rested on the arm of her chair; "it was mine, when I bore you from the water, and laid you safely on the bank. I can conceive only one degree of happiness greater than that."

"My strength was so completely exhausted," said Hilary, drawing away her hand to pass it across her forehead, "that had I not been relieved from the weight of Nest, and released from her struggles, I must have sunk in another moment."

"Poor little thing! she was unconscious how she increased your danger," replied Charles; he could not bring himself to say the words of praise to his rival's presence of mind, which were his due, and which Hilary half hoped to hear. Presently he added, looking up suddenly:

"And you *will* go to-day! is that kind, Miss Duncan, to hurry away the moment you can move; at any risk to leave my house, rather than oblige me?"

"You know, Mr. Huyton," replied Hilary, "we have sometimes other things to consider, besides obliging our friends; but it can not justly be called unkindness to do our duty; and mine takes me home to-day."

"Of course, if your *duty* takes you away," was his answer, "my pleasure or happiness must not interfere with it; they have no right to be considered for a moment."

"I am sure my father would tell you that the two can not really be at variance," answered Hilary, earnestly. "If we both follow the road of duty, we may be certain that we shall not come into dangerous collision. They are lines which never clash, except through carelessness or mistake. They may diverge widely, they may run parallel, but they will have no unsafe crossings, if we take conscience for our engineer."

"True, dear child," said Mr. Duncan, "as your favorite poet says:

"'Duty, like a strict preceptor,
Sometimes frowns or seems to frown;'

still, when we have the courage to look her calmly in the face, we shall find the frown is our mistake; a mere shadow cast by fear or over-anxious wishes."

Mr. Huyton make no further objections, and the family were permitted to return to the Vicarage, as had been proposed. Nobody, however, could prevent his riding beside the carriage the whole way, or to forbid his being there to hand Hilary out when she descended from it; it was very disagreeable to her, but he would not see that; and even when she entered the house, he appeared extremely reluctant to take his leave, and allow her to rest in peace.

Once more in her place at home, and gathering strength, every hour, from the pleasure of being there, Hilary could not avoid immediately perceiving the extreme depression of spirits which overpowered Maurice; and with a woman's quickness, made more acute by her own recent experience, she decided that his unfortunate attachment to Dora, must in some way be the cause. Of the existence of this attachment she had been for some time aware; but not guessing what had really passed between them, she concluded that it was his own sense of its hopelessness which oppressed her brother. Eager to bury those too-encroaching thoughts of another person, which were continually creeping into her mind, she would yield nothing to the lassitude of recent illness, would allow herself no rest, lest memory should be engrossed by one image; but resolutely engaged in all her usual occupations, and threw herself with more than her former zeal into the cares, hopes, and pleasures of those around her. Of these, naturally, Maurice was the first, after her father; and his affairs, indeed, were peculiarly prominent just then. Captain Hepburn had written to say, that he had received the promise of Maurice's appointment to the *Pandanus*; so that they might now expect his removal any day. But however excited or restless, anxious or happy, such a prospect might make him, his sister saw clearly this was not all; and earnestly hoping that a confidence she had so long enjoyed would not now be withdrawn, she watched him with affectionate attention and silent pity.

It was not till the day following, that she received from him an explanation, which told her how truly he deserved the pity she had already bestowed, and how much real, though unacknowledged, sympathy there was between them.

They were sitting together on Tuesday afternoon, just arranging about an expedition to be undertaken by Mr. Duncan, his son, and Gwyneth, when the Drewhurst carriage drove up to the door. At the first glimpse of the liveries in the distance, Maurice had started up; but when the carriage passed the window, he sat down again quietly, and whispered to his sister, there was only Miss Barham in it.

Isabel entered alone. She came to inquire after Hilary; it appeared that she and her father had driven over to "the Ferns," expecting to find the Duncans still there; and that on discovering the mistake, Mr. Barham had decided to remain with Mr. Huyton, having some magistrates' matters to talk over, while his daughter proceeded to the Vicarage. Isabel said that Mr. Huyton had offered to accompany them; but her father thought that such an incursion in the Vicarage drawing-room would be overpowering, so after luncheon she had come alone. She would not, therefore, remain very long, as papa would be expecting her back to pick him up; but she was delighted to see how well Hilary was looking, quite like herself again! getting home must have done her a world of good. When questioned about her sister, she answered that Dora was not well; she thought the hot weather disagreed with her; she complained of head-ache; could not eat, and was very pale; a common effect of heat on her constitution. Papa talked of sending her to some friends in the north, for change of air. He meant to remain at the Abbey himself, for the present, and of course Isabel must be with him; he could not spare her; but Lady Margaret would take Dora to Scotland, or Scarborough, or Germany; it was not quite settled which; and she believed they would go very soon.

"Now I must go," exclaimed Isabel, starting up, "or papa will not trust me alone again. Oh, by-the-by, Mr. Maurice Duncan, I thought you were gone to sea. Surely Mr. Huyton told us you were appointed to some ship."

"Perhaps I maybe," said Maurice, trying to speak carelessly, then remembering that what he said might be repeated to Dora, he added, "I expect it any day: I heard it was to come, and of course, it will be soon."

"Well then I wish you *bon voyage*," replied Isabel, lightly; "I am so very glad to have seen you once more before you go, to say so. Good-by, Hilary, dear! mind and get well. Do you know, papa wants Mr. Huyton to stand for the county, and I dare say he will; and with papa's interest, I have no doubt he will succeed. He ought to be an M.P. Papa says, few people know how really clever he is, he is so quiet and modest. But we want such men for the country. So papa says. Good-by."

Hilary watched the carriage drive away, and as Isabel's pink and white feathers disappeared in the distance, she sighed to think what would she not give to be able to hope that Mr. Huyton would really transfer to the heiress of Drewhurst Abbey the affection which he had hitherto wasted on herself.

It was with the utmost difficulty that poor Maurice was able to command his attention and spirits sufficiently to be the usual cheerful companion to his father. But on his return he hurried into the garden, and there, when Hilary was able to seek him, she discovered him stretched on the sloping bank of the terrace, with his face covered by his arms. She sat down beside him, and gently passing her hands through his curly hair, she whispered,

"Dear Maurice!"

He turned his face toward her, and she, putting her lips to his cheek, again whispered,

"I was afraid you were very unhappy."

"Oh, Hilary, I am such a wretch, such a thoughtless, selfish, cruel fellow! If you knew all—" was his exclamation, with a passionate misery of look and manner most unusual to him.

"Indeed, dear Maurice, I can not believe you. You may, perhaps, have been thoughtless, though that is not like you; but cruel, selfish! never. Oh no, I know you better!"

"You don't know, dear; you could not guess what I have done; how I have pained and half-broken the dearest, warmest, most loving little heart in the world; how I have dimmed her smiles, and clouded her sunshine, and made both her head and heart ache. Yes, it is all my fault; mine, mine entirely."

"Yours, dear Maurice!"

"Yes, Hilary, she loves me; it is no idle vanity which misleads me; she said it—she owned it with tears and sobs—with fear and trembling, and yet in spite of both grief and terror, that she loved me; she, the bright—the rich—the beautiful; she loved *me*! and what has it brought her? Grief and pain, sickness and fear; and all for me! I, who though I would lay down my life for her, am not worthy to touch the tip of her little finger! I, who have no claim, except that of deep, doting, devoted, never-ending love for her. Oh! Hilary, is she not an angel to love me!"

"But why, dear Maurice, why be so miserable then, if she really loves you? does Mr. Barham object?" asked Hilary, not quite understanding his incoherent exclamations.

"We dared not ask him."

"Dared not! Maurice, that is not like you!"

"No! Dora dared not. What is there that I would not dare for her that honor did not forbid? Oh, Hilary, if you only knew how I love her!"

"But it is a pity—nay, surely, Maurice, it is wrong if you love thus, not to tell Mr. Barham! concealment never can be right, and must be doubly painful!"

"Yes, Hilary," said her brother, rising upright and looking steadfastly at her, "if we went on with it; but when I found how it was, that I was not only using up my own feelings, but acting on hers—not only making myself unhappy by indulging a presumptuous passion, but involving her in the same hopeless misery, I saw there were but two ways open to us. One to explain all to Mr. Barham, and cast ourselves on his compassion; the other to part! I would have taken the first, there would have been far less of suffering and misery; she judged otherwise, and we parted on Saturday. You heard what Isabel said to-day."

"Then you have been neither cruel nor selfish, my dear brother, but strictly honorable and right. Imprudent, perhaps, but who can control the heart by prudence, Maurice; or prevent the growth of love, where there is sympathy and community of feeling? We can not either compel or forbid its existence, can we?" and Hilary blushed deeply, as she propounded a doctrine taught her by her late experience.

"I do not think that is right, Hilary," replied her brother thoughtfully, considering his own circumstances, and not suspecting from what feelings she spoke. "I believe we ought to control all our passions; and if we have not the power, it must be that we have willfully thrown it away. Love is like ardent spirits, perhaps, we may refrain altogether, but if we do imbibe it we must be responsible for the ungovernable evils it produces. And, oh, Hilary!" added he, throwing himself down on the grass again, "I am a wretch for having plunged Dora in such a depth of trouble—a selfish, miserable wretch; because, even now, I can not wish her not to love me; I would give the world, I would give my hopes of promotion, that she had never begun; but I can not, try as I will, really wish her now to leave off loving me. And yet it is only sorrow and pain to her."

"But, Maurice, better times may come—why should you despair so? who knows what may happen to induce Mr. Barham to approve of your suit, and then what happiness for you?"

"What happiness indeed! I wish Dora would let me speak. I am sure it would have been better, don't you think so, Hilary? We could but have been refused; have had to part, and to wait; we *might* have been happier. We had better have spoken."

"Yes, I am sure of that," said Hilary, emphatically, "certainty would be better, and candor and openness must be the safest, because the truest path. She should have let you speak."

"I don't know, though," resumed Maurice, with a strong dislike to hear even an implied censure on his idol, "she must be the best judge of that; the evils, the pain of coldness and displeasure, would have all fallen on her. She would have been the sufferer. It was natural she should shrink from the disclosure, it would cost her too dear! If I could only have borne all for her!"

"I can not imagine that she would have met with any thing half so bad as the trouble of concealment and the pain of mystery. Mr. Barham might not approve your attachment, and then he would have separated you, sent her away, or something of that sort; but that is no more than has now happened. The dictates of honor are as imperative as the commands of the sternest parent. If he had refused his consent, you must have given up all hope, and you might both trust to recovering in time from an unfortunate love."

"Hilary, you don't know! Love like mine lasts for life," was his determined answer.

"But perhaps it might not with her; and you know you must really wish her to be happy. If she had no hope she would gradually recover her serenity; at least I think one must if hope were really gone; but now she will not only have the sickening misery of protracted suspense, but the fear of discovery, and the pain of acting a part—of in appearance deceiving her father."

"Deceiving! how unjust you are; she is incapable of deceit."

"I only said the appearance, dear Maurice; but why should she fear to own her love? You are not unworthy of it; noble birth, indeed, you have not, but, except that and money, you have every thing a man can want! Education, profession—why, Maurice, your profession has been followed by a king!— person, manners, temper, principles. Oh, what could Mr. Barham ask better; and you have no low connections—nothing to shock aristocratic prejudices; the son of a gentleman, and of an old, good family! Why should Dora fear to own you—to acknowledge her love? A love returned, confessed as yours is, and Mr. Barham never prevented your being together. Dora has been allowed to come here as she pleased. Surely she must be mistaken in her judgment on this occasion."

"I wish you could persuade her so."

"I will try when I can see her," said Hilary.

"But it must be before I go, dear," returned Maurice, eagerly. "If I am ordered off, and have to leave this unexplained, it would be base and cowardly then to throw all the burden and pain on her alone. I could not do that!"

"I think even then, at any rate, it would be right to avow it all, and let the consequences follow as they might. Every week's delay must add to the evil."

"If you could but see her, Hilary! but she will not come here, I know. Where could you meet her? Could you go to the Abbey?"

"How, dear Maurice? I have no means," said Hilary.

"Perhaps Mrs. Paine could take you over, or Miss Fielding. If you could contrive it! do think about some way of meeting!"

Eager to fulfill her brother's wishes, Hilary turned her mind entirely to the means of their accomplishment; and in her self-devotion to his interest, contrived to forget, in a great degree, her own feelings of suspense and anxiety. She would not indulge in contemplation, she would not listen to the whispers of hope, or to the cold insinuations of fear and doubt. She put away all retrospective glances, and stilled her mind with a calm, but fixed resolution, to wait in patience, and trust for the future, whatever its result might be.

She sent a note to Mrs. Paine to ask if she could drive her over to the Abbey the next day, saying, that having heard from Isabel that Dora was suffering, and likely soon to leave home, she was very desirous of seeing her. Maurice carried the note, eager to do something, and finding action less painful than quiet and thought. But the owners of Primrose Bank were out when he arrived there; and after wandering for some time in the vicinity, in hopes of meeting them, Maurice was obliged to return home without a reply.

It was about twelve the next day, as the family at the Vicarage were sitting together, that the carriage from "the Ferns" drove up. Much to Miss Duncan's relief, she saw at a glance that there were only the two ladies in it; and in a few minutes Mrs. Fielding and her daughter were in the parlor, the one as full of kindness, and the other of energy and gayety, as usual. They were delighted to find Hilary so much improved. As well as ever they said, no trace of languor or paleness visible. This was true, for the sight of them excited her, and they could not tell that the pink hue in her cheeks, and her apparent self-possession and activity, were the result of high-wrought, but concealed, feelings of suffering anxiety. Victoria's object was to take her out for a drive, Mrs. Fielding to remain with Mr. Duncan while his eldest daughter was away.

No answer had come from Mrs. Paine; Hilary saw Maurice look at her with imploring eyes; and although hardly liking to ask the favor of Victoria, she was strongly tempted to beg at once to be driven over to the Abbey. It was, however, by no means improbable that any minute might bring the answer from Mrs. Paine, and until that arrived, she could decide nothing. She could only explain to Victoria how far she was pre-engaged; and while doing so, Mr. Paine himself walked in, bringing an excuse from his wife. She was not well, and the poney-carriage had met with an accident; but if to-morrow would do, it should be at her service. To-morrow, Hilary thought, might be too late: Maurice was in an agony of impatience, Victoria was urgent and persuasive, and she herself, afraid of yielding to selfish feelings, and sacrificing her brother's happiness to her own scruples, gave way at length to the united influence of her companions, and prepared to accompany Miss Fielding.

Certain thoughts as to what Captain Hepburn would think, if he knew she was driving in Mr. Huyton's carriage, were put away as intrusive and selfish; there was no occasion to connect the latter at all with the act, the obligation was conferred by Victoria alone, and need concern no one else; and as she hoped to be of use to Maurice, there was every excuse for taking her present step.

CHAPTER XIII.

"She moves slow; her voice alone
Has yet an infantine and silver tone.
But even that comes languidly: in truth,
She seems one dying in the mask of youth."

Iseult of Brittany.

Hardly had the carriage driven from the door, when Hilary had reason to repent of having yielded.

"I shall go home first, if it is the same to you," said her companion, calmly; "on several accounts; one of which is, that you must not go without your dinner, and we shall be sure to find luncheon ready when we get there."

Hilary remonstrated, and assured her she should have no appetite; and she did not wish her to go out of the way on that account. But Victoria was one of those gayly-selfish and cheerfully-obstinate individuals, who are never really turned out of their way, or persuaded out of their opinion. She listened with a smile to Hilary's remonstrances, and agreed to her remarks, but never in the smallest point altered her mind or her conduct. To "the Ferns" she meant to go, and accordingly to "the Ferns" they went; avowedly for Hilary's comfort, actually for Miss Fielding's pleasure. On first reaching it the master was invisible, and Hilary, for a few minutes, entertained the hope that, though thus forced against her will into his house, she should escape meeting him. But this hope soon proved vain, for presently he entered; and not only did his tone and manner in addressing her speak of the feelings she did not wish to encourage, but they evinced so entire an absence of surprise at her visit, as made her unavoidably suspect that the whole had been a scheme between the cousins to entrap her into coming there with or without her will. This was confirmed by the fact of his bringing in with him a basket of most beautiful flowers, which he began arranging as he sat by her, observing, as he did so, that he wished to replace the bouquet she had lost on the day of her accident.

What a world of thoughts rushed through her memory at these words, and dyed her cheek with hot crimson blushes. How Charles interpreted her confusion she did not know; her ideas flew off to another person; there was another voice ringing in her ears—a voice which petitioned, in never-forgotten whispers, for one violet; and then she wondered, as she had often done before, not only what had become of those flowers themselves, but of the feelings they seemed to express, and the hopes they had awakened; had that bunch of violets sunk, where she had so narrowly escaped, and were they to be the type, the emblem of the fate which would attend her own shy affections, and shrinking, undeveloped expectations?

"You do not know," continued Charles, after watching her downcast eyelids and flitting color for some minutes, "that I saw the remains of that bunch of flowers, scattered, soiled, withered, floating on the water two days afterward. I tried to secure the peristeria, which I should have valued for the associations connected with it. It was near the bank, and I could see one snowy dove, sitting on her little nest, unsoiled and peaceful. I tried to grasp it; but I failed, and not only plunged my own feet into a treacherous hole, from which I had some difficulty in escaping, but pushed the flower itself under water, and it did not rise again!"

"It was hardly worth the risk," said Hilary; "you, who have so many fair flowers in your own houses, should have allowed those which accident had scattered on the water to float on, until they became the prize of a less wealthy individual."

"Had they been mine still, or rather, had they never had another owner, been pressed by another hand, I might have done so, Miss Duncan," was his significant answer.

"I still think it was not worth the risk," replied Hilary, quietly; "but we are told that we may learn lessons from every thing, and certainly life is full of emblems, if we do but read them right."

"I know how fanciful you are, Miss Duncan," replied he, in a lighter tone; "what moral would you deduce from this incident for my benefit?"

She hesitated a little; seeing which, he added more gravely, "Nay, do tell me; since I lost the flower I coveted, let me profit by the loss in some way; do not let that pretty dove-blossom have sunk uselessly beneath the waters; tell me of what it is the emblem!"

"No, excuse me," replied Hilary, seriously, "I can not undertake to give lessons in morality to you." And then, turning away decidedly, she raised her voice to address Victoria, who was just reading a note, which she had found waiting for her on her return.

Perhaps Miss Fielding did not think the countenances of the other two indicated that their conversation could be prolonged with benefit to themselves; for she came forward almost immediately, and suggesting that luncheon must be ready, led the way to the dining-room.

The carriage was ordered round, as soon as the meal was concluded, and Hilary, who had been on a mental rack, while obliged to undergo the pointed civilities, and the overpowering assiduities of both cousins, began to breathe more freely, in the hope of escaping to a more genial atmosphere, and putting a continually increasing space between the soft voice and half-reproachful dark eyes which now followed her so tenderly.

It had required all her self-command, and her regard to duty rather than impulse, to avoid showing in her manner how exceedingly she had been annoyed by what had passed, or how entirely she was at "the Ferns" against her will. Her sense of what was due to herself, as well as her hosts, had compelled her to be courteous, and the recollection of what she owed to Charles Huyton, increased her resolution to endure. Victoria knew she had come unwillingly; she could assure Mr. Huyton of the fact; and now she hoped the penance would soon be over, and the painful struggle between gratitude and dislike, or something very near it, might be put away at least for a time.

Greatly, therefore, was her annoyance increased, when she heard Charles say, that having some papers to take to Mr. Barham, he should accompany them, and would order his horse at the same time.

"Do so, by all means," remarked Victoria, "if you prefer riding; but otherwise, you know, you could just as well come with us in the carriage. However, perhaps you like being independent."

"What does Miss Duncan say?" said Charles, looking at her.

"Miss Duncan can have no choice," replied Hilary, trying to look indifferent; "since both carriage and horses belong to Mr. Huyton, no one can dictate to him which he shall use."

"But perhaps you have secrets to discuss with Victoria," said he, playfully, "and then I should be sadly in the way. Is not that the case?"

"No, I have no secrets with her!"

"Then, since the right of choice is mine, and you will say nothing to direct me, I choose your company, ladies; and if I choose wrong, the consequences be on you, who refused me your advice and counsel."

Hilary wished she had only had the courage to say that he had better ride!

The drive to the Abbey would have been pleasant after all, could she have forgotten both the past and the future. Mr. Huyton was not disagreeable; on the contrary, he was once more in one of those moods which made her doubt whether her former fears had not been the mere illusions of vanity. Kind and just quietly attentive to her, to Victoria he devoted all his gallantry, and pretty nearly all his conversation. They were both in good spirits, and without being particularly clever or witty, they were exceedingly amusing and pleasant. But the painful uncertainty which these abrupt variations of manner occasioned, was not to be allayed by an hour's calm, or by a temporary remission of his attentions. She was uneasy and anxious still, doubting the wisdom of her own decision in accepting Victoria's invitations, and only succeeding in putting away harassing and useless perplexities, that they might give place to other feelings at least as painful. Dora and Maurice! their difficulties and distresses were too real and too new not to deserve undivided attention, and she felt as if she were even unkindly selfish, as she reverted to them, in having allowed thoughts for herself to occupy her mind.

Fast as the four horses swept along, they hardly went quick enough for her impatience at last, when she remembered the grief and anxiety from which her brother was suffering at home. She tried to still herself, and be patient and quiet, knowing well that eagerness and impetuosity were not the qualities wanted on this occasion to carry her point. But, with all her efforts, every nerve was thrilling, and every pulse seemed beating through her frame, as they drove up to the Abbey; and engrossed in her own thoughts now, far away from recollections of herself, she was unconscious of her abstracted and very pensive air, and quite unaware of the glances cast on her, and the meaning looks interchanged by her companions.

Charles and Victoria were very far indeed, from guessing what was the subject which occupied her mind; as far as Hilary herself was from supposing that they attributed her nervous and uneasy expression to pique at his manner, or jealousy of Miss Fielding.

He left them in the hall, to go to Mr. Barham's library, while the young ladies were shown into Isabel's morning-room, where she and Lady Margaret were sitting together. Miss Barham's reception was a very warm one; she was delighted to find Hilary was equal to the exertion, and for some minutes her delight prevented her taking any real notice of how unwell her friend appeared. The paleness of her cheeks, and anxiety of her manner, did at last strike Isabel; and Hilary, who had been nervously waiting for a pause, in which she might find time to inquire for Dora, was prevented from doing it at all by an exclamation—

"After all, you look very tired and exhausted, Hilary, dear; I shall forbid you mixing in conversation, and insist on quiet and repose for you. Suppose you were to go to Dora's room. It would not excite you too much, and you do not look as if you would overwhelm her."

Hilary gladly assented, and after telling Victoria to send for her when she was ready to go, she followed Isabel from the saloon. In her pleasant dressing-room, with windows open and jalousies closed, making a cool and grateful twilight, Dora was stretched listlessly on a sofa; her beautiful long hair all tumbled about her pretty face, and her whole appearance, and even her attitude, betokening a restless and miserable impatience. Isabel had put Hilary in at the door without speaking, and then herself retreated; and, on hearing a noise, poor Dora did not raise her head, but only asked who was there. Her friend did not answer, advancing gently to the sofa, but uncertain how to announce herself. Dora then removed the hand which covered her weary eyes, and raised her head. With one little shriek of satisfaction, up she sprang, and Hilary was clasped in her arms, with warm kisses rained on her cheeks and lips, and tender embraces, and choking sobs, and smiling, tearful words of endearment and welcome, and blushes which ran up quick and hot to her temples, and even dyed her finger tips with pink, so deep they were.

Poor Dora! hers was the sorrow and the emotion of a child.

They sat down together on the sofa; Dora with her arm round Hilary's waist, and nestling in close to her, as if there she might find peace, or at least support.

"How are you all at home, Hilary? and who is there?" were her first coherent words, and down went her looks upon the carpet, and up came, redder than ever, the blushes to her cheeks.

"Well—all well—and Maurice has not left us yet!"

There was a little start, and the fingers which held Hilary's hand were pressed more closely than before; there was a fluttered pause, and then the trembling girl said—

"Do you know, Hilary?—has he told you?"—and the eyes asked even more eloquently than the words.

"Yes, Dora, he has. I came here on that account."

Dora threw herself upon her companion's neck. "Good, dear, sweet Hilary! what do you think of me? are you shocked? oh, don't say I am wicked to love him. Is it, can it be wrong? I could not help it Hilary; indeed, I could not!"

"Do you think *I* could blame you for loving my brother?" said Hilary, tenderly.

"Ah, dearest Hilary! how good you are. Then you do not think me wrong; oh, what a comfort. If *you* say I am right, then I feel sure indeed that I am."

Miss Duncan's eyes were cast down, and there came a graver expression over her face, which Dora immediately remarked.

"What is it, Hilary?" eagerly inquired she; "what is wrong? Why do you look so? If you do not blame me for loving Maurice, what do you mean?"

"It is not for loving Maurice," replied Hilary, hesitating, and pressing Dora's fingers closer. Their eyes met, and then bursting into a passion of tears, Dora once more hid her face; but this time it was with her hands, away from her friend, and she faltered out, between her passionate sobs, "I know—I know—but oh, Hilary! I dare not—*dare* not! You do not know what I should have to bear. I knew, I thought you would say this—but I can not—can not."

Hilary again kissed and soothed her, and spoke soft words of sisterly tenderness, and did not try to argue or persuade, until Dora's own vehemence exhausted itself, and she became calm. Then Hilary spoke of openness and truth, firmness and endurance, and tried to show her that there was no hope but in candor; and to convince her that her cowardice was wearing out her own feelings, and throwing away the happiness of one she said she loved so well. And her father, too, how could she reconcile her conduct with her duty to him? and how could he bear it, when he learned that his young daughter had given away her affections to one whom she dared not own—had done what she was ashamed to acknowledge—had listened willingly to words she blushed that she should hear? could this be right?

Dora threw herself upon the sofa, burying her face in the cushions, and lay there in powerless grief, her very attitude and air telling of the prostration of her mind, of her entire helplessness and irresolution.

"Oh, if I could—if I dared—if I were you—had your strength, Hilary—but you do not know what coldness and unkindness are—you never felt my father's frown. Any thing but that I could bear. I could die for Maurice—I shall die for him, I know. I do not wish to live without him; but I dare not tell myself—I dare not own it all."

"Then you are quite resolved, Dora, to conquer your affection—to give him up entirely? You can never see him again; and, I may tell him you have determined on this course—that you sincerely renounce his love, and bid him forget you if he can."

"No, no! cruel Hilary, don't talk so! in all my grief, to know he loves me, is my only comfort: give it up indeed! but he will not—he can not—he never can forget me."

"Nay, Dora, for both your sakes he must, and he will, too. Maurice will do his duty at any hazard, and the love he may not own, he will not nourish. He would endure any thing for you, and your good; and even that, the greatest suffering of all, the crushing of all hope, the renunciation of all claim on you, the extinction of his affection, he will bravely battle for, because he knows that all this is better for you; more truly, lastingly good for you, than the growth of a secret, a clandestine, and, therefore, a disgraceful attachment. He will fight, and he will conquer, too; though the victory may be won only by the sacrifice of youth's brightest, dearest hopes."

Dora's sobs were her only answer.

"He loves you better than you love him, Dora," continued Hilary. "He would do and suffer any thing rather than renounce you, except what he knows to be wrong."

"Then he will never speak of giving me up," said Dora, with decision.

"He will never seek to see you again, until your father knows all," said Hilary, firmly. "Never—he said so; and why, dear Dora, why not speak?" added she again, in tones of most winning tenderness; "you can have no other hope."

"Then I can have none! for my father's anger I will not brave. Maurice I shall love to my dying day; but if he will leave me, and will never see me more, be it so; if he would only wait—only trust for the future, something might arise, some sudden turn or change; but if he is impatient, let him go."

It was no use arguing with Dora; she felt she was wrong, but she would not dare to do right; nor was it till with tearful eyes and trembling lips, that Hilary attempted to say farewell, that her temporary indignation died away, or she softened into regret. But when she saw her friend's deep, unspoken emotion, pride again was banished by tenderness, and springing up, she clasped her arms round Hilary's waist, and faltered out a loving, sad adieu.

"Yes, tell Maurice I am entirely unworthy of him—tell him to forget me—but for me, I will lie down and think of him forever. My heart is crushed, broken, Hilary; and to part from you, the last tie to him—it is agony. I am going away very soon. They think change will do me good: well, well, I do not care. Leave me now, Hilary."

And the little weeping, petulant beauty threw herself once more upon her couch. Hilary lingered still, and then Dora, looking up, said—

"You blame me, I know, but do you think I shall be happier than he? Will wealth, or jewels, or the empty pleasures heaped on me, or the whispered nonsense of those who seek my fortune, or the idle life I lead, will all those make my heart lighter? Compare our fates, and tell me which is most to be pitied. I know, though mine may be bright to look at, it will be all sorrow and misery within."

"But Dora, dearest Dora, why must this be? All this misery might be spared if you would but speak, or let Maurice speak. There need be no hidden grief then, and even if your father disapproved (which he might not), at least you would have done right, and then trustful patience, and resignation, and brighter hopes might come again. And peace can only be won by walking straight on to it. Believe me, Dora, you can have none unless you take this course."

"Go, go," cried Dora, impatiently; and Hilary, hoping that her absence might do what her presence had failed to effect, prepared to withdraw. She met Miss Barham's French maid at the door, who informed her that Mademoiselle Fielding desired her not to hurry, but she was quite ready to go; whereupon Miss Duncan immediately descended.

Charles Huyton and Mr. Barham were in the room, but she soon discovered that the former was engaged to stay and dine at the Abbey, and Victoria, evidently weary of her visit, was pleasantly bent on hurrying away. Hilary left Mr. Huyton apparently in earnest conversation with Isabel, though, to own the truth, the conversation was all supplied by the young lady; but this, Miss Duncan did not remain to notice; and it was a satisfaction that they were spared his company on their return to Hurstdene. Victoria announcing that her friend was too tired to talk, desired her, laughingly, to be silent, on pain of her high displeasure; and herself taking up a book, their return home was accomplished with scarcely another sentence uttered by either.

Weary and dis-spirited Hilary was in the extreme; she had over-tasked her body, over-excited her mind, and had failed of securing the object which alone had tempted her to set aside her own feelings, and do what she so very much disliked. Now that disappointment was added to weakness and fatigue, she was inclined to take a most unfavorable view of her own conduct and to doubt whether even success would have justified her in her own eyes, in the step she had taken. At all events, she resolved that nothing but absolute necessity should induce her in future to incur any obligation to either of the cousins; and whatever their wishes or motives might be, she determined that her own rule must, for the future, be strict and invariable.

She would neither be betrayed nor tricked into giving the appearance of encouragement to one she never could love.

A shake of the head, and a little glance of concern, was her first intimation to Maurice of her want of success; nor was there time or opportunity for more definite explanation, until late in the evening. When the rest of the family had retired, Maurice drew a large chair toward the moon-lit window, and placing Hilary there, he sat down beside her, and silently kissed her cheek. She laid her head upon his shoulder, and the pent up feelings which had been struggling all the evening for expression, found a channel in a shower of tears.

Silently the sister wept, and silently the brother smoothed her hair, and kissed her forehead, and clasped her closer and closer to him. She was the first to speak.

"Oh! Maurice, I could do nothing, I am so sorry."

"Did you see her?" was his first question.

She repeated, as far as she could, the particulars of her visit while he, drawing a little away from her, leaned his head on his hand, and so concealed his face in the deep shadow which the fingers made in the moonbeams. She could not read the expression of pain, of disappointment in his eyes; he did not mean she should—she had suffered enough for him without that; but she *knew* what he was feeling, by the innate sympathy which love and experience give, and she grieved afresh. He was silent for a while, when she ceased speaking, and they sat together that calm summer night, as still and grave as two carved figures, except when the soft night breeze, blowing through the open window, rustled in her dress, or lifted the long brown curl from her neck.

"Oh, Hilary! why did I ever know her?" was at last his exclamation. "Only to make her unhappy! dear, darling Dora!"

"And what will be the end?" whispered Hilary; "what will you do?"

"Hope! hope! hope! love on and love ever, while she remains single. We may not meet, but who knows what patience, perseverance, time, love, constancy, fortune may do! who can foresee what may happen? No, I will never despair, while there is room to hope!"

"Dear Maurice!" was at once her most eloquent and consolatory interjection.

"And, Hilary, if I sacrifice love to duty, if I deny myself now every opportunity of intercourse, every gratification of my affection until I may ask it fairly, honorably, justly, surely I may hope for brighter and better times. Only if Dora did not suffer!"

He fell into a reverie, which he ended by abruptly exclaiming,

"You do not love Charles Huyton, Hilary?"

"No, and never shall. Would you wish it, Maurice?"

"I don't know; no, I think not, I would rather—"

"What?" exclaimed she, looking eagerly at him.

"Never mind!"

"What makes you talk of it, Maurice?" said she, after a moment's reflection.

"He told me himself, the day of your accident; he spoke then of his love for you. I wondered I had never seen it before; but I had fancied him engaged to Miss Fielding. It is natural he should love, more than that you should not. Are you sure of that?"

"Perfectly so, and so is he. If he persists in loving me, it is at his own cost; it never will be returned. I have long wished him to give it up; and like you, once thought it was going away. Till Sunday, I believed him engaged to Victoria! Did he really tell you he had not changed?"

"Yes, and he was most emphatic in his expressions!" replied Maurice.

"I am sure Mr. Barham wishes him for a son-in-law; and Isabel would suit him so perfectly. I wish he would think so too," continued Hilary, speaking slowly and thoughtfully. "I wish he would; I should be so glad."

"And do you still mean never to marry, Hilary?" said her brother, turning and looking gravely in her eyes. "Do you keep unchanged?"

"Leave the future, Maurice," was her quiet answer. "I never mean to marry Mr. Huyton, nor will I leave my father for any man now living."

The brother and sister parted for the night, after lingering long; for Hilary, tired as she was, could scarcely bear to shorten the few hours which they might yet have to spend together.

And the morrow's post brought the dreaded, the expected change; the summons to duty, which, for his sake, Hilary welcomed with a smile, a cheerful tone, an energetic kindness. But when the parting was over, all her strength gave way, physical weakness asserted its supremacy, and she was forced to allow depression and pain to take their course. She could not raise her head from the sofa all that day, and when Charles Huyton called, she was too ill to see him. There was some comfort in that; it partly paid her for her nervous languor, for her aching head, and fevered frame; she was able to be invisible, without a fear of ingratitude.

The strong stimulus withdrawn, the occupation ended, the anxious suspense for Maurice terminated, her own thoughts would turn to her own affairs. It was a week, only a week, since the memorable Thursday, the day when she had last seen Captain Hepburn; how long it seemed; double that time, at least. She had to tell herself it was only a week, to suppress the rising impatience, to quell the incipient murmur. Duty with him must be first; public before private duty; patriotism before feeling; honor before love; his country before his friends. This she knew right well; and she ought not to feel herself neglected, or fear herself forgotten, merely because a week had passed without direct intercourse. No, not if vanity did not mislead her, not if she had understood him rightly, and read his character correctly. He did love her! that she believed, but there were other doubts more harassing than to doubt his love. Her present torment was to doubt what her duty should be.

Had she not resolved, promised, bound herself to sacrifice her whole time, care, and affection to her father and sisters? this had been her most solemn determination. How had she kept it? By yielding to the first impulse of affection; by allowing her mind, her fancy, and her feelings to be engrossed by another; by one who, a fortnight ago, was an entire stranger to her; by one who had never told her that he loved her; by one whose professional duties might make an engagement to him, even if he offered it, incompatible with her own domestic ties. What was she wishing to do? where were her resolutions, her promises, her intentions of self-devotion and self-forgetfulness? Forgotten at the very moment when they were put to the test. Thoughts such as these, self-torturing and reproachful thoughts, were not of a nature to still her throbbing pulses, or cool her aching brow; they were hardly more medicinal than the hot tears which the parting with her brother cost her.

Her sisters watched her with affectionate care, and forced her to take such bodily repose as her actual weakness required; playfully declaring, if she attempted to exert herself again, they would tell her father of her pale cheeks and heavy eyes; so she felt it her duty to lie still, although stillness of mind was for some time quite unattainable.

But quiet and repose brought strength of body, and with it came back more command of her spirit also. She saw her way, she understood her duty, and right well she knew that duty was truly the safest, smoothest path that she could tread. To put away thoughts of the past, to bend her attention to her domestic cares, to control her memory and curb her fancy, this she resolved, Heaven helping her, to do. Could she not? Yes; the events of the last ten days had not surely robbed her of the mastery of her mind. She could govern it still! What else had she been learning all her life? and should she now give up the attempt because the task was less easy than heretofore? should the charioteer drop the reins because the road was narrow and rough; or the pilot abandon the helm, just when the vessel came amid the shoals and breakers?

So argued Hilary; and if the expectation of a happy result, as men say it does, aids greatly in the performance of a difficult task, that, perhaps, was one source of the success which now attended her efforts.

Her strength slowly returned, her equanimity came with it, and although she was somewhat paler and more languid than formerly, although she still had struggles against depression, and fits of painful recollection, they were not apparent to her companions, who only saw that she was more easily tired than formerly, rather more silent, and a good deal less excited when Maurice's letters arrived.

It was a very quiet week which followed. The Barhams left the Abbey, the master of "the Ferns" was also absent. He had accompanied his aunt and cousin to London, from whence, Victoria told Sybil when she called to take leave, the ladies were going on to the sea-side, perhaps, or possibly to the north of England, and it was by no means unlikely that Charles would go with them.

Hilary did not see any of them again before they left; but when she was certain that event had taken place, she felt an unspeakable relief come over her, which made her troubles seem easier to bear.

She was able now to leave her room, and stroll about the garden, wander on the green, or rest on her favorite seat by the chancel-window, without fear of meeting any one whom she would rather avoid. The calm summer air under the shady trees always did her good; and an afternoon spent in solitary reflection, or in quiet, half-cheerful, half-grave chat with her father, was a mental tonic which never lost its power.

The liveliness of the family party depended on the younger ones; they were untamed by sorrow yet, and soon recovered parting from Maurice. To their view, life was like the beautiful vistas in their own wild forest, across which the sloping sunbeams played between the shady trees, turning all they touched to gold.

CHAPTER XIV.

"You 'never loved me!'—No, you never knew—
You with youth's dews yet glittering on your soul—
What 'tis to *love*. Slow, drop by drop, to pour
Our life's whole essence perfumed through and through,
With all the best we have, or can control,
For the libation! cast it down before
Your feet—then lift the goblet dry for evermore!"

Anonymous.

One afternoon, Mr. Duncan and two of his daughters had gone over to Primrose Bank, Hilary being left with only Nest as her companion. The child had been reading to her sister until she was tired, and then leaving her to reflection and silence on the green bank of the terrace, she strayed away to the garden-gate. She looked across the green, with no very particular expectation of seeing any object worth her attention, but with a vague childish curiosity, which was always prepared for a marvel or a pleasure. She saw some one approaching; a gentleman, a tall man; perhaps it was Mr. Huyton, perhaps Mr. Paine, or may be, thought she, it is Maurice: she was too young to consider probabilities, or understand the troublesome restraints of propriety and decorum; and too well known, and too much petted generally in the parish, to have any fear of a repulse, or dread of a rebuff. The gate was unlatched; out she ran, and skipped across the turf to meet the individual in question. After advancing a hundred yards, however, she saw that she was mistaken; Maurice it was not: no, nor Mr. Huyton—it was a fuller figure, a firmer step; she slackened her pace one minute, and shading her eyes with her hand, looked at him attentively. It was!—yes—it was one of whom her sister had spoken much! one to whom her father had told her she owed her life; one whose name had been joined with those of her own family in her prayers for blessings on his head. It was Captain Hepburn himself! She rushed on joyfully; and breathless with her race, eager, excited, with flashing eyes and crimson cheeks, she reached him, caught his outstretched hand in her little fat fingers, and covered it with grateful kisses.

"Dear Nest!" said he, raising the child in his arms, and looking at her glittering eyes, "how are you? how are your sisters—all?"

"Oh! Captain Hepburn, I am so glad to see you; now I can thank you," was her only reply: and she threw her arms round his neck and laid her cheek close to his.

"For what, dear child?" said he. His thoughts were of Hilary, and he hardly remembered that Nest had any thing to be grateful for.

"For picking me out of that horrid black water," said she, in a whisper. "I have so wanted to see you since; but you know you went away without saying good-by to me or Hilary."

"Do you remember that day, Nest?" said he, walking slowly on, with her in his arms.

"Oh, yes! so well; my slipping down, and the bubbling water, and the cold, and the choking feeling here in my throat and head, and such a pain, oh, dear! I dream sometimes now, at night, of the bank, and the gurgle of the waves, and wake with such a start. I did not like to wash my face for some days afterward. But is it not odd, Captain Hepburn?—I can remember nothing about you taking me out. I should not have known you did, if they had not told me so!"

"Who told you?"

"Papa and the others?"

"Hilary?"

"No," replied Nest, gravely; "they will not let me talk to her about it. Sybil told me not; and she never has spoken about it at all, since she has been ill."

"She is well now?" said he, inquiringly.

"Better, but not well. She can not walk much. She is in the garden."

"Will she see me, do you think?" said he, stopping at the porch, and setting Nest on one of the benches.

"I don't know," replied the little girl, gravely. "She has seen nobody but Mr. Paine, for days. She could not see Mr. Huyton, when he came last, though he sent me to ask her; and you know he pulled her out of the water, as you did me. She said she was too ill."

"But she is better now," said he, earnestly; "perhaps she will not mind me. Is your papa in?"

"No, only Hilary, and she is in the garden. I will go and ask her, if you like; or you will come, and she must see you then."

He hardly thought such a surprise desirable, and suggested that Nest should go on first. But Hilary, who had missed her sister, had risen to look for her, and met the child the moment after she turned the corner of the house; so that the gentleman had the opportunity of ascertaining that he might, so far as an abrupt introduction was concerned, almost as well have presented himself at first.

"Oh, Hilary! will you see Captain Hepburn?" was her exclamation.

"Nest, what do you mean?" he heard in a hurried, fluttered accent, and he was sure she had stopped short in her approach.

"Don't be pale, Hilary—don't be frightened," said Nest, coaxingly. "You have not seen him since that horrid day, I know; and when I saw him it made me remember all, and made me feel funny, I do not know how; but it goes off, and now I am only glad."

"But, Nest," he heard her saying, and there was a catching in her voice, which, to his anxious ear, told of a struggle with excitement and surprise, perhaps of deeper feeling too, "have you seen him?"

He could stand still no longer. Advancing from the porch, he met her on the lawn. She was stooping over her sister when he turned the corner of the house, but she raised her head at the sound of his feet, and stood still. She really could not take one step toward him, and had not her hand rested on little Nest's shoulder, perhaps she could hardly even have stood at all. There was a beating at her heart, a throbbing in every pulse, which seemed to suffocate her; there was a mist and confusion before her eyes which, for a moment, blended sky and earth, trees, shadows, and Captain Hepburn, in one wavering cloud of darkness. She had no thought or feeling, except a wish to stand upright, and a sensation that to speak was impossible. How they met she did not know. The warm clasp of his hand on hers was the first thing of which she was quite aware; he was by her, he was looking at her, but he was silent as herself.

The first words he spoke were not those of greeting, but as if they formed a part of a long preceding conversation, and in a tone that implied a whole world of tenderness and anxiety.

"Come in now and sit down; I grieve to see you are still so weak!"

He drew her hand within his arm and led her toward the porch, while she revived to the comforting conclusion that perhaps he thought her agitation was the effect alone of bodily, not mental weakness. She yielded to his guidance, wishing heartily that she could speak, but doubting her power too much to make the effort.

When he saw her safe in a large easy chair, he sat down by her, and said, in a quiet voice:

"I left Maurice quite well yesterday, very busy and enthusiastic about his ship."

"Happy, too," ejaculated Hilary, her thoughts instantly reverting to her brother's cares and troubles, and forgetting at once all her own embarrassments. "How are his spirits?"

"Variable, perhaps; at least I fancied so, when he was not actually employed; but better than at first."

She looked at him, anxious to try and ascertain what he knew or suspected of Maurice's feelings; but meeting his grave, dark eyes, she was recalled to a recollection of herself and him; she colored again, hesitated, and broke off a half-uttered word abruptly.

He waited to allow her time to recover, then finding she was silent, he said:—"Were you going to ask how long we should be fitting out? I think in three weeks more we shall report ourselves ready for sea!"

The easiest thing for her to do was to repeat his words, "Three weeks!"

"Come here, Nest," said the Captain, "Maurice sent you his love, and a great many kisses. Shall I give them to you?"

"Did Maurice give them to *you* first?" inquired Miss Nest, with a look half coquettish, half demure, and holding back from him.

Even Hilary smiled at the idea, but he went on.

"He wants you to send him some of those double violets which grow in your garden. You are to put them in a letter which is to go by post."

"I will go and gather some," screamed she, in an ecstasy of delight at the idea, and darted away.

He turned to his other companion.

"Do you remember?" said he, bending a look on her she could not meet.

"What?" in a low, trembling whisper, was all she could say.

"These, and what preceded them!" and he drew out and opened a paper, and showed her the contents.

She did remember; she saw the withered flowers, the white ribbon tied in a peculiar knot. They recalled all: the whispered words, the gay festival, the alarm, the accident, the agony of fear, the rescue, and the parting look. Embarrassment and personal feeling were merged in one sentiment, stronger still, gratitude! Clasping her hands, and raising to him a look of trustful earnest, tender gratitude, she exclaimed: "And I have never thanked you; let me now. Oh, Captain Hepburn! you who risked your life for Nest and me, what do we not owe you?" Her tearful eyes said more, far more than her words.

"The risk was nothing," said he, hastily; "do not speak of that; and the prize was all that I hold dearest on earth!" He had said it at last; she had almost intuitively known what was coming, and she did know what must follow now. She gave him one shy glance, and then hiding her face upon her clasped hands, she tried to conceal the blushes which burnt upon her cheeks.

"Yes, Hilary, it is the truth! the world does not hold another object so dear to me as you. Are you displeased with me for saying so? For you, for your happiness, your welfare, your peace, there is not the thing which I would not dare or suffer myself; and to win your love! if I only knew how to do that!" —

He stopped and made a gentle effort to take her hand; it was yielding unresistingly. He ventured to draw a little nearer, and said: "Will you not give me one look, one word, at least, to show me that you are not displeased with my presumption?"

She looked up at him; there was an earnest expression in his eyes, a deeply-anxious tone in his voice, a humility, a self-mistrust in his whole air and manner, which told that it was no set form of self-depreciating words without meaning, no assumption of suspense to conceal real assurance and hope; he was at that moment truly suffering from struggling doubts and fears; he was putting his happiness to the test, to win or lose it all.

The look she did give him was not discouraging: it was not likely to be, with her feelings. Fears as to the past, doubts for the future, present anxieties, weakness, uncertainty, were all swept away in the rush of gratified feelings and tender satisfaction. He loved her; he, the good, the wise, the brave, the courageous man; he who could deliberately and unflinchingly face danger, and confront death, not only in the tumult of excitement, amid the plaudits of the multitude, but also in the chamber of sickness, by the bed of infection, in the stillness of the hospital, where none but true courage or dull apathy could remain unmoved by fear; he was now waiting, in trembling suspense, for her decision, and deprecating her displeasure with a humility he would hardly have shown to a monarch.

She saw the immense power which she had over him, and she saw it with delight. Not the delight of gratified vanity, the satisfaction of the coquette who rejoices in giving pain; but the pleasure of a loving and grateful heart, exulting in the discovery that it has the means to confer happiness where it has felt deep obligation, and the gentle triumph of maiden modesty, at last assured that it has not bestowed affection unauthorized and unwished for.

She owed him her life, and her sister's also; and she had that in her power which he said would repay the benefit. He had placed his happiness with his heart at her disposal, and she could reward the generous gift by a single word.

With an air of the most betwitching modesty and confidence, she raised her head, she held out both her hands, and said, "Captain Hepburn, you have made me happy by the assurance of your love;" then fearing she had said too much, she would have drawn back, but she was not allowed; his thanks and raptures were too warm, too energetic to be interrupted.

"I could not leave England," he said, presently, "without explaining my mind, small as my hope of such an answer was; I trusted, that perhaps you would think of me, let me try to deserve you, let me endeavor to win your love. I feared that silence and absence might lead to misconstructions, might make you doubt my sincerity, blame and mistrust me. Believe me, I dared not flatter myself that you felt more than a friendly interest; what have I to tempt you, Hilary, that you should condescend to love me? It is only your own goodness, your sweetness, which inclines you to listen to me favorably. If you knew me better, I fear you would value me less."

She shook her head a little, and with downcast eyes, and lips just parting into a smile, she said, "I do not *love* all those whom I have known much longer."

He knew it well; for he knew he had a rival, and she might almost have seen that he did so, had she been able to look at him.

"Hilary, I know you will be true to me, while I am at sea; I feel that I may trust you once and forever; and when I return, you will become my wife."

"I will never leave my father, Captain Hepburn; I will form no engagement—plight no promise, which can in the least interfere with his comfort, or my attention to him. His claims first, and then yours may be considered. You think me right, do you not?" added she, anxiously, laying her hand on his arm, and looking up in his face, where she fancied she saw a shadow gather. On that question she felt all her happiness depended.

"Right, Hilary, in your estimation of your duty; only wrong in your estimation of me. Do you think I would tempt you away? or that I could look for happiness with you, if it was bought at the price of neglecting your first duty? I hoped you knew me better."

Her answer was to lay her head upon his shoulder, and whisper gently, "Had I thought so, you would not be what you are to me, Captain Hepburn.

I trust you entirely; and promise, one day, to be yours. When, we can not tell."

"And hear me, dearest, renew the vow I once made, never to ask you to give me your hand, unless our marriage can be compatible with your father's comfort. I will wait—I will be patient—I will consider only your happiness and your peace. Since you have condescended to promise me your faith, I feel that no sacrifice on my part can be too great to repay you. It is so good of you to love me. I have no better home, no fortune, no worldly station, or importance to offer you. I have so little to tempt you. Ardent, devoted love, and a share in an unblemished name, that is nearly all; and if you condescend to accept this, shall I not agree to your terms, and consult your pleasure? Indeed, it seems to me such a wonder that you should love me, that I feel tempted to ask again, are you sure you do? What have I done to deserve such happiness?"

"Done! if I were not afraid of spoiling you by praise," replied Hilary, smiling, then stopping; she added, after a minute's pause, and in a tone of emotion, "done! who saved me, by saving Nest? who dared what others hesitated to do? do I not know you brave, and prompt, and energetic?—no, do not interrupt me, many *might* have done as much, perhaps; but who saved Maurice? whose watchful care preserved my brother? who sat by him when others feared infection, or shrank from the terrors of delirium? You may have known me only for a fortnight, I have known and valued you, Captain Hepburn, for many, many weeks—for months, indeed."

"It shall ever be my humble prayer, it shall be my most earnest endeavor, Hilary, not to disappoint your trusting love; and Heaven helping me, I hope to repay it in kindness, in affection, in guarding you from evil all your life long." He spoke very gravely; he was much moved by her warmth. "Words are too poor to paint my gratitude to you for the honor you do me. And so they are to describe my implicit trust in your truth, your constancy, your prudence, and your affection. That I have to ask you to wait, that I am forced to leave you to the anxiety and trouble which I fear our separation may cause you, gives me great pain and grief for your sake; I would gladly spare you every shadow of care, I would gladly devote my life to you from this time. I grieve, but I trust you entirely. Will you believe as fully in my constancy as I do in yours, sweetest Hilary?"

"Yes."

That single word satisfied him completely.

When Nest came back from the garden, and the clergyman and his daughter from Primrose Bank, they interrupted a very happy conversation;

one full of all the sweetness which confidence and affection, hope and gratitude, can inspire.

It may be easily believed that after this explanation Hilary recovered both strength and spirits with a rapidity which surprised and delighted her sisters and friends: it may be readily imagined, that young ladies of Sybil's and Gwyneth's ages entertained their own theories, and formed their own opinions, when they found Captain Hepburn once more at the Vicarage; opinions and guesses which proved to have been surprisingly near the truth, when we consider their age and education. Mr. Huyton's acquaintance had existed so long, and his friendship had been so diffused in the family, that they had never thought of him as a suitor to their sister; but, from the first, they had settled between themselves, that Captain Hepburn must fall in love with her. There was every thing to recommend such an arrangement in their eyes. He was grave and quiet, the nearest approach they could hope for to a mysterious and suspicious character; while, on the contrary, Charles was so lively and talkative, that they could imagine neither concealment nor reserve in his case. Then, too, their favorite hero was comparatively poor, and had a profession which would be attended by possible danger as well as renown, would certainly occasion long absences, and might give rise to romantic incidents, doubts, distresses, and heroic difficulties. All this was a charming contrast with Charles Huyton's fortune and station in life; who besides, as they thought, not caring for Hilary, could only, had he wished to marry her, have offered her a matter-of-fact, readymade, and every-day sort of home; it would have been an engagement, presenting no difficulties except that of getting her wedding-clothes properly made, and offering no romance, except their first meeting, now nearly forgotten.

Not that the girls wished their sister any harm, or had the slightest dislike to seeing her happy; but at their age the quiet monotony of a prosperous life seems dull in prospect, and they had no idea that misery and misfortune, anxiety, suspense, and sorrow were not the most pleasant accompaniments of life, when occasioned by sufficiently romantic and poetic causes. They did not know how reality strips suffering of romance, not only to the individual who grieves, but to the spectators who witness it: and that mourners who go about the daily affairs of life, hiding a broken heart under an outward calmness, may be extremely interesting to read of, but hardly excite so much actual sympathy and compassion, as one who has to walk through the world with a wooden leg.

But all this these two girls had yet to learn; and in the mean time they were greatly rejoiced when they understood how rightly they had guessed, and learned that the evident and marked devotion with which Captain Hepburn had listened to Hilary, watched her footsteps, conversed with her, and finally saved her life (for they always gave him the whole credit of that adventure, and were, perhaps, for his sake, a little unjust to Charles), when they learned that this was finally to be rewarded with her love and faith. In short, the engagement gave them perfect satisfaction.

Mr. Duncan was very well pleased; yet he certainly would have preferred the richer *parti*: he liked Charles, perhaps, a little better than he did the other; and there could be no doubt as to which, in common language, was the best match. If Hilary was happy, there was nothing more to be required; but he would certainly have wished either that Captain Hepburn had been in Charles Huyton's place as regarded position, or that Charles Huyton had been the accepted suitor.

But if Hilary was happy, that was enough. And she was happy, exquisitely happy; for the five days that her lover was able to remain, she was as joyful and blithe as a bird. She recovered her health, of course; she went about her daily tasks singing and smiling, making every body near her partakers in her gayety. She felt she had one to trust to now, on whom she should have a claim; she looked forward with pleasure, and saw the future very bright. In the happy hours they spent together, she found one to whom she could express her past difficulties, her bygone sorrows and trials, one whose firmness strengthened, and whose tenderness comforted her. Oh! what delightful seasons of confidence these were; dearly prized at the time—more dearly still in memory.

Maurice had told his friend his troubles and sorrows; so Hilary could discuss his prospects with her lover; and though perhaps a little shocked at the depreciating view he took of Dora's conduct, the earnestness with which he hoped that Maurice would recover from his attachment, and the certainty with which he predicted that the lady would probably forsake him, she would not have been a true woman had she not speedily adopted his opinions, and become a convert to his views even before she had quite done combatting them. One subject there was on which they did not touch; one topic on which Hilary, supposing him to be ignorant, herself preserved silence, and on which he, aware of her reserve, respected her feelings of delicacy too much to intrude.

The knowledge that Charles Huyton had been perseveringly repulsed, that wealth and station, abilities, personal charms, flattery and importunity, had failed to gain the heart which was now his own, was very sweet. If there is the man in the world whose pleasure in his own success would not be enhanced by such considerations, let him triumph in his conscious stoicism. I do not believe that there is; some might plume themselves on their own superior fascinations, some might rejoice in the lady's disinterested love;

some might value themselves—some her the more for such knowledge, but satisfaction of one kind or other, I imagine, every one would feel. For the present, however, Captain Hepburn concealed this source of satisfaction with as much scrupulous care as Hilary herself; and, but for an occurrence which even on this topic broke down their reserve, they would, probably, have parted when his leave of absence called him away, without any allusion to the matter.

Captain Hepburn had letters of business to write; and Hilary, taking advantage of the opportunity, set off to pay some visits in the village. The night had been stormy, but the morning was fair and bright, and Hilary, walking briskly, was soon at a cottage about half a mile on the road toward "the Ferns," whose inmates it was convenient for her to visit alone. The food, the clothes, and the advice all given, she was just issuing from the garden gate when she was addressed by Charles, who, throwing himself from his horse, advanced quickly to greet her. She was surprised, for she had believed him still absent from the country; and a mixture of other feelings, which his sight recalled, gave her an air of emotion, sensibility, and bashfulness, which he readily interpreted in the way most flattering to himself. Had he known whom she had left writing letters at her little table at home, he would perhaps have been as anxious to avoid the interview as herself; but ignorant of what had passed since they last met, he very joyfully took his horse's reins upon his arm, and walked himself by her side. The usual form of questioning about friends and relations, recent occupations, his journey and his return, was gone through, and was followed by a silence of some duration. This was broken by Hilary, who, casting an anxious look at the clouds now gathering ominously overhead, observed, that she was afraid there was going to be a storm. She had hardly said the words when down came the rain in large drops, rapidly increasing in number every moment. There was a sawyer's pit at a short distance with a shed beside it, and as this seemed the only shelter within reach, and the rain appeared likely to be violent, they quickly agreed to take refuge there; hoping that the shower would be as brief as it was sudden. She was most anxious to get on home; perhaps Captain Hepburn would have done work, and would miss her; perhaps her father might want her. So she thought, as she stood for a minute or two at the entrance to the shed, looking wistfully up at the clouds, and watching those flitting gleams of brighter sky which occasionally seemed to promise a clearing up. Still the rain went on, and as drops began to penetrate through the slight roof where she stood, he said,

"Come further in, Miss Duncan; it will not clear the quicker for your watching; and here is a nice block of wood, which will form a seat for you, where it is quite dry."

The easiest thing to do was to comply; she sat down accordingly, and he placed himself beside her. Then a sudden conviction came over her that something was to follow; and with a sort of desperate hope of stopping him, of avoiding a renewal of what was so painful, she began to talk of other things, the season, the harvest, the people, any thing for a subject. He listened in silence; his eyes were fixed on the open doorway; he might have been counting the drops which fell from the eaves, so steadily did he gaze that way. Her ideas, unsupported by any help from him, necessarily came to an end; and when she paused, it was his turn to speak.

"Hilary, tell me, once more let me speak; has my changeless devotion no influence on you?"

She shook her head.

"None! yet of late you have seemed to encourage me; you have accepted—at least you have not repelled—my attentions; you have allowed me to distinguish you as my first object; you have permitted those advances from my family which were intended to show how they would welcome you as one of themselves; you have graced my *fête* with your presence; your name has already been whispered round the neighborhood as the object, as the recipient of my vows: has not all this given me a right to hope; does all this go for nothing, for unmeaning form with you?"

"I do not understand your language, Mr. Huyton," replied Hilary, in great suprise; "your tone and manner are alike new and unpleasant. May I ask you to drop this subject while we are compelled to remain together here!"

"You would ask in vain; my happiness, my welfare in life, every hope here and hereafter is bound up in the thoughts of you, in the wish to make you my wife!"

She tried to stop him as he spoke, but her gentle interruption was quite unheeded as he poured out his vehement declarations.

"Why have you refused to see me, shut yourself up, and banished me from your house? What makes you, one so tender, loving, gentle as you, what makes you so hard, so unpersuadable to me? What have I done that you will not love me? What is there in me, about me, belonging to me, that makes me disagreeable? And why this coquetry; at one time readily listening, calmly permitting, if not encouraging, my devotion, then denying me all interest, all concern; repulsing me entirely? Is this fair! just! right! Hilary! Do you think those who witnessed your peril, and your rescue, in my park, doubted the motives which nerved my arm and warmed my heart? Do you think their plaudits were valued for any thing besides the worth they might give me in your eyes? And, Hilary, is my reward to be ever the no! no! no! which dooms me to misery, despair, and heartless solitude?"

Mr. Huyton rose as he spoke, and stood before her in magnificent desperation. She looked at him amazed; he was strangely altered. He was no longer the humble suppliant; he seemed to think he had earned a right other, that she was his in equity.

"Mr. Huyton, you are unjust, and such language as this is strangely unpleasant to hear. I do not know what claim you have to speak so. I have never intentionally done any thing to give you hopes that I should change as you wish. Again, I must ask you to be silent, or I shall leave this shelter; I would rather encounter the storm without, than listen to such words."

"You do not know my claim? It is the claim of love, constant, unchanging love, the love of years. Not the feeble growth of a week's intercourse; the every-day admiration, which at one moment distinguishes its object, the next leaves it without a sigh or a struggle; it is the passionate glowing devotion which rises beyond every earthly consideration, which sets neither honor nor duty above it—which knows no honor, owns no duty except that of loving unchangeably and deeply. This is my claim, who can produce a better? who has striven harder, longer, more devotedly, to make this love apparent?"

"I will neither listen to, nor answer such language," replied she, decidedly; "let me pass."

"I will not," said he, placing himself in the door-way; "do you suppose I would allow you to go out in this storm, expose yourself to such risk? Sit still."

"Then," said Hilary, reseating herself, "as you are a man and a gentleman, be silent."

"You were not always so sternly resolute, Hilary!"

"Nor you so—" she stopped.

"So what? speak out, say what you mean at once," said he, advancing close to her.

"No, I shall not," replied she, more gently; "I am sure that you do not wish to give me pain, and that this unpleasant topic will be dropped henceforth."

"But do you not pity me?" ejaculated he, seating himself again by her side, and clasping her hand so firmly that she could not withdraw it.

"Yes."

"And nothing more, Hilary? esteem, regard, kindly feelings, are all these gone, or did you never entertain them toward me?"

"You did not ask for these, Mr. Huyton; you asked for love, which alone I could not give."

"Are you sure?" said he, gazing intently at her. "Are you certain that it is not pride of consistency, or ignorance of your own feelings which misleads you? Do you know what love is, Hilary?"

"I do," said she, in desperation, resolved, even at the risk of raising an indignant jealousy, which she instinctively dreaded, to end his painful importunity. "I know what love is, and that I do not feel it for you."

"Hilary! Hilary!" cried he, in the wildest excitement, and more firmly than ever grasping her hand; "do you mean!—what am I to understand by that avowal?"

"That I have no love to give you, Mr. Huyton—my hand and my heart are another's." Her blushes confirmed her words.

"And who has dared to step between me and my object?" said he, slowly, while his face grew dark with rising passion and jealousy. "Is it, can it be Captain Hepburn?—there is no other."

"It is," she tried to say, but the words hardly passed her lips; she was frightened by his look and tone.

"Has *he* dared!—what, when he was warned, when he knew my wishes, my intentions; ah, he did not know *me*! Did he think I would be balked of my object? Does he think it is safe to come between me and my aim? Hilary, dearly shall you rue the day that you give your hand to that beggarly sailor. Bitterly shall you repent the deed! While you are still Hilary Duncan, you are unspeakably dear to me, and for love's sake, while there is hope, I will be whatever you may wish; but once destroy that hope, once take from me all possibility of winning you, and I tell you, you will wish rather that a demon had crossed your path, than that you had thwarted me."

Indignant and offended, she raised her eyes to bid him leave her instantly, and they fell on the figure of Captain Hepburn himself, whose step on the wet turf had been inaudible, but who now stood in the door-way looking at them. Her start and exclamation made Charles release her hand and turn round too; and Hilary, profiting by her freedom, sprang toward her lover, and clasped his arm as if to claim his protection.

"Take me away," she whispered, in an agitated voice.

Silently and gravely, he threw round her a cloak which he carried, and carefully wrapping her in it, he drew her hand under his arm, and prepared to leave the shed.

She gave one glance at Charles; he was standing with his arms crossed, and a look of haughty indifference, which she believed to be affected. In another moment they had turned away, and were taking the path homeward; but before they had gone a hundred yards, they heard the sound of his horse's hoofs at a sharp gallop, dashing along the road to "the Ferns." The sounds died in the distance, and Hilary, relieved and overpowered at once, very nearly burst into tears.

The storm was passing away, the rain had not quite ceased, but the sunbeams were struggling through the clouds, and every tree and shrub was fringed with glittering drops of light, while the effect of the flitting shadows chasing each other over the distant landscape was beautiful to see.

"There is no hurry," said Captain Hepburn, gently checking the impetuous steps with which Hilary had at first proceeded. "Do not agitate yourself, we are quite safe. The storm is all but over now, and you may walk quietly. It is pleasant to be together here, Hilary."

A gentle pressure of the arm on which she leaned, was her only answer, she had not quite self-command enough to speak.

"I wish I had come a little sooner to look for you," added he; "had you been long there?"

"I don't know; it seemed long, it was so disagreeable," and her voice was checked by a sob. But recovering by an effort, she added immediately: "However, it is over now, and we need not refer to it."

He did not answer for a little while, but at last he said, very gently, but with a manner which seemed to indicate that his mind was made up on the point. "Hilary, I do not think that is right, either by me or yourself, in our relative situations. If I were to remain with you, to protect and watch over you, I would not ask your confidence on that point. I could act for myself and you too. But since I must leave you so soon, and in the neighborhood of that man, whose bad passions are all raised by your refusal of his addresses, at least let me know all. Let me understand exactly what has passed, that I may form some idea of what there is to dread. Indistinctness of outline always magnifies objects. Let us view the matter calmly and clearly."

"How much do you know?" said she, looking up at him. "I never told you that."

"You did not, dear, but Miss Fielding told me at 'the Ferns,' that her cousin had been in love with you for years, had been refused by you once, but that he still hoped to win your love; and that the *fête* which so nearly cost you your life, was devised and carried out as a compliment to yourself."

"Had I suspected that," said Hilary, emphatically, "do you think any persuasion would have induced me to go there? Oh, no!"

"I thought that at the time, dear Hilary; and but for the abrupt conclusion to your share in the amusements, I should have taken the opportunity that afternoon, there in the very midst of my rival's splendor and all the riches and temptations which he displayed to bribe or buy your love, to offer you my hand, and a share in my humble fortunes."

"What consummate vanity!" said Hilary, smiling up at him with eyes that told a very different tale from her words; "could not your triumph in forcing me to like you be complete without the glory of such a contrast?"

"Presumption I would plead guilty to; but if you knew the doubt and hesitation with which I contemplated the effort, you would not think it was the easy feeling of satisfied vanity, Hilary. To plunge after you into the lake was a trifle, compared to the plunge I meditated at the moment. But now I will not be baffled by smiles; tell me, if you love me, all that passed between Mr. Huyton and you just now."

With crimson cheeks, she repeated as well as she could the dialogue in the shed, until he stopped her by saying, "His last speech I heard! I never liked him or his cousin; there was a something of intrigue and manœuver in her which shocked me; and for *him* — perhaps I was unjust, however. But his unmanly violence to you now, is hard to forgive. Is that what he calls love? or can he suppose affection is won by threats? Dear Hilary! for your own sake, I am glad you did not love him."

"There never was any danger that I should," said she, calmly.

"Yes, there was great danger; young, simple-minded, and inexperienced as you are; too pure to suspect evil, too ignorant to know it, there was the greatest danger that this man, handsome, clever, rich, ardent, devoted, with every advantage which seclusion and leisure, time and place could supply, should have won your heart before you could rightly read his character. That your affections should have continued disengaged until I had gained them appears to me a wonder, and a thing to fill me with gratitude. Dearest Hilary! how can I be thankful enough?"

"You can not imagine," said Hilary, after a pause of gratified feeling, "how great a shock it has been to me to find that he has shown himself what he is; I never could have loved him, but I did esteem and like him. I thought well of him in many respects, and to find that he is so desperate, so self-willed, so violent, has really given me great pain. Oh, I hope he will leave the country now, that we shall never meet again!"

"It was ungoverned temper, Hilary, made him speak as he did; a disposition quite unaccustomed to be checked or thwarted. It will wear off. When he really sees that it is hopeless, I do not think he will continue to vex himself about it. The quick, fiery passions which explode so vehemently are not those which are the most lasting and effectual in their results. Do not vex yourself, dearest, about it. Time will smooth down his asperity, perhaps. At any rate, he can do you no harm, he can not alter my trust in you, nor, I should hope, shake your confidence in me."

Hilary's smile showed how entirely she agreed with her lover's opinion, which accordingly they continued to discuss, with great satisfaction, till they reached home.

CHAPTER XV.

"When I was young, my lover stole
One of my ringlets fair;
I wept, 'Ah no, those always part,
Who, having once changed heart for heart,
Change also locks of hair.'"

Anonymous.

The next thing that Hilary heard of Charles Huyton was, that he had quitted "the Ferns," having dismissed his establishment, shut up the house, and intimated an intention of not returning for many months. This information was obtained by Captain Hepburn, and was received with great satisfaction, not only by Hilary, but by the reporter himself. He was very glad, as he was forced to leave her in so unprotected a situation, to feel that so violent and determined a lover as Mr. Huyton threatened to be should have removed himself from her immediate vicinity.

His leave of absence, prolonged to the last possible moment, ended, of course, much too soon, and the parting was naturally painful; but Hilary's cheerful and affectionate disposition supported her. She was certain of his love, and that was happiness enough to supply resignation and hope. Of the misery of protracted suspense, the pain of an uncertain engagement, the long anguish of patience, she knew nothing. She felt unlimited trust in her lover's constancy, as well as his character, and a calm dependence upon that merciful Providence to whose care she committed her future prospects. She was thankful, deeply thankful that she had been saved from being captivated by the very engaging qualities of one whose principles she could not trust, and that another to whom she could look as a guardian, a director, and a guide, had been brought within the circle of her acquaintance. If there was happiness to be found in this world she believed it would be in his society; and beyond, far beyond this world, there was that sure and certain hope which could support through the most stormy scenes of life, by pointing onward to a bright and peaceful "forever" together. So she parted from Captain Hepburn with sorrow, yet with hope, and the tears which the former caused to overflow were checked by the whispers of the latter; and neither her grief nor her love made her a more careless daughter, or a less kind sister, nor occasioned any visible want of consideration for the feelings or wishes of others.

How often, in her leisure moments, the short, black curl which lay in a small gold locket, his parting gift, was contemplated or kissed, it is not necessary now to say; nor is there any means of ascertaining whether it received more attention than did the long shining, wavy lock with which she parted in exchange, and which accompanied a pretty water-colored likeness of herself, originally done by Mrs. Paine for Maurice, back to the *Pandanus*. One thing was certain, that Maurice was very good-natured and obliging, and allowed the picture which had been intended to ornament his cabin to hang in the Captain's instead, where it may be supposed to have served as a public avowal that the owner was indeed an engaged man.

Months rolled on, and brought no apparent change to the family at Hurtsdene Vicarage. Nothing more was heard of Charles Huyton, except that he was incidentally mentioned in Isabel Barham's letters to her cousin, Mrs. Paine, as much in their society in London; then as accompanying them on a trip to Paris; then as having taken a moor in Scotland near one of her father's estates: and of their expectations of seeing him during their autumnal residence in Argyleshire.

The younger girls lamented his desertion of "the Ferns" and the loss of his library; but to Hilary these months were days of peace and happiness compared with preceding excitement; and she tried hard to persuade her sisters that Mr. Paine had as many books as they could read, and more than they could remember.

One other slight diversion they had, namely, the reappearance of Mr. Farrington, who came down for part of the long vacation, and took lodgings in the forest. He was an old acquaintance and friend of Mrs. Paine's, and was a great deal with them at Primrose Bank, and consequently often in the society of the sisters at the Vicarage. Not quite so often, perhaps, as he could wish; for Hilary, grown wiser by experience, began to suspect that young men did not seek the society of girls entirely without an object, and became shy of encouraging a kind of intercourse, which, within her knowledge, had more often ended disastrously than otherwise. She could not help seeing that the young barrister admired Sybil exceedingly; but she knew, that though her sister was womanly in manners and appearance, she was childlike in disposition and character. Not quite sixteen, she was too young to think of matrimony; and while she continued indifferent to Mr. Farrington and quite careless about his attentions, Hilary did not wish him to become more demonstrative.

Mrs. Paine agreed with her, indeed this caution originated with that lady; and one day she took on herself to communicate to the gentleman the extreme youth of the object of his admiration. This brought on a confidential conversation between the lady and the gentleman, in which he informed her that he was quite willing to wait a year or two, but that he was bent on making Sybil Duncan his wife hereafter. Then, if his business continued to flourish as it had done lately, he should by that time have a fair income to offer her, so he implored Mrs. Paine in the mean while, to give him a good character to that discreet, matronly, elder sister, who now looked as suspiciously on his attempt to be agreeable as if she had to defend from desperate fortune-hunters an heiress of ten thousand a year.

Mrs. Paine laughed, and promised to speak pretty well of him; and when the vacation ended, Mr. Farrington was obliged to return to London, where, in spite of his love for Sybil, there seems no reason to think he was either miserable or morose.

So passed the autumn and early winter. Christmas brought the Barhams to the Abbey, and Hilary was thinking with much interest and much curiosity of Dora and her feelings, for it was some weeks since she had heard from her; when a servant from the Abbey brought over a note to ask Mr. Duncan and his eldest daughter to pay them a visit, with a promise of the carriage to fetch them one day, and to take them back the next.

Hilary felt doubtful about accepting the invitation, anxious as she was to see Dora; but a little postscript to Isabel's note, not at first discovered, compelled them to decide in favor of going; it was to the effect that Mr. Barham desired to see Mr. Duncan on business, which could not be discussed in a morning visit; so an answer was written, agreeing to the proposal. Her sisters all declared it was nonsense of Hilary being so unwilling to go; it would be very pleasant; the Abbey was, probably, full of pleasant people, besides Isabel and Dora, and Mr. and Mrs. Paine, who, it was known, had gone over on Monday, and were to stay till Saturday. What more could she want to be sure of an agreeable visit?

She could only repeat that she had preferred their society to any the Abbey could promise, and that home was pleasanter than any other place; at which her sisters only laughed, and said "Let her try."

To the Abbey they went, arriving there, by particular desire, in time for the two o'clock luncheon; and there they found assembled, besides Mr. Barham and his two daughters, only the Paines and another gentleman, a young clergyman, whose personal appearance immediately attracted Hilary's notice; he being the first individual of a peculiar class with whom she had as yet met. There was something odd in the arrangement of his hair, in the appearance of his neck-cloth, and in the shape of his coat-collar, which gave an idea of singularity rather than sanctity, and made her more inclined to wonder at than admire him.

She had not much time, however, to form conjectures relative to this gentleman, for the young ladies almost entirely engrossed her. Each, in her different way, appeared delighted to see her again, and really Isabel's more measured accents, and stately welcomes, were hardly less kind and cordial than the *mine caressante* and endearing words of Dora, who scarcely knew whether to laugh or cry at meeting, and could not express her affection and joy with sufficient emphasis to please herself.

The afternoon was fine, although it was mid-winter, and the ladies, having seen the four gentlemen adjourn to Mr. Barham's private sitting-room, determined to go out for a refreshing walk. The sun was just setting in a clear green and amber sky, the air was sharp and frosty, with scarcely a cloud visible over-head to dim the beautiful half-moon hanging in the eastern heaven; there was no wind to make it feel cold, and the ladies soon walked themselves into warmth and spirits, such as can only be known to those who are blessed with health and strength to enable them to enjoy active exercise in the free air.

"Now, Hilary," said Dora, as they turned their faces homeward, and slackened their walk into a comfortable strolling pace, "have you the least idea why papa sent for you?"

"Some kind of business with my father, I know," replied Miss Duncan, quietly; while Isabel exclaimed,

"Dora, how you talk! I wanted to see you, Hilary."

"So did I," replied Dora, "but not a bit would that have availed, had not papa had business; it is about that Mr. Ufford, you know!"

"Dora, how can you interfere! do, Fanny, tell all about it, for really Dora ought not," again exclaimed Isabel, a little impatiently.

"I did not mean to say any thing at present," replied Mrs. Paine; "but, as Dora has said so much, I will explain. Hilary, dear, we are going to leave you!"

"Leave us!" said Hilary, amazed; "dear Mrs. Paine, what do you mean?"

"The Rector of Copseley is dead, and you know my husband had the promise of the living."

"Oh! I remember; I am very sorry; that is, I am glad for you, but sorry for us, for my father, for all: it will be hard to part;" and the tears came into her eyes as she spoke.

"Do not trouble yourself to be glad," said Mrs. Paine, affectionately, "I shall be most truly sorry when the time comes to part; but it will not be yet; we shall not move till the spring, I believe."

"That is a comfort," said Hilary; "what has Mr. Ufford to do with it?"

"Nothing at present," said Isabel, quickly, as if to prevent Dora from answering. "That depends on your father, of course. But if Mr. Duncan could like him for a successor to Mr. Paine, we should be very glad!"

"Oh!" was Hilary's answer. On such a point she had little to say. She knew that Mr. Paine's opinion would have great influence with her father; and she thought his judgment might be trusted. If he approved of Mr. Ufford, all would be right; and this she should soon learn from his wife.

"Mr. Ufford is a man of very good family," said Isabel, presently. "He is the third son of Lord Dunsmore; and though his fortune is small for his rank, I think you would find him an acquisition at Hurstdene. He is very pleasant, and really a good clergyman."

Perhaps the thought how little either fortune or rank had to do with this latter recommendation which passed through Miss Duncan's mind, prevented her answering this rather complicated speech. She felt sure also that Mr. Barham must have some private motive for interesting himself in the curate of Hurstdene; so she resolved to wait before she gave any opinion relative to her own feelings on the subject. It was one which too nearly concerned their own domestic comfort to be lightly treated, had there been no higher motives, or more important objects connected with it.

The road to the Abbey led them up a thick avenue, where the leafless branches of the trees threw a most perplexing checker-work of darkness across the white moonbeams as they lay on the ground, or fell on the figures of the ladies. Suddenly they saw a gentleman approaching them. Isabel uttered a little exclamation, indicative of very pleased surprise, before her companions recognized the new comer; but the next moment Hilary saw with a mixture of uncomfortable feelings that it was Mr. Huyton himself. The dread of meeting him had been one motive for her unwillingness to go to the Abbey, and great had been her relief on learning, soon after her arrival, that he was not at all expected. By what unlucky accident he chanced to come at the very time when it was least desirable, she did not know; but she saw from the manners of Miss Barham, that though very welcome, he was yet quite an unlooked-for guest.

It was impossible in such a light, to mark any expression of features or changes of complexion, so Hilary's varying color was safe from notice. How they should meet she could not guess; but nothing was left to her decision.

Mr. Huyton advanced, took Isabel's proffered hand, made his excuses with grace, spoke easily to Dora and Mrs. Paine; and added, as he turned to her,

"And I have the pleasure, too, of seeing Miss Duncan. I hope you are quite well, and all your family."

If ever Hilary was surprised in her life, it was at the composure and calmness with which her hand was taken, and these words were said. She would gladly have avoided shaking hands, but that was impossible; he went through the ceremony with such perfect grace and self-possession, as prevented it being awkward even to her, but with an air of indifference which amazed her when she thought of the past. As they returned to the house along the moon-lighted terrace, she could catch indistinct glimpses of his face, while he conversed gayly and courteously with her companions; and there was neither look nor tone which could convey the impression that her presence was a matter of the smallest consequence to him. Could he have quite recovered from the infatuation of past years! had he learned to regulate his affections and govern his feelings, to acquiesce in her decisions and participate in her indifference? Might they associate on an easy footing, as friendly acquaintance, without awkwardness or reluctance? She would have gladly believed this to be the case; but she feared to trust too entirely to appearances, when she remembered that more than once before she had been misled by his assumed calmness, to believe in the extinction of feelings, which seemed to have been only the fiercer for suppression.

No, she could never be comfortable with him again; she dared not trust him, so long as he continued single. If he would but marry some other woman, what a blessing she would esteem it. As she walked along musing thus, she only heard the sound of his voice mingling with the tones of her companions; she did not understand a word they said; her memory was away in the sawyer's hut in the forest, and to her imagination, she was again listening to his threatening accents, or again clinging to that dear arm, which so tenderly supported her from the unpleasant scene. She was so engrossed in these thoughts, that when Mr. Huyton turned to her, and observed that he had seen Mr. Duncan in the house, and was glad to find him well, she really, at first, hardly knew what he was talking of, and her answers betrayed her wandering thoughts so clearly, as to make Dora and Isabel both laugh at her absence of mind.

It was late enough when they reached the Abbey porch to make it quite allowable that the young ladies should retire to their several toilettes; and then Mrs. Paine begged Hilary's company at hers for a moment, to explain some circumstances which she could not so well speak of before their hostess. It appeared that the intelligence that the living of Copseley was vacant, had reached the Paines the day after they arrived at the Abbey, and that Mr. Barham, on learning it, immediately expressed a strong wish to secure the future curacy of Hurstdene for Mr. Ufford. Why he was so anxious about it, or what particular inducement there was to place that gentleman in so retired a position, Mr. Barham did not mention; but this was avowedly his object in sending for Mr. Duncan. He wanted to settle it all immediately. That he had some ulterior motive, nobody who knew Mr. Barham could doubt, and Mrs. Paine had her own ideas on that point; but she did not think it right to mention mere conjectures; so she said she should leave Hilary to guess for herself. As to Mr. Ufford, she saw no harm in him, he seemed to be zealous, and talked well; but she was rather doubtful of his sincerity; he had a way of not speaking his opinions frankly, which made her uncomfortable, and she half-suspected him of extreme views, which might lead to injudicious innovations. But she was not sure of her own opinions, and most people were captivated by him; even Mr. Paine thought him a most excellent young man; so that it was, perhaps, bold in her to say that she did not quite like him.

"But he strikes me," continued she, "as having an *idée fixe* of his own extreme personal importance and dignity; and you know, Hilary, that even very good men do often go very much astray, and become exceedingly inconsistent and strange, from having an ill-balanced character; from allowing one notion to overgrow their mind, and so warp or conceal other estimable qualities."

"Very probably," said Hilary; "but you say Mr. Paine likes him, and I expect my father will be guided by him. Oh! how I shall miss you! Mr. Ufford can never be what your husband has been to us; and there will be no compensation at all for the loss of you! Well, it is no use thinking of it; there are still three months left, I will not make them unhappy by anticipating the evil day; time enough when it comes. How do you think Dora is now? She looks very well."

"I do not know that she is otherwise; they thought her delicate in the summer, but I fancy she quite recovered both health and spirits before she joined her family in Scotland, and she has not been ailing since."

Hilary thought that this account did not agree with certain little notes she had received from time to time from Dora, speaking of a general disgust of life, an extreme want of spirits, and an inevitable tendency to a heart-broken death. But it was quite in accordance with her personal appearance, and her air of health and cheerfulness.

Dinner at the Abbey was always a grand and stately affair. The guests felt they were assisting at an important and solemn ceremony, a guaranty of the respectability of the ancient house of Barham; a remnant of the feudal times and the pomps of former days, when baronial ancestors had been served by squires and pages themselves of noble birth. Clinging to almost the last remnant of those by-gone days, Mr. Barham was particular about his livery-servants: they were many, they were well-trained, and their costume was as handsome as good taste could make it. In that gorgeously lighted room, contrasting as completely as wealth and elegance could suggest, with the ancient refectory, or the convivial board of olden times, it was impossible to find a shadow of concealment; a screen of any kind, to preserve blushing cheeks or troubled eyes from the glance of the curious, or the inspection of the sharp-sighted. So Hilary found to her cost; the round table brought every one in sight of each other, and made every observation audible to the group.

It was at this particular time that Mr. Huyton addressed her with a question regarding Maurice; he hoped he was well?

She replied in the affirmative, trusting that no one in the circle would care enough for her brother, or so little for herself, as to pursue the subject. She was mistaken. Mr. Huyton forced her to tell him what was the name of his ship, and where she then was, which she could hardly do without naming Captain Hepburn, although to speak before him of her lover was peculiarly distressing. On this, Mr. Barham took up the subject, by asking if he had not seen the young man at "the Ferns;" a talk, dark man, about thirty; older a good deal than Miss Duncan? Hilary, blushing exceedingly, and conscious that more eyes were fixed on her than she liked to meet, said *that* was not her brother; he was young and fair.

On this Isabel, smiling graciously, observed that she thought papa was thinking of Mr. Duncan's captain, not himself; to which Mr. Barham observed, with his usual majesty, that it was by no means improbable: who might his captain be?

Hilary gave an imploring look at Isabel, but for some occult reason she did not choose to speak. Mrs. Paine's attention at the moment was not directed that way, nor, indeed, had she been disengaged, instead of listening to a remark of Mr. Ufford's, could she have interposed without awkwardness. Dora's eyes were on her china plate, which she was minutely examining, and Mr. Barham was looking at Miss Duncan for an answer. How she wished her father had been present to have answered for her, but he did not dine with them, as he had a nervous dread of being troublesome or unpleasant from his infirmity. She felt she must reply; indeed, it was but a moment that she hesitated; a moment was enough to feel a great deal of embarrassment; another, to resolve to brave it all; and although conscious that Charles Huyton's eyes were reading her countenance with a deliberate intentness, which she thought quite cruel, she answered her host's question with sufficient distinctness, that his captain's name was Hepburn.

"Hepburn! Hepburn! that's a good name, an old family name, Miss Duncan, one long distinguished in Scotch history," observed Mr. Barham. "Did we not meet somebody of that name in Scotland, Isabel? You who are such a genealogist and historian, you must remember, I am sure."

Isabel did remember accurately the whole genealogical table of the gentleman in question; and while she was relating some interesting historical anecdotes connected with the family, Hilary's cheeks had time to cool, and she trusted the name of her lover would not again be forced from her.

But when Isabel had finished her graceful little narrations, her father again turned to Miss Duncan with a question as to whether she knew if her brother's captain belonged to this ancient house. It was important, perhaps, for Mr. Barham's comfort, since he had done Captain Hepburn the honor of recollecting him, that he should be proved worthy of so great a compliment, by possessing the lineage of a gentleman. Hilary replied briefly, that she believed so.

To her very great astonishment, Charles Huyton spoke.

"Whether Captain Hepburn can prove his descent from honorable ancestors or not by genealogical records, he certainly does by his chivalrous conduct and noble bearing, if honor and courage are the attributes of high birth. He is as brave and gallant a man as I have ever seen."

Hilary gave one quick, grateful glance at her *vis-à-vis*, as he spoke these words, which was not thrown away. She knew better than any one else the effort it must cost him.

"Ah! I know to what you allude," said Isabel, with a sweet smile; "but if I remember rightly, Captain Hepburn was not the only one who displayed courage and daring on that occasion. Even Hilary must admit that there was another strong arm and bold heart then and there. The spectators at least saw both performers, although the immediate actors in the scene were, perhaps, only conscious of a part of what passed."

Hilary again looked up timidly at Mr. Huyton. She felt that thus appealed to, she ought to make some response; but she hardly knew what it would be safe to say. There was a shade on his brow, a sort of frown, as if Isabel's words called up some bitter thought—as if he were struggling with painful feelings.

"You are quite right, Isabel, it was an occasion when it would be invidious to draw comparisons, or to do any thing but give equal thanks to the one who saved my sister, and to the one who saved myself."

Hilary's voice trembled slightly as she spoke.

"If that had been the only occasion on which Captain Hepburn had shown his courage and dauntless spirit," replied Charles, "I should still say that he was first in honor, for he led the way; I did but follow his example. But I know this is not the case; I know that it is only one of several such instances. I have heard that he has dared a leap into a wild tossing sea, in a dark and stormy day, to save a helpless fellow-creature. Is not that the fact, Miss Duncan?"

With glowing cheeks and quivering eyelids, Hilary assented.

"Perhaps," said Isabel, "there are braver acts done quietly and almost unnoticed even than that, heroic as it seems. Acts which require a more generous heart and noble nature than the human courage which would lead a sailor to dare the storm, to help a shipmate in distress."

Mr. Huyton rather looked than asked for an explanation. Isabel went on.

"To throw oneself from the pedestal of glory in order to place another there, to refuse the honorable distinction due to courage that it may be transferred to a companion in exertion, is a quiet heroism, a generous self-devotion, which requires a firmer and braver heart than the mere defiance of bodily danger."

Mr. Huyton bent down his eyes upon the damask table-cloth, and only showed, by the silence that followed, that he understood the lady's meaning. Hilary could not avoid looking at him; she knew better than Isabel the extent of generosity which could induce him to praise a successful rival. No words which he could have spoken could have so moved her heart toward him as this commendation of one whom she had supposed him to dislike. It was noble, candid, high-minded; she had not given him credit for such feelings; she had been unjust to him in her imagination; she wished to make amends. She gave him a look which expressed some part of her feeling; and while with lips trembling with emotion, and eyes sparkling with pleasure, she glanced at him, he suddenly raised his own eyes, met hers, and read her heart.

Isabel Barham little suspected the hidden emotions of the man to whom she was carefully studying to be agreeable. If she had at one time, for a short period, feared the influence of Hilary, such fears were entirely dissipated by the intelligence which had reached her, of her friend's engagement.

She little dreamed how often the Vicar's daughter had refused the hand to which she was so willing to reach out her own; or that the affections she would so gladly have won, had long been passionately and hopelessly devoted to another.

The heiress of the Abbey would not have deigned to stoop for a heart which her inferior rival had refused to accept; she would have scorned the acquisition had she really understood the position of affairs. Had she *loved* Mr. Huyton, her feelings would have been different; but love had nothing to do with the matter; it was a desirable connection, that was all. She might be capable of loving, perhaps, if she had the temptation; but as yet it had never occurred, and Charles Huyton was not the man to captivate her nature. The vagaries of affections are incomprehensible, and unaccountable by any rule; but the effects of ambition, love of importance, and worldly position, are much more easy to calculate. By these, at the present moment, Miss Barham was governed.

The dinner was over at last, and Hilary, released from the position *vis-à-vis* to Mr. Huyton, rejoiced to devote her attention to her father, who was waiting for them in the drawing-room. The rest of the evening went by without emotion of any trying nature. Mr. Huyton had a good deal of conversation with Mr. Duncan, during which Hilary escaped to the other end of the room; she had no wish to throw herself in the way of the young man, although she was pleased that he should show attentive deference to her father. Isabel Barham was also carefully kind to the clergyman, and it was a pretty contrast to see her standing beside his chair, with her graceful figure, and queenly air, talking with elegant animation, reading in the best-modulated voice in the world short passages from some new book she was discussing, and raising her head occasionally, to put back the long, dark ringlets which swept her well-turned shoulders, and would fall over her cheeks, as she stooped to refer to the work before her.

Mr. Ufford joined Hilary at the table where she was standing, turning over a book of prints, and entered into conversation on the topic of Hurstdene, its village, population, schools, church, and such particulars as might naturally be considered interesting to him. She found him, as Mrs. Paine had said, pleasing and gentle in manners, with a peculiar way of winning from those he conversed with their opinions; while he seldom committed himself by stating his own. It did not strike her at the time so much, but when she subsequently came to reflect upon their conversation, she found that she literally knew nothing more of his tastes, habits, opinions, and inclinations, than might be gathered from the courtesy with which he had listened to hers. It rather seemed, on review, as if he had been judging her, and for that purpose had succeeded in inducing her to develop her own views and feelings. She was not sure that she liked him; she hardly thought this fair, and she resolved, if they met again, to preserve greater equality in their steps toward a friendly acquaintance.

They kept rather late hours at the Abbey; it was midnight before the party broke up, although there was nothing particular doing to entertain them. When, however, the ladies did retire, Hilary watched, with an indescribable interest, the greeting between Isabel and Charles Huyton; she could not keep her fancy from speculating on, and her heart from seriously wishing for their union, and she half hoped that the long conversation which had engrossed them both, after Mr. Duncan had left the drawing-room at his usual hour, might be indicative of an approach to the sentiments which she desired.

His last words to her were spoken as easily, and in as disengaged a tone, as to Mrs. Paine herself, and Hilary went to her room, with a persuasion that the meeting was less uncomfortable than she could have expected. She drew a low chair to the fire, and sat down to think; but her reverie was soon interrupted by a light tap at the door she had not previously noticed, which, on opening, disclosed Dora Barham in her dressing-gown, with her long hair all hanging about her shoulders.

"Our rooms adjoin, you see, dear Hilary," said she, closing the door, and coming up to her friend. "I have sent my maid to bed, and now let me talk to you."

She threw herself on the carpet at her feet, laid her arm in Hilary's lap, and looked up in her face with a wistful expression.

"Oh, I am so unhappy! I do not the least know what to do. What ought I to do?—do tell me?"

"My dearest Dora! how can I?" replied Miss Duncan, caressing the soft round cheek, and lovingly putting back the glossy hair which spread over her knee.

"Oh, you do know a great deal. They want me to marry, and I can not, will not; you know why. But they do so want me to marry."

"Who do?"

"Papa and Isabel, and Lady Margaret. Oh, it's dreadful; you do not know what I have gone through these six months."

"To marry!" said Hilary; "what, to marry in a general way, or is there some one in particular? You talk vaguely."

"Oh, one man in particular: Mr. Ufford!"

"What, this clergyman?"

"Oh, no, his elder brother, a much older man, a widower, too, with one little girl; think of wanting to make me a step-mother."

"And do you not like this gentleman?"

"No, not much, pretty well; he is pleasant, and good, and kind. I like him better than his brother here; he is much more open and generous; only if he would have been so obliging as not to fancy himself in love with me, I should have liked him much better."

"And now, where is he? is he still wanting to marry you?"

"He says, of course, if I am so averse, he will not press his suit; but he shall and must love me to the end of time; and papa says I am a silly child, and do not know my own mind. And oh, Hilary, he said—'Dora, if you loved another, I would not have pressed you to accept this offer; but since your heart is disengaged, there is no reason that you should not marry a man of such a character and such a position as Mr. Ufford!'"

"And what did you say, Dora?"

Dora hid her face and sobbed, then said—

"I complained of his age, his daughter, my youth, my indifference, but I got no pity. They would not admit these to be objections."

"Then you could not plead that your affections were pre-engaged, Dora?"

Again the face was hidden, and there was silence.

"Dora!" said Hilary, stooping and kissing her, "do not be ashamed to say so, if you are indifferent to *him*; I shall not blame you, if you have conquered an imprudent inclination; speak to me, say is that the case?"

"No," cried she, with vehemence, and raising her flushed face suddenly, "I have not. I love your brother better than ever; absence, time, separation, make no difference. I love him now, and I shall love him forever!"

"Then why not tell your father? had you owned it then, you would have been able to explain all."

"I was going to. I intended to have told him; I was only thinking how to begin, when he silenced me by adding, 'I say this, Dora, because I feel assured any daughter of mine would be incapable of forming or owning to an unworthy passion; of encouraging an affection beneath her, of consulting wild and childish fancies, rather than the claims of her family, the advancement of her best interests, and the maintenance of that elevated position in society, in which she has been placed by her birth and fortune.'

What could I say after that, Hilary? Own that I loved a poor lieutenant! I dared not."

There followed a long silence. To urge on her friend measures which, if they did not altogether embroil her with her father, would be so much more advantageous to Maurice than to Dora, was impossible for Hilary. She had given her opinion of right and wrong, she could do no more; so the two girls sat together, looking at the fire, and each plunged in thought.

"What must I do?" at last sighed Dora. "I sometimes think of going into a convent; if I were only a Roman Catholic, I would."

"My dear Dora!"

"Then," continued the willful little penitent, "I think of telling Mr. Ufford that I love another, and so getting him to give me up. What do you think of that?"

"I do not know."

"Hilary, would you, for all the riches and titles in the world, marry any other than Captain Hepburn? tell me."

"Certainly not; I could not."

"Nor will I than Maurice; our cases are exactly similar."

"Not quite."

"Yes, they are; we each love one, and that feeling makes it wrong to engage ourselves to another. There is no difference."

"A little. I have my father's consent to my affection and engagement. If I had not, I should try to obtain it."

"And if you could not?"

"I should try to conquer my affection."

"What! and leave your lover to suppose you faithless, changeable, treacherous? I will not."

"Yes. If it is not right to love, it matters little what he thinks of you, in comparison of doing right. Your duty is to conquer an improper, unauthorized affection, and the sooner the better."

"But it is not improper; it is right to love as I do."

"Then tell your father, Dora."

"I dare not—*he* will not think it right."

"Nay, then it is wrong."

"Cruel, cruel Hilary!"

"I am sorry to seem so, dear Dora; but it appears to me so plain. There are but two things to do. Own your attachment and abide by the consequences; or conquer it, and give Maurice up entirely."

"I have nothing to give up; I am not bound to him, nor he to me, except in unalterable affection. That is all."

"A most unhappy affection. How much better for you both, if you could renounce it entirely. Continued as it is, it can only make you discontented, miserable, unable to adopt any path in life. If you could but overcome and forget it!"

"And marry Mr. Ufford? Never!"

Hilary was silent again.

"I never thought to hear such words from you, Hilary," continued Dora. "Have you no regard for honor and principle, that you advise me to marry without love? have you no affection left for Maurice that you bid me abandon him? none for me, that you desire me to perjure myself? Oh, shame, shame on you, Hilary! You do not deserve to be Maurice's sister."

"I do not deserve such reproaches," replied Miss Duncan steadily, looking at her friend's glowing face, as she started to her feet before her. "I never proposed, or prompted such ideas."

"What did you mean, then?"

"That you should really and honestly try to conquer your unfortunate predilection for my brother. Surely there is no virtue in obstinate constancy; the passion denominated love, has no such merit in itself, that it should be clung to at the expense of all other good qualities; that candor, and filial affection, and self-denial, and self-control, are all to be sacrificed to it. What is it, after all, but often a merely selfish inclination, a determined perseverance in our own way, this constancy which is so much praised and extolled? And as to making one happy, what can be a greater delusion! It seems to me that persisting in an unfortunate attachment, is very like persisting in entertaining some wearing illness, which makes you uncomfortable in yourself, and uneasy to those around you."

"But, Hilary, one can not help these things; love may be a disease, but it is an incurable one—at least, in cases where the infection is really taken."

"I do not believe that, Dora. We are not sent into this world to be the sport of our passions; and I am convinced that our natural affections need no more be fatal to us, than our necessary acts, such as eating and drinking. We may, by mismanagement, bring our bodies or our minds into such a state, that the things which should conduce to our health and happiness, may produce fatal consequences; but then who is to blame? Consider the end and object of this life; to prepare for a better, a peaceful, blissful state, where darkness, doubt, and distress can not come; where tears shall disappear forever: and can you suppose that we are necessary victims to deplorable passions which must so entirely interfere with this great object? that love, which is intended to assist us onward, can of its own nature be ungovernable and incurable? Oh, no; we may learn to command every passion, even the strongest, if we seek aright."

"You are just talking enigmas to me; you know very well I never learned any thing about self-control; and Maurice loves me as I am. I shall go and take the first opportunity of telling Mr. Ufford I love another; for I never could bear to be step-mother to a girl of twelve years old. It is too absurd of papa to expect it at all."

She quitted the room, leaving Hilary to meditate at leisure on what had passed; to grieve over the mutual infatuation of her brother and her friend, and to comfort herself that at least Dora's pettish injustice would not last, for she could not bear to quarrel with her.

CHAPTER XVI.

"Her moods, good lack! they pass like show'rs.
But yesternight, and she would be
As pale and still as wither'd flow'rs;
And now to-night she laughs and speaks,
And has a color in her cheeks— —"

Iseult.

Hilary knew Dora better than this wayward little thing knew herself. She came back very penitent and humble, before she could sleep; and after a great deal of kissing and crying for her crossness, she ended by insisting on sleeping with Hilary, and taking that opportunity of keeping her friend awake half the night, talking alternately of Captain Hepburn and Maurice.

The morning hours after breakfast passed rather heavily away. The ladies were together in their sitting-room, the gentlemen were all invisible, nobody exactly knew where. Isabel was grave, Dora was languid, and Hilary was thoughtful.

"Where's Mr. Huyton?" yawned Dora; "how stupid of him not to come and talk to us! I am so tired. What's become of him, Isabel?"

"Really I do not know; perhaps he is in the library."

"No, I went in there, just now, and Mr. Ufford was all alone, reading St. Augustine, I believe, and making extracts. You may guess I did not disturb him. Where is your father, Hilary?"

"He and Mr. Paine are together," said Miss Duncan.

"Oh, how tired I am," said Dora, laying a very pale cheek against the crimson back of her easy chair.

"Mr. Huyton never goes away in general, where can he be?"

"I should not wonder if he has gone to 'the Ferns,'" observed Mrs. Paine.

Isabel looked up. "What makes you think so, Fanny?" asked she.

"I heard him order his horse to be ready immediately after breakfast, and you know he left the table early."

"Ah, I dare say he had business, and that brought him down into the country," said Miss Barham, quietly; "he feels so much at home here, that as his own house is not habitable at present, he naturally resorts to ours, when he wants a brief habitation."

From all which Hilary gathered, that when with the Barhams, either at the Abbey or elsewhere, he was accustomed generally to make himself agreeable.

"I wish something would happen!" said Dora, presently, with another yawn.

"What?" inquired Mrs. Paine.

"Oh, any thing, an event! something to rouse and excite one; to give one a fillip. I do not quite want an earthquake, but I should like something!"

"Poor child!" said Mrs. Paine, laughing; "it wants a new toy, or a nice cake."

"No, it is sick of cakes, and tired of toys," said Dora; "it wants good wholesome food, and a little work instead of play. I should like to lose my fortune, and have to work for my bread. I think I could be happy then."

"Pretty work you would make of it!" said Isabel; "I wonder how you would begin."

"Why, really, that is a problem worth solving," replied Dora; "I wonder too. What part of my education do you suppose was intended to fit me for the storms of adversity? which branch of the distorted and grotesque plant, which forms my small portion of the Tree of Knowledge, would be of the slightest use to me in distress? I think I might, perhaps, be capable of engaging as a ballet-dancer; but as to any thing else, I am sure I can not guess."

"How can you talk so?" exclaimed her sister; "it is quite improper. You have had a very good education for a lady!"

"Well, I happened to see one of the maids cleaning the grate to-day in my room, and she looked so busy, so happy, and was chirrupping so cheerfully to herself, that I could not help stopping her to ask her what made her so merry; and she said in a frightened voice, as if excessively ashamed of herself, that she had no time to be unhappy, so she could not help it; for she had so much to do, that really, if she had a mind to fret, she should not have a minute to spare, for she was quite an underhousemaid, you see, and had to do the work, while the others looked after her. I told her I envied her."

"You ought not to put such ideas into their heads, Dora; it is republican and leveling."

"I do not think what I said will do any harm, Isabel. Hilary, if you had to work for your bread, what would you do? Should you not like it?"

"I believe I do it pretty much now," replied Miss Duncan; "and I do not particularly wish for a change."

"Well, I do," said Dora, closing her eyes, and sinking into profound silence.

The morning past, the luncheon hour arrived, and not till after that did Mr. Huyton make his appearance, nor did he publicly account for his absence, or at all explain where, or how he had spent the three or four hours during which he had disappeared. The Duncans were to return home after luncheon, and as Hilary was proceeding up the long stairs to her room, to prepare for her departure, she encountered him at the top of them.

He stood back a little, as if to let her pass, but turned and joined her in the gallery.

"Are you going?" said he, wistfully looking at her.

"Yes, presently; you have been riding, have you not?"

"I have been to Hurstdene."

Hilary looked surprised.

"Yes, I spent the morning there; I longed, with an inexpressible longing, to see those scenes again, to tread those walks, look at those walls once more. You were here, my presence at the Vicarage could not disturb you; could excite no anger in you; I ventured to gratify my wishes. To take one more view of the place I dearly loved, where I was once welcomed as a constant, and only too happy guest."

"Did you see my sisters?" asked Hilary, embarrassed and pained.

"Yes, they were as kind as ever. I have at least one thing to thank you for—you have kept my secret well. Dear girls! they little knew, when they playfully reproached me for my long absence, whose wish it was it should be so! It is noble of you, Miss Duncan, to allow me to retain their good will; not to teach them to view me with aversion; not to inspire them with the cold dislike you entertain toward me yourself."

"Indeed, you do me injustice, Mr. Huyton," replied Hilary, gently, and pausing, in the gallery through which they were passing; "it is not aversion that I feel for you."

"And when we met yesterday by moonlight, could I not even then read the expression of your face? the chilling indifference of which it spoke, haunted me all night; and your hand, too, did it not tell the same tale? those fingers which once used to return the pressure of mine, now coldly suffer me to touch them, passively submitting to a form which is demanded by good manners, not expressive of sympathy. Do you suppose I am insensible, or indifferent to the change? Would to Heaven that I could annihilate the last eighteen months, and stand once more by your side the friend I once claimed to be!"

"Would that we could, Mr. Huyton, so far as you are concerned," replied she, gravely; "but the wish is idle and vain! we are what we have made ourselves, and feelings, words, actions, can never, *never* be recalled. Would that it were possible to begin anew our acquaintance!"

"I would still be your friend, Hilary," said he, in a more gentle voice; "may I not be that, may I not sometimes see you on these terms?"

"I believe you would; I know you are generous and noble; I can not forget your words last night, and I can honor the feeling that dictated them."

A flash of joy passed across his face at these words, and fixing his eyes on her, he said:

"And may I hope that you will still see me, receive me as a friend—let me sometimes visit your father, sometimes converse with you?"

She shook her head. "Not now; not under present circumstances."

"Not for your father's sake? he loves me, you know," said he, persuasively.

"I dare not."

"Dare not! which then is it that you will not trust, my honor or yours, Hilary?" There was a shadow gathering on his brow.

"Why should we peril either," replied she; "mine, yours, or that of another who is far away? You know my faith is pledged to him, to what end then *our* meeting, until you too have chosen another object for the love you have so unfortunately misplaced? Then we *may* meet perhaps as friends. Till then, let us part as friends."

"You have nothing more to fear from me, from my love," replied he, bending down his eyes to conceal their expression. "But neither has any one aught to hope from it! For me to love again is impossible. Let it be enough that I resolve to extinguish a vain, hopeless passion. I ask now to be trusted as a friend only. Can you not believe me so far as that?"

"It is wisest not to try," said she, slowly.

"What makes you so mistrustful?" questioned he, looking earnestly at her.

"Experience!" was her answer; while the color deepened on her cheeks, as she thought of past scenes.

"Are you quite candid now, Miss Duncan? is it not, rather, the injunction, the wish, perhaps, I should say, of *him*, of Captain Hepburn? Did not he bid you shun me? It can not be your own nature to be so newly suspicious; tell me it is his."

"No, indeed, he laid no restriction on me: he trusted entirely to my prudence, and I will show I deserved it."

"I would rather it had been his wish; I could have borne his suspicions better," said Charles, sadly. "But surely, could he see me now, he would not fear me. I only aspire to be your friend, I only ask for calm and quiet intercourse; I have no pretensions now which could create jealousy, or make him suppose me a rival. I own his superiority, I admire, I esteem him; my own hopes being gone, I may at least rejoice that one worthy of you has won you; I am resigned to my loss; why should you make it more bitter than necessity requires?"

She was silent, but she drew back when he tried to take her hand.

"If he did not mistrust me, why should you? *He*, at least, knows us both better, does more justice both to you and me. Why should you hesitate? It is such a small favor I ask. For your father's sake, let me come sometimes and see him."

"No, Mr. Huyton, I can not. Unlimited trust deserves unwavering prudence. Do not ask again, it is decided. At Hurstdene, and on purpose, I will not meet you. Let me say now, farewell. It is hard to refuse one to whom I owe so much; it is hard to seem ungrateful; but it is best. But you shall always have my best wishes, my earnest prayers for your happiness; I will never forget that the hand I hold assisted to save my life."

"Would that I had perished then and there!" cried he, losing self-control for a moment. "Would that the water had closed upon us both—that I had gone down with you in my arms, rather than—" he stopped abruptly; footsteps were heard ascending the stairs, he was recalled to a thought of where he was; he only stayed one moment to press her hand in both of his, to kiss it with a warmth, a passionate ardor, which did not speak of cold friendship; to give her one sad, reproachful look, and then he rushed toward his own dressing-room, which was in an adjoining corridor, leaving Hilary to enter her apartment, near the door of which they had been standing, and there to conceal her excitement and her fears.

She had proceeded but a little way in her preparations for departure, when Dora rushed into the room, her bonnet in one hand, and her cloak in the other.

"I am going with you, Hilary, for the drive," cried she; "the horses must stop there to rest; for I have made papa agree that it was more civil I should go home with you."

She seemed in great spirits, and danced about at intervals, while she was pretending to dress.

"You are awake now, Dora," said her friend, smiling; but her voice betrayed at once that her own tears were not far off.

"What is the matter?" exclaimed Dora, stopping to look anxiously at her friend; "what have you been crying about, Hilary, tell me?"

"Nothing worth talking of—my own folly," replied Miss Duncan, turning away, and stooping to look at the lock of a carpet bag.

"I have long known," said Dora, gravely, "that you were a very foolish child, always crying about nonsense and trifles; so I can easily believe you. No doubt you hurt your foot against a step, or pricked your finger with your brooch, and that made you cry."

Hilary laughed a little, and did not answer otherwise.

"I want to come and stay with you at the Vicarage for some days," continued Dora, in another voice. "Do ask me, I should so like it. Tell papa you want me."

"I am afraid Mr. Barham would think I was taking too great a liberty in asking you, Dora."

"Oh, no, he would not mind; you ask me, and he will let me go. You do want me, do you not?"

"Very much," said Miss Duncan, kindly; "it would give me great pleasure indeed to have you there, but I hardly think you are likely to be permitted."

"Oh, we will see," said Dora; "now I am ready; are you? then come down."

Mr. Huyton was down stairs with the other visitors when the girls descended; calm, self-possessed, and courteous; listening gracefully to Isabel, who was discussing a question on political economy with Mr. Ufford; while Mr. Barham sat by with a look of paternal pride.

Hilary ventured to make the request dictated by Dora; it was graciously received, treated as a very great kindness and honor, and if Miss Duncan liked to trouble herself with such a wild, thoughtless little child as Dora, he should be very happy at some future time; they would think of it.

"Mrs. Paine returns to Primrose Bank on Saturday," suggested Dora, "let me go then to the Vicarage; it would suit Hilary very well, I know."

Dora settled it all her own way; Isabel did not disapprove; it was true that Mr. Ufford was to leave them also in company with the Paines, but Mr. Huyton had promised to remain some time longer, and she was just as well pleased that her sister should *not* be there during this visit; for so carefully did Charles balance his attentions, and so strictly impartial was he to both sisters, that the eldest never actually felt sure whether she was or was not the one preferred.

Very glad indeed was Hilary to be back in her own home, and away from the grandeur and restraints of Drewhurst Abbey. She never felt so much at ease with Mr. Barham as with any one else, and the sight of Charles Huyton made her unhappy. The great surprise which her sisters expected to afford her, turned out a failure; for she had already heard of their visitor; but it was news to Dora, who had not guessed where he had been, and who did not fail on her return home to charge him with it.

Saturday came, and brought the younger Miss Barham to take up her abode at the Vicarage, as she had promised, much to the delight of the sisters there, who could not make enough of her. She was in great spirits, laughing and chatting rather wildly, and making them all laugh, too, with her nonsense. Her grief and anxiety sat lightly indeed on her. The Paines and Mr. Ufford accompanied her, the latter to be introduced to the Vicarage; he was to preach the next morning. Mr. Duncan appeared extremely pleased with him, and there was every prospect that Mr. Barham's plans would be carried out.

Two or three days passed; Dora was still at the Vicarage, very happy and amusing, when, one morning, Hilary returning to the drawing-room, after a brief absence, found two visitors there, one of whom was a stranger. However, from his resemblance to his companion, she guessed him to be the elder Mr. Ufford, before Dora, with some blushes and embarrassment, introduced him as such.

He was a pleasing and sensible-looking man, with an air of elegance becoming his birth, but with nothing in the slightest degree affected, or wearing the appearance of dandyism. He was simply in the best sense a gentleman, and a very good-looking one, too. Hilary liked him very much. Neither was he so immensely old, as Dora had represented him; to look at him, you could hardly believe him eight-and-twenty; and but for the certainty of his having a daughter, she would never have given him credit for a greater age. Possibly the representations of Dora had overstepped the facts, and this obnoxious child might not be quite so much as twelve years old.

Mr. James Ufford, the clergyman, was the bearer of a message from Mrs. Paine, who was desirous to see Miss Duncan on some parochial matters, but was detained at home by cold and headache: he had, accordingly, set off to bring this message; and on the way had been overtaken by his brother, who had ridden over from Drewhurst Abbey that morning. It was proposed, partly on Dora's suggestion, that they should all walk over to Primrose Bank together, and accordingly they presently set out, Hilary and Gwyneth with Mr. Ufford, junior; Dora under the care of the elder brother.

These two did not attempt to keep up with the others, and Hilary soon lost sight of them. Perhaps, concern for her brother made her quick-sighted, but she could not help fancying that, in spite of her assertions, Dora was by no means unwilling to receive the admiration or permit the attentions of her companion, and she could not anticipate any other conclusion to the affair than what Captain Hepburn had predicted as most probable.

She was so much engrossed by these considerations as to afford but indifferent company to Mr. James Ufford, who, in consequence, devoted himself to Gwyneth, and succeeded in convincing that young lady that he was, without exception, the most delightful man in the world, even before they reached Primrose Bank.

Hilary went straight in-doors, and sought Mrs. Paine, who was in her own room; but the other two, tempted by the fineness of the day, lingered on the little lawn, looking at the blossoms of the laurustinus bushes, and planning imaginary changes in the flower-beds, until they were rejoined by the others, who loitered behind.

Mrs. Paine and Miss Duncan having finished their business, came down stairs together, when they found the drawing-room full. Besides those for whose presence they were prepared, Charles Huyton was there, whose visit was unexpected by either; he had, however, come over from the Abbey in company with George Ufford, and while the latter had followed his brother, he had been wandering about with Mr. Paine, inspecting the outhouses, which wanted some alterations, and planning other improvements in the place.

He was now gayly conversing with Dora Barham, and even after he had advanced to greet the two ladies, he again returned to her side; while she, with more coquetry than Hilary had suspected her of feeling, seemed encouraging him, either from actual preference, or to pique George Ufford; it was not easy to decide which. Miss Duncan made up her mind that day, that constancy and earnestness were not a part of Dora's nature; that her conduct depended on her feelings; while her feelings appeared entirely under the influence of chance or accident varying at every turn.

Perhaps Dora was afraid of her friend's reproaches, for after their return home, where they were escorted by James Ufford alone, the other gentlemen being obliged to ride back to the Abbey, she carefully avoided any occasion of having a confidential discussion of the past. In a very few more days she was to return home, and Hilary hoped sincerely they might part without any further reference to her personal affairs. But this was not the case. Miss Duncan discovered accidentally that in a letter Gwyneth had been writing to Maurice, Dora had persuaded her to insert so many messages, so much of reminiscence and kindness, as must tend to delude Maurice, as it perhaps deluded herself, into the idea that she was still constant to him in her affections, and unchangeably bent on loving him alone.

Hilary felt obliged to remonstrate.

"Please don't, Dora, another time. It is not right to any one; to Gwyneth, or to Maurice, or yourself, or your father; if I had known it in time, I should have stopped the letter."

Dora looked half-vexed and half-foolish.

"You are so precise, Hilary; you are not like any body else."

"Perhaps not; but we are not talking of myself, but of Maurice and you."

"I quite wonder you consider it correct to put us in the same sentence, when you seem so determined to keep us apart," continued Dora.

"Now, please, dear Dora, do be reasonable," said Hilary, imploringly; "can I ask you to come here that you may carry on a clandestine correspondence with my brother? What would your father say?"

"My dear Hilary, every body has their peculiarities; yours is to be haunted with the idea that every body is doing something improper, unless they will proclaim their deeds at the market cross."

"What is clandestine must be wrong," said Hilary, decidedly.

"But can you not comprehend, my dear young friend, that there is a difference between secrecy and improper concealment? It is not necessary to publish every thing one knows, neither is it wrong to avoid some topics. Even to a father there may be things which it is better not to repeat; there may be subjects concealed from the best of motives."

"This is all very true, perhaps, but the difference between discretion and dissimulation is positive, Dora. If you feel sure that when he knows your conduct he will approve it, and consider your secrecy was justifiable and proper, you may venture to practice it, I suppose, without fear."

Dora was silent.

"Neither is it fair to Maurice," continued Hilary; "you are misleading him; I do not blame you for learning to prefer another, but—"

"No," interrupted Dora, "you could hardly do that, at least with justice, since it is not the case."

"Dora, you deceive yourself, surely; your manners to Mr. Ufford—"

"Dear Hilary, don't tell me my manners encourage *him*," cried she, rather alarmed; "I assure you I do not mean it in the least; but what can I do? He is so gentle and amiable, I can not be cross to him, and you would not have me rude, I am sure; so then I turn round and flirt with Mr. Huyton to get rid of the other, and you look at me with such fault-finding eyes: are you jealous, Hilary, it is that? I believe Mr. Huyton loves you all the time. Oh, Hilary! what a blush, my dear girl! you are jealous, then: what will Captain Hepburn say?"

"If I did not know that you were talking all this nonsense merely to get rid of my remonstrances, I should be seriously displeased with such foolish language, Dora; as it is—"

"As it is, Hilary, you must bear with me! I love Maurice, and Maurice only, but Mr. Huyton amuses me when I am dying of *ennui*; he is pleasant and clever, and I know well that he has no heart to bestow, to have any dread of entangling it. Do you think I have not seen how he loves you! how he follows you with his eyes, listens to your voice, even while he is talking to others; worships your shadow, and haunts your footsteps? I never could make out why you did not like him; for although I do not myself, I think you might suit him, and he you."

"All this has nothing to do with what I was talking of, Dora; you know Mr. Huyton is nothing to me; but while I retain any regard for you (and that must be always), I can not help wishing to prevent your doing wrong, and deceiving yourself and Maurice."

"Well, I will not deceive Mr. Ufford; I will tell him plainly my opinion the very first opportunity!"

"Are you quite sure what your opinion is? are you certain that when you send him away, you shall not regret what you have done? Do you really wish to give him up?"

"I would give up twenty such men for Maurice."

"Consider, Dora, if you were to marry my brother, you would become the wife of a poor man, one who must immediately curtail all the luxuries and indulgence which have become habit to you. Are you seriously bent on this—prepared for it?"

"I should like poverty—riches and luxury disgust me; I am weary of indulgence."

"But think what it would be to lose your place in society, which you must do when you ceased to be Miss Barham, of Drewhurst Abbey, to step down into retirement and neglect; to lay aside your elegant style of toilette, to give up your horses, your carriages, your journeys here and there at pleasure; your multitude of attendants, your luxurious rooms. To have to wait on yourself, order your own dinners, put up with indifferent and awkward servants, consider before you spent even five shillings, calculate which joint of meat is most economical, and how to make it last longest and go furthest; perhaps even to repair your own wardrobe, certainly to walk about on foot; and to live in small rooms, with the certainty of not being able to travel for change or diversion. Could you patiently put up with all this, and smile away difficulties and *ennui* in such circumstances?"

"I suppose I could as well as another woman, unless you mean to infer that your brother and his wife must be unhappy; I do not see that I should be more so than any other."

"You might, because you would have so much to renounce; while all these things would be natural, and therefore easy, to one brought up as I have been. You say you would like poverty, Dora; try. Allow yourself the gratification of no whim, deny yourself every superfluity which arrests your fancy, rise early, live plainly, do some useful work; for instance, make a flannel petticoat for a poor woman, or a cotton frock for a baby, and try for a month, or a fortnight even, how you like such a life. It would be sad to make a mistake, and find it out too late."

"But it would be quite different, Hilary, to play at being poor myself, or to be really so with Maurice."

"I admit that; you could go back at any time to riches; the step would not be inevitable."

"And so it would be unreal, and therefore could do no good. The motive would be wanting."

"I do not see that; the motive would be to try whether you could manage without riches; to understand yourself, and form a right judgment of the value you set on wealth. If you could not do without indulgence to this modified extent, and for so short a time, you would have no right to engage in such a situation for life."

"Besides," said Dora, "I do not believe it can be necessary; for though Maurice is not rich, I should have my own fortune, which will, probably, be large. Papa told me he would give me handsome settlements if I married Mr. Ufford."

"And how much would he give you if you married Mr. Duncan?" inquired Hilary, significantly.

"Oh, I don't know! The same I suppose! why not?"

Hilary looked doubtful. Dora went on.

"And then, after all, nobody in my station really is poor; it is all a romance of your imagination. I dare say Maurice would contrive as other people do, to get along and keep up a respectable appearance. I need not have bad servants, I would hire good ones; and I would manage my ménage so that it should be no trouble, and I should rather like the pleasure of ordering dinner, and contriving nice little surprises for him in the way of eating. I am sure I could be happy."

"Of one thing, Dora, we are quite sure; without your father's consent, you will never try the experiment; and if he wishes you to marry Mr. Ufford, he is not likely to approve of your engaging yourself to Maurice."

"You dreadfully matter-of-fact girl! how you knock down all my delightful castles. Oh! Hilary, I wish you had been crossed in love, and then you would have had some pity for me."

And so the discussion ended. Hilary had not learned as yet, that to contradict a youthful passion, to argue against it, to overwhelm it with unanswerable reasons, and endeavor to extinguish it with detailed proofs of its absurdity or unfitness, is certain to strengthen and increase its power; so red-hot iron is hardened into tempered steel by plunging it suddenly into cold water.

CHAPTER XVII.

"In the woods where the gleams play
On the grass under the trees,
Passing the long summer's day
Idly as a mossy stone,
In the forest depths."

Tristram and Iseult.

Time passed on, as time will do. Eighteen more months went by; Hilary hardly knew whether to say they went fast or slowly. Fast, very fast, it seemed, when she thought of the changes it had brought. It was only two years since they had first seen Mr. Farrington, and Sybil was now his wife. The child had grown up and loved, and married, and left her father's house; and yet how short a time it seemed since she was yet a child, dependent on Hilary's care. Now she was in another home, the center of her own system. She was very happy; so, though her absence caused a gap, it was not to be lamented. Very fast, too, time seemed to move with her father; how rapidly he had aged, how infirm he had grown in these two years. It saddened Hilary's heart to look at him; he had always been old for his age, he might have been eighty in appearance now; and fear whispered to the daughter, that she could not, must not, hope for lengthened days for him. She dared not look forward, so she turned away her eyes.

But slowly, slowly it seemed to move, the time which was to bring her lover home. Two years of his absence had gone, perhaps more than another might have to pass ere his return. She began now to understand what was meant by hope deferred; she knew what waiting was now. Now and then her bright hopes seemed to fail her, and she was ready to murmur that he should still delay. But better feelings usually prevailed; he was doing his duty; he was acting right; he was denying his strongest inclinations, and should *she* give way, she who had neither storm, nor danger, nor anxious responsibility, nor thwarting cares nor vexatious counteractions, nor any other difficulty to contend with? She could stay with those she loved in her sheltered home, and pray for him in the parish church, knowing so little trouble, feeling no doubt of her duty. Shame on her false heart, her feeble trust, her fainting patience, if they failed her at such a time.

The other changes besides those mentioned were slight. The Paines indeed had gone, and Mr. Ufford now filled the office of curate. He had much more absolute power than Mr. Paine had exercised. Mr. Duncan was incapable of doing much, so Mr. Ufford ruled supreme, and, except that he had contrived to offend many of the farmers' wives, and quarrel with their husbands, had driven away the old schoolmistress, and considerably diminished the school, had scattered the congregation and half-emptied the church, every thing might be considered to do very well. Hilary saw much of this with sorrow, Gwyneth with wondering indignation; not at the clergyman, however, but at the people who disagreed with him. What any one could find to quarrel with in him, she could not imagine. So good, so quiet, so full of plans for the good of every one; it was wonderful that every one would not submit to be led as she was, and would not on every occasion give up will, wish, and reason to the control of Mr. Ufford.

She could not understand why, but certainly Mr. Ufford had an unfortunate faculty, both for giving and taking offense, for finding himself injured, and feeling himself neglected, which did not smooth his way in the parish. It is foreign to my story, to relate how he quarreled with the village choir about the Psalms, and the church-wardens about the poor-box; how pews became a lively subject of discussion, and churchings a source of dissent. He had Mr. Duncan's ear, and could persuade him to what he pleased; and he was so plausible in his statements, so well-intentioned in his theories, that, of course, it was impossible he should contradict him.

Nothing could exceed the almost paternal kindness with which he had been welcomed and treated by the vicar; and Hilary, conscious that her engagement was known to him, fearing no evil, and thinking no harm, had received him nearly as a brother, and done every thing she could to smooth his way with the people. Such influence as he had, he owed to the Duncans.

As to Gwyneth, ever since their first interview, she had given him credit for every virtue under the sun, and invariably believed him to be perfectly right, let who would differ from or disagree with him. She was the confidante, consequently, of all his theories for the improvement of his people, of all his wishes that they were very different from what they were, and of all his doubts of ever making them any better. His theories certainly were beautiful: it was unfortunate that they should be based on the most ideal foundations, and so be generally impracticable. It was unfortunate, too, that those changes which he did introduce did not work well. For instance, as I said before, his attempt to re-model the school ended in the secession of the schoolmistress; but as his plans were never sufficiently fixed to be acted on, the new schoolmaster fell into his own ways, and the routine became rather more inefficient than before, while Mr. Ufford, in disgust, pretty well ceased to visit it.

And so it was in every thing else; things did not suit his fancy, were imperfect, or inappropriate; he made violent changes, was opposed, was determined, carried his point, made enemies, gradually grew indifferent, and gave up his object, contenting himself with strolling about the Vicarage garden, detailing impracticable schemes to Gwyneth, and drawing imaginary pictures of what might be.

He was one of those people who never have time for any thing, and who, from want of *reality*, do nothing in the end, although avowedly always busy. What could be effected by others in his plans, was well done; what depended on himself alone, was well talked of. Yet he was a great favorite with many, especially with recent acquaintance, and his friends always formed the highest estimate of his powers, and the liveliest expectations of their results.

Hilary was most anxious to think well of him. She discovered in time that he was expecting to succeed her father in the living; and this created a strong source of interest in him, and a most ardent wish that he should prove all that he was supposed to be. She shut her eyes to his deficiencies, excused any mistakes or neglects, labored to supply the care and zeal which were occasionally wanting, and to reconcile all apparent inconsistencies or short-comings. She had often hard work, and did sometimes feel as if she were endeavoring to make ropes of sand, although she laid all the blame of failure on her own mal-adroitness and ignorance.

Left as Hilary was almost entirely to her own discretion, it was not surprising that she sometimes made mistakes of conduct, acting on an innocence and ignorance of the world beyond her own village, which made her singularly unsuspicious of evil, and blind to imprudence. It certainly was a mistake to allow such unlimited and unreserved intercourse between Mr. Ufford and her own family; or rather, perhaps, the mistake was in those who placed so young a man in a situation where such intercourse was unavoidable. She herself heartily wished he were married; she missed Mrs. Paine more every month of their separation, and especially after Sybil had left Hurstdene; for Gwyneth was so much more reserved and silent than her sister, besides being younger, that she could not entirely fill her place; and her feelings were so enthusiastic, and so little regulated by reason, when she did express them, that Hilary had some trouble in guiding her at all.

Of course, Miss Duncan's bright spot in the future was the *Pandanus*; for however unremitting and unreserved a correspondence might be, it was impossible for the letters of a lover in the West Indies to supply all the daily counsel, the prudence, and the judgment which she needed to guide her; and what could possibly stand instead of the charm of his personal presence?

Mr. Ufford's father had died about a year after that gentleman had settled at Hurstdene, and his elder brother, after some occasional and rather lengthy visits to the village, had just gone abroad, partly for his own health, which was precarious, still more for his daughter's, which was decidedly delicate. Their mother had died of consumption, the second son, too, had shared the same fate, and many people thought the present Lord Dunsmoor had inherited the same weakness. James Ufford appeared the most robust of the family, and there seemed considerable probability that the title would eventually devolve on him.

Not that this idea had ever occurred to the sisters at the Vicarage, who, from seeing him every day, observing his simple habits, and quiet, gentlemanlike indolence, quite forgot that he belonged by birth to another sphere than themselves, and might some day rise to a circle where they could not hope to reach.

Meanwhile the Barhams had been sometimes at the Abbey as usual, and sometimes absent for months. It was evident Lord Dunsmoor avoided them, and Dora, in confidence, told Hilary, she had let him know that her heart was engaged elsewhere. Charles Huyton, too, was often there. Hilary met him too often. He was a great friend of James Ufford's, and frequently at Primrose Bank; of course, Hilary could not prevent that: she could not help, either, falling in with him in her walks and visits, but it was always painful. He was ever the same. Humble, gentle, only begging for friendship, entreating for tolerance, pleading for simple intercourse, if she remonstrated at these meetings; if she took them quietly, and tried to treat them as things of no consequence, he would use the opportunity to say or do something to oblige her. Papers which contained any intelligence of the *Pandanus* were always forwarded to her, and she knew the hand which directed them: news was obtained through the Admiralty of every change of the vessel's destination, and transmitted through James Ufford for her information. It was impossible to show more disinterested desire to please her; more anxious concern to win her confidence, and prove himself her friend. It was hard to repulse his attentions, and to seem unjustly suspicious; yet she could not trust him, she feared him too much, to be at ease—she was never sure of his sincerity.

Victoria Fielding had not since been seen in the neighborhood; she had married and settled in Cheshire, as had been intended. Charles often went there to visit her, and messages of friendship from her to Miss Duncan were not unfrequently the excuse for some interview.

It was summer again, and every thing was sparkling in a brilliant morning sun. Miss Duncan was in the garden before breakfast, cutting some flowers, stooping over a rose-tree, to select the blossoms which could best be spared; Gwyneth was making the tea in the parlor, while Nest was demurely talking to papa, occupied meanwhile in needle-work of the first importance.

"Hilary!" said a voice behind her which made her start. Down went the basket, the flowers, the scissors, all disregarded, forgotten. She was in another moment gently, tenderly clasped in Captain Hepburn's arms. Surprise was swallowed up in delight, she could not even ask how he came, she was so happy to see him there.

When the first excitement had passed away and explanations were demanded, it appeared that the machinery of the *Pandanus* having been found defective, she had been ordered home to refit, and having arrived after an unusually rapid voyage, the captain had obtained forty-eight hours' leave, and traveled down in all haste to spend the time with his affianced, bringing the first news of his own arrival in England, as both he and Maurice, it appeared, had been too busy to write to announce it.

Maurice, too, was in England then; he was well, but could not leave the ship for more than twenty-four hours, so for the present he must content himself with seeing Sybil in London. It was possible that the steamer might be paid off; "and if so," said Captain Hepburn, "I should be free for the present; perhaps it might be months before I should be employed again, perhaps years, and in that case, Hilary—" his eyes finished the sentence which his words left incomplete, as he stooped his head to take a view of the pretty blushing face, which was trying to conceal the feelings it could not suppress, and drooping so gracefully close beside him.

"You all seem very glad to have the captain with you again," said Mr. Ufford, laughingly to Gwyneth, during his usual forenoon visit. Hilary was in the garden with her lover. "He is a great favorite, apparently. I affronted Miss Nest just now grievously by saying that I did not think him the nicest man in the world; not so pleasant for instance as Charles Huyton."

"Nest loves him dearly," replied Gwyneth, "and it is natural she should, for you know he saved her life in the water."

"If that sort of obligation were always productive of dear love," replied he, "my friend Huyton would occupy the place just now filled by Captain Hepburn there."

"Perhaps he might have, had he wished it," said Gwyneth, innocently. "But Hilary was not likely to bestow it even from gratitude, if he did not ask for it himself."

"*If!*" exclaimed Mr. Ufford, amazed. "Is it possible that you, Miss Gwyneth, can be ignorant of his wishes, and his disappointment? I thought those sort of triumphs were always boasted of between young ladies with peculiar delight."

"I can imagine no delight in disappointing an amiable man, nor any triumph in pleasing a bad one," was Gwyneth's answer. "So in any case there could be nothing to boast of."

"And did she never tell you?" added he, curiously looking at her.

"No! and if there was any thing to tell, the same delicacy which prevented her naming it must prevent me from discussing it. At the same time I think it must long have ceased if there ever was any attachment. Hilary has been engaged these two years, and Mr. Huyton apparently has attached himself to Miss Barham since that!"

"Miss Barham!" repeated Mr. Ufford, with a curl of his lip; but he did not finish the sentence.

The next morning, when Mr. Ufford as usual walked over to the Vicarage, he was accompanied by Charles Huyton himself. There was a little embarrassment and hesitation in his manner as he presented himself, indicative, perhaps, of uncertainty as to his reception, but which was quite unusual with him. But with Captain Hepburn beside her, Hilary could venture to be frank and friendly; and the kindly inclination shown by this visit toward one who had been his rival won him a smile and a gentle glance, such as he had not met for a long while. Charles came to congratulate them on the safe return of the *Pandanus* to England, to express his good wishes, and to shake hands with Captain Hepburn once more. So he said; and he did give a prolonged and friendly grasp to his rival's hand, such as no true English heart could give or receive if a shade of evil feeling remained behind. It seemed to speak of deep heartfelt congratulations, and an earnest, trusting commendation to his care of the fair being whom they both had loved, and one had loved so hopelessly though truly. So Captain Hepburn interpreted the action, and gave him credit for generosity and submission, and true nobleness of mind.

They were wandering about in the garden, when Captain Hepburn noticed some changes which had been made there. Hilary said they had been suggested by Mr. Ufford, and principally effected by Gwyneth, who had adopted the ideas; for herself, she liked the old way best.

"So do I, Miss Duncan," said Charles, gravely. "The old garden had great charms for me; do you know, Captain Hepburn, I have only once been in this garden since you left England."

"Indeed!" replied the sailor; "whose doing was that then?"

"It was this lady's wish," said Charles, "but I thought it hard. Will you not make interest with her, that I may not be excluded in future? Trust me a little."

"I can not interfere with Miss Duncan's rules or regulations as to her visitors," replied Captain Hepburn, in a tone that might pass for jest or earnest. "If I had any power I might exercise it in your favor: at present, you know, I am only a visitor myself, and can say nothing."

"Papa wants you, Hilary," said Nest, just then running up; and she, taking her little sister's hand, returned to the house, rather glad at that moment to escape.

The gentlemen remained together looking after her, as they stood under the old lime tree on the lawn.

Mr. Huyton was the first to speak.

"We have been rivals, Captain Hepburn, but we need not be enemies; I would gladly prove myself not only your friend, but the friend also of the woman whom I may not love."

His companion thanked him for his professions.

"While you have been gone, it has been my wish still to watch over her happiness, and to guard her in every way. She can tell you that from the day I learned how your success had forever deprived me of hope, I have never breathed a word, nor done a single action which has spoken of any sentiment of which you could disapprove."

"I have no doubt of it," replied Captain Hepburn, frankly; "and allow me to thank you for your many acts of kindness. But you must also permit me to say, that it is for the sake of your own happiness alone, I can form any wishes regarding the extinction of your attachment to Miss Duncan. No doubt it is better for you that it should sink into friendly feeling; otherwise your sentiments toward her, though they may interest, could not disturb me. Her manner of receiving them is all that concerns me, and that has my most entire approval!"

Charles Huyton colored deeply, and bit his lip in silence.

"Excuse my frankness," continued the sailor, "I do not intend to hurt your feelings; I only want to assure you, that I entertain no jealousy or mistrust, and can feel none, while she continues what she is. But you must understand, that my confidence does not arise from your refraining to seek her love, but from her own rectitude and delicacy. Your honorable intentions I have no right to doubt; but my happiness is not dependent on your honor, nor on that of any other man. If she could not guard her own, your forbearance and generosity would avail me little."

"Of course! of course!" said Charles, eagerly, having recovered his composure and complexion; "in her you must have perfect confidence; I hope you may have the same in me. You may, perhaps, be leaving her again; her father's health is failing fast; in the event of his decease the daughters must leave their present home, and I shudder to think of the distress which will befall them. Give me permission at such a time, or in any other moment of trouble, to watch over them with a brother's regard, and extend to them a brother's care. Let me plead your authority for interesting myself in their welfare, and doing whatever may be within my power to comfort and protect them."

"Thank you," said Captain Hepburn, quietly, in reply to Mr. Huyton's earnest enthusiasm. "I am obliged to acknowledge the same thing. Mr. Duncan's health is, I fear, failing rapidly; and sorrow is probably in store for them on that account. She will suffer greatly."

"And will you authorize me to do what I wish; the little that is in my power to protect or shield them in trouble, to comfort and befriend them?"

"You can hardly need my authority, Mr. Huyton, to enable you to act the part of a friend, so far as the usages of society allow. Beyond this, of course, you can not wish to go. Where the world has placed its ban on incurring obligation, or accepting favors, there it is not only prudent but proper not to trespass."

"Oh, my dear sir, the usages of society are narrow and restricted; the ban of the world is cold and cruel; they are invented to excuse selfish indolence, and silence the claims of the helpless and dependent. I would wish to set these aside, and act on my own judgment, as true friendship and kindness may require, regardless of what others may think."

"Excuse me, sir, but the injunction to 'Provide things honest in the sight of all men,' requires that friendship and kindness should regard what may be said of others. The usages of society are founded on a long experience of facts and results; and though they may only aim at controlling appearances, they are not safely to be trampled on; neither is the world in general so very strict in its requisitions as to make it too difficult to comply with them. Depend upon it, they are founded on right principles, although only in themselves the very shell of what is fair and good."

"All I ask is to be trusted; to act as the adopted brother and sincere friend of Miss Duncan and her sisters, in case of trouble."

"So far as Miss Duncan herself will authorize you, I can make no objection, Mr. Huyton: but nominal adoption and confidential friendship between individuals situated as you are, are mere delusions, and have been most judiciously placed in the category of unsafe and unadvisable things, although they may not be actually considered incorrect."

"The fact is," said Charles, with a slightly bitter politeness, "you are afraid to trust me. Well, so be it. If your suspicions interfere to prevent Miss Duncan having a friend in need, I can at least assure you she shall have my best wishes; that is all I can give her."

Hilary returned at this juncture and Mr. Huyton felt himself obliged to take leave, although it was evidently with reluctance that he went.

Fast flew the hours, bright and fast, which Captain Hepburn might spend at Hurstdene; his professional duties too soon forced him away; but he was leaving with the hopes of speedily returning, perhaps for a longer time, perhaps to remain entirely, so the separation could be bravely borne.

"My dearest Hilary," said he, the evening he was to start, for he saved time by traveling all night, "do you know what you are doing by allowing that young man to be so constantly here?"

He looked toward James Ufford, who was loitering as usual on the lawn with Gwyneth and Nest.

"No! What?" was her answer.

"Do you not see that Gwyneth has fallen in love with the curate?"

"No," said Hilary, coloring crimson, "has she?"

"So it appears to me."

"Well, and what then? How could I help it? What must I do? Why should it signify?"

"Signify! do you think Mr. Ufford intended it?"

"I do not know. I am sure Gwyneth has not such an idea in her head; perhaps they are both unconscious; but don't you like him?"

"Not much. I do not think he is *real*. He should talk less, and act more. He may be half in love himself with Gwyneth; but it is in that aimless, purposeless way, which will never grow to any good end. He likes to keep her to himself; he likes to talk to her; but while he can amuse himself as he does, enjoying her admiration and devotion, and feeling sure of her preference, he will not ever care to exert himself for more."

"But what can I do?" said Hilary, distressed.

"Now a clever, active, manœuvering mother might fix him directly. Any one, in fact, who would condescend to use the requisite arts and exertions. There is a tact in managing these affairs, which few girls possess. They are sincere, ardent, yet shy, modest, undemonstrative; they can do nothing but waste their own affections. It never succeeds with a character like Mr. Ufford's, compounded of much good, alloyed by selfish and self-indulgent vanity."

"But, Captain Hepburn, would you have me manœuver to secure a wavering heart for my sister? I can not stoop to that."

"No, Hilary, I would not have you different from what you are: but I wish Mr. Ufford went further off. I have no confidence in him. It is a pity that you admitted him to such constant intercourse."

"I am very sorry," said she, humbly: "it was my imprudence. I did not know better. I am so ignorant; but perhaps you do not understand Gwyneth aright. She is enthusiastic and ardent in her fancies, but they do not always endure. What could I do now to prevent an intercourse which has grown up so naturally out of our relative situations?"

"That is exactly the question that I have asked myself again and again, without seeming to be at all nearer finding an answer. I am afraid it is one of those imprudences which are irretrievable: which, in fact, are only proved to be so by the result. You know there are steps which once taken, can not be retraced, and actions of which we can not choose but bear the consequences. This is poor comfort for you, dear Hilary; but do not distress yourself so, my love; perhaps the effects on Gwyneth may not be evil. I may have imputed too much to her."

"She is so young," said Hilary; "oh, I hope I have not helped to make her unhappy."

"Yes, she is very young; young enough to recover from an infatuation of the kind, should she find her idol is only made of clay, and to be better and wiser for the experiment."

"I do believe her admiration is the result of religious feeling; she would think little of him if he were not our clergyman. It was that attracted her."

"These two feelings are constantly acting and reacting on each other, in rather a confusing way in women. Personal regard for the minister is either the origin or the result of attention to his doctrines; and one is constantly increased by the other."

"It seems so natural, so unavoidable, to care for one who teaches us our highest duties; instructs us in our dearest interests," interposed she, apologetically.

"Yes, it is essentially the nature of woman's religion, to seek to expand itself, pour itself out on some visible object. Hence has sprung the influence which, in every system, the clergy attained over the female world. It matters little whether it is the priest in the confessional, or the Presbyterian minister in his congregation. The degree of power may differ occasionally, but its source is the same; and where weak heads and lively feelings meet, the result is perpetually an effervescing enthusiasm, often troublesome and unsatisfactory at the time, and liable to wear itself out, leaving deadness and flatness behind it."

"You are hard upon us."

"Am I? I do not mean to be unjust: and though I admit there is a great deal of folly exhibited by those who are guilty of this idolatry, I respect it in comparison with what I feel toward those idols who consciously encourage the worship. I should not choose to express my opinion of those men, who, taking advantage of this feminine peculiarity gratify their vanity, or indulge their love of excitement, by winning, under the cover of religious instruction, affections which they never intended to justify. My words would shock you!"

"Are such things done, out of books and plays? in real life?"

"Are they not? but you, dearest, can but little answer such a question; and the flagrant examples which come beneath one's own knowledge, are not what one can quote or repeat. Suppose you were to call Gwyneth in at this moment. Can you not make an excuse for interrupting that eternal wandering under the trees?"

"Oh, yes, I really want her, and I, too, am wasting my time here; there are some things to be looked out for Maurice, which you ought to have to pack up. Would you tell her, please?"

Accordingly, Gwyneth was summoned into the house, and Captain Hepburn joined the young clergyman on the lawn.

"How beautiful this place looks under a setting sun," observed the former, gazing round.

"Yes—pretty well. I shall make a great change, though, if ever it is mine. Many of these trees must come down, and the flower-garden must be modernized; it is in wretched taste."

"It seems to me to suit well with the house; are you a gardener!" inquired Captain Hepburn.

"Not personally in the least; but I like to have things nice, only somebody must do the work for me; I know nothing of details," replied Mr. Ufford.

"I always think a practical knowledge and love of gardening, give a certain reality and sincerity to a man's character, which is singularly useful; especially in your profession, Mr. Ufford."

"It would be a curious speculation," replied the other, "whether facts bear out your idea. I will take it into consideration, whether the best gardeners of my acquaintance are the best clergymen, and the most practical men. Would not a love of construction save a man's character? I have a great fancy for building, I own; and I expect some day to realize my plans on the Vicarage. That old house must come down. I could not live in it."

"I have received so much kindness here," replied his companion, "that I can not contemplate such a change without regret. It is a comfort, however, to think that when an event so trying to the Vicar's daughters arrives, as that which will make you master here, they will have a friend, and not a stranger, to deal with."

"Poor things! I am really sorry for them," said the curate; "it will be a sad trouble. I think an Elizabethan house would look best here; would suit the place and country. Don't you?" eyeing the old Vicarage as he spoke with an air of consideration.

"I have not thought about it at all," replied Captain Hepburn, with internal disgust. "I fear they will be sadly forlorn and unprotected; their brother away, perhaps, and they so young and ignorant of the world."

"You are unnecessarily anxious about them, Captain Hepburn; they will find friends, depend on it. I can understand your feelings of interest, however, although I can take more cheerful views of their prospects. Believe me, nothing on my part shall be wanting. I have strong motives to influence me—my sincere gratitude—remembrance of kindness received—regard, honor; in short, make yourself easy. Their comfort and happiness shall be my first object. I pledge myself to that. Pray trust me!"

Roused out of his selfish dreams, Mr. Ufford spoke what he felt at the time, and meant all that he said. Captain Hepburn could understand his words and tones to have but one meaning; his admiration for Gwyneth was sincere, and his purposes settled. If he had not the steadfast, straightforward strength of will, which the sailor possessed, he might yet have sufficient firmness of character to secure his own respectability, and Gwyneth's happiness. One must not quarrel with a man because he is more cautious in his movements, or more slow in his decision, then one's self. Captain Hepburn hoped the best from him, and while he trusted his warning to Hilary might not be useless, he flattered himself that his fears might be entirely unfounded.

"I shall trust implicitly to such an assurance, satisfied that they will have a friend in you. They have their brother-in-law in London, to take care of them in case of need," continued Captain Hepburn; "I have a great respect for Mr. Farrington; from what I have heard of him, he must be a very well-judging man."

"I must be going," said Mr. Ufford; "if the young ladies are busy, I dare say they will not care to see me just now; pray make my excuses to them. I wish you a good journey;" and he went accordingly.

Two hours afterward, Captain Hepburn was also on his road to London, speculating a little on whether he had done more good than harm, by what he had ventured to say about Mr. Ufford. The first result of his observations was, that after a great deal of indecision, Hilary took courage to hint to Gwyneth, that now she had really grown up, and was neither in years nor person a child, she should be careful to behave as became a young woman, and that it might be as well, perhaps, to adopt a little more reserve toward Mr. Ufford, and not spend quite so much time in his society. Gwyneth heard her quietly, took in her meaning, and secretly deduced from it the assurance, that Hilary probably thought the curate was falling in love with her, a notion which had not before crossed her mind. Hitherto her admiration had been, so far as she knew, purely of a spiritual nature; but this observation gave it another turn, and from considering Mr. Ufford in the light of a superior being, raised above human weaknesses, and only to be admired at an humble distance, she suddenly discovered that he was a gentleman, an unmarried man, and a young man, and one whose affections and future intentions might be subjects for speculation and doubt.

That he was heir-presumptive to a barony, and might look for rank and fortune in his wife, if he chose to have one, occurred to her at the same time with a sudden chill, which depressed her spirits to a painful extent; it was little likely that he would stoop to a portionless and undistinguished girl like herself, unless—and the thought gave her peculiar pleasure—he should really have fallen in love with her, as he told her Mr. Huyton had done with Hilary. The contrast between herself and the clergyman was not greater than between this other couple; and if love had been so strong in one case, why not in another?

So she reasoned with herself, and concealed her feelings, and resolved to wait and watch his conduct. Apparently, Mr. Ufford was anxious to justify his promises, and prove his friendship to the Vicar's daughters. His visits were for the next two days quite in the usual style, quietly walking in just when it suited him. Hilary, however, was more watchful, and allowed no more of those unrestricted rambles which had latterly been so greatly extended. Gwyneth had more occupation at home, and was obliged to be quiet and useful.

The third day brought an entirely new set of ideas. A letter came from Captain Hepburn, which was of some importance to their plans. The first page of this letter, though, no doubt, gratifying to the receiver, need not be transcribed; what relates to my narrative ran as follows:

"The result of the survey is that the boilers are found in a very bad state, and need so much repair, that in the mean time the whole ship's company are to be turned over to the *Erratic*, a sister-ship, just getting ready for sea. This alters my plans, and puts an end to all hopes of a few months' rest on shore. We shall probably be off again in less than a month, and for who knows how long! no prospect of another leave long enough to reach Hurstdene; I could almost regret the change of ship, and do heartily wish she had not been in so advanced a state. However, it would be foolish, as well as wrong, to murmur at what most men would consider a singular piece of good fortune. But, my darling, shall I not see you again? can you not all come to London? We talked it all over, Sybil, Maurice, and I, yesterday, for I got your sister and her husband to come down and look at the steamer, and she is delighted at the plan. They can take you all in, she says, and she, of course, would be gratified by a visit from her father. It is almost your only chance now of seeing Maurice. Do arrange and come immediately."

There was a letter from Sybil to the same effect, and a most pressing one from Maurice, urging the proposal most warmly.

There was no room for hesitation, and no time for delay. Arrangements were made in haste, and the evening of the next day saw the family domiciled for the present at Mr. Farrington's.

Maurice was there to receive them; the captain had sacrificed his own pleasure, and allowed the leave to his first lieutenant, which they could not both have at once.

It is not my intention to narrate minutely all the events which occurred in London; the interviews between the lovers, the excursions to Woolwich, to inspect the *Erratic*, and many other particulars not directly bearing on the result to Hilary. Days passed rapidly, and except for the parting in prospect, would have been very happy. There was a charming uncertainty about the chances of meeting, which increased the pleasure; and besides, there was enough of novelty in the great change to three girls from the forest, to excite and interest them.

Mr. Duncan never would allow his inability to accompany them on many excursions to interfere with their enjoyments; he had his own share, he said, in the different accounts they brought back to him, and it would be a positive loss to him, if either of his daughters were to shut herself up on his account; he had long ago learned to read by himself, and although he had never attained the fluency and ease which some blind persons acquire, perhaps from beginning so late in life, he was yet independent in some respects, and able to occupy his lonely hours by the study now dearer to him than any other, of the Book of Life, which had been his consolation and support in all his trials.

"Shall I, or my rival, have the pleasure of your society to-morrow?" said Hilary, laughingly, to her lover, one evening. His visits were generally made after the hours of work in the dockyard were over.

"Are you jealous of the wandering lady at Woolwich, Hilary?" was his answer.

"Perhaps I might be, if I did not know that, as you deserted her predecessor, and transferred your attentions to her, so you would be equally ready to forsake your present favorite on detecting some defect in her constitution or her powers."

"A sad specimen of inconstancy," said he, playfully.

"No, not inconstancy," replied she, "because the feeling remains the same; it is devotion to your profession which actuates you, and the ship, though well-beloved for a time, is cared for only as an embodiment; a visible symbol of this feeling. It is your profession which is really my rival."

"You are wrong, love; to which did I devote myself first?"

"Ah! you mean that I am the rival," said she, looking up, with a smile.

"My profession is my duty, Hilary," said he, gravely; "would you rival that? I hope not."

"Never!" was her energetic answer. "And yet, am I only your plaything?" it was spoken with hesitation.

"That depends on yourself, Hilary!"

She looked as if to ask how; but pondered in silence.

"You may be, I trust you will be, my good angel! my better self! to inspirit, cheer, guide me in the path of honor; not the weight to draw me back, the bait to allure me to forget the grand object of life."

"That is not professional honor!" said she, doubtingly.

"No, it is to do my duty in the state of life to which it has pleased God to call me," was his quiet answer. "And, Hilary, professional honor is only dear to me, I trust, in so far as it may reflect light on a profession dearer still—that of a Christian warrior."

"Ah! I felt that was the foundation of your zeal."

"The only sure foundation, love; the feeling, or rather the principle, which will carry one unflinchingly through danger, difficulty, trouble of every kind. Life to every one is full of deep mystic meaning; the life of a sailor above all. The troubled waves, the wearying calm, the changeful winds, the uncertain currents, the dangerous rocks and shoals, the tedious length of voyage, the joyous arrival at home, all realities to us, are figures appropriated to mystic subjects. Then we have the lonely watch, the strict discipline, the hardships and self-denial, the temperance, the necessary obedience to superiors; ought not each one of these to remind the Christian of the duties of his calling? each in itself a religious duty exemplified!"

"Like the chivalrous devoirs of the knightly warriors of old," said Hilary; "an actual realization in deed of the intangible theories of the Christian faith."

"Yes! the whole of a sailor's life is an allegory; an acted picture of things unseen. But that is not what I meant to speak of when alluding to a possible rivalry between duty and you. Hilary, while health and strength are granted to me, they must be at my country's service when required; and no domestic tie, not even that of a wife, dear as it may be, may interfere. Not from the old heathen pride in patriotism which made one's country's glory the idol of life, but for the higher, holier reason, the belief that my path has been appointed by my Heavenly Father; and that to follow it with all my might, is but doing my duty in its simplest form. Do you not think me right? Life itself, were I called on to lay it down on service, would be gladly devoted; not to win the praise of men here, but to testify to the truth and sincerity of my profession!"

Hilary's eyes filled; and as she sat silently thinking on his words, almost unconsciously her fingers pressed the ring which he had placed there as a sign of their betrothal. He watched her countenance anxiously.

"You are not satisfied," continued he; "your look asks where you come in my estimation of life. Is not that it?"

"Am I selfish? I did think that."

"First of this world's objects; reward of labor and peril here in hours of rest; companion for ever in that life where duty will involve no sacrifice, and love will bring no pain or tears."

She could not answer, except by the quivering lip and drooping eyelid, which spoke of strong, but suppressed, emotion.

"I had not loved thee, dear, so much, loved I not honor more!" continued he, taking her hands in his, and speaking in a voice of ineffable tenderness.

"I believe it! I feel it!" she answered, eagerly. "I know that while Heaven has the first place in your heart, I am sure of retaining my rightful portion there. I am not, indeed, I am not jealous of your devotion to what is so high and holy—only—"

"Only what?" inquired he, as she hesitated.

"Only I would rather you should serve your country, mankind, and above all, the cause of religion, by living, and not—" her words failed her again.

"To every man upon this earth death cometh soon or late," was his reply; "and, Hilary, ever since I can remember, it has been my dream, my wish, my hope to devote my life—I do not mean to *live*, but to *die*—in some great, high, holy cause, something which may show that a Christian, with the hope of salvation and the promise of Heaven, is not afraid to do and dare all that a heathen warrior might have done with the poor promise of an earthly glory. But to no other ear than your own would I breathe this aspiration; who else would understand my feelings? In confiding to you the deepest passion of my soul, Hilary, I prove to you how I have merged my life in yours. To ordinary companions such thoughts do not find words to express them."

"They do better," said she, with a glowing cheek and sparkling eye; "they find actions. You have proved your sincerity again and again in your dauntless defiance of danger. Yes, and I will not draw you back; woman though I am I will not weaken you, nor bid you pause for my sake: rather let the thought of me nerve you in the hour of danger, make you stronger, braver, more intrepid in a worthy cause. And should our hope be fulfilled— ah! believe me, I will try to follow your example, and bear the agony for your sake, that you may wear a martyr's crown!"

"My own, true-hearted love!" was his only answer.

CHAPTER XVIII.

"Love, I feel thy bitter smart
Wildly throbbing through my heart,
Waking, sleeping,
Smiling, weeping,
Still I think of thee!"

Mr. Barham and his daughters were in London at this time, and a few days after the Duncans' arrival, Hilary and Sybil went together to call on them. The girls were very cordial and glad to meet, especially Dora, who had ascertained that the *Pandanus* had arrived in England, and was, in consequence, in a desperate state of internal anxiety to hear some news of Maurice.

While they were chatting together, Mr. Barham himself walked in, very gracefully gracious when he discovered who the visitors were; quite surprised to learn that they were visiting Sybil, and in London, without his knowledge, and taking some civil interest in the present object of their chief concern.

"I do not know any thing about these new steamers," observed he, "I have never had an opportunity of studying these subjects; yet it is an important one, one which deserves the attention of those who hold a large stake in their country's welfare; being a subject which must strongly affect the interest of a great naval power. I must take the matter into consideration."

"I am sure my brother would be happy to show you his new ship, if you would honor the *Erratic* with a visit," observed Sybil, very proud of Maurice and his steamer also.

"Well, Mrs. Farrington, that would be a good idea; what do you say, Isabel? suppose we were to make an excursion to Woolwich!" observed he.

"It really would be worth while," said Miss Barham; "as you say, sir, one ought to know something about the great means of defense for our nation. I think it would be a proper thing to do; and as we know both the captain and lieutenant a little we could not have a better opportunity than now."

"Be it so, then," was his answer. "How shall we arrange about time? it might be we should go at an inconvenient hour, without some previous arrangement. How can you communicate with your brother, Mrs. Farrington?"

"He will be up with us this afternoon, I expect," replied Sybil; "shall I send him to you if he comes? That would be simple."

"Exactly! that would simplify the matter, as you say. Isabel, the gentleman might dine with us, I think. The table will not be too full."

Hilary listened and said not a word; Dora, too, sat in silence, but her deep interest in the subject could not be concealed from one who suspected its existence. Finally, it was settled without her intervention, that Maurice should be there for a seven o'clock dinner, and if he liked, Miss Barham added, to accompany them to the opera afterward, they would be very much honored. Would not Hilary join their party? They would be nearly alone, only Mr. Huyton would be with them.

It was fortunate she mentioned him, or the temptation to accompany Maurice would have been irresistible; but that name was enough. Hilary decidedly declined, and wondering much what the result would be, the ladies took leave, and returned home.

"I can not go, Hilary," said Maurice, when he heard the invitation; "must I?" He looked exceedingly disturbed. Sybil, perfectly unaware of any private reasons, pressed it warmly. He must, it would be so rude if he had no reason to give; and then it did not matter, however dull it might be to go, he could not escape this visit to the ship, and it would be much better to be civil, and they were always kind, even though Mr. Barham was tiresome; and he would like to meet Mr. Huyton, who was to be there, and really the two young ladies were worth seeing, they were so pretty!

Maurice laughed off his embarrassment, by declaring Sybil's arguments were exemplary *non-sequiturs*; but at the same time suffered himself to be persuaded into what he wished above all things.

His ideas of time that evening before setting out, were somewhat wild, and the pains that he took at his toilette were not to be told. He succeeded in reaching the house rather early, and found, as he had perhaps guessed by intuition that he should, Dora alone in her drawing-room! Their meeting had all the flutter and emotion of forbidden pleasure; time had not changed his feelings in the least, and although hers had by no means been so invariably constant, she fancied that they had, and told him so, and that did pretty nearly as well. The sight of the handsome lieutenant, with his pleasant smile, and captivating manner, revived her somewhat declining affections, and the conviction that during two years of absence, she had yet retained all her former power over him, gratified her vanity, as well as her tenderness toward him.

Their interview was short; another knock at the door warned them of intruders, and sent Dora hastily from the room, while Maurice turned round to greet Charles Huyton, whose entrance he had been prepared to expect. Dora did not reappear until the moment dinner was announced, just in time to be consigned by her father to Mr. Duncan's protection, and she had pretty well recovered her complexion and her serenity when they took their places at table.

How delightfully the evening went, need not be told; the delicious little momentary interviews, while cloaking the ladies for the Opera, the whispered words, the meeting of hands with a thrilling emotion, the pleasure of sitting beside each other in the carriage, the intervals when other persons claimed Isabel's attention, and allowed Maurice leisure to devote himself to Dora; the stolen glances, the intelligent, and yet hidden smiles, in fact, all the dear and dangerous sweets of a clandestine affection, need not be dwelt on. Then there was the grand, crowning hope of another meeting, the plan for the excursion to Woolwich, which was fixed for the ensuing Tuesday, when it was settled that a large party should unite to inspect the *Erratic*; affording Mr. Barham and Isabel, and such patriots as were concerned for the good of the nation, an opportunity of improving their knowledge on an important subject, and providing for others who were satisfied with more personal and less philanthropic views, an occasion of a pleasant social meeting, and an agreeable refreshment. The Duncans, of course, were to join the party, and Mr. Farrington, if he could steal a day from briefs and business. Charles Huyton was to be there also. Isabel asked him; they were to go down by water, and the point of rendezvous, the hour, and the various other particulars were all settled with accuracy by Mr. Barham himself.

It was not destined, however, to take place quite so soon. A slight indisposition on Mr. Barham's part obliged him to defer the engagement; for however anxious he might be to benefit the nation at large, by his practical knowledge regarding screw steamers, yet he believed himself to be conferring a still more important advantage on society, in taking care of his own health; at least, this was the reason assigned for the change of plan, which considerably disappointed some of the party concerned.

Be his reason good or bad, the excursion was put off for a week, and in the mean time, each day that Maurice happened to be in town, he considered it his positive duty to go and call in Eaton-place, to learn how the invalid was, and when it would suit him to fulfill his promise. Once or twice too, it happened, through some contrivance of Mr. Huyton's and Dora's, the families met in excursions for other objects, and Hilary was occasionally thrown into company with Charles; but as there was never any thing in his behavior to distress her, she was beginning to feel hardened regarding such meetings, and to view them with much indifference.

Indeed, her feelings were too deeply engrossed by other matters to have much thought to bestow on her former lover. Dora and Maurice made her very uncomfortable; they seemed perfectly infatuated now; were more desperately in love than ever; and Hilary could not help expecting that some grand discovery and consequent domestic disturbance would be the result. She wondered neither Isabel nor Mr. Barham appeared to notice it. That Charles Huyton had, she knew, for he had hinted it to her, with a significance and expression not to be mistaken. But it was not really so evident as her fears and consciousness made her imagine; Charles discovered it partly by former observations of his own, but more now, by watching her eyes, and reading their anxious and troubled looks.

But the hour of parting was drawing near: the *Erratic* was almost ready for sea; the crew were on board, and she was reported fit to sail in four days more. Now then must be the Woolwich party, or never. Mr. Barham was well—agreed to the plan once more—the weather was fine—the day and hour came, and they started. It was not to be expected that Mr. Barham would expose his daughters to the contaminating mixture of society to be met with in an ordinary river steamer; they had one hired expressly for the occasion, and every thing was in as first-rate a style as possible.

Fair shone the sun on the river Thames, as they steamed down its waters, so famous as a channel of commerce and a subject of indignant complaint to the citizens of London; and merrily the party were dashed along, while Mr. Barham descanted learnedly on the subject of trade and landholders, Britain's position, privileges, and duties, and the grand part which a resident proprietor, and one who did his duty to his country, filled in the vast affairs of the nation; while Isabel leaned on his arm and approved, and Charles Huyton cast anxious glances at Hilary, and longed to place himself beside her; and the others moved about, and talked nonsense at random, and with great enjoyment.

They reached their destination at last, landed, and were met, as had been agreed on, by the captain of the *Erratic*, who conducted them forthwith to the dock where the steamer still lay. The happy first lieutenant received them at the gangway, authorized by every circumstance to take Dora under his peculiar care, even as her elder sister was the natural charge, for the time being, of the captain.

To the quarter-deck they went first, where they all remained to chat and discuss their voyage, to peep over the bulwarks, and ask questions about the vessels lying alongside; or to gaze up with admiration and wonder at the complicated ropes and spars towering overhead.

The Barhams were quite new to such a scene, and Isabel was rather more ignorant of the realities of sailor-life than Dora, who was supposed never to know any thing at all, so that Captain Hepburn had his time and attention fully occupied by the questions and observations of Miss Barham and her father, and could only contemplate Hilary from a distance. Maurice had lost nothing in personal appearance by his uniform, which Dora, for the first time, saw him wear; his crisp brown hair looked particularly fascinating, curling out from under the gold-laced cap which sat so gracefully, she thought, upon his head. Hilary, too, looked at her lover with feelings of admiration; but it was not merely for his personal charms; she loved to watch the quick motion of those fine dark eyes, the intelligence and kindness they conveyed, agreeing so well with the firm, yet sweet expression of the mouth; she loved, best of all, to see those eyes settle on her with a deep, grave look, and to know that it was concern for her interest, and anxiety for her happiness, which filled them with such unutterable tenderness; a tenderness that would have prompted him, she knew, to sacrifice any thing of this world, any pleasure, any advantage, any hope to secure her happiness and welfare.

Admiration for Maurice's handsome face had much to do with Dora's love, but Hilary's admiration was rather the result than the source of hers.

A summons to luncheon in the captain's cabin called them to the first serious concern for their visit; and when the repast was concluded, it was judged appropriate to perambulate the whole ship, and inspect every thing worth seeing. This ceremony concluded, the party landed, determined to walk round the dock-yard, and see some of the works carried on there.

Out of his own vessel, Captain Hepburn by no means considered that duty any longer attached him to Miss Barham, and by a little skillful arrangement, and judicious patience, he succeeded, for the first time, in securing Hilary as his own companion. Sybil was tired, and wished to sit down, while the greater part of the visitors continued their investigations; and her elder sister was not unwilling to remain with her under the special guardianship of Captain Hepburn, whose uniform was a certain protection against the inquiries and suspicions of correct policemen, anxious to secure her Majesty's dockyard from the possible evil designs of unknown ladies and civilians.

"Now, Hilary, I have one thing to say, one request to make, which, had I time to spare, I would either omit, or produce with a proper preface; but I can not do either."

So began he, as soon as the others were out of hearing. Hilary raised her eyes to his face with a look of questioning anxiety.

"Sybil, I trust you will support my petition," continued he, "so I shall speak before you without hesitation; Hilary, my prayer is, that you will become my wife before I leave England."

"Captain Hepburn!" ejaculated she, coloring.

"Why not? you have already promised one day to be so; why not fulfill that promise at once, and let me know you irrevocably mine before I leave you?"

"Do you doubt me, then? do you mistrust my faith?" asked she, hesitatingly.

"If I did, Hilary, I should never have urged such a request; if *I* thought you would change, I should have small wish to make you my wife. No, it is no selfish desire to secure any good to myself, or to gratify a jealous and mistrustful affection, dearest; it is your own comfort and welfare which occupy my mind."

"I believe it," said she, frankly, placing her hand in his; "and as I have promised to be one day your wife, I will make no foolish and idle objections. But—"

"But what, love?"

"I do not see the reason, the occasion, the propriety of this step; so sudden—I had not thought of it."

"I am aware that there are objections, but they seem to me slight compared with the advantages of the measure," said he, gravely. "What say you, Sybil, does it shock you so much?"

"No, indeed!" cried she, speaking with all the enthusiasm of a happy young wife, "I think there would be no harm, if there is time."

"We could manage that, unless Hilary is very particular about her gown and bonnet," said he, smiling; "and even such things can be got in London, on the shortest notice, if she wants them."

"Ah, no, I do not care for that," said Hilary; "but tell me what you ask, and why, and give me time to think and breathe; if I were to—to do this—I can not leave my father, even to follow you, Captain Hepburn."

"No, that is not what I mean; don't be so frightened, and look so pale, dear Hilary; we move out of dock and drop down the river on Saturday, probably about the middle of the day; what I ask is, that early on that morning, you would meet me at the church here, and become my wife;

the business part I will arrange. Your whole party could come with you to Woolwich, your father and all; and Maurice would be there too; surely that would secure respectability enough! and then when I leave you, you shall be as much your own mistress with regard to your movements as ever. Hurstdene can be your home during your father's life, Hilary; but should you lose that, before I return, you would have at least the additional protection which the name of a married woman can confer; and in this country that is of no small importance. And, Hilary, then you would be forever safe from the intrusions, the attentions, the insidious friendship of Mr. Huyton."

"Do you fear him?" said she, looking up.

"I mistrust him; as to *fear*, that is not the word. Once my wife, and you will be safe, there will be nothing for him to hope more, and, perhaps his passion will really expire; but till then, I am certain he will continue to haunt you, and his disposition makes me tremble."

"You judge him hardly," said Sybil; "you are a prejudiced rival."

"Not a jealous one, at least, Sybil: but I watched him to-day; I saw his face darken and his very lips grow pale, as his eyes fell on the portrait of Hilary, in my cabin. I saw a world of evil and envious passions pass over his brow as he stood and gazed at it. He said the truth when he declared in the hut in the forest, that while you continued single he would never cease trying to win you. Let me place one insurmountable barrier between you and him, and let us extinguish the last faint hope of your changing. He will then leave you in peace."

Hilary paused, pondered, and hesitated. "It is so soon," was all that she could say in objection, there really seemed no other to urge.

"However long you defer it, if your wedding day is ever to come at all, we shall eventually come within four days of it," observed he, smiling a little.

"So sudden!" ejaculated she again.

"I thought you had been contemplating it these two years past—I am sure I have," was his answer.

This time she could not forbear smiling a little herself, and the day was won by her lover.

"Really," observed Sybil, "I think you are quite right, nobody can call it sudden after an engagement of two years; and if the next three days allow all necessary arrangements to be made, the time is as good as a month or two."

"I do not suppose many people will concern themselves about our wedding," replied he; "and those who do, may have facts explained to them."

It was agreed to before the rest of the party rejoined them, and the thanks and gratitude of the gentleman were also sufficiently expressed.

It made Hilary very grave and thoughtful for the whole way home, although Captain Hepburn was by her side, and trying to cheer her. She was reviewing what she had undertaken; yet it was by no means alarming. There was no new anxiety or responsibility thrown on her at present; nothing which need break in on her quiet course of life, or disturb her care for her father and sisters. His absence would not be more painful, nor occasion greater uneasiness, and she should at least bear his dear name, have an open, acknowledged claim to care for him, an avowed interest in his welfare and prosperity. And at some future time, she might hope for protection, support, assistance from him, to guard and guide her through life's troubles when they came. Such were her thoughts, as she leaned upon his arm, and spent the time in a dream which left her no notice to bestow on those around her.

When the plan was announced in the family party that evening, it was highly approved by all; even Mr. Farrington gave his opinion in favor of the arrangement, especially after he had some private conversation with Captain Hepburn respecting settlements and such lawyer-like affairs. To arrange these matters effectually before Saturday, was impossible; but the lover had no intention of profiting by the haste he urged in a pecuniary way.

Hilary's portion, being her share of her mother's fortune, was five thousand pounds; and the whole of this, with an addition that nearly doubled it from himself, he promised to settle on her, empowering his future brother-in-law to see the business arranged, and granting him such legal authority as he recommended, to proceed about it. But of these matters Hilary knew nothing, and she never gave the subject a thought; whether she would be richer or poorer for the marriage, she did not know; the wealth of love and protection she was acquiring satisfying her for the present.

Had there been no peculiar necessity for haste, in the conclusion of the marriage, nothing would have been further from Miss Duncan's wish than to have a public wedding. A cortège of bridesmaids, a splendid breakfast, a grand assembly of fine bonnets, and fine dresses, seemed to her simple and youthful mind altogether inconsistent with a solemn religious ceremony, although perfectly befitting the more worldly view in which this engagement is too often considered. Quietness, simplicity, and solemnity, would have been her objects, such as would neither invite criticism, call for observation, nor serve as a display for vanity and pomp. She would have been the last to desire to publish their intentions, or to call on her neighbors for congratulations or envy. But the same delicacy which would have made her shrink from display now acted somewhat differently, in producing a fear that a clandestine appearance might be the result of this haste. There were few, indeed, who would concern themselves about her or her proceedings; but it was these very few whose opinions she valued, or whose censure she wished to avoid. It was this feeling which induced her to impart her intended marriage to Miss Barham and her sister when they met on the Thursday afternoon. The young ladies were extremely interested in the narration, and expressed a great desire to be present at the ceremony themselves. Dora first started this idea, but Isabel was pleased with it, and finally it was settled that if their father did not object they should join the wedding party; although Gwyneth and Sybil both laughingly declared they would never be able to rise early enough.

"Rather than not do that," exclaimed Dora, "I would sit up all night!"

Hilary thought she understood the secret of Dora's extreme anxiety, and hardly knew whether to be most sorry or glad that Maurice and she should have the dangerous pleasure of another meeting. It seemed to her to be only laying up additional stores of sorrowful remembrance and hopeless regret. But the company of the sisters was offered and pressed in such a way as to leave little real choice to her on the occasion. Yet, why Isabel Barham should so wish to be present, as to propose taking the trouble of rising much earlier than usual, and driving all the way to Woolwich before ten o'clock, was a little incomprehensible. Sybil said privately that Isabel liked a freak as well as any body where it did not compromise her dignity, and that this little exertion had a degree of novelty about it which made it irresistible to one weary with the platitudes of polite society and elegant decorums. Even Isabel had her portion of romance in her character, and though she would never do any thing incorrect herself, she yet enjoyed the sort of secrecy and mystery which naturally attended the present affair.

Mr. Barham made no objection to his daughters' plans, and according to the latest arrangements, the carriage from Eaton-place brought the two young ladies over to Mrs. Farrington's in very good time to take an early, though rather hurried breakfast, with the bridal party, before starting on their long drive to Woolwich.

It all seemed unreal and strange to Hilary, as she sat by her father's side during that drive. Her thoughts were very busy, and yet would not settle on any thing steadily. The purpose of the present meeting, the engagement she was about to contract, occupied her less than the parting which must immediately follow. Happiness was very far from her heart; patience and hope were what she needed. The most unwavering confidence, the most perfect dependence and trust prevented her having any misgivings as to the step she was taking. She had no hesitation in bestowing her hand where her heart had long preceded it. Up to that point her path was easy and bright, and could he but have remained with her she would not have had a shadow to dim her serenity. But that inevitable absence, what a chasm, what a dark, impenetrable abyss it seemed; what an abrupt termination to the sunshiny road she had been lately treading; how uncertain its length and its depth? All she knew of it was that it was dark and dreary in prospect, and that she must pass it as best she could, bridging it over with hope, and faith, and patience, and an earnest steady perseverance in daily duties. These would bring her to that other side, which now seemed so dim, so uncertain, so distant, and yet which appeared to the fancy, through all the mists of futurity, fair and pleasant in prospect.

So her mind wandered away while her eyes were fixed on the passing houses and the flying trees, to scenes where all would be certainty, and enjoyment, and peace; and as she looked upward at the clear, blue sky; unsullied by the smoke, and undisturbed by the noise and bustle of the vast city, whose long suburbs they were traversing, she thought of that future which alone may be depended on, that love which never wearies or grows cold, that protecting care which can not err nor cease. She remembered that her lover and herself had alike anchored their hearts there, with the sure anchor of Hope, her restless fears dispersed, and her heart grew calm and quiet.

There was no hinderance, no delay; the drive to Woolwich had been so accurately calculated, that they reached the church within two minutes of the time appointed; the gentlemen were ready, waiting their arrival, and after a very brief interval more, the couple stood side by side, and hand in hand, to answer those words which bound them for life to each other.

Concentrating every feeling in the present moment, giving her whole heart and soul to the words she was repeating, and the prayers in which she was called on to join, the bride forgot all that was immediately to follow, and went through with a calm, grave, self-possession her part in the short and yet impressive ceremony.

And they were pronounced to be man and wife; and it was over, and the party gathered in the vestry to sign the register, and whisper a few subdued words of good wishes (for who could talk of congratulations or joy at that moment?) and Hilary awoke to a consciousness that it was all real. She leaned against the end of the table, while her husband held her hand in silent, speechless, subdued emotion; as if nerving his whole frame, gathering all his strength of mind for the great trial before them. It needed not words to tell her how he felt; she knew it in the close and tender clasp of those fingers on her own; she read it in the grave, sad look of his eyes, in the lines of emotion about his mouth, which his utmost efforts could not conceal.

However, the parting need not be immediately, there was yet an hour of reprieve; the tide would not serve till afternoon for the steamer to leave the dock, and it had been before arranged, that the wedding guests should all go to the hotel, where a second breakfast, most acceptable to those who had left London so early, was prepared for them by the bridegroom's orders; as in the *Erratic*, in her present state, it was not convenient to receive such a party. But what was the use of lingering at such a time? true, every minute was precious, and yet every minute was pain. Little mirth and little conversation was there at that board, where even yet the time, though dull, went all too fast.

They rose from the table, and, as if by one consent, the guests betook themselves to the balcony overlooking the river, that the parting between the husband and wife might at least be undisturbed. None remained with them, save the blind father, who was sitting, as if in a reverie, in a large arm-chair.

Hilary hung on her husband's neck in speechless grief; ah! this was a different thing from parting two years ago; and yet why? now that he was all her own, why did it make it so infinitely harder to let him leave her?

"My wife, my own dear wife! we shall meet again!"

She tried to smile a "yes," but tongue and lips alike disobeyed, and tears alone answered her best efforts to be calm.

"Hilary, your brother-in-law will tell you about settlements, what, as my wife, your income will be; I can not speak of money now; only I am thankful that I can assure you an independence, which to your moderate wishes will be comfort, and almost wealth. Now farewell, my own, my best-beloved, my darling! God guide and bless you—once, and once more! and now farewell!"

He placed her on a sofa, hurried to the balcony to see his other friends, whispered to Sybil to take care of her precious sister, and wrung the hands of all the bridesmaids in silent sorrow and repressed feeling; then he returned to the parlor. Hilary sat as he had left her, absorbed in an endeavor to conquer her despairing grief, by thoughts of hope and aspirations for patience. She heard her father call Captain Hepburn to him. She heard the warmest blessings invoked upon his head; she listened almost as if in a dream, as if it concerned some other than herself; but when her husband's step again approached her, she roused herself at once; with a short exclamation, speaking of unutterable struggles within, she sprang up, threw herself into his arms, held him for one moment in silence, and then withdrawing calmly from his embrace, she said, with energy —

"Now go! I will never be a hinderance to you in the path of duty. Go, we shall meet again in happier times, and then! — "

"And then: ah, Hilary! — "

Eyes and lips finished the sentence, but not with words, and he was gone!

Maurice must go next; there had been but little intercourse between him and Dora; he had seemed to shun her, and to devote himself to his younger sisters. This was very natural, perhaps, certainly very prudent; for Dora's share of self-control was small, and she would easily have been betrayed into exhibitions of feeling, equally unwise and unsafe. But Dora could not reason calmly, and was as unwilling to allow that others had higher claims on Maurice than herself, as she would have been to admit her influence was declining. Foolish and excitable, she felt angry and ill-used, that he should shun her, or that when she had taken that early drive for his sake, he should have either looks or thoughts for his sisters in preference to herself.

What right had he to be more cautious than herself? why should he draw back when she advanced? In her desperation at the idea of parting, she had rather wished that their secret should be discovered; though she had not dared to tell it, she would have liked that it should be found out; and now he was, all of a sudden, so careful, so reserved, so cold. Ah! she would be cold too. She tried, but not very successfully; she could not assume the tone of indifference she wished; then she grew angry; vexed with herself and her feelings, which she fancied so much warmer than his; she became careless, flighty, and wild in manner; she laughed and talked one moment in an idle way, the next she was silent and dull; to him she was absolutely cross, and very nearly rude; yet he was calm and unmoved, as she thought, only turning with a graver, lower, more subdued tone toward his sisters, or his father, and decidedly avoiding her. What he was really suffering, the various emotions and changeful feelings which were torturing his heart, she did not know: she gave him no credit for an endurance which was little short of martyrdom; and was indignant at a self-control assumed almost entirely for her own sake. Not to compromise her any further was his object, and although he greatly feared that she was displeased, he had resolved that before the eyes of Isabel, no demonstration on his part should betray a secret she had but recently enjoined him to keep at all hazards.

The very last time they had met, he had again ventured to urge an explanation with her father, fearful from a chance remark of Charles Huyton's, that their secret might otherwise be betrayed to him; but this she had again forbidden; and his earnest prayers and expostulations had been silenced and set aside. He had been disappointed, and though forced to yield, he had warned her that evil would come of it. It was this which had made her so eager to go to the wedding, and it was this which so bitterly affronted her, when she found him coldly reserved. She thought him sullen, but he was only firm, and thus they parted; she with her girlish heart swelling with pride and mortified feeling, a sense of wrong on her own part, unavowed to herself, and therefore rankling deeply; a wounded conscience, to which she would not attempt to apply the only balm that could have cured her. He with pain and grief, doubled and trebled as he calculated all the circumstances; a pain greater than quitting his sisters, severer than saying a long farewell to his father; the pain of a noble mind, feeling it has done wrong, and condemned to suffer and repent in silence. He saw she was angry, and he writhed under the notion, but what could he do? she had forbidden him the step which could alone make reparation for his conduct; the alternative to renounce all claim on her he had fairly stated, and although she had denied the necessity of so doing, she could not alter his determination.

So they parted, with formal phrases of courtesy from him, with averted eyes, and unwillingly extended hand, and tones of coldest civility from her; and he dashed away, to busy himself in professional duties, while she drove back to Eaton-place, with a flushed cheek, and an aching brow, and a heart wildly throbbing with a strange mixture of remorse, anger, and regret.

CHAPTER XIX.

"There stood a wretch prepared to change
His soul's redemption for revenge."

Rokeby.

The day after the excursion to Woolwich, Charles Huyton had left London for a short time. Perhaps had he been still in town, Isabel Barham would not have so readily engaged to attend the ceremony. For the last two years it had been the secret object of her life to make herself Mr. Huyton's wife; yet she was often obliged to confess with regret, that she seemed no nearer to it than before. She managed well, too, with much prudence and discretion and perhaps had not the heart she besieged been pre-engaged, she might have been successful. But such a pursuit could not elevate the tone of her mind, improve her good feelings, or increase her susceptibility to generous emotions. There was no heart in it; it was simply a mercantile transaction.

The unconscious worship which Gwyneth bestowed on an idea, embodied to her fancy in the person of Mr. Ufford, was a far more ennobling sensation. She was admiring, sincerely admiring virtue and worth; and though deluding herself in supposing that these were inherent in an extraordinary degree in her idol's character, she was perfectly unselfish and true in her feelings. When her time came to be undeceived, she would not, at least, have to confess that she had been mean and mercenary, that she deserved to be disappointed, and had no right to complain. Not so Isabel Barham; she was entangling herself, in her own endeavors to catch another; for if she escaped with feelings uninjured by love, she had, at least, a mind debased by cunning efforts, a heart soiled and profaned by being bent on mean objects—worldly pomp and worldly riches. Disappointment was impending over her. Disappointment of the bitterest kind!

Mr. Huyton came back to London rather earlier than had been expected; and soon after walked up from his lodgings to Eaton-place, where, as we have already noticed, he spent much of his time. Mr. Barham was within, and after some discussion of political questions, in which he had of late been trying to interest Charles Huyton, the elder gentleman observed casually—

"Miss Barham and her sister are gone down to Woolwich!"

"Indeed, again! not to the *Erratic*, I suppose," said Charles, carelessly.

"Not exactly; but connected with the steamer, I believe their engagement is."

"There must have been some strong attraction there, to draw the young ladies out so early."

"Why, yes. I understand that one of Miss Barham's young friends was to be married this morning to an officer at Woolwich; and as a graceful compliment to one whom she esteems as rightly occupying her proper station in society, my daughter consented to attend as bridesmaid."

"*Who* is the bride?" inquired Charles, with quickness; a strange, wild thrill of anger, pain, and bitter jealousy shooting across his heart: something forewarned him whose name he should hear; it was with difficulty he could control himself.

"A young lady you know, I believe; the daughter of the Vicar of Hurstdene: a most respectable man he is, and one whose connection with our family entitles him to more consideration from *us*, than it is exactly requisite to show to others in the same station."

"Ah!" cried Mr. Huyton, suddenly starting up. "I am sorry I have forgotten—I have an engagement—I must hurry away, or I shall be too late!"

"Shall we see you again to-day? my daughters will be sorry to miss you," said Mr. Barham, looking with a sort of speculative wonder at Charles's countenance. It was not surprising, that his face should catch the attention of even the egotistical and self-centered man. There was something so wild and strange in the expression.

"I don't know! perhaps, if I can—; may be I shall leave town," was the incoherent reply, in a low, changed, husky voice.

"You are ill, I fear," said the other, frightened, and laying a hand on his arm; "let me ring for something."

"No! no! only hurried, my dear sir," said Charles, with a painful smile. "Good-day."

He hastened away. There was war in his heart; anger, jealousy, outraged feeling, hopeless love; sickening pain, a burning desire of revenge; a vindictive determination to do—he knew not what; any thing, every thing, however miserable to himself, so that he might return agony for agony; that he might make those suffer who had injured him. Unconscious of external objects, he gained his own apartments, and there locked in and safe from interruption, for hours he gave way to his fiery passions. Words could hardly describe the convulsive vehemence of the feelings that tore and shook his soul. The old Greek fables of men possessed by the furies, seemed realized in him. He was mad with rage; frantic with disappointed love; frenzied by a wild jealousy—cruel, insatiable, dark, pitiless as the grave itself. Whatever of hope he had hitherto entertained now rose to his mind, but to torture him more; his very plans and expectations, built on the uncertainty of his rival's profession, and his chances of supplanting him during a prolonged absence, now recurred to his memory as a mockery and a torment. Lost! all lost! every chance, every hope, every deep-laid scheme, swept away before the flood of his hated rival's success. Baffled, outwitted, triumphed over, scorned; such, no doubt, he was. The sailor had understood his projects, seen through his offers of friendship, and now laughed at them, having made sure of his bride.

And was there nothing left for him yet; no hope! no revenge? Was he helplessly the object of contempt; the disappointed, the rejected lover; could he do nothing? Ah! the cold heart he had failed to touch with love, might yet be bent by sorrow; and though he could not make it his prize, he could, perchance, make it his victim!

He could wound her through another; and he would. No matter what it cost him, no one should say he was the mourning lover, victim to an unrequited affection. No! he would dash aside his love for her, forget it, trample on it if needs must; but he would have revenge. If there was one sentiment in the mind of Hilary, one affection which could rival her attachment to her husband, he knew it was her love for her brother; nay, he believed that it was the strongest, the deepest of the two. It had been planted by nature, nursed by tenderness and sympathy through every year of her life; it was one with which no contemporary love could interfere, with which no past friendship could compare, which no future regard could in the least degree replace.

The happiness of her brother was Hilary's greatest joy; his disappointment and sorrow would be her most bitter grief. And this he had in his power, or, at least, he might have if he chose. He had made himself master of Maurice's secret, he had seen and understood his passion for Dora, and he believed that to defeat him there, would indeed be a bitter blow.

He could do this! he was convinced that he had only to speak, and Mr. Barham would most gladly close with his offer; and as to Dora, he thought too lightly of her affections to suppose them invariable. Opposition he might meet with at first, but this would not daunt him; the support of her father he might rely on, and time and perseverance would do the rest. He did not doubt of ultimate success!

As to the result to himself, the securing a wife whom he neither loved nor esteemed, he did not stop to calculate that; he saw nothing in his mental visions but the feelings of others; he considered nothing but the suffering he was preparing for those who had offended him. By a strange misappreciation of the character of the woman whom he had loved so long, and ought to have known so well, he even fancied that an ambitious desire to see her brother united to the daughter of the rich Mr. Barham, had influence with her: that she who had been unmoved by the temptation of wealth and station for herself, had yet been open to covetous desires for her brother's advancement in life; and that regret and mortification for the loss of the heiress, would help to embitter the grief which a lover's affection must occasion.

His plans determined on, his mind made up, and his spirits calmed by resolution and despair, he returned to Eaton-place to dine with the Barhams; and for the first time since the commencement of his long intimacy with the family, he made a most marked difference in his treatment of the two sisters. His manners to Dora were expressive of a desire to please, such as he had never betrayed before, and such as excited some surprise and disappointment in Isabel's mind, which required both spirit and good breeding to conceal.

How Dora herself received this change of manner might be gathered from Isabel's speech to her as they stood in the drawing-room afterward.

"Well, Dora, I really think you are the greatest and most relentless flirt I ever saw."

"Am I?" said the younger sister, languidly throwing herself on a sofa, and turning away her face; "what have I been doing now?"

"Flirting to a degree beyond good manners with Mr. Huyton," said Miss Barham, looking at her own deepening carnation in a pier-glass opposite to her.

"I was only paying him in kind," replied Dora, undauntedly; "if he meant nothing, nor did I; if he was in earnest, I have no objection."

"You don't mean to say that if Charles Huyton were to propose to you, you would accept him?" said Isabel, turning full on her sister.

"Would not you, Isabel?" was Dora's reply.

"Our tastes are not usually so similar that that should be any answer," said Isabel.

"Well," said Dora, starting up, "I mean what I say; I was not flirting with Mr. Huyton more than he was with me."

"And if he were to ask you to marry him, you know you would say no, as you did to Lord Dunsmore!"

"No, I would accept him on the spot," cried Dora, giving way to a desperate fit of pique and mortified feeling. "You need not look so scornful, Isabel; I mean what I say."

"Luckily you are not likely to be put to the test," replied Miss Barham. "But we must go and dress, or the countess will be here before we are ready to go with her."

Dora, however, did not follow her sister's example; but when the other quitted the room, she remained reclining on the sofa. Her head ached, her heart ached still more; affection wounded, vanity and pride alike outraged; sorrow, real sorrow, a sense of injustice in herself, and of having been all through in the wrong, made her bosom throb, and flushed her cheek, and really rendered her quite unfit for society.

She was still sitting languidly thinking, when her father and his guest entered the room.

"What is the matter with you, Dora?" said the former, in a voice of unusual kindness; "what makes you look so pensive?"

"I am very tired, papa."

"And where is Isabel?"

"Dressing to go out."

"And you," said Charles, approaching her, and standing beside her sofa with looks of devotion, "are you going?"

"No, I am tired."

"That expedition to Woolwich was too much for you," observed her father.

"I believe it was," said she, with tears, half sorrow, half anger, starting to her eyes.

"Ah, we will have no more such freaks, little Dora," said Mr. Barham, "will we, Mr. Huyton? we must take more care of you, my child, in future."

The unusual kindness of her father's tone went to Dora's heart. Would he only have been always so, she would have been saved from how much unhappiness; she felt choking, and could make no answer, only laying down her burning cheek upon the pillow.

Mr. Huyton drew a chair close beside the end of the sofa, and leaning over toward her, was in the act of whispering some gentle sentiment in her ear, when Isabel entered.

"What, Dora, you not dressed! and Lady Fitzurse has been announced as waiting for us."

"Never mind Dora, my love," said Mr. Barham; "she is not going out to-night; she is over-tired, and had much better stay at home. I shall remain with her. How well you look, Isabel."

So Miss Barham was forced to depart alone, and with rather a rebellious heart, at leaving Dora and Mr. Huyton in such strange proximity. There is sometimes an intuitive perception of what is about to happen, which, against our will, seizes on the heart and forewarns us of evil or disappointment. Isabel, in spite of every wish to the contrary, felt at that moment that Charles Huyton was lost to her: and Dora, with a tumult of emotion she could not attempt to understand, perceived that his intentions were more serious than she had supposed.

Anger against Maurice for being more conscientious than herself; regret for her own share in the past; gratified female vanity; a desire of retaliation, disguised under a pretense of repentance, all urged her on at this moment; and she allowed the advances of her new lover with a graceful and encouraging simplicity, which at once surprised him, and pleased her father.

"Mr. Barham," said the visitor, after awhile, "I am going into the library to look for that book you promised me; I know exactly where to find it, I believe."

He went, and the father taking immediate advantage of his absence, with no small degree of gratified pride and ambition, which he mistook entirely for parental affection, proceeded forthwith to detail to his daughter the pleasing intelligence that Mr. Huyton had that very evening made proposals for her hand; that nothing could be more agreeable than such an alliance; it was a noble offer, and made in a noble spirit; the settlements would be every thing that could be desired; and as to the gentleman himself, there could not be two opinions as to his character, or two sentiments as to his good qualities.

Dora listened in profound silence, with rosy cheeks and downcast eyes, and fingers nervously playing with the tassel of the sofa cushion; but, in spite of her external quietness, there was the fiercest war in her heart. Love, anger, remorse, ambition, fear, doubt, vanity, all struggled there. To refuse at once, and without a reason, a suitor whom but just now she had visibly encouraged, was, she fancied, impossible; to assign the real cause of the reluctance, she could not but feel was more so still; better, she thought, it would be to temporize, to adopt half measures, to conceal what she dared not own, to brave what she could hardly endure to contemplate; to secure peace and tranquillity for the present at least, come what would of the future. To say yes, now, was not to bind herself irrevocably; to accept Mr. Huyton as a suitor, by no means made it inevitable that she should become his wife; circumstances might occur, unforeseen, incalculable, to release her from an engagement; and meantime, perhaps Maurice would regret his conduct, would wish he had not refused the promise she had offered to make, would—she hardly knew what she wished or expected, except the single desire to alarm him and arouse his jealousy, by making him fear to lose her.

With these ideas floating in her mind, she at length brought herself to the point of speaking, and when her father closed his harangue, she looked up and said:

"Please, papa, tell Mr. Huyton I am much honored and happy, and—and all that sort of thing."

"You need not agitate yourself so, my dear little Dora," said he, smiling graciously, for Dora ended by a fit of tears; "there is no occasion to be unhappy, I am sure; you do quite right to accept Mr. Huyton's proposal; but although I am ready to be your messenger, we must not forget propriety and honor in the message. Desirable as the connection is, we need not rush at it, as if we thought ourselves receiving, and not bestowing a compliment. You must allow me to alter the words, although not the meaning of your answer."

"As you please, sir," said Dora, faintly; rebellious recollections were rising in her heart; and she had a struggle at that moment not to shriek out a negative.

"I shall go and speak to Mr. Huyton," said the father, quite unconscious of his daughter's agitation.

She was left alone, and burying her face in the cushions, she gave way to the bitterest tears.

She was insensible to outward objects; memory had gone back to the sunny days at Hurstdene, or tortured her with the happy hours so recently spent on board the *Erratic*; she sobbed and trembled violently, then thought again of the past, and thought was followed by fresh agitation. In this state she was lying when her hand was touched by some one, and starting up, she saw Charles Huyton beside her.

She felt guilty, and hurriedly tried to hide her emotion and drive away her tears; could she have seen into his heart, she would have discovered that these accompaniments to their betrothal were but too suitable and fitting. She did glance at his face, and saw how little his eyes wore the expression she thought that love should wear. They were gloomy, sad, full rather of harsh resolve than joyful hopes. An idea struck her suddenly. This abrupt proposal, this unhappy appearance, whence did they spring? Had he loved her long, did he really love her now? Was not Hilary the real object of his affections? Had this new resolve any thing to do with her marriage? It rushed through her mind that it was despair, not love, which prompted him, and that though she might now accept his hand, he would himself, when the moment of pique was over, be the first to regret this step, and, perhaps, would not only be ready to cancel the engagement, but would be glad to resign her to another.

She dried her eyes; he cleared his brow; he spoke of love, esteem, honor; she listened, blushing, and faltered out an acquiescence, which he read her too correctly not to see was half reluctant. But the reluctance neither surprised nor distressed him. He knew he had a rival to supplant, and it would have been but half a triumph to have had her accept him readily. More decided opposition would have been not unwelcome. But he knew her to be light and volatile; her sailor-lover's feelings were of a firmer texture, and so were his sister's also, and these were the hearts he sought to wound.

So the farce of that engagement was played out. He made love, and she listened and assented; and when Mr. Barham rejoined them they had exchanged promises of love and faith, while the heart of each, in secret, entirely belied these spoken words.

It had been settled that the family party from Hurstdene should return home on the Monday after Hilary's marriage; and the girls having taken leave of their friends, the young ladies of Eaton-place did not expect to meet them again. Captain Hepburn had privately urged on Hilary the advantage of inducing Gwyneth to remain some time longer with her sister in London, and Sybil was extremely anxious to detain her; but no persuasion or argument had the slightest effect upon Gwyneth herself, who, having her own reasons for wishing to return, was not to be induced to change her determination by any thing which could be urged by the others. She said very little in reply to the suggestions or wishes of the family, but calmly and passively persisted in her own way; and, much to Hilary's disappointment, they all returned together as they had gone. The same evening saw Gwyneth once more strolling on the green terrace with Mr. Ufford by her side, detailing to him all the events which had occurred in London, and hearing in return most pleasant assurances of how much they had been missed, and how glad he was to have them home again. Gwyneth was very glad then that she had not staid in London.

Hilary would not have minded being left to do all the necessary arrangements, consequent on resettling at home, without help, if her sister had been employed in a way which had been less questionable in its utility; but she could not prevent it now; for though she sent Nest to beg Gwyneth's assistance, the young lady only promised to come directly, and then apparently forgot all about the request.

"Poor Mr. Ufford!" said she to Hilary, when the curate having taken leave, she had time to rejoin her sister, "he is in great distress!"

"Indeed," said the elder sister, "what is the matter?"

"He has had such bad news from Italy; his little niece is certainly dying, and her father, his eldest brother, seems very nearly as bad. He has a great mind to go to them."

"He should talk to my father about that, not to you, Gwyneth," said Hilary, gravely; "but why does he not? I am sure he had much better, if Lord Dunsmore wishes it."

"I told him if he could get help in the parish I was sure papa would agree most readily," continued Gwyneth; "and I think he means to propose it. There is some idea of a college friend of his taking the curacy, if papa approves, just to allow him time to go abroad."

The next morning Mr. Ufford called again, and this time he mentioned to the Vicar his half-formed scheme of going to Italy. Of course Mr. Duncan could make no objection, but entered kindly and warmly into the young man's anxieties.

It required a great deal of talking, however, before Mr. Ufford could decide on any plan. He came to the Vicar with only a great mind to act, and he left him, having arrived no nearer to forming a definite intention, or seeming to Hilary to have any serious idea of acting as he talked! She felt a little annoyed at his indecision; it would form an indisputable excuse for many visits, and much dawdling, and a reason for putting off some useful plans regarding village improvements, and deferring some alterations and amendments in the church, which had been projected, and for which Lord Dunsmore himself had contributed funds. She longed to put a little energy or decision into his mind and actions; she wished she could make him resolve either to go or stay, or that at any rate she could enlighten his understanding sufficiently to make him comprehend his own desires, and not pass the time for action in lingering between duty and her sister Gwyneth.

The sort of expectations to which his conduct gave rise in the village was more than once significantly hinted to Mrs. Hepburn, when receiving the congratulations and good wishes of the many attached parishioners who had known her from a child. The fear perpetually expressed that her marriage would remove her from the neighborhood, as Miss Sybil's had done, was pretty generally followed by a more or less broadly-worded hint that Miss Gwyneth's choice would be a better one for them, and that they hoped one of their young ladies at least would never leave them; for young as Miss Gwyneth was, she was quite womanly in her way and look, and was as well fitted to be mistress at the Vicarage as young Mrs. Hepburn herself. And a remark which closed one of these commentaries the first time they met her taught her what accurate and penetrating notice those apparently indifferent spectators took of their superior's ways and proceedings.

"But bless you, miss," said one old woman, "it would have been far better for us had you taken the young 'Squire at 'the Ferns,' instead of this captain from foreign parts. And they do say he will be fit to hang himself, whensoever he comes to hear of your being married to another."

Hilary tried to look unconcerned, and to speak on some other subject.

News travels fast, and it soon became known to the village gossips that Mr. Huyton did not intend to commit suicide on the occasion of Hilary's marriage.

But the first intelligence which reached the Vicarage of his plans came directly from himself, in a letter to Mr. Duncan, which the writer knew well must be read by Hilary herself.

"Dear Mr. Duncan,

"Although I am just on the point of leaving England for some weeks on most important business, I must steal a few moments to write to you, lest indifferent and gossiping tongues should convey to you the report of what I wish to be the first to communicate. Former friendship and bygone events convince me that this intelligence will be received with some degree of interest by the family at the Vicarage. I am about to marry; it is no use seeking for elegant turns of language to announce it; that is the plain fact. The lady, who is already well known to you, has particularly commissioned me to give you the information; and when I tell you that she is no other than Miss Dora Barham, you may form some idea of the happiness which gilds my future prospects. I believe the ceremony will be celebrated immediately on my return from Germany, or as soon after as can be conveniently arranged. You can imagine the pleasure with which I contemplate settling quietly at 'the Ferns' once more, with such a companion and friend; and I trust her anticipations are as pleasant and vivid as my own. Among these must, of course, rank very highly the opportunity it will afford of carrying on the friendly intercourse with your family, which has already been so conducive to our happiness in past years, and which it will be equally desirable and delightful to establish on a permanent footing for the future.

"With kind regards to your family circle,

"Believe me ever,

"Yours faithfully,

"Charles Huyton."

It was well for Mr. Duncan's peace and comfort, that loss of sight had prevented his cognizance of many things which must else have come to his knowledge: it was well, too, that he could not see his daughter's face as she read this letter. The bitter irony of those words was concealed from him, but she felt it to her heart.

"Going to marry Dora!" said Mr. Duncan; "I am surprised. I thought he would have taken Isabel."

She was silent; she could not speak; the effort to read through these words in an unbroken voice had been almost too great for her; she was now recovering herself as well as she could.

Mr. Duncan thought a little, and presently observed—

"Well, I am glad he has resolved to marry at last; and to have your young friend settled at 'the Ferns' will be pleasant for you, Hilary, as long as you stay in the neighborhood. You must write him an answer by-and-by, and we will tell him of your marriage, my child."

"Do you want me just now, my dear father?" said she, compelling herself to speak; "if not—"

"No—no, not at all at present; let Nest come to me in half-an-hour."

Hilary escaped to her own room, carrying the cruel letter with her.

Engaged to Dora Barham! incredible! monstrous! could he ask her? could she accept him? it seemed impossible: where was Dora's love for Maurice? where Charles Huyton's knowledge of that love? Till this moment she had not known how much she had depended on her constancy; how completely she had built her hopes for her brother's happiness on some fortunate turn to their affairs. Well she knew how deep, how true, how tender were her brother's feelings, how entirely he had surrendered his heart to this hapless affection; and though aware that no engagement had passed between them, it seemed to her that their recent intercourse in London had increased their mutual attachment. Oh! what could Dora mean then by thus abruptly abandoning him! What would Maurice feel when he learned her inconstancy! If she had been sincere to him, if her sentiments had been real, where was her faith to Mr. Huyton! by what name could an engagement with him be designated? and if she had been all this time trifling with Maurice! if she had been gratifying her own vanity at the expense of his happiness—but that was impossible! Dora was volatile, thoughtless, imprudent, but she was not deceitful, she was not heartless, she was not wicked. Hilary could not endure to think ill of her; there must be something unexplained; there was some secret which had not reached her yet. Perhaps compulsion had won from her an unwilling assent; moral force, parental authority, persecution, might have been employed; she knew Dora was weak, possibly she had not the strength of will to withstand such influence; she might rather deserve pity than blame.

But for Mr. Huyton himself, what excuse could be urged! Maurice had been his chosen friend; a hundred times had he made professions of regard, or declarations of esteem for him; and he knew, or, at least, he was strongly suspicious of this esteemed friend's attachment to Dora Barham! It was not a violent affection which misled him, and blinded his eyes; Hilary believed him at the best, indifferent, regarding Dora; he had always rather despised her intellect, and slighted her charms; no! love for her was not his excuse: there was no love in that cruel letter which Hilary now held in her hands. As her eyes slowly perused the words again, her fancy presented to her mind the terrible expression of his face when he had first heard of her own engagement. It seemed to ring in her ear once more, the bitter tone in which he had exclaimed, "You will wish rather that a demon had crossed your path than that you had thwarted me;" and as she remembered this, she felt that it was revenge he sought; a revenge for his slighted affection, which she could not choose but feel deeply.

The happiness of Maurice and Dora was sacrificed, perhaps, to her own; it was her hasty marriage which had brought this impending grief on her darling brother!

"Oh, Maurice! Maurice!" sobbed she, as she buried her face in her hands, "why am I to be a source of misery and disappointment to you? Oh! brother, you who have never done any thing but comfort and love me, are your hopes now to be blighted for my sake? Why did you love so truly and so well? Why did you surrender that generous heart to one who dared not own the affection she had created! Was it a crime to love, that she should blush to be claimed by you! Oh! weak, foolish Dora, your idle, childish terrors have caused all this."

Very bitter the blow was, and rendered more so by the insulting tone in which the news had been announced. Could this be Charles Huyton, the man whom she had known so well, who had seemed so amiable, who had professed such love for her! She shuddered as she contemplated such a character, and tried to persuade herself that she had fancied more than the truth. But yet in her secret soul there was something which told her otherwise, which impressed on her the conviction that it was a bad, unholy feeling now actuating her former lover, and that misery must be the result to those concerned.

Oh! how she longed at that moment for the comfort of her husband's sympathy and love; how her heart ached to pour out its fears and sorrows to him, knowing that there they would be understood and borne with, and perhaps reasoned away, but this intense longing must be checked, put aside, kept under, or it would soon grow up into an overpowering cloud, darkening her hopes, numbing her feelings, paralyzing her actions, and obscuring from her the bright sunshine of trust and cheerful faith.

She turned her thoughts once more to Maurice and Dora; but what could she do for them? Nothing but pray for them; and sinking on her knees she did pray, long and earnestly, that if sorrow must come on her beloved brother it might be borne with patience, and so bring a blessing with it; and for the others, too, she prayed, that the angry feelings might be softened, and the unkind intention converted into a better mood; that the weak might be strengthened, the erring restored; that they might both be saved from sinful weakness and sinful passions; and that if their own willful ways brought suffering on them, that suffering might be sanctified to a happy result.

Little thought the angry and vindictive man for whom she prayed, of the only return she made to his unkindness; and little deemed he that if his cruel letter had given her pain, it had also afforded her the occasion of exercising faith, meekness, and charity; that her soul rose the stronger for the blow which he had hoped would prostrate it.

She forgave him the injury he had, perchance, intended; and to forgive from the heart is alone the blessed gift of that Spirit whose presence brings peace and consolation.

CHAPTER XX.

"Let her have her proud dark eyes,
And her petulant, quick replies;
Let her sweep her dazzling hand,
With its gesture of command,
And shake back her raven hair,
With the old imperious air."

Tristram and Iseult.

"So Charles Huyton is really going to marry Miss Dora Barham," said Mr. Ufford to the party at the Vicarage. "I wonder whether she is satisfied now."

"How did you hear that?" was Hilary's reply.

"Oh! I had a letter from Huyton this morning, announcing his good fortune; hoping my poor brother would not take it amiss that he had succeeded where George had failed. I own I am more surprised, however, at Huyton's proposal than at the young lady's answer."

"You have not heard any thing more from Italy, I suppose?" inquired Hilary, to whom the other subject was distasteful.

"I heard this morning that Lord and Lady Rupert, that is Dunsmore's sister-in-law and her husband, have left Florence, and must now be at Naples with my brother."

"I am glad of that," said Gwyneth, eagerly, "it will be a relief to our mind to know he has some one with him; and you like Lady Rupert, I think."

"Yes, I do not feel it so necessary to start immediately, and as George was so very anxious to hear that his projects are put *en train*, perhaps it would be better to make some definite arrangements regarding the church and school, at least before I go."

Accordingly papers were produced, plans and estimates looked over, calculations made, and statistics gone into. In the midst of all, while Gwyneth was busy noting down for Mr. Ufford some important calculations, and Hilary was explaining to her father the plan ultimately decided on, Gwyneth suddenly observed,

"I wonder Dora is going to marry before Isabel; I am so surprised that she should remain so long single. What do you suppose is the reason?"

"I really do not think such things are worth speculating about," observed Mrs. Hepburn, who particularly wished to avoid the subject.

"Miss Barham's position is peculiar," said Mr. Ufford, "and so is her character. She is too proud to marry a mean man; too rich to marry a poor one; too great for a humble man; too clever for a foolish one; too independent for a mercenary man; and too good for a bad one."

"Well, that only proves that she must have a wise, clever, rich, and noble husband," said Gwyneth, laughing a little; "and I suppose with so many claims, aided by the addition of grace and beauty, the probability that she might meet such a one is not very small."

"Perhaps! but then, this wise, good, clever, rich noble man may not perhaps submit to be governed by his wife; and I have a notion that Miss Barham has been too long accustomed to be her own mistress, to like to give up the privilege, or to be at all ready to lay down her scepter."

"Oh, you do not do her justice!" cried Gwyneth; "besides, any woman who loved, would resign all her prerogatives readily to one who deserved them."

"Gwyneth, my love! have you finished those extracts?" said her father.

Gwyneth went on with her work in silence.

"There's the Abbey carriage crossing the green," observed Mr. Ufford presently, he having sauntered away to the window, while the young ladies managed the details of business.

Hilary changed color; she felt reluctant to meet Dora. "I had no idea they were in the country!" she observed, in a voice of discomfort.

"Only Miss Barham is," replied Mr. Ufford, looking with a little curiosity at Mrs. Hepburn's face. "Miss Dora is gone to visit some friends in Northampton, I believe with her aunt, Lady Margaret, while the happy Huyton is in Germany. The carriage is coming here."

It did come, and Isabel entered the Vicarage exactly the same as ever in appearance; her sister's engagement had made no outward change in her. It had been a disappointment, but she was too well-bred to show it; and, except in a hasty abandonment of London, there was no perceptible effect of the news. However, Dora herself could not be much more unwilling to discuss the affair than Isabel was, so it was a mutual accommodation that the sisters should part for the present. Miss Barham found herself suddenly weary of the London season, and much in want of rest and fresh air; to face

Hilary, to see Hurstdene, to exist even at home, Dora felt impossible; and she arranged a hasty plan for accompanying her aunt into Northamptonshire, hoping that change of place and entire novelty would smother the thoughts which were burning in her heart, and diminish her regret, despair, and self-reproach.

Miss Barham was immediately interested in the details of the business which had just been occupying the others; and both touched and grieved by the account of the precarious state of the first projector of the alterations. She had a right, she said, to be interested in any improvements of a church, which had so long formed part of their family property, and she insisted on having it all detailed to her. Mr. Ufford accordingly went through the plans, while she listened with a most graceful and marked attention. Then she asked, in a pretty, injured tone, why her father had not been consulted; and was hardly appeased by the assurance that Mr. Barham having done so much for the chancel a few years ago, nothing more was required at present, nor could they feel justified in calling on him for assistance in a matter of ornament which was purely the wish of Lord Dunsmore.

"Was nothing more really wanted?" inquired Isabel; she should like to see the church, and judge for herself. She asked Gwyneth to walk down to it with her; Mr. Ufford, of course, accompanied them. They sauntered about there for a long time. Isabel was very enthusiastic, suggesting all sorts of expensive plans for ornament and effect; Mr. Ufford himself was quite carried away by her zeal, entering into her ideas with almost equal warmth. It was a subject that exactly suited him; ideal, imaginative, combining beauty, poetry, and all the unreal, sentimental, religious feeling, in which his spirit always delighted. He could arrange a symbolical device, and revel in an illustration of some fanciful theory, much better than he could go through a dry detail, or endure a self-denying, sober perseverance against ill-success.

Isabel was mistress of the elements of her subject; she was acquainted with the fashionable theories and modern language of church architecture; she could discourse elegantly on stringcourse, and reredos, lecterns, open-sittings, equality of ranks, chants, and responses: galleries and parish clerks were her aversion, and a choral service her delight. Gwyneth could think and feel, but Isabel could talk; while the continued references to Mr. Ufford, to his taste, opinion, wish, decision, not only compelled him to listen, but were so very flattering to his own self-love, as to convince him that hitherto he had greatly undervalued Miss Barham's good qualities.

They lingered long together, and when he had handed her into her carriage, and watched her drive off, he said a hasty farewell to the family at the Vicarage, and walked home, leaving the young ladies to put away his papers at their leisure.

Gwyneth was thoughtful and silent the rest of the day.

The curate came the next morning to the Vicarage soon after breakfast; but hardly had poor Gwyneth time to be glad to see him, when her joy was dissipated by his words.

"Oh, Mrs. Hepburn, will you give me those plans and sketches for the new buildings? Mr. Barham wants to see them, and I am going over to the Abbey this morning to consult about them with him; and shall probably not come back till to-morrow."

He went, and for some little time there was occasionally a change in his tone and manner toward Gwyneth Duncan; his words were often few, and hurried; there was no more loitering on the terrace, or dreaming over books of religious poetry with her. He did not absent himself from the Vicarage, but she was no longer always his object, even in the undecided and indolent way in which she had formerly been. His whole mind seemed engrossed in the decorations of the church, and things connected with it, including Miss Barham. Isabel promised a great deal toward providing funds; the chancel was, of course, her peculiar care: and deeply interested as she was, it was natural that she should be constantly driving over, to see how the work progressed. There was scarcely a day in which it was not necessary that the curate and the lady should meet; either at Hurstdene to consult on the spot, or in the library at the Abbey, to examine books on decorative art, or illuminations copied from old MSS.

Hilary saw it all, and watched them with a careful eye. She often felt hurt at the proceedings, on her father's account, whose tastes and wishes were perpetually over-ruled; he did not like the idea of these new decorations, he feared that the quiet gray church, so dear to him in its serene simplicity, might assume too fanciful an appearance under their plans. The coloring of the walls and ceiling, talked of by them, he thought unsuitable. But he loved peace and hated dissension; and when Mr. Ufford argued on one hand, and Isabel coaxed on the other, he could not resist, but gave them their way.

As yet, however, the greater part of the decorations were only existing in idea, much repair was needed first of a substantial and important character, and it appeared probable that the autumn and winter must pass before Fancy could exercise her power on the colored decorations and ornamental scrolls. Meanwhile, Isabel drew patterns, and Mr. Ufford applauded.

Gwyneth Duncan had at first noticed this unexpected coalition with considerable uneasiness; the fear she felt of Isabel as a rival, showed her how much her own feelings were interested in Mr. Ufford's. She wondered that nothing more was said of the journey to Italy, and wished most heartily that the curate had set out before Miss Duncan's return to the country. By degrees, however, she became more easy; he resumed much of his old manner to her; when Miss Barham was not by, he sought her opinion, claimed her services, and courted her approval almost as much as formerly; and she began to hope that, however he might admire Miss Barham, or be flattered by her condescending notice, that his real preference was confined to her. She was very quiet, and more reserved than ever; not even her sister could penetrate her secret; she never became demonstrative, least of all to him.

Anxiety for Gwyneth's happiness, and concern for Mr. Ufford's uncertain conduct, were not the only sources of trouble to Hilary's mind at that time. Her thoughts would follow her absent sailors. Love would make the heart tremble, although faith whispered of patience and hope, and her husband's spirit, his devotion to the cause of duty, his calm courage and high aspirations, inspired her too: but yet they could not always check the intruding chills which woman's weakness threw over her. Generally, however, she was calm and trustful, although the blank of his absence was a sorrow which constant exertion, and devotion to the good of others, could alone alleviate. But for Maurice, poor Maurice, there was more painful thoughts still. His first letter was at once longed for, dreaded, and received with a mixture of feelings which it would be difficult to analyze.

The *Erratic* had remained some days at Plymouth, quite long enough for Hilary's letters, with the news of Dora's engagement, to reach her brother. She had written with the tenderest concern, the most sympathizing sorrow, and yet, fearful of augmenting his disappointment, she had hardly dared to express what she really felt. To her husband she could confide all; but to Maurice, it seemed to her, that either to pity or to blame, to question Dora's past or her present feelings, to suppose her faithless or deceitful, untrue either to him or his rival, would be equally inappropriate, unkind, or unwise. She dared hardly do more than state facts, and express anxiety regarding his feelings. Then came his letter, like himself, generous, warm-hearted, high-minded, loving. He had, he said, no right to complain, she had broken no faith to him; he had asked for none; they had parted on the understanding that she was free, disengaged. He had never deserved her, and it would be unjust, then, to claim a place in her memory as any thing beyond a friend; he had no wish to make her unhappy, and since their union appeared to her impossible, she was at perfect liberty to act as she had done. It was like herself, too, if she had endeavored to please her father; it was an engagement which he, no doubt, would perfectly approve; and there was much offered by it to influence and tempt her beyond common inducements. That she would not marry for the sake of rank or fortune alone, she had already proved; beyond a doubt, she had good reasons for her conduct. His most earnest wishes for her happiness, his constant prayers for her, were all he could now give; these she should have. He charged Hilary not to allow her to suppose he felt ill-used, or that he judged her harshly, or blamed her; nor need her affectionate heart grieve for him; she had done him no injustice, no wrong; and the inevitable evils of life he hoped he could bear. A sailor must expect storms in his voyage, and should know what to do under them. A sudden tornado had come down on him, catching him, perhaps, with too much canvas spread, going on too gayly before a light breeze; but should he therefore give up all for lost, and allow the hurricane to overwhelm him without an effort? No, he would shorten sail at once, and trust, by vigorous and timely exertion, to remedy the danger to which incautiousness in fair weather had exposed him.

"Not that I can ever forget her," continued he, in conclusion, "or am at all likely to find one to fill her place. Her memory will live in mine, as we think of one dead; and her name will ever have a charm for me beyond all other feminine appellations. But do not fret on my account, dear Hilary; you have enough care, without taking another load on your shoulders for my sake."

But Captain Hepburn told his wife how great was the struggle in the mind of Maurice, how severe the shock had been, and how glad he should be when they had left England, as this weary detention from day to day, kept them all in an irritating state of idle uncertainty. Hilary knew Maurice must feel, yet his letter was a comfort too. If he could so bravely face his disappointment, the severity of the blow would be greatly lessened. If no angry feelings were lurking there, he would escape the bitterest portion of disappointed love; and perhaps, after all, the abandoned lover might be less an object of pity than his successful rival.

Affairs went on at home, for some weeks, much as has been described. Isabel Barham was the most devoted friend to Gwyneth; constantly at the Vicarage, to talk over the building plans, or consult about the embroidery she was occupied with for the church. Penelope's web hardly gave rise to more discussion and anxiety than did the cushions which Isabel thought she was working. They traveled backward and forward, several times a week, between the Abbey and the Vicarage, in Miss Barham's britchska; that young lady always expecting to find time to set a few stitches during her visit, and generally proving mistaken in the result; so that the only progress the work made was when Gwyneth sometimes herself took it in hand; indeed, the cushions might be said to live chiefly on the road, if they had actually any other existence than in the imagination of their projectors.

The curate was not excluded from the cabinet councils held on these topics, and he rarely absented himself. None of the lookers-on could at all make out the meaning of the several parties; even Hilary doubted what were Mr. Ufford's views and intentions; and as to Miss Barham, when at Hurstdene, she seemed to care little for any thing but the vicar's daughter. The accounts from Naples, meanwhile, were most unfavorable; there seemed scarcely a hope of Lord Dunsmore's life, which faded and flickered apparently like a dying lamp; but as his sister-in-law and her husband were devoted to him, his brother was content to remain in England.

It was a wild and stormy day, such as not unfrequently breaks up the fine weather at the commencement of August; the curate had not presented himself the whole morning at the Vicarage, and the family supposed him confined to his house by the tempest.

The church bell began to toll, and its long, mournful vibrations seemed to come sadly and awfully, with a warning sound, across the furious blast; sometimes swelling loud in a transient lull, sometimes almost swept away by the violence of the roaring gale.

"That is old Martha Blake's funeral," observed Hilary; "what a day for the poor people."

"Yes; and Mr. Ufford, too," observed Gwyneth.

The bell tolled on, and by-and-by Nest, who was watching from the window, remarked that the party had just appeared. Slowly, and with difficulty, the black group made their way across the green, the wind violently opposing their progress, and threatening at every moment to overpower their feeble and tottering steps. Gwyneth's eyes were fixed on the procession as it wound its way along; she expected to see Mr. Ufford issue from the church to meet the mourners; but they paused at the Lychgate, set down the corpse, and sheltered themselves as well as they could beneath the walls. It was evident the clergyman had not yet arrived. Five minutes passed; ten, a quarter of an hour; still the bell tolled on; and still the mourners stood huddled together by the gate of the dead.

"How wrong to keep those poor people waiting there," said Hilary, a little indignantly.

"I dare say there is some mistake about time," replied Gwyneth; "and I am sure they have often kept Mr. Ufford for an hour or more."

Still time went on; at length, after a long hour, a messenger came to the Vicarage, to ask what should be done; they had sent to Primrose Bank, but the clergyman was out, and had left word that he need not be expected back.

"Then I must go and bury my old parishioner," said the vicar, rising up. "Hilary, my hat and coat, please, love; old Martin will guide me down to the church; so do not disturb yourself."

Hilary was thunderstruck; for her father to go out in such weather might be fatal; he had not been so well as usual for some days. She knew not what to do; ah, could she but have exposed herself for him! Vain wish; she watched him preparing with a sad presentiment, then resolutely threw on her own black cloak, and determined to accompany him. The storm which he must encounter, she too would brave; perhaps she might assist, or shelter him from its fury.

With many sorrowful charges from her to Gwyneth to have a fire lighted, and dry, warm clothes in readiness, the couple took their way together, although the father earnestly remonstrated against Hilary's exposing herself to such needless inconvenience. It was vain to attempt to hold an umbrella; petticoats flapped wildly in the wind, and caught the dashing torrents of rain as they fell; but under the churchyard wall, there was a little shelter, and rain alone comparatively inconvenienced them, during the out-of-door service.

When it was over, Hilary, bidding the poor women, all so wet and draggled, to come up to the Vicarage to dry and warm themselves, hurried her father home as fast as infirmity and tempest would allow him; and wet, breathless, exhausted by the contest with the elements, they reached the house at last. But the struggle had almost overpowered him, and on his arrival, he was attacked with a sort of faintness which greatly alarmed his daughters. He revived after a short time, and smiled at their solicitude; but although he seemed to rally, he complained once or twice in the evening of extreme chilliness, and before night it was quite evident he had caught a violent cold.

Morning did not bring the comfort which he had endeavored to persuade his daughters would accompany it; sore throat and fever were apparent, and Hilary, in great alarm, dispatched a hurried messenger for the doctor. Gwyneth was most miserable; her father's illness overpowered her feelings, and that it should be caused by the apparent neglect of Mr. Ufford, aggravated her distress. She wearied herself in inventing unsatisfactory excuses for his absence, each one of which was abandoned as unlikely, after being entertained for a short period; and the conviction that he would call that morning to excuse his absence, was so strong, that every moment she fancied she heard the latch of the wicket-gate.

The doctor came, prescribed for his patient, shook his head, and avoided giving a definite opinion; contenting himself with observing, he had taken a chill, and they must make him better if they could. Hilary kept her own thoughts to herself, unwilling prematurely to alarm her sisters; but she wrote to Sybil. The vacation was so near, that she thought Mrs. Farrington would easily arrange to hurry her departure, even if she were obliged to leave her husband behind for a few days.

The day passed heavily away; the storm had ceased, but the sky was dull, and the earth damp and dreary; and the exterior dullness was well answered by the blank within. All there was dull indeed.

Many parishioners came toward evening to make anxious inquiries for their pastor, and Gwyneth had to see and answer them; and many and deep, though not loud, were the murmurs that his reverence, who never spared himself, should have been forced out in such a storm, through the inattention of one, who—Gwyneth had to stop them abruptly, to charge them not to judge hastily, to make excuses, and invent possible reasons for the mistake; which sometimes brought her such an answer as,

"Ah, well, miss, I dare say you doant like to hear 'um blamed, but 'ees not like his reverence, and will never fill his shoes."

An observation which brought the color into her cheeks more than once.

"Belike, miss, ye doant know Mr. Ufford was gone over to the Abbey yesterday?" said one old gossip to her; to which Gwyneth replied, with as much unconcern as possible, she did not: but there was something in the tone and manner which startled her.

The second morning of Mr. Duncan's illness brought Gwyneth a note from Isabel. She was sitting with Hilary beside her father's bed, when it was placed in her hand. She opened and read it; then silently laying it down before her sister, she left the room.

Mrs. Hepburn hurriedly perused it. It was to announce, in most graceful and well-chosen words, the fact that she was engaged to Mr. Ufford. She was sure the intelligence would interest her friends at the Vicarage.

Hilary had hardly time to understand this announcement, and none at all to calculate its effects on Gwyneth, when her attention was called to her father. He awoke suddenly, in such intense pain, that every thought had to be given to his relief. She was obliged to summon more help, and Gwyneth, hearing the subdued bustle, came out of her room. Her countenance was white as marble, and almost as composed as a statue; there was no other sign of emotion than the shadow under her eyes; her whole attention was devoted to her father; and her energy was astonishing. The alarm of the daughters was great, though intensely quiet; and an urgent message was sent to the apothecary to come immediately. Much to their relief, he was met near the house, and hurried forward. Every application which skill could devise, or care employ, was made use of to relieve the patient; but for hours the sisters, though working with untiring energy, saw no beneficial result. At length, however, there came a cessation of pain, followed by sleep.

Now Gwyneth insisted Hilary should rest. She had been up the whole of the preceding night; she must take repose. Gwyneth's black eyes burned with a fever fire as she spoke; her cheeks were white, but her hand did not tremble, nor her lip falter.

"And you, Gwyneth," said Hilary, kissing her, as she listened to her low, yet impressive whispers; "do you not want rest?"

"No, not now, not yet; when I am tired I will rest, but it would be useless to try now, and I would rather be doing something."

"There are carriage wheels," said Hilary, listening. Gwyneth's face flushed for one moment, but the color died away as her sister said: "It must be Sybil!"

It was Sybil, not alone either; she was accompanied by her husband's uncle, a physician whom she had brought with her from London, a gentleman they all knew and liked exceedingly. The relief which the sight of the travelers afforded was very great; but as the patient was sleeping quietly, there was nothing else to be done but to welcome and refresh them.

Mr. Wild, the apothecary, was to call again in an hour or two; he had already hinted at the propriety of calling in more advice, and would, no doubt, be glad to have Dr. Symons to share his responsibility.

The sisters clustered together round the drawing-room fire, for the evening was so chilly that the travelers were glad of its warmth, and spoke in low, anxious tones of their hopes and fears. Sybil's indignation at the cause of this illness was less suppressed than her sisters; and murmurs of "careless," "thoughtless," "unpardonable," crossed her lips.

Then came Mr. Wild again, and a consultation between him and the physician; and then the sinking spirits with which they listened to the faint encouragements and doubtful words of the doctors. However, it was no time to give way; feeling and fear must be crushed down into the smallest possible space, anticipation must be prohibited, action and energy were what were now required. Gwyneth took the watch; her sisters were to sleep, and they could sleep all the more quietly, knowing that Dr. Symons was within call, if necessary.

There was scarce a shadow of amendment the next day, to cheer them; but there were no worse symptoms in the sick man; he slept much and heavily in the night, but when awake, pain was lessened, and consciousness more alive. The day passed in slow hours, marked by the changes in the sick room, as one sister after the other took her seat beside the bed. Gwyneth's restlessness increased hourly, when not stationed there; nothing else seemed to afford her a moment's quiet. Whatever of active exertion was required, she was the doer of it; she never tired, except of being unemployed, and her quickness of eye, readiness of thought, and lightness of finger, were much praised by Dr. Symons, who little guessed the source whence this unfailing activity sprung.

It was on the afternoon of Saturday, the third of Mr. Duncan's illness, when, as Gwyneth was crossing the vestibule, the pleasant sunshine streaming in at the open door, tempted her for a short space to pause in the porch. She lingered a minute, the next, as she turned away, a step caught her ear; it was Mr. Ufford. Her first inclination was to draw back, her next, and the governing one, was to advance composedly with extended hand.

There was, perhaps, a little confusion in his countenance as he looked at her; a little surprise at the deadly whiteness of her cheeks, the strange glance of her dark eyes, as he greeted her.

"You have been long coming," said she gravely; "my father has asked for you several times."

"I am sorry; I am but just returned from the Abbey. I will go to him now," he said, in great confusion and haste.

"No, you can not, he is asleep, now; Sybil just told me so; and Dr. Symons would not have him disturbed for the world." She spoke with an effort; she dared scarcely allow her breath to come, lest it should overpower her self-command. Each nerve was stretched, each muscle rigid in the exertion to seem calm.

"Asleep—Dr. Symons! Good heavens! what is the matter?" inquired he, startled into forgetting his own concerns, and really thinking of her words.

"Do you not know?" she paused. "Walk in, I will tell you when I can!" Another pause, during which she tried to strangle some heaving sobs, she overpowered some rebellious flutterings. "I think I will call Hilary!" she added, quickly, as a last resource, and hurried away from the room door. He entered. Nest was there alone. She rose, but would hardly speak or come forward.

"What is the matter, Nest?" exclaimed he, abruptly.

"Papa is no better," replied the child, looking down; "no better at all; and Dr. Symons, who came here yesterday, does not know how to make him better, and Sybil says, Mr. Ufford, it is all your fault!"

"My fault!" cried he; "how in the world? what have I to do with it?"

"Your being away, and obliging him to go out on Wednesday to the funeral, in all that storm; nobody knew where to find you, so poor papa had to do it himself."

A very unpleasant conviction accompanied the light which his understanding received by Nest's plain speaking. He colored, sat down, and was silent for some minutes.

"How long has he been ill?" said he, at last.

"Ever since Wednesday evening, when he caught cold; but here is Hilary."

Mr. Ufford rose, feeling singularly uncomfortable and embarrassed.

"I can not tell you how shocked I have been, Mrs. Hepburn, to hear of Mr. Duncan's sudden illness," said he; "I had no idea of it!"

"Did you not receive a message from me? we sent yesterday to beg you would come as soon as you could, as my father asked for you several times."

"I am but just returned from the Abbey!"

Hilary was silent and grave. Her looks were more of a reproach than any words she could have uttered; they spoke so plainly of grief, anxiety, and patience. He felt obliged to say something in excuse or apology; and with ever-increasing embarrassment, he said:

"I am so sorry it should have happened; but I quite forgot the notice, and all about the funeral—it was most unfortunate!"

Still Mrs. Hepburn was silent.

"My housekeeper ought to have reminded me, when I told her I was going out," continued he; "it was excessively careless of her to forget; I shall speak to her about it."

"If you usually depend upon her for those sort of things—" began Hilary, and then stopped suddenly.

"Besides, who could ever have supposed that people would be so mad as to go out in such weather at all?" added he, determined to be angry with somebody. "These old women have no more sense than a post; it was irrational, and I really think they must have intended to vex and annoy me."

"I think they are hardly to blame for keeping an appointment," said she; "they could not tell you would not be there, and, perhaps, were as much inconvenienced by the weather as you could have been, had you been present."

"I don't know that; they are used to rough it; and there is a sad spirit of spite and ill-will prevalent among them; a more selfish, ungrateful, thankless, obstinate set, I never met with. They are equally devoid of sense and affection."

"You do them injustice, I am sure; you would not doubt their affectionate feeling, if you heard their anxiety for my father. But I can not stay with you now. Can you wait here on the chance of my father's waking, or will you call in again by-and-by?"

Mr. Ufford was too glad to make his escape at that moment, and promising to call again in an hour's time, he walked off, trying to drown his own sense of wrong, by throwing the blame on every body in the parish except himself.

Mr. Duncan's attack proved an influenza of a most dangerous nature; and no skill or care from physicians or nurses, could arrest its progress or prevent its effects. He lingered on for nearly three weeks, and then darkness and silence fell on the Vicarage, sorrow and tears filled the village dwellings, for the father was taken from his children, and the pastor from his people, and the place that had known him would know him no more.

The sisters sat together in the gloomy rooms during those long summer days which intervened between the death and the funeral, each, perhaps, going over in silence in her own mind the scenes of childhood so deeply impressed on memory; the happy hours, the kindly-given lesson, the birth-day treat, the pleasant surprise, all coming from him who was now gone from them; each one a joy that never could recur again, but which, although now receding into the shadowy regions of the past, was yet even in recollection a thing to be valued and to be grateful for.

They had some great comforts also. Mr. Paine and his wife contrived to come to them, and he was dearly welcomed, both as friend and priest, and she was an unspeakable solace to Hilary. Their brother-in-law had joined them the week after Sybil came, and his presence relieved them of the painful intrusions which funeral arrangements gave rise to.

Hilary knew that support and comfort would come alone from a higher source than earthly friendship, or domestic affection; but the gift of these latter was received as a favor to deserve gratitude, a token that He who provided even for temporal blessings, would not forsake his children, nor withdraw from them the necessary help.

Her greatest anxiety was for Gwyneth now; and, perhaps, her bitterest sorrow was caused by Mr. Ufford.

The latter, indeed, had deeply disappointed her by the coldness and reserve which, like a damp, wrapping mist, had crept over him. His visits had been few and hurried, except when absolutely sent for; his words cold, stiff, and unwillingly given. His time was principally devoted to riding over to the Abbey, which swallowed up most days in the week. His own prospects, of course, chiefly occupied him, and, no doubt, the visits at the Vicarage were painful for more than one reason; yet, when they remembered the past, their father's kindness to him, his previous conduct, and friendly professions, and his connection with their sad loss, they all felt that something more was due from him than they received; perhaps he, too, was conscious of ingratitude, which made the sight of former friends unpleasant; perhaps he was simply self-engrossed, and thoughtless regarding the sorrows which did not touch him.

But Gwyneth was a nearer, deeper trouble, and Hilary could not look at her without fear. The same stony composure wrapped her still. Ever since her father's death she had shed no tear; but her dark eyes looked blacker than ever by contrast with her white cheeks; she spoke little, never of her feelings; she rested little; but with a strange, untiring energy, she seemed always engrossed by some object for the good of others. An ordinary observer would never have guessed the amount of agony and endurance that pallid brow concealed; but Hilary read it in her silence, in her downcast eyes, and in the burning touch of her fevered fingers, and she read it with fear; for such unnatural suppression of feeling, such intense and over-wrought calmness must, she knew, break down at last: and what would be the end of it?

CHAPTER XXI.

"Chill blows the wind, the pleasaunce walks are drear,
Madcap, what jest was this to meet me here!
Were feet like those made for so wild a way?
The southern chamber had been, by my fay,
More fitting trysting-place for us to-day!"

Tristram and Iseult.

Mrs. Hepburn's fears for her sister were not immediately realized; for weeks there was no symptom of the reaction she had dreaded. Gwyneth threw herself with a passionate energy into all the preparations, the business, and the distressing bustle which must follow the decease of a clergyman. The necessity of leaving the home of their whole life, the doubts where to go; the troublesome technicalities of dilapidations, and other matters of the same kind; the anxiety regarding what Maurice would wish done in his absence; the misery of parting with all the treasured relics which a family mansion contains, of knowing that all they had loved and valued must pass into other and careless hands, painful as they were, did not daunt her spirit. Her one wish was to leave the place; her answer, when Hilary begged her not to overtire herself, was generally, "I can not rest at Hurstdene."

No, she could not rest there, now she knew that she must, eventually, leave it; now that her pleasant visions had been so rudely overthrown; that her day-dreams had proved more evanescent than the sunset glory on the tree-tops; rest in *his* house, she could not; knowing, as she did, that he only waited for their quitting it to pull down the whole, from ridge-tile to door-sill. Rest there! where he, who was now whispering soft things to another, had once said and looked such words, such meanings to herself, as she dared not now recall. She was incessantly urgent to be gone; but nothing would persuade her to go first; she would not yield so far as to seem unable to remain. Sybil took Nest back to London with her, Gwyneth remained with Hilary.

The marriage of Mr. Barham's daughters was approaching; one ceremony was to unite the two couples, and the country round re-echoed with gossip on the subject. The owner of "the Ferns" was at home, Dora, too, had returned to Drewhurst Abbey; all there looked as bright and gay, to outward seeming, as the affairs at the Vicarage showed dull and sad. The black crape of the mourners, and the orange wreaths of the young brides, were but the symbols of the apparent contrast between their present prospects.

Yet, perhaps, all was not as it seemed; there might be throbbing hearts and wrung feelings under the folds of the richest brocades; there might be bitter tears in secret, shed over the elegant baubles which custom dedicates as fitting presents for a wedding; there might be a shadow upon the mental vision, through whose thick gloom the bridal finery might appear but as a ghastly mockery, more fearful, more dismal, than a funeral pall.

And there are consolations for unselfish mourners, which bear up the heart, and support the drooping spirit, and make the feeble strong; sweet thoughts of peace, which fill the void that death occasions, and make even memory a comfort and a blessing, though it calls up scenes never to be repeated here. No, the parting which a hopeful death occasions, is not the darkest shadow in this world of sorrow!

Isabel Barham in due time paid a visit of condolence to her friends at the Vicarage. Hilary met her alone, Gwyneth was busy, and did not appear. Miss Barham seemed really touched as she saw Mrs. Hepburn's pale cheeks and black garments; perhaps the contrast of their present situations struck her, perhaps she remembered how much of pain and sorrow had followed Hilary, since the time when she had been a bride.

She spoke kindly and affectionately, and inquired with great interest as to their intentions.

"We shall leave this next week," said Hilary. "Maurice and Captain Hepburn are both desirous we should be nearer the southern coast, and we think of a house not very far from Southampton. Mr. Farrington has a sister settled there, and though we should not like to live in a town, it would not be convenient to be very far from one."

"Then we shall lose you quite, I fear; I was half in hopes we should have had you settled in this neighborhood still. I was talking to Mr. Huyton about Primrose Bank for you, but he did not seem much to like it."

"Thank you for thinking of us; but to have us within an easy distance of either London or Portsmouth is my husband's object, and Southampton unites both. He and my brother are my sister's guardians, and we shall, I hope, always continue to live together."

"That will be very nice; and Hilary, you will not mind my asking as a friend, you will be comfortable as to circumstances—income I mean?"

"Yes, we shall do very well; we have never been accustomed to luxury, and we shall not have much to resign of that kind."

"I see you have been packing up," said Isabel, looking round.

"Yes, such things as we take with us; Maurice would like us to keep all, but there is much that it would not be worth while to move. He has left it entirely to my discretion."

"And this will be my farewell visit then; I am afraid I shall be too much occupied to come again. By-the-by, Dora told me to ask if you would see her; I wanted her to come with me, but she had some scruples, I could not understand what, and only sent a message."

"Yes, I should," said Hilary, with warmth, "I should indeed like to see her, pray tell her so. How is Lord Dunsmore now; have you better accounts of him?"

A shade passed over Isabel's face.

"Why, the accounts lately have spoken of his being better; he has seemed to rally a little since the death of his child, but those sort of partial revivals are not uncommon in pulmonary complaints, and I can not imagine that, ill as he has been, he has any real chance of recovery."

"I thought," observed Hilary, "that it was doubtful whether his was a pulmonary attack."

"I believe one or two physicians pretended to doubt it," replied Isabel, a little impatiently; "but the most eminent declared it hopeless, and no one could see him, I should suppose, and question his having every appearance of a victim to consumption."

"Can I not see Gwyneth?" continued Isabel, after a pause.

"I will try to find her if you will excuse me for a few minutes."

Hilary had no little difficulty in persuading her sister to appear; she made some excuses about business and unfitness of dress, but finally yielded, with the air of one who resigns herself to walking to the stake. Her heart revolted from meeting her successful rival, and when she remembered the visits of former days, when her company had been assiduously sought as a screen and an excuse for other interviews, when she had been made so unconsciously to administer to her rival's objects, and her own disappointment, it did require no small share of resolute fortitude to go through the ordeal before her.

It was borne, however, as many other trials had been borne, by putting away thought and feeling, by avoiding to scan her own sensations, and simply taking pains to do the present duty rightly; as a traveler among precipices, on a narrow path, refuses to look down into the unguarded gulf below him, and keeps his faculties steady, by engaging every one in the task of setting the next footstep safely.

The next day, as Hilary was busily engrossed in writing, she thought she heard a step behind her, and looking round, saw, to her surprise, Dora Barham standing there alone.

Apparently she had just ridden over from the Abbey, but her hat was thrown off, and her long hair was hanging somewhat disordered down her pale cheeks, while she stood, with parted lips and fixed eye, and hands half raised, as if hesitating whether to speak, or to retire.

"Dora, dear Dora!" said Hilary, holding out her hands. In another moment Dora was in her arms, hiding her face upon her shoulder, and sobbing out incoherent words of tenderness, sorrow, and self-reproach. Her friend did not speak, but caressed her softly, and waited until this ecstacy was over, well knowing, from experience, that Dora's moods were somewhat changeable.

At length she raised her head, and with downcast eyes, and tears trembling on the lashes, she asked, in an agitated voice, "Oh, Hilary! what do you think of me?"

"That you are very kind to come and see me, dear," replied Mrs. Hepburn, smiling gently.

"Ah, well! perhaps it is wisest to say nothing of the past, we will talk of something else. This dear old place, this happy, happy room, that beloved garden. Oh, Hilary, Hilary! my heart will break."

"It is very painful to leave it," replied Hilary; "it is always hard to give up scenes to which the heart clings, and I understand Mr. Ufford means to pull it all down, and build a new and larger vicarage. He can hardly make it grand enough for your sister's habits, without making it too grand for the living."

"I dare say not," said Dora, abstractedly. "You have removed the pictures?" Her eye had sought for one portrait which used to hang in that room.

"Yes, most things are packed up, ready for removal: we go ourselves very soon."

"Ah, me! ah, me! and how is—how are your sailor friends?" Her cheeks varied from red to white.

"Well, quite well."

"Hilary!"

"Well, dear, what?"

"Tell me! oh, tell me!—in another week I may not ask, or even think of him—tell me now in mercy—" she put her hand to her head.

"Yes, but what am I to tell you, Dora? he is well, quite well."

"Tell me what he thinks of me; tell me or I shall go mad! Does he hate me, despise me, as an idle, giddy, trifling coquette, a heartless, ambitious girl, content to sell my hand and person? Does he not loath me from his heart? He must, he can not help it."

"No, indeed."

"Has he mentioned my name to you? What did he say? What *could* he say but words of contempt and scorn!"

"No, neither contempt nor scorn; far from it he says. I will read you what he says;" and turning to her desk, Hilary presently produced the letter containing the allusions to Dora's marriage. She read his message, while Dora, listening, held her breath as if afraid to lose a word.

"Good, noble, honorable Maurice, too good, too kind," said she at length, "happy, happy for you that you are not bound to so worthless, so feeble a creature as I am! Ah! I am glad, glad, most glad that you are not miserable. Read it again, Hilary, once more; or no, let me see for once, only once, his blessed writing." She caught the letter from her friend, and began to read it herself. Mrs. Hepburn remonstrated, but Dora held the letter with both hands, and read, eagerly devouring the words with her eyes, and totally deaf to her companion's voice. Then, when she had done, she passionately kissed the paper, pressed it to her heart, looked at it again; and again, with streaming eyes, put her lips to the signature.

"Wretch, wretch that I am!" she cried, frantically; "oh, Hilary! I shall die, my heart will break, I know I shall! I often have a burning pain here in my bosom, or my head, which can not last; iron, flint, granite, breaks or pulverizes; surely human life is not harder, not more tenacious than those. Tell me, shall I not die?"

"Yes, Dora, one day; we must all die once: but death is a solemn thing, not to be met unprepared; and these wild and passionate expressions are not a fitting preparation for this great reality. Give me back that letter."

"No, let me keep it; it is mine, for me, concerns me most."

"You must not, Dora; remember, you are to be another man's wife next week."

"Next week! ah! when I am, I will send it to you; let me keep it now."

"To keep it now ought not to be any object to you. Give it me back. If you value it, you must not retain it; if you do not, you will not wish to keep it."

"Till the last—till my—my wedding-day!" said she with a ghastly smile.

"If you wish for happiness, if you value peace, return it!"

"Happiness! Peace! we have long parted company—I lost them when the *Erratic* sailed; happiness, as the wife of a man who does not care for me—for whom I have no regard; peace with a husband who weds me while his heart is another's, knowing, too, that mine is pre-engaged; who seeks me from pique; whom I have accepted from cowardice. Yes, ours will be a home of happiness and peace, the hearth of domestic felicity, the very center of all true and happy virtues."

"Dora! Dora! how can you talk so!" cried Hilary, shocked and dismayed.

"Talk! ask me how I can act so! what does talking signify! ah me!"

"But, Dora, is it possible that with such sentiments, such feelings, you can be really going to marry? oh, think before you take an irrevocable step; before you deceive yourself and him, too far!"

"I am not deceiving him, Hilary; he knows what he is about; come, I will tell you all, only listen."

She threw herself on the ground at her friend's feet, her favorite attitude, and poured out her story.

"We parted coldly, I was offended, vain, foolish thing! I misunderstood the very devotion of his heart; then came Charles Huyton, tempting me with wily words. I knew he did not love me. I knew it was you he worshiped; I saw through his motive, and trusting that he would himself weary of so unsuitable a union, I said yes! I was mad—provoked; but I did not mean it, I thought I should have escaped. But I knew not his resolution in evil; his stern purpose, his dark determination; day after day have the toils closed round me; the net in which I wound myself has entangled me more. I can not shake myself free; he *will* marry me; and I can not, dare not, say *no*. Oh, Hilary! do you know his dark expression, did you ever see how his eyes can glow and sparkle with gloomy fire? Once I did not dislike him; now I dread him beyond measure, and compared with Maurice! don't tell him how miserable I am, it would make him sad; at least, not till it is over! when I am dead, then, then, tell him that my heart was broken. Ah, Hilary!"

"Dear Dora! what can I say to you? do not go on with this; not for Maurice, not for his sake, but for your own. For your conscience, your honor, your virtue, do not risk all by such a fatal step. Think, pray — pray for strength, for light, for guidance, and stop before it is too late."

"Pray! what, when about to do what is so wrong?" murmured Dora; "would such prayers be heard?"

"Yes; prayer to do better, to have grace to repent! prayer is always heard."

"Nay, then, I will pray for death! that would be the greatest boon to me."

"Dora, if you had stood as I so recently did by a death-bed, if you had witnessed how solemn a thing it is to prepare to render up the soul, how the weakness of the body prostrates the powers of the mind, and how even the humblest, truest faith, does not exclude bitter penitence for failings long past and errors known besides only to the Great Creator, you would not, you could not, wish to rush unprepared to such a solemn work as dying. Think, Dora, if after such a life as my father's, there was so much regret for misspent moments, such humble acknowledgment of unfulfilled duties, think what it would be to face our end, because we are too weak to suffer for the truth; what madness to call on death to save us from earthly fears, and dare to face our Judge, because we will not do our duty here, from dread of a fellow-creature's censure! oh, Dora, consider!"

"Tell me about your father, Hilary," said Dora, in a broken voice, and hiding her eyes against her friend's knees; and Mrs. Hepburn thinking that, perhaps, to turn her thoughts from herself might be useful, related such particulars of Mr. Duncan's death-bed as she believed might soothe and interest her auditor. She was seriously alarmed for Dora's state of mind. There was a restlessness in her eyes, a nervous twitching of her muscles, a variation in her complexion, and other similar symptoms, which she thought indicated extreme mental excitement; and her wildly variable manner, her sudden changes of subject in conversation, and her extraordinary tones, confirmed these fears. She appeared, so far as Hilary could judge, like one on the brink of a violent fever; and the thought passed through her mind, that, perhaps, the marriage she so deeply deprecated, might, after all, be arrested by causes over which even Mr. Huyton had no control.

Dora sat for some time profoundly silent, and, except for the occasional deep heaving of her breast, quite composed outwardly. At length, when

Mrs. Hepburn ceased speaking, she slowly rose, and after kissing her two or three times, she walked away to the window, and stood there looking out in silence. Then she said, but without turning round:

"Hilary, if there is one person whose influence could induce Charles Huyton to break off this hateful marriage, one who could soften his heart, and lead him to have pity on me, on Maurice, on himself, it is *you*. If you would intercede for us!"

"Dora," said Hilary, hurriedly interrupting her, "you mistake; you are not thinking of what you are saying. I can have no such power as you suppose; and for me to interfere in any way with him, would be alike useless and impossible. I can do you no good."

"Ah, you do not know—his former feeling for you is still—"

"Hush, Dora; if former feeling for me exists, it is an insult and a wrong to hear of it; an insult to me, a wrong to my husband. What influence could the wife of Captain Hepburn exercise over the mind of Mr. Huyton, in such a cause?"

"It might not be a wrong influence; I meant no harm! I know that, though angry at your marriage, he still looks up to you, respects you, esteems you above all other women; and a word from you, such as you have spoken just now to me, would, perhaps, awaken him to a sense of right and wrong, might arouse some remorse and repentance before it is too late."

"Dear Dora, I believe you to be most entirely mistaken; and even could I with propriety speak, the opportunity may never occur, and your conduct, your decision, ought not to depend upon the chance of my speaking, or the possibility of my influencing him. Act for yourself; follow your own sense of duty, and dare to be true even at last."

Dora sighed heavily, and turned away. More Hilary said to the same purpose, but in vain; Miss Barham continued uncertain and miserably undecided, and when at length she quitted the Vicarage, it was with no assurance that she would not, after all, pursue the dangerous road that she was treading.

Her last words were:

"Oh, Hilary, why did you not love and marry him, then we might all have been happy!"

The sisters' residence at the Vicarage was rapidly drawing to a close. A long farewell had been said to every well-known forest nook and glade, each beloved haunt of bygone days; a sad leave had been taken of each parishioner, each lowly friend and affectionate well-wisher, many parting tokens had been humbly but kindly offered, from those who had known them from childhood, or begged as precious memorials of the late Vicar and his daughters, by the sorrowful parishioners, who still grieved for their best friend. The last Sunday came, and they knelt for the last time on the spot where for years their devotions had been offered up. Every look was now a pain, every action almost caused a pang, and both sisters ardently wished the time were come which should put an end to the sorrowful dream in which they now seemed to move. There was no outward demonstration of their grief, it wore the calm, grave, torpid aspect, that a dull November day presents, when the sky is all shrouded in a somber vail of gray, and the distant hills wear the same heavy tint; while no wind moves through the half-bare trees, or wakens the waters to life. Over such a scene silence and stillness brood, the silence of death-like sleep, made only more apparent as the soft rustle of a falling leaf catches the ear, or the eye is attracted by its movement, as it calmly floats to the dull earth beneath.

The afternoon of Monday, the last afternoon they were to spend in their old home, Hilary walked down alone to visit for the last time the graves of those so dear to her, and look once more on the favorite spot where many a peaceful hour had been spent.

She walked slowly and softly all round the western end of the church, scanning its gray tower, and casting loving glances at each well-known window. The workmen had not been there for several days, but their poles and scaffolding encumbered the place, and spoke of decay and change, of old things being replaced by new, of all passing away and being forgotten in turn. Her mind went off to scenes where change is unknown—where rust and moth do not invade—where decay comes not—where, blessed thought! distance is not, separation can not grieve, where there is no more sea! Her thoughts were with her husband then, as she must, at least in idea, share all gentle, happy thoughts with him; but her hopes were not bounded by earth; they had gone on into futurity, and time seemed but an atom in space, while she gazed on the vast prospect of eternity.

Slowly and softly she trod over the grass, among the graves of hundreds who had loved, and suffered, and wept as she had, and then lain down to sleep and be forgotten. She passed the northern transept, and turning the corner, came forward, with inaudible footsteps, to the eastern end. She was startled suddenly from her reveries, for there, under the old lime-tree, whose yellow leaves now thickly strewed the ground, stood one whom she little thought to see there at such a time; Charles Huyton stood beside her father's grave.

Roused by her footsteps, he looked up suddenly, and starting as he saw her, he raised his hat, with an air of almost haughty defiance, but stood still.

Old memories flashed thick and fast on each, as they stood there once more together, and their eyes wandered away to the church-wall, and to the Virginian creeper, whose long sprays still showed some crimson leaves clinging to their parent stem, waiting their turn to fall to rest. Then their looks met, and they each aroused themselves to speak.

"Mr. Huyton," said she, advancing a step, "we are both changed since we stood here once before; and after all that has passed, there is, perhaps, no spot on earth so appropriate as this for us to part. Here, by the grave of one who loved you, and whom I know you must have esteemed and valued in return, let us bury all that may have caused pain to either, and exchange a farewell and forgiveness together."

"I do not agree with you," replied he, coldly, and making no offer to receive her hand; "it does not appear to me that any two people on this earth can have less reason to wish to speak, or that a spot so unfortunate for a meeting could be found."

She was silenced for a time; he stood gloomily looking at her; at length she said, very gently:

"We leave this place to-morrow morning, and I am come now to pay a last, a final visit, to this solemn spot. Need I say more, or need I ask you, as a gentleman, not to intrude on a seclusion so sacred; not to persecute me here with unkind and unholy emotions!"

"Have I wronged you, Mrs. Hepburn, that you talk of forgiveness?" said he, sternly.

"If *your* conscience can acquit you, Mr. Huyton, it is not necessary for me to recall unpleasant recollections. Do not let us discuss the subject."

"Forgiveness implies a sense of injury," persisted he; "I have a right to know how I have incurred the charge."

"When we last parted," said she, after a pause, looking at him with gentle eyes, "you asked earnestly and urgently to be considered as my friend. What have I done since, to cause this change in you; that now, when we are parting, perhaps for ever, you will not say one kindly word; will not bid me good speed, nor let me give you my good wishes?"

"If my memory serves me rightly, you refused those urgent entreaties, you declined decidedly, the friendship which I offered. Am I to conclude that your refusal was insincere, and that you wished to keep me at your feet, even while you affected to repulse me?"

"You are cruelly unjust, Mr. Huyton," was her answer; "I told you that intercourse between us must cease, until—I am sure you must remember the condition—nor have I even now, when that condition is about to be fulfilled, the slightest wish to carry on the acquaintance; I only asked for an exchange of parting words; and my only wish now is, that you should leave me in peace. At least do not profane this spot with bitter words. I pray Heaven to bless you, and lead you to true happiness here and hereafter."

"Yes, the condition *is* about to be fulfilled," repeated he, as if in a dream; then starting, he said, with more animation; "and the fulfillment of this condition then meets your entire approbation?"

He fixed his eyes on her with a piercing glance, under which she shrank and colored. "The choice you would not make yourself, you approve of for your friend, do you?"

"If you think you can make Dora happy, Mr. Huyton, if that is your wish, your determination, all your friends and hers must approve of your choice."

"Happy!" repeated he, scornfully, "oh, yes! very happy; as happy as she deserves, and you know how much that is. Tell me now truly," coming a step closer to her, "would you rather see the object of your idolatry, of your passionate devotion, happy with another, forgetful of your affection; or know her miserable, but constant at heart?"

"Real, devoted affection must wish its object to be happy; it is a very selfish love which can endure no pleasure which it does not share," said she, gravely.

He seemed to be pondering her words, then answered: "That may be woman's love; a man's is different. I do not believe the man exists who would make such a choice."

"I know you are mistaken," she said, and her looks told him where her thoughts had flown.

"Answer me one other question," said he; "I know you can not choose but answer sincerely. Tell me has my intended marriage occasioned you either pain or pleasure?"

She hesitated. Dora's wild words crossed her mind. Would her answer have any influence on her friend's fate? could it be that he regretted the grief he had occasioned, and would repair it even now?

"Speak, I implore you," added he, as she waited to consider.

"Would my reply make any difference in the result? would the knowledge of my opinion influence your conduct?" she asked, looking up at him.

"Try," said he; but it was with an expression of eye she did not like.

"No, I will not. I see no good could come of the answer!"

"Thank you, that is enough!" said he, with a bitter smile; "I know that could Hilary Duncan have expressed any pleasure or even unconcern, she would have done so at once; and I do not suppose Hilary Hepburn is less sincere."

She colored again, and after a momentary hesitation, she said: "I believe you may be right in your inference, but the cause of the pain must be unknown to you."

"Is it? do not fear that I should attribute it to piqued feminine vanity, or disappointment of selfish triumph, which would gladly retain the love it does not return. I know you better than that. I know that thoughts of self did not mingle with your pain; the disappointment Dora's marriage cost you, has but little to do with mine."

"Much of the disappointment I have felt, arises from regret, Mr. Huyton; regret to see a mind formed for better things and nobler, holier tempers, a mind which can appreciate the beautiful, the true, the good, perverted by an unwise and ungoverned passion, till it could stoop to malicious retaliation and mean revenge, for imaginary injuries; to deception and hypocrisy to carry out its objects. Whatever other sorrow I may have felt, my keenest has been to lose the power of esteeming one whom I had known so long." Tears started into her eyes as she spoke, and she looked at him with an expression of pity he found it hard to withstand. She thought she saw a wavering, uncertain glance, and she hoped that, perhaps, even now he might relent. She ventured to speak again.

"Forgive me for uttering what may seem harsh; my words were, perhaps, too strong; but let me say one thing more. In three days you are, they say, to give your hand to Dora Barham, and with your hand to promise your love! Is it affection for her that actuates you? and shall you be sincere in the vows you plight her? If not, what hope of happiness is there for you or for her?"

"I neither know nor care," replied he, hastily; "all I know is, that Thursday I will wed Dora, and that no persuasion, no argument of yours, shall move me from my purpose. No, Hilary! you were deaf to my prayers, cold to my earnest love, you turned from me with indifference, again and again. Now—" He did not finish his sentence, but raising his hat from his forehead, he bowed low, and then strode hastily away. Hilary sat down on the bench under the lime-tree, and wept bitterly. It was long before she raised her head from her hands; when she did, and looked round, twilight had fallen on the earth, and her last day at Hurstdene had closed in.

Startled to find how late it was, she rose to return home, and with a lingering glance at the swelling turf and white tombstones, she walked toward the church-yard stile, her heart full of deep and holy thoughts, of heavenly aspirations and hopes. Her mind was brought back to present things by one of those rude contrasts which jar so painfully at such a time, while they recall the sad reality of sin in its coarsest aspect.

Lolling upon the stile over which she had to pass, she saw through the gloom the figure of a man who, as well as she could judge, appeared to be a stranger, perhaps a traveling peddler, for his pack was on the wall beside him. He did not move as she approached, but seeing her, he said, in a voice which betrayed that he had been drinking,

"A pleasant evening, my dear!"

Hilary felt alarmed for a moment; but she had the courage of a brave woman, which, though it does not make her insensible to danger, even in the moment of alarm leaves her the calm possession of her faculties. She believed that to seem gravely self-possessed was the best check to vulgar insolence; and remembering that there were cottages close at hand, whose inmates she could summon by a cry, she said, in a calm voice, which would have influenced a sober man immediately—

"I will trouble you to allow me to pass, my good man."

The ruffian, however, was insensible to the tone and manner of her appeal, and only quitted his position to grasp her arm, swearing that he always made a pretty girl pay toll.

Hilary started back, and raising her voice, called by name upon the inhabitants of the nearest dwelling for assistance; but hardly had she uttered a single cry when a strong arm was thrown round her waist, and so powerful a blow at the same moment was discharged in the face of her assailant, as leveled him to the ground. Half-lifted, half-voluntarily springing over the stile, she found herself safe upon the green, while Charles Huyton, whose arm had so opportunely defended her, supported her in silence toward her home. At the same time other steps were heard approaching, and the cottager on whom she had called, hurried up to demand whether any thing were the matter.

Hilary paused, and though with some difficulty commanding her voice, she replied,

"There is a man in the church-yard who has had a fall, Martin; go and see if he is seriously hurt."

"And tell him," added Mr. Huyton, "that if he does not instantly decamp, I will send a constable after him to-morrow, and punish him for his conduct. The atrocious ruffian!" added he, in a lower voice, which yet trembled with passion, "to dare to insult you with his vulgar insolence. Thank Heaven that I was there to save you!"

Hilary could not answer for a little while; her nerves were unstrung, and tears were following each other down her cheeks, choking her voice, and agitating her whole person. They walked on for some yards in silence; but by resolute efforts she so far conquered her emotion as to be able to speak.

"I am much obliged to you; I need not detain you longer, I am quite safe now!"

She would have drawn away her hand from under his arm, but he retained it still, and finding he was resolved to accompany her, she seized the opportunity to make one effort more.

"Mr. Huyton you are indignant at the man who, in his stupid, half-insensible brutality, has just alarmed me by his coarseness; but is it more inexcusable than the refined and considerate cruelty which tortures the feelings and wrings the hearts of those who having never offended, are yet sacrificed to the revengeful determination of another?"

He made no answer at all; but she fancied, from the motion of the arm on which she rested, that he was contending with suppressed agitation. It was too dark to see his features distinctly.

"I know," she continued, softly, "that you have good and noble sentiments left in your heart; your interference for my rescue shows that; your evil angel may whisper dark thoughts to you, but the promptings of a better spirit are still heard; oh! listen, and yield to it; and, not for my sake, but for your own, your happiness now, and your welfare in eternity, banish revengeful thoughts; forgive *me* for the fancied injury which you resent, and make poor Dora happy!"

They had reached the wicket gate. She paused, and held out her hand.

"Say one kind farewell, and let us part as friends!"

He grasped her hand so firmly as almost to cause unbearable pain, hesitated, and then said in a wild tone,

"No—no, I have sworn, and will not falter from my word;" and throwing her hand from him, he rushed rapidly away.

CHAPTER XXII.

"Or perchance has her young heart
Felt already some deeper smart
Of those that in secret her heart-strings rive,
Leaving her sunk and pale, though fair."

Iseult of Brittany.

Wearied in body, and exhausted in mind, Hilary entered the house with slow and lingering steps. Gwyneth met her in the vestibule with an exclamation of—

"How late you are, Hilary!"

"Yes," replied the latter, looking fixedly at her sister. "What is the matter, dear?"

She saw, by the glow in Gwyneth's eyes, and the deadly whiteness of her cheeks, which looked like marble by lamplight, that something had occurred to stir her feelings. Gwyneth laid her finger on her lips, and then whispered, as she motioned to the drawing-room door,

"Mr. Ufford has been waiting for a long time to say good-by."

They entered the sitting-room together. Mr. Ufford was standing by the chimney in a fit of abstraction apparently, turning over the leaves of a small prayer-book belonging to Miss Duncan, which he had found on the table. They had, as I have said, seen but little of each other since the late vicar's death. He was devoted to his visits at the Abbey, which every week had seemed to engross him more and more, while the curate, whom he had engaged as soon as he had the power to do so, had taken almost the entire charge of the parish. Excepting chance meetings, therefore, their interviews had been few and short; but now he had called to say a last farewell.

Rousing himself when he saw the sisters enter, he tried to say something kind and friendly, but his words came stiffly and unwillingly; and his sentences, instead of flowing with their usual ready freedom, broke down generally in the middle. Hilary was sorry for him; more so, perhaps, than he deserved, but she did not study to suit her commisseration exactly to his merits; she helped him all she could, by ready politeness, and a free, disengaged air; turning the conversation, so far as was in her power, to safe topics, unconnected with sentiment or feeling. She told him that they had already engaged a house near Southampton, situated, as they understood, on the borders of some forest land; that Mrs. Lawrence, Sybil's sister-in-law, had been most kind in superintending the arrangements; that Sybil herself had been down there to see that all was ready, and that they expected, therefore, to find the house perfectly habitable on their arrival.

Mr. Ufford expressed the warmest satisfaction at this intelligence. He was delighted to think that they would have friends in their new home. Then he looked round the room, where he had spent so many hours, and inquired if they were not going to have a sale of the furniture.

It was, perhaps, fortunate for the composure of the sisters, if not creditable to the feelings of the gentleman, that this question was put in so matter-of-fact a way. It had been a sore trial to them, only to think of parting with the loved old furniture, companions of childhood, witnesses of their former life, bound to their affections by so many ties of association. Scarcely a chair but was filled by the shadowy memory of some well-known form, or a table but was connected with some of their daily habits. It had been a struggle to resolve to part with any thing; but prudence and justice prevailed over inclination. Much of it, such as side-boards, cabinets, and book-cases, were extremely heavy, and though old-fashioned, was valuable from the beauty of the time-stained wood. All these had been readily purchased by a cabinet-maker of the next town; and as Maurice had given the whole furniture to his two youngest sisters, the value of these articles made no inconsiderable addition to their very moderate portions. Still it was a painful subject, especially to Gwyneth, and perhaps, had the visitor evinced a shadow of sympathy in his tone, her composure would at that moment have given way.

He spoke, however, in a voice as indifferent as if he had been merely discussing the renunciation of a worn-out garment, and his companions felt at the moment almost surprised at caring so much for what ought to be so easy, and nearly convinced that it was the simplest affair in the world to break off half the ties and reminiscences of a life-time.

Hilary answered that the sale was to take place next week; whereupon he observed that he should then probably be at Paris, as he and Miss Barham had agreed to pass through France, intending to go by way of Marseilles to Italy, and to spend great part of the winter at Naples, with Lord Dunsmore. Accounts from him continued very variable, and it was his uncertain state that made them desirous to have the wedding a quiet one.

Hilary was surprised. "A quiet wedding!" thought she; "I wonder what they would have had." She had heard of guests to the number nearly of a hundred expected at church: she had heard of feasting of the tenantry, and ale and bonfires, garlands, and flower-strewing, processions of children in new frocks and bonnets, and other gayeties, which Isabel seemed indefatigable in planning in the most poetical style, and arranging in the most symmetrical manner. It seemed very right and suitable for those in the rank and station of Mr. Barham's daughters; perfectly consistent with their future expectations also, for they were co-heiresses of a large property, and held a leading position among the county society. Mrs. Hepburn had not a word to say against the facts, but it amazed her to hear such proceedings styled "quietness;" so she contented herself with observing that she had no doubt but that it would all be extremely elegant, and kept her other opinions to herself.

Mr. Ufford seemed to take for granted that his auditors felt a strong interest in his proceedings, and accordingly conversed for some time with fluency on his bride's various plans; but at length, remembering that he must go home, he took leave, with sundry good wishes for their welfare, and a kindness of manner which would have been very pleasing, had there been no private unacknowledged feelings to turn it into pain.

Gwyneth, whose face looked in a white heat, perfectly intelligible to those who knew her well, watched him out of the room, and listened for the closing of the house-door, then turning away, she murmured, with a sigh of relief, "To-morrow."

The morrow came, and early in the dull morning the sisters, accompanied by one attached domestic, who had lived with them from girlhood, when she waited on Hilary's mother, and was now an active and respectable woman, a little above forty, set off on their journey to meet some branch of the complicated iron framework which ramifies so widely through our land, and which, after a due number of changes, a sufficient degree of waiting at some stations, hurry at others, and misunderstanding at all, of trouble, of anxiety, and of delay, landed them safely within as short a distance of their future home as they could hope to attain.

Mrs. Lawrence kindly met them at the station, and her carriage conveyed the somewhat dispirited and weary travelers from thence to their new abode. It had been a mournful day, and one which required every support that trusting love and humble faith could afford, not to overpower composure. After catching the last glimpse of those dear old trees, Gwyneth had drawn down her thick crape vail, and long after that time no unnecessary word had passed her lips; but whether she were crying or not her sister could not tell.

Hilary had so many important trifles to attend to that she could not give her mind wholly to thought or feeling, and for some time she scarcely realized what had occurred. Still, in those periods of tranquillity which intervened, when she could think composedly, there was ever a light rising up clear and pure, although distant far, which brightened the gloom of her prospects, and prevented her being overwhelmed with sorrow. Hurstdene was not to her the whole world, as it was to Gwyneth; and though tender remembrances and buried affections must hover round the graves of the dear ones lying there, her heart was not at the Vicarage now: the tie that had bound her was broken, and another and a stronger bore her on in hope. It was her husband's wish she was fulfilling, and she felt as if, now that she was brought more entirely to depend on him, they were more closely united than ever. She might now give him the first claim on her thoughts, which before had been shared with her father; and though hardly yet accustomed to the void which their recent and great loss had occasioned, she had hope and tender love to fill it up. Every step seemed to bring her nearer to her husband, since every step was in obedience to him, and although the parting from her old home had been a bitter effort, she was able to throw her mind forward, with some degree of cheerfulness, to the future.

And more than all the earthly love which brightened her path was that high and holy, that deeply reverent affection, of which conjugal union is but a type and an emblem; that trust and simple faith which can always support the most lonely, and soothe the most sad.

"Yes," thought she, "if it is so easy to do my husband's bidding, and follow his guidance, how much more easy, how infinitely more sweet ought it to be to submit to the Hand which can not err, to trust to the Eye which never closes, to obey the Will which has surely promised good to those who humbly wait on it; only let me stay myself on that great support, and all will be, all must be well at last."

And so she charmed to rest her mournful thoughts, and took readily and thankfully the good which still surrounded her. In imagination, she scanned what her future occupation might be, and half wondered what work would arise to fill the place of those happy labors which had formerly engaged her. The education of her youngest sister would, of course, be her principal occupation, that would supply employment for many hours; but there must be other duties also to be discovered and followed up; doubtless they would show themselves in time; and though her work might not be so obviously laid before her as in her own home and former situation, she believed that if she faithfully followed the most apparent duty, and did her best in that, others would present themselves in time, and make good their claim on her attention, even as you may reach the extremity of the longest chain, if you have once secured the first link.

It was from meditations such as these that she was roused by their arrival at their destination; and she was able to come back from them with cheerfulness, to greet the kind and thoughtful stranger who had taken such pains to show them friendly feeling and good will. Mrs. Lawrence did not enter with them their new residence; she judged that the sisters would be glad to rest, without feeling constrained to exercise civility; she therefore left them at the door, with a promise to see them to-morrow, and trusting they would find all right, she departed. Hilary took Gwyneth under the arm, and they walked in together, leaving the two maids to arrange the trunks, while they took the first view of their new home.

Small it was, but very comfortable, and the furniture had been arranged by tasteful and loving hands. On the table stood the tea-service just ready for the weary travelers, and on the cheerful fire bubbled and hissed the little kettle. Flowers were in the vases too, and the sofa was wheeled up exactly at the most comfortable angle, while their books, and some well-known drawings of Sybil's own, prettily framed, completed the pleasant aspect of their room, and spoke audibly of love and remembrance.

Gwyneth looked round for a moment, then, with a sigh, she threw off her bonnet and cloak, and sinking on the sofa, buried her face in the cushions. Hilary took in at a glance all that it was intended she should read there, the gentle thoughts, the sisterly zeal, the kindly-meant attention, and refreshed and strengthened as she drank in such pleasant feelings, she turned her eyes on Gwyneth.

There was that in her attitude which told of utter prostration, both bodily and mental, which showed that the spring which had moved her hitherto had lost its power, and that her energies were now suffering a collapse as entire as their former strained motions had been unnatural. Hilary went round to the back of the sofa, and stooping, kissed her cheek with gentle love. That soft touch overpowered Gwyneth; her resolution to conceal her emotions at all hazards gave way; her customary reserve thawed, and she burst into an agony of tears, startling and alarming from their vehemence.

But Hilary felt that even this storm was better than the smothered fire which had for weeks past been burning up her sister's heart, and consuming her life by a slow torture, so she rather encouraged than attempted to stop its progress; by kind caresses and gentle words of endearment, she increased the flow of feeling for a time, that so the source of grief being dried by exhaustion, a real and permanent calm might be the result.

Gwyneth wept till she had no power to shed tears; and when her mourning hushed itself into a quiet, low sob at intervals, and she was able to listen, her sister spoke.

"Dear Gwyneth! this is my fault; your sorrow comes of me, my carelessness; ah, how ill I have fulfilled my charge."

"Your fault!" cried Gwyneth, "how? you are not to blame for the fickle temper and the hollow friendship which have cost me so dear. I shall be better now; this is the last moment I shall give to regret; to-morrow I will begin a new life."

"Then I hope that will in part consist, dear Gwyneth, in letting me know and share your feelings. Do not fear that I shall encourage you to weak expressions of regret for the inevitable past, only do not shut yourself up in that frozen reserve."

"Am I reserved? am I cold to you, Hilary? I did not mean it. But to talk of the past can do no good. I would rather forget it altogether."

"If you can: whatever leads to discontent, you ought to forget."

"So I will: Hilary, I was deceived in him and in her. She has been treacherous, and he was—ah, I can not tell you what he was to me. I thought him all but perfect, and now—" she hid her face again.

"He has much which might have been good in him," said Hilary, gravely; "much which steady principle would have brought to rich fruit; but his character is marred by his visionary turn of mind; his want of practical, hard-working earnestness, and, too, his high thoughts of himself. He spends his life in dreams of good, and disgust at the faults of others. But he does nothing to remedy the evils which disturb him."

"You have been disappointed in him, too, Hilary; I have seen it long."

"I have. I doubt whether Isabel will make him happy; but it is his own choice."

"No, it is hers, Hilary; she had set her mind on it. I have been their plaything, but I will not be their victim. He will never know what he has cost me."

"You must not dwell on thoughts of injury or unkindness done you, Gwyneth. Second causes must be forgotten, if you wish to forgive. I was highly imprudent in allowing so much intercourse, and shall not cease to blame myself as the cause of your sorrow."

"No, you have done nothing to blame yourself for, dear Hilary. The past is gone—let it go. Hope for this world, and love, with its bright fancies, and all the youthful visions in which I once indulged, have been dissipated forever. Henceforth my life will be one of quiet devotion, and charitable exertion, and such other occupation as may suit a calm and contemplative existence. To marriage and all its attendant joys and sorrows, I have said farewell forever. For you and Nest, all my cares shall be; and my hopes shall be fixed on an immovable futurity. We will never mention this subject again."

But Gwyneth's frame was not equal to her resolution; Nature would have its way, and the long-continued exertion, followed by a sudden relaxation of the strain, told now in a severe attack of nervous fever, which prostrated her for many weeks.

Hilary's first work in her new home was that of sick nurse to her sister.

Languid and restless, too weak for exertion, and too excited for repose, Gwyneth saw the day arrive which she knew was to unite her cold-hearted and successful rival to the man she once believed attached to herself. She could not turn her thoughts from what she supposed to be then taking place at Drewhurst, and her imagination, morbidly active from her illness, presented to her mind the whole scene. She saw the picturesque park, with its ancient avenues and groves, glowing in the sunshine of a fine autumnal day; every leaf tinted by the early frost, which had changed the hue of the foliage while yet thick, and given the most glorious shades of orange, gold, and pale lemon, to the majestic oaks and beeches.

So had looked her native woods, as they last met her gaze, and the picture dwelt in her mind. Then she fancied the assembled friends, the gay groups of patrician beauty, the humbler concourse of tenantry and laborers; she seemed to see the broadly-smiling faces of the merry throng, to hear their joyful shouts, their clamorous good-wishes for their young ladies' welfare. She pictured those two fair girls, in all their bridal splendor, flushed with triumph, or coloring with bashful feeling; she saw the bridegrooms standing by their side, she heard the words pronounced which decided their future life's history; she followed in imagination to the banquet, she listened to the speeches of congratulation; she saw Isabel's proud bearing, and unwavering self-possession, as she passed from her father's halls, amid admiring guests and shouting dependants; she saw her enter the carriage, whose four noble horses stood prancing at the door, half startled by the bustling throng; she saw her wave a graceful farewell to the crowd—and then she started with a sigh, to awake to the consciousness of her own quiet room, its simple furniture and cheerful aspect, and Hilary's soft voice and tender hand, presenting to her the draught which it was needful she should take.

Yet when her head was again laid upon the pillow, the same vision returned, still the sound of wedding bells seemed to float in her ears, the shouts of the crowd seemed to ring around her, and the flutter of bridal robes and bridal vails seemed ever wavering before her eyes. She did not know that they were the idle visions of a fever which so distressed her; but in her weak and nervous state, she almost fancied herself endowed with some preternatural sense; she believed herself the victim of some strange power of *clairvoyance*, and could not distinguish, in her languid condition, truth from error, reality from fancy.

Several days passed, and Hilary felt half inclined to wonder that she had not heard from Dora. Her friend still had possession of the letter from Maurice, on which she had so resolutely seized, but she had repeatedly promised to return it on her wedding-day, and the arrival of that letter had been looked for as a token that the sacrifice was complete. Why did it not come? Had her resolution failed her at last, and was she weakly unwilling to resign a memento which she had now no right to retain? Or had any circumstance occurred to delay or prevent this unwilling and unpropitious union? The former seemed most probable, and Hilary blamed herself again and again, for having done what she really could not help, but which she felt now as if she ought to have prevented.

One morning, it was at least a week after the day fixed on for the double wedding, the letter arrived; but it was not Dora's hand which had directed the envelop, and there was also a note inclosed for herself: she read it hastily.

"My Dear Mrs. Hepburn,
"You have, no doubt, heard of the strange and unexpected calamity with which it has pleased Providence to visit my household. Great as the trial is, I am thankful to say my daughter Isabel is supported under it wonderfully, and the poor sufferer herself is making slow progress to bodily health. The inclosed portion of a letter, I imagine, belongs to you: as there was no address, I had no idea, until perusing it, what it was; though it appeared to have much mysterious connection with the sad event I have referred to. It has, however, furnished some clew to the melancholy catastrophe; but permit a most unfortunate parent to express his regret that it should have come into her hands; and in addition to say, that though highly applauding your brother's fine sense of honor, I must consider it most lamentable that he should have scrupled to make known his views and wishes to me,

now that the result has been so disastrous; it is evident that the struggle between duty and feeling has been too much for my daughter's tender frame; had I been aware how the case stood, or at all foreseen such a conclusion, my conduct would have been (as that indeed, of any affectionate father would be) extremely different. Trusting that you and your family are in good health, in which wishes my eldest daughter joins,

"Believe me," etc. etc.

Hilary's astonishment and alarm at the receipt of this letter were very great, almost overpowering her self-command. What awful event, what terrible catastrophe had occurred to Dora, so to humble Mr. Barham's tone, so to affect his mind, as that he would have preferred encouraging Maurice's suit could he have foreseen the result? The most fearful ideas entered her mind, and she could hardly sufficiently abstract her thoughts from this perplexing and agitating subject, to attend to the wants of her sister, whose state of weakness required the most incessant care.

Had the marriage really taken place; why was Isabel still then at the Abbey? where was Mr. Huyton or Mr. Ufford? what had Dora done? it was all perplexity, darkness, and fear. Her only resource was to answer Mr. Barham's letter by a simple acknowledgment that she had heard nothing of the events at Drewhurst Abbey, and would be grateful for intelligence concerning her friends. "I have deeply regretted," she continued, "that my brother's letter accidentally met your daughter's sight. The difference in rank and fortune between him and a Miss Barham, in his opinion, placed an almost insuperable barrier between them; the attachment which he could not avoid feeling, he endeavored to subdue or control; and as she refused to allow him to refer the matter to you, they parted with no expectation on his side of meeting again. His own present happiness has been sacrificed to a purely unselfish desire for her best good; and if he has been mistaken, I am sure it will increase to an inexpressible amount the sorrow he has already experienced."

So wrote Hilary, anxious to state the truth, fearful of compromising Dora, ignorant of what had happened, and thoroughly alarmed and distressed by what she dreaded to hear.

Isabel replied to her letter, and gave all the explanation in her power. Hilary knew the rest, better even than her correspondent did!

Very different, in truth, had been the scene at the Abbey, from what Gwyneth's imagination had depicted. The ceremony had, indeed, been gone through, and Isabel herself did not seem more composed and calm than her younger sister; Dora's pretty face was white as her vail and robe, but scarcely an eyelash quivered, and her voice, though low, was steady. Kisses and congratulations she bore with perfect self-possession, she graced the breakfast-table with her presence, and went through its ceremonies as if they concerned her not; but when the moment came for rising from the feast, she trembled visibly, uttered one piercing scream, and pressing her hand to her head, she sank down insensible. Her husband caught and supported the death-like figure, and would not resign the charge. She was carried by him to her room; no one dared to dispute a right to attend her, which he fiercely asserted; he continued by her side, and when she opened her eyes they fell immediately on his gloomy countenance. The effect was unfortunate; she was attacked at once by terrible hysterical convulsions, repulsing him with evident horror, raving at intervals, wildly and incoherently, of strange and alarming topics, and calling for Hilary Hepburn, in piercing tones.

The greatest fear was entertained by the doctor, who was summoned, of the result; he declared that unless she could be calmed, reason, if not life, might be the forfeit, and insisted upon every thing in the slightest degree connected with the late ceremony, being removed from her sight. Gradually her fits subsided, and she sank into a state of torpor, supposed by her attendants to be sleep.

This alarming event, of course, delayed the departure of Mrs. Ufford, who could not quit the house, with her sister in that state; and while the rest of the guests took a sorrowful leave, Mr. Barham, his daughter, and son-in-law, endeavored to console each other in their mournful terror.

Charles Huyton, yielding to the solicitations of the doctors, agreed to banish himself to "the Ferns" for the present, lest some unlucky circumstance should reveal his presence to his distracted bride, and so bring on a relapse.

"When Mrs. Ufford entered her sister's apartment the next morning, the attendant told her, in a whisper, that the patient slept. Then, in an unadvised moment, she added:

"We found this letter yesterday, in the bosom of Mrs. Huyton's gown; had you not better take care of it, madam?"

It was an unfortunate whisper; Dora was not sleeping, only lying in a half-unconscious, dreamy state of exhaustion; but the mention of her hated name, the allusion to that too-dearly valued letter, roused every emotion again, and a terrible scene ensued. Her fearful screams brought her father and the medical attendants, but it was too late, the sudden shock had quite overset her reason; and from that time she had continued for several days, alternately raving wildly of the letter and of Maurice, or bewailing distractedly over her broken faith. That she was in the worst access of a terrible brain fever was their only hope; it was possible that could that be subdued all would yet be well.

The unfortunate letter had been placed in Mr. Barham's hands, and he began to examine it, under the idea that it had been addressed to Dora herself. He had previously entertained occasional misgivings as to his daughter's feelings; he had once or twice fancied she entertained a preference for the young lieutenant; but pride would not listen to the notion, and her ready acceptance of Mr. Huyton's addresses had, for a time, relieved him from alarm. On Dora's return home, however, still graver doubts had risen; her manners to Mr. Huyton were of a kind which spoke of indifference, if not dislike; and there was so entire an absence of confidence between the two, such coldness in the gentleman, such waywardness in the lady, so little interest or concern for each other, that he had often feared a violent and complete rupture would be the result. Mr. Barham had thought himself a happy man when, the marriage writings having been signed, the young couple had turned away from church united for life. Such is happiness based on a worldly fabric; such are human calculations, human foresight.

Now he would have given any thing to cancel the ceremony, could he by that means have recalled his daughter's reason, and insured her life. Now he fancied that had he known of her prior attachment, he would gladly have gratified it; and struggled to believe that he would have really bestowed her hand and fortune on Mr. Duncan, had he been aware how deeply her happiness was concerned. Vain self-delusion; indulged in only to palliate, to his own reproachful conscience, the fact that he had never consulted her feelings, or really considered her happiness. It was easy to say what he would have done under circumstances which had not happened, and not very difficult to persuade himself that had Maurice made formal proposals for his daughter's hand, he would have been listened to with ready acquiescence, and not rejected with polite contempt.

Days rolled heavily on, and brought no change for the better. The fever gradually subsiding, left the unhappy bride weak as an infant, in body, and little stronger in mind. Her intellect seemed lost entirely, and it became an anxious question, whether returning strength would bring back memory and reason, or whether every faculty of the mind had been for ever annihilated in the struggle she had undergone.

Hilary's sorrow was intense when she heard this sad narrative. Oh! the misery that pride and passion, that weakness and want of principle, that sin, in short, brings into this world. What a wreck had Charles Huyton's wicked vehemence occasioned! How mournful that such suffering should be brought on others by the willful folly and self-love of one. No doubt good would arise in some inexplicable way from all this fearful train of sorrow and pain: no doubt, to those who received it humbly and faithfully, even this terrible event might prove a blessing. Still it was awful and almost overpowering, filling all those concerned with sadness and distress; and turning to bitter mourning an event which had been expected to make them glad.

Oh! how she thanked Heaven that Gwyneth's sufferings were of a lighter kind, that her illness was so far more hopeful; that her mind was so humbled and purified by her trial.

"I do not deserve to be so waited on," said Gwyneth, in return for her sister's care. "I am not worthy of giving so much trouble; you are too good to me, dear Hilary!" And her only care then seemed to be to lessen her sister's fatigue, and repress all symptoms of suffering which might distress her. And days increased to weeks, and she began gradually to amend; her strength slowly returned; her appetite, her spirits improved. She had laid down her disappointment and regret on her sick bed: she did not resume them when her powers of mind returned.

The autumn had found her a romantic and heart-broken girl; the spring left her a sober, thoughtful, and yet cheerfully-active woman.

One day very early in the spring, before Gwyneth's eyes had yet lost their languor, her cheeks the pallid hue of sickness, and her attenuated figure had acquired its former elasticity and vigor, they had a visitor at their house, who, of all their former acquaintance, they perhaps least expected to see again. This was no other than Lord Dunsmore, who, instead of dying in Italy, as his friends had anticipated, had entirely recovered and returned to England.

Those were right who said that his disease had nothing to do with the lungs; his lordship was now in the enjoyment of good health, with no other remains of his former illness than a slight degree of pallor which suited well with the refined and aristocratic style of his countenance; it gave him an interesting appearance, which distinguished him at once among the many coarsely-colored complexions, thick features, and dumpy figures, so prevalent among Englishmen of plebeian birth.

How Mrs. James Ufford had borne the recovery of her husband's elder brother, the sisters did not know: people do not like to have their predictions falsified, and Isabel had confidently expected that he would die; but, as she had never even mentioned the subject of his return to Hilary in a very recent letter, they were only able to draw what conclusions they thought most probable from her silence.

Lord Dunsmore told them he was settled at Southampton for a few weeks, for the accommodation of yachting, which he intended to pursue as soon as the weather permitted, and he hoped during that time Mrs. Hepburn would allow him occasionally to visit at her house. He looked with great interest at the traces of recent illness on Gwyneth's face, and on her leaving the room he inquired with a degree of particularity as to the commencement, the duration, and the cause of her loss of health, that compelled Hilary to own it was sorrow and over-exertion which had been the origin of her nervous attack.

Lord Dunsmore made no further comment on that topic; but observed, that of all remedies for such complaints, sea-air was the most efficacious; and he hoped Mrs. Hepburn and Miss Duncan would try what effect a few excursions in his yacht would have toward bringing back the color to her cheek, and the symmetry to her figure, which he had once before so much admired. Hilary smiled at what she considered an idle compliment, and let the matter drop.

With a little hesitation of manner, he then mentioned that he had been to Hurstdene; he was almost afraid to enter on the topic; but Hilary was not overpowered by the reference, and gladly questioned him of her old home and neighborhood. He told her all by degrees.

The Vicarage had been entirely pulled down, and a modern house was now erecting on the spot; why, Lord Dunsmore said he could not imagine, he was sure his sister-in-law would never live there when it was built; she would not like to give up the importance of being mistress of the Abbey; which eventually would, in all probability, be her own property.

He paused, and a shadow passed over his face. "Poor Dora!" sighed he, presently. She looked up at him, and then averted her eyes; but he read the glance.

"No, I do not need your pity, Mrs. Hepburn," said he, with a half smile, and then immediately resuming his grave and feeling air; "the sentiments which would have given me a personal interest in her melancholy fate, died out long ago. Before I went to Italy you must have seen that I was cured of that complaint. No one with an ordinary human heart can do otherwise than pity a creature so young, so fair, so interesting, struck down by such a fearful blow; but I have no regret for her which the wife of Charles Huyton might not justly inspire."

He went on to describe her condition as he had learned it from his brother. She was usually calm and quiet, in tolerable health, sometimes sunk in the profoundest melancholy, sometimes showing the indifference and carelessness of a child; but memory seemed completely gone; she was subject to the strangest vagaries of fancy, and though generally gentle and obedient, occasionally betraying a violence at contradiction which proved she was not to be trusted. They talked of removing her in the spring, and trying the effect of traveling and change of air; her husband, who was strictly prohibited her sight, was gone abroad already; her maiden name alone was used to her, and not the slightest allusion suffered to remind her of her marriage or preceding history. Her favorite companion was the lady who had formerly been her governess, in whose presence she seemed to feel herself once more a happy child.

Hilary shed many tears over the melancholy fate of one whom she had so greatly loved, and Lord Dunsmore himself could not detail the particulars without emotion. He told her that Isabel was become an object of extreme aversion to her sister, who was, however, very fond of her father, and her aunt, Lady Margaret.

"And poor Mrs. Ufford must feel it so much," observed Hilary.

"Isabel is so accustomed to hide her feelings, if she has any," said he, quietly, "that one can hardly tell. Mr. Huyton's conduct surprises me most."

Mrs. Hepburn looked up quickly.

"He absolutely and most vehemently refused to have any measures taken to pronounce the ceremony void, which, under the circumstances, the father wished to adopt. He declares that the insanity is simply the effect of fever ensuing after the marriage; that she was completely in her right mind at the time; and that should she recover, of which he professes to entertain the strongest hopes, she is still his wife. It was with difficulty that her father persuaded him to leave her in his keeping, but I believe every expense of her separate establishment is defrayed by himself, and he seems wildly anxious to assert his title as her husband, and proper guardian, wherever the opportunity offers. Yet the physicians unanimously declare that in her present state, to meet might be to hazard her life, and would, at least, in all human probability bring on a hopeless relapse."

Hilary was silent, but her features told of a strong mental emotion, with difficulty subdued.

"For my part," continued Lord Dunsmore, "I look on him as little less insane than his unhappy wife, and can not help fearing but that some day he will prove even more so."

Hilary heard Gwyneth's step on the stairs, and had only time to give her companion a hasty caution to avoid the subject, when her two sisters entered together.

Their visitor seemed so little anxious to go away, and altogether remained so sociably with them, that Mrs. Hepburn could not avoid asking him to join their early dinner; which he agreed to with an alacrity that bespoke either a good disposition for their society, or a good appetite for his meal. Nest had a hundred questions to ask him about Hurstdene, when she learned he had been there recently; and his replies were so interesting, that even Gwyneth was drawn into the conversation, and found herself inquiring about old friends and old haunts, although, theoretically, she would have concluded that it was a subject she could not approach.

From that day Lord Dunsmore often was their guest; their little house and modest establishment seemed to have peculiar attractions for him; and he was continually doing something to show his concern for Gwyneth's delicate health, and to expedite her recovery.

He was most anxious that they should take advantage of his carriage, horses, and servants, which he declared were idling away in uselessness, as he never wanted them; he made his sister-in-law, Lady Rupert, who was staying with him, call repeatedly to carry them out for drives in the country; he induced them, as the weather grew warmer, to make excursions in his yacht, and in many other ways testified his friendly feeling toward them.

Best and most delightful of all, he one day brought them news of their brother's promotion, a circumstance which, as he was not appointed to any ship, would probably bring him home in less than a month.

He did not say that it was his interest which had procured the step, but the sisters felt that it was, and thought that they had good reason to be grateful.

CHAPTER XXIII.

"Hear the loud alarum bells—
Brazen bells!
What a tale of terror now their turbulency tells!
In the startled ear of night,
How they scream out their affright!
Too much horrified to speak,
They can only shriek, shriek,
Out of tune,
In a clamorous appealing to the mercy of the fire—
In a mad expostulation to the deaf and frantic fire;
Leaping higher, higher, higher,
With a desperate desire."

Edgar Poe.

The long northern winter had nearly passed, and the breaking up of the cold weather was daily expected at Halifax. To the fair Haligonians themselves this season had been one of unusual enjoyment and gayety, for more than one British ship had, during this time, visited them, and the *Erratic* had passed the whole period in their harbor. The political disturbances which had made this arrangement advisable need not here be detailed; they have nothing to do with my story, and did not in the least interfere to stop the festive meetings, in which those far-famed belles are said to delight, while they added to their parties the unusual presence of merry young naval officers, always eager to assist by their company in social amusements.

It was true that the captain of the *Erratic* was married, and therefore uninteresting; the first lieutenant, too, was so grave and reserved, that, though interesting, he was inaccessible. It was whispered that he had been crossed in love, and was not to be consoled by any of the fair young beings, who, in their warm compassion, would readily have undertaken that task. But though disconsolate, he was not ill-natured; he was always ready to accommodate more happy individuals by exchanging duties, or such other kindnesses as were required, so that all agreed that Duncan was the best fellow in the world.

It was evening, a social party surrounded the Governor's table, among whom sat Captain Hepburn, who was a special favorite there. Suddenly the alarm of fire in the town was raised, no uncommon event when nearly the whole of the buildings were of wood. But there was on this occasion apparently more danger, or more fear than usual; the sounds of the uproar reached the dining-room, where Sir Charles was entertaining his guests; and in a few minutes the table was deserted, the whole party of gentlemen sallying forth to see what was going on.

There was reason for the outcry. The dark canopy of heavy smoke, reddened up to the zenith by the reflection of the fire; the crackling long tongues of fierce flames, which shot up high above the roofs, and leaping madly off, like disembodied spirits for a moment visible, ascended to the sky; the loud pealing of the startling alarum; the cries and shouts; the rush of many feet; the heavy roll of the fire-engines, tearing helter-skelter to the spot, all combined to show that this was no common conflagration. One whole block of houses was so completely in a blaze that to isolate the flame by pulling down others, and cutting off communication, seemed the only thing left to do. There were no lives in jeopardy, but property to a large amount was in danger; the presence of the Governor gave a stimulus to exertion, and all worked with a will; sailors, soldiers, firemen, towns-people and strangers.

The scene was awfully grand, as scenes where fire has the mastery must be. Other elements are majestic in their might, but none have such a character as fire. The energy, self-will, malice, and cruel vigor of this fearful power, give the beholders an idea of life which no other can present. Yes, living fire is its fitting appellation. Living: a life instinct with the spirit of mischief, such as nothing earth-born can compare with. And while all worked as if for life and death, and the enemy still rose and triumphed, seeming at once to invite and mock their efforts—another alarm was raised of the same nature in a quarter at some distance from the first.

Whether the fire had crept along the ground, or been carried by a burning brand, or sprang up from some internal cause, could not be known; it was too certain that there it was, and part of the crowd moved off in that direction to ascertain the cause.

"For Heaven's sake, Hepburn!" said Sir Charles, "go down and see what new trouble is this. I will come in five minutes, if more help is needed."

At the word, Captain Hepburn disengaged himself from the press, and hurried off. On his way he met a boat's crew of his own "Erratics," who, headed by Maurice, were hastening to afford assistance, and who now, with a joyous cheer, as they saw their captain, placed themselves under his orders. They reached the spot; one house was on fire; a large store belonging to three women, which had been but recently built of brick, and now stood alone, the first of a new block.

Oh, horror! there were the forms of the wretched inmates at an upper window, whither they had fled from the flames below; the stair-case was consuming; their retreat was cut off. Already had a messenger been sent for a ladder, and as the party of sailors came up, men were seen approaching with one on their shoulders. But at this moment a cry was raised, from whence it came they knew not, that there was powder in the house, and the crowd shrank back in terror. "Better three women than hundreds should perish," was murmured round. The flames flashed brighter, the black smoke curled thicker every moment. Captain Hepburn sprang forward, and laid his hands upon the ladder which the dastards who bore it had thrown to the earth in their hurried retreat.

"What, my men! 'Erratics' afraid of powder when a woman is in peril! You have all had *mothers*!"

"Ay, ay, sir!" shouted the gallant fellows to a man, and assembled round him. "We'll heave up the ladder, sir," said one noble seaman, "if *you* will keep out of danger; ay, and if needs be, go aloft ourselves. 'Erratics' fear neither powder nor smoke;" and as he spoke, the ladder was carried to the house, and in a second run up to the roof, where the three terrified women had crept for safety from a garret window.

Captain Hepburn stood at the foot to steady it; Maurice was by his side. In a few, but peremptory words, he ordered all his men back; he would remain alone: the instinct of obedience prevailed; slowly and unwillingly the sailors retired, scarce condescending even then to stand out of danger. The ladder was so frail that the least experienced eye could see that it would not bear the weight of two persons at once, and yet the women, even in their perilous position, half hesitated to trust themselves to their only chance of escape.

"Down! down!" shouted the men, in an ecstasy of impatience, "every moment you delay you risk the captain's life."

Captain Hepburn tried to speak words of encouragement, and at length one, the boldest, ventured the attempt and descended in safety.

"Go, Maurice," said Captain Hepburn to his brother-in-law, as they together watched her progress; "go back with her; you are not wanted here."

"Never while you are in danger," was the lieutenant's resolute reply.

"Go," repeated the other with more emphasis, "for Hilary's sake; if I perish, tell her I fell in duty—why should she lose us both?"

"Never!" was still the answer. "Go, you, dear Hepburn, for *her* sake, it matters nothing what becomes of me."

By this time the second woman had nearly reached the ground; the third, with feeble, tottering step, was commencing the descent, seemingly more alarmed at this attempt than at the awful danger which had menaced her. Another minute and all would be safe, when just then a fiercer burst of flame issued from the window, as some new impulse was given to its fury, and another shout arose amid the crowd, "The powder! the powder!"

At the same time another form was seen, a man laden with a heavy box issued from the garret window, and although the last woman had but advanced a few steps, he began, with frantic haste, to descend the ladder.

"Back! back!" was the word which swelled in a shout from the indignant spectators; "wait for your turn, as you are a *man*!"

It was no use; even as the cry rose in the air, the ladder snapped like a reed, and man and woman were hurled in one helpless writhing heap upon the gallant officer who had tried to save their lives. Maurice was unhurt. Another prolonged shriek echoed the voice of the falling wretches, and then came the silence of horror, only broken by the fierce crackling of the madly exulting flames. At the same moment the governor arrived on the spot.

The sufferers were lifted from the ground and borne away; the fractures or contusions of the two who were uppermost did not render them wholly insensible, but the captain wore the appearance of a corpse; hurriedly they carried him from further danger, and the next moment, with a fearful explosion, the house blew up, the ruins of the front wall covering the spot where the two bold men had so recently stood. No more mischief was done.

"Would to God that I had been in his place!" sighed Maurice, as he covered his insensible brother-in-law with some of the blankets readily produced. He was lying on a door, which his men tore down to carry him.

"He is not dead," said a surgeon, as he felt the pulsations of that heart which had beat so bravely. "Don't smother him. Quick, with him to the hospital. His best chance! I will go on, and get matters ready."

"Forward, men; steady, my boys!" and they bore their dearly-beloved burden onward.

There were tears among his crew. Tears trickled down rugged, weather-beaten cheeks; tears from eyes which could have confronted an enemy's battery without flinching; but good captains make good men; and sailors, rough and hardy as they are, have often hearts within soft as a woman's.

He did not die then; he recovered his consciousness, and heard unflinchingly from the surgeons the fate which would probably be his.

"Maurice, do you know what they say?" inquired he, as his brother-in-law visited him. The lieutenant hesitated to answer.

"My professional career is over," resumed he, calmly. "I may return to Hilary, and die in peace."

Maurice concealed his face.

"Yes, death may be slow, but it will be certain; so it is to all: only I *feel* his cold finger touching me. The spine is irrecoverably injured, and I shall never stand on the quarter deck again."

"Poor Hilary!"

"Yes, poor Hilary; she will suffer: it will be your duty to comfort her when I am gone; but I trust I shall see her again. Maurice, you need not pity me very much. One can not live on earth for ever, and to die for duty has been my first wish."

"Hepburn, I must go home with you."

"Maurice, you must not! you can not! there is your profession!"

"I don't care, I will renounce it—quit the service—give up any thing to be of use to you."

"Madness—think of your sisters; you know they look to you for help—of your honor! your prospects in life! would you give up all, and do me no good? I will not hear of it."

"What steps shall you take?" said Maurice, resolved, yet unwilling to dispute the topic.

"I shall apply for a survey in due form; there is not much question of the incapacity of a man who can not stir a step, nor stand upright; and go home next packet."

"And the ship?"

"Ah, dear old *Erratic*. I have, I suppose, taken my last leave of her. Thank my men, Duncan; thank them from me, for their zeal and care. I fear I shall never see them again, nor hear their farewell cheer as I go over the ship's side for the last time."

He turned his face a little more toward his pillow, and whispered something about Hilary, which Maurice did not catch.

However things were ordered somewhat differently.

The next day, Maurice hurried to the hospital, with a face in which various feelings contended strongly, though pleasure might be seen flashing up amid pain.

"What has happened?" inquired the senior, as he saw his countenance.

"I shall go home with you, after all," said Maurice; "I am promoted!"

"Ah! how glad I am, my dear fellow, I wish you joy; promoted! how?"

"From home; *how* I don't know! I have no interest, you know, and none to care for me *now*."

A shade came over his face, as he thought how his other step had been gained.

"Well, you deserve it, Maurice, as much as any one; there is no need of considering it the result of interest; your own merits have, no doubt, been the cause; and it is come in time to reward your bravery the other night; for your sake, *all* your sakes, I am glad. How your sisters will rejoice; dear Hilary! But I wish you had been appointed to a ship out here, to have served your time at once."

"I am sure I don't. The best part of it is the being able to go home with you. I should care little for it otherwise. But I must tell you what the Admiral said. You know he came in yesterday about sunset; and the mail arrived this morning."

"Yes, I heard the salute yesterday evening. That will make it much more easy to have the survey; I had been wondering how it would be best to manage, there were so few of the right people. I should have had to apply to the Governor."

"Yes—well, this morning the Admiral landed, and then sent for me. He asked me no end of questions about the fire, and said some very handsome things about us both; then he added, 'The Lords of the Admiralty, with their usual discrimination in discovering merit, and promptness in rewarding it, having moreover, no doubt, had penetration enough to foresee what has just occurred, have sent out this as your reward. Commander Duncan, I have great pleasure in presenting you with your commission from their lordships, and beg to add your epaulettes from myself as a mark of esteem!' I thought he was joking, till I saw the commission in my own hands. What a queer old fellow he is; and as kind as he is odd."

"And what did you say?" said Captain Hepburn, smiling.

"*I* say? I am sure I don't know. I felt ten thousand things at once; I was choking with joy, and all sorts of feelings. Going home with you was, I think, my first and last thought, though. He took my mutilated thanks very civilly; but demurred to the idea of our going home in a packet. Only think, the *Erratic* is ordered home at once."

"No! is she really; what for?" The color flashed up in Captain Hepburn's pale cheeks, and he made an effort to move his helpless form. Maurice raised him tenderly, the tears standing in his eyes, as he saw the utter prostration of that strong man's strength. His arms were free and living, but his lower limbs were as if dead.

After swallowing down his emotion, and arranging his brother-in-law more comfortably on the pillows, no easy task, for there were many contusions to be cared for, besides the great injury to the spine, Maurice went on.

"The Admiral says you shall go home in your own ship, Hepburn; you need not invalid until you reach England; you can command her from your couch, and I will be your nurse and passenger."

"But what is she going home for?"

"I did not hear; what do you say to his plan? He told me to mention it, but he is coming here himself this afternoon; he and the Governor, for the latter came in just before I left, and told me he meant to come and see you. I must not repeat what he said to the Admiral about it all; but he was very kind, and shook hands, and wished me joy of my promotion; and talked as if I had done any thing at all."

"You did as much as any body," said Captain Hepburn, "except getting your back broken; and I suppose may share equally in the merit, whatever that may be. The result can not affect that!"

"But about the *Erratic*, you will keep the command?"

"I will answer the Admiral, Duncan!"

"Ah, then I know you mean to give up; well, perhaps it will be best; if you do, he will put his nephew in with an acting order to take her home; he is a nice, gentleman-like fellow, and the ship's company will get on with him. However, I should not wonder if they were paid off at home, they have been out three years altogether!"

Captain Hepburn did not seem to be listening; he was considering some other subject.

The Admiral and the Governor came together to visit the captain of the *Erratic*.

"I am sorry to see you here, Captain Hepburn," said the former, as he shook him cordially by the hand. "Why must you go and do the firemen's work, and get into this pickle yourself?"

"Well, if there had been any one else, I would not have interfered," replied the young officer. "You see I must pay the penalty for extra-professional zeal, by quitting her Majesty's service."

"Not quitting, I trust; a little rest and time will set you on your legs again. Go home to your wife, and let her nurse you for six months, and then you'll be as well as I am."

The sufferer shook his head.

"Never despair, never despair," added the Admiral; "here is Sir Charles here, was telling me how his cousin recovered from an accident quite as bad as yours; so why should not you?"

"We shall see," replied the other, quietly.

"That man who tumbled on you, ought to be run up to the yard-arm," pursued the admiral, warmly; "what are you going to do with him, Sir Charles?"

"I believe he will be tried for burglary," replied the governor, "as soon as his arm is well. He was endeavoring to make off with stolen goods, and must have broken into the house before the fire began."

"Ah well, I hope he will be punished! but, Captain Hepburn, you need not invalid; I'll tell you what; those sagacious gentlemen at the Admiralty have ordered me to send home the *Erratic* at once, to take his Excellency, Lord Somebody or other, to some court or kingdom; you keep the command, at all events, till you reach Spithead; time enough to invalid then, if you must. You might go to Haslar first, for six weeks, and who knows what might happen!"

"You are very kind, sir, but I have really no chance of recovery; and am so entirely incompetent for exertion, that I think I had better keep to my first resolution."

"Exertion—you need not exert yourself! leave that to the master and first lieutenant. Why, what do half the captains do now-a-days, but live on shore, and only go off to the ship when there is a man to be flogged, or some other excitement!"

"There are such instances, but they are hardly the rule, sir."

"And you must know your friend here too well, to expect him to follow such exceptional courses," said Sir Charles, smiling at the admiral.

"I don't mean to say it's right; but a captain with a head like Hepburn's, even though he had no legs, would be better than many a big lubber all legs and arms, without any head to bless himself with. And I know such on this very station; depending entirely on their first lieutenant."

"Still I would rather have my own way," said the captain.

"Obstinate fellow! Think of the pay; you have a wife and family, have you not?"

"A wife, sir; but I will not take pay for work I can not perform!"

"One of your absurd romances, Hepburn. I know you of old."

"Not very absurd, I think: simply honest. And if a captain is of any thing beyond nominal use, let the *Erratic* have one for the voyage who can move himself without help, either mental or personal."

"Ah, well, I'm the gainer, you know; but what good will it do you at the admiralty? will they thank you for your self-denial? Not they; they don't know what such fine feeling is. Boards are always half-grained, tough, and intractable."

"I am beyond caring for their praise or censure now, sir; my accounts must soon be rendered at a higher tribunal."

"Don't be down-hearted, my dear fellow!" said the admiral, gulping down something which seemed to stick in his throat. "I hope to have you under my command again some day."

"I am so glad Duncan has been promoted," observed Captain Hepburn.

"Ay, there's a piece of interest, depend on it. How does he manage to get on? Not but what he is as fine a young fellow as need be; but then *I* know how things go. I would bet you any thing you please, Sir Charles, that there is a lady at the bottom of that. I *know* he got his lieutenant's commission because a little girl, having admired his handsome face, got a great man to speak for him to the First Lord. That's the way the service goes on. Eh, Captain Hepburn!"

"You are not quite correct in one matter, sir; the young lady had never seen Maurice Duncan; she did it out of love for his sister."

The admiral laughed.

"His sister is my wife," continued the captain.

"Ay! indeed! I was not aware of that!"

"He is a fine, intelligent, brave-hearted young man," said Sir Charles, "a credit to the service any how. His regret for your accident, Hepburn, was touching the other night!"

"Well, I suppose the young lady has been to work again," observed the admiral; "for here's his commission come out to-day."

"She has had no hand in it this time, sir, at all events," replied the captain.

"Eh! how do you know that?"

"Poor thing! she is ill—married and ill—deranged, I believe, brain fever, or something of the sort—at all events, quite out of the question," said Captain Hepburn, gravely.

"Ah, indeed, poor thing! I did not know that! Well, you are quite determined to give up, and invalid, are you, Hepburn?"

"Quite, sir, thank you for your kindness and consideration. Thank you very much. You have been my friend, and you too, Sir Charles; and if, as you are pleased to say, you are satisfied with my conduct, all I ask is, be friends to Duncan, if in your power. It is, perhaps, the last professional favor I shall ask of any one."

"Well, my dear fellow, I promise you," said the admiral. "But, don't be down-hearted; you will soon be well. Good-by."

"Poor fellow!" said the admiral to the governor, as they left the hospital; "he's booked for death as sure as fate. I am sorry for him; and if he *is* to die, he might as well have died within my command, and I could have given the vacancy to my nephew."

"We'll hope he may get home alive," said Sir Charles; and so he did.

Lord Dunsmore had been absent from Southampton for some days. He was visiting at the admiral's at Portsmouth, and the sisters did not at all expect to see him, when one afternoon, a fly stopped at their door, and he, issuing from it, was shown into the house. There was something strange, excited, sad in his look, which startled both ladies, and made them glance anxiously at him; yet he seemed trying to speak as usual.

"We did not know you were come back," said Hilary.

"I am but just arrived by train from Portsmouth. I wished—that is, I undertook to bring you word"—he paused; she looked, but could not speak. "The *Erratic* arrived at Spithead at day-break."

The beatings at Hilary's heart choked her; she leaned back in her chair, white as the cambric she held in her hands. She felt, she *knew* there was more; there was bad news behind. He started up.

"A glass of water, Gwyneth," exclaimed he.

Mrs. Hepburn tasted the water, and then whispered—

"Go on."

"I saw both your brother and your husband; here is a note for you!"

Hilary caught it; it was from Maurice, and she noted Lord Dunsmore change color, nor did he tell her not to be alarmed; so there *was* cause for fear! She forced herself, however, to look at the note.

> "Dearest Hilary,
>
> "We are here; will you come to your husband? he wants nursing. Lord Dunsmore has promised to bring you by next train. Come at once. I will not leave H.
>
> > "Yours ever and ever,
> >
> > > "Maurice Duncan."

"Southsea Common."

"I am ready," said she, rising at once. "I will go directly."

"There is a train leaves in an hour. I kept the fly; we should start for the station in twenty minutes or less."

"I will be ready," said Hilary; she withdrew.

"Go and help her, Nest," said Lord Dunsmore. "Please stay one moment, Miss Duncan."

"Call Sarah, Nest," said Gwyneth; "tell her Mrs. Hepburn wants her. Now, my lord."

She turned to him for information. He threw himself on a chair, and seemed to control his feelings with difficulty.

"You ought to know," said he, hurriedly, "she will be long away, perhaps. He is very ill; has had an accident; lost the use of both legs—may be in great danger. Think what you will do in her absence."

"Stay here," said Gwyneth, decidedly.

"No, dear Miss Duncan, your brother mentioned it, approved my plan; let Lady Rupert fetch you to-morrow. I will arrange it all."

"Oh, what matters about us! it is for Hilary we must think; you go back with her?"

"I will take charge of her to Portsmouth; will you not let me provide for your comfort too?"

"You are very good to think of me! Now let me go to Hilary!"

Mrs. Hepburn looked bewildered, stunned; she was trying to dress for her journey, while Sarah and Nest were packing a small carpet-bag.

"Law, ma'am, don't take on so; I dare say it is not so bad. Why should you expect the worst?"

"I do not know what I expect, Sarah; please make haste. What I do not take, Gwyneth, you must send, if I want it. I don't know now. Surely, it is time to go."

"Your shoes, Hilary, those slippers will not do for traveling," said the sharp-eyed Nest. "Give them to me that I may pack them up; here are your boots!"

The exchange was made; in two minutes more she was in the fly with Lord Dunsmore; than whom her own brother could not have been kinder or more considerate.

They were just in time at the station, and were saved all the agony of delay. Once in the train, Hilary began to ask some questions; and Lord Dunsmore had to explain how he came to be connected with the affair. The news had been telegraphed early that the *Erratic* was at Spithead, and then came the captain ashore in his gig—not the captain whom Lord Dunsmore, remembering Hilary, expected to see, but another, who brought the news that Captain Hepburn was sick, on the invalid list; on this the admiral immediately offered his tender to bring him on shore, and Lord Dunsmore had gone out in the vessel, partly from anxiety for the invalid, to take him late news of his wife, and partly, perhaps, from other motives.

He introduced himself to the two passengers, offered his services in any way that would be of use, was most kindly received, and it was soon settled among the gentlemen that, while Maurice attended his brother-in-law to the lodgings in Southsea, which he had already sent on shore to secure, this new friend should set off by the next train, to bring back Hilary to the longing husband.

"Lodgings!" said Hilary. "Can he not be moved home!"

"I should hope he might eventually; but the first thing was to get him safe on shore. The lodgings are only taken for a week!"

"And he—tell me—I can bear it now, what is the matter?"

Hilary's face showed how she had, by a strong effort, brought her mind to bear, and her lips to utter these words.

"It was an accident, I understood; he hurt himself, and can not, at present, stand or walk; though I should not have known from his face there was any thing the matter. He is helpless."

This did not sound so very bad; Hilary's imagination for a moment suggested to her a variety of possible accidents, which might merely disable him for a time; and for a little while her previous alarm seemed unfounded. Then her memory again presented her companion's manner, the fixed gravity, the mournful glance, the utter absence of all attempts at lessening her terror; he had never bid her hope, he had never said she was too uneasy; he named no serious cause for alarm, perhaps, but he felt it, and he meant her to feel it too. It was what he did *not* say, rather than what he did, which aroused fear; and the cold, heavy weight of hopeless though undefined dread sank on her heart and threatened to crush it quite.

But there was a Refuge to which she could flee, a Covert from the tempest which now beat upon her head, a Rock on which she might safely build her hopes. This thought it was that kept her calm; a feeling rather than a thought. It was the impulse of her soul, a part of her life, to trust and be still; she had trusted long; and confidence did not forsake her now. That was her strength indeed.

"You were with him when he landed?" said she, presently, after sitting for some little space with hands clasped and head bent down.

"I was! he bore it well; those things are easily managed by sailors."

He did not tell her, for he could not trust himself, the scene on board the *Erratic*, when he took his leave of the ship. He had been carried out on the quarter-deck on his couch, to say farewell to his men; there he had thanked them for their zealous services, their obedience, their orderly conduct, during the three years they had been together, and bade them all go on, though he was taken from them, to serve their Queen and their country as nobly as before. Then, calling up the crew of the second cutter, who had been with him on shore on that eventful night at Halifax, he thanked each for his undaunted bravery in the moment of danger which they had shared together; for their concern for his safety, and their ardor for his rescue, saying, that he believed it was to their promptness in assisting him that he owed what little life was left him, as, perhaps, but for their ready aid, he might have been buried under the ruins of the fire, and never seen his country again. And now he charged them all to live sober, steady, honorable lives, to strive to do their duty, and mind what the chaplain taught them, "And so farewell, my lads; God bless you all! and if we never meet again here, may we all reach the shores above, where there is no more sea."

They tried to give him the hearty cheers which he had once longed to hear, but it would not do. The cheer broke down into one universal sob; and brave, strong men, whose hearts might have been thought as tough as the oak planks on which they trod, turned aside to conceal their tears, or leaned against the bulwarks for support, as they wept like children. They loved him well, those gallant fellows, and they knew that he was going home to his young wife, from whom he had parted on his wedding-day, only to die! and they mourned not only for him, but for her, whose gentle beauty, in the short glimpses they had had of her, had been strongly impressed on their romantic fancies.

"But if I am to be even a week at Southsea," said Hilary, presently, "what is to become of my sisters? they are too young to be left there quite alone."

"I thought of that," said her companion, eagerly, "and so did your brother; and we proposed—only perhaps, it would worry you to talk about it now"—leaving off abruptly.

"Oh, no! indeed, their comfort is my first duty; I wish I could think of any thing; my mind is not very steady; but it is not like our old home now; it would have been nothing to leave them at the Vicarage."

"Well, I thought, if you approved, might they not go to Lady Rupert's; I know she would like it; she is so fond of Gwy—of your sister."

Hilary raised her eyes, and gave him one look, so penetrating, so steady, that, had he not deserved her confidence, he could not have met the glance.

"Are you in earnest, Lord Dunsmore?"

"Earnest, yes—perfectly so, from my heart! but I do not wonder you ask, after what you saw in my brother!"

Hilary looked down.

"It seems hardly a time to speak of such things *now*," continued he, eagerly and rapidly, his pale countenance glowing with emotion; "but yet, perhaps, after all, it might remove distrust and doubt, perhaps lighten your anxiety in some respects, if I am open. Let me tell you, then, my feelings, and see if you will trust *me*. I do love her, and I do hope to win her. Even before I went to Italy, I preferred her; but then I thought James did too; I thought he was in earnest, so I left; but that as much as other things took me abroad; and when the news reached me of his intended marriage, I own it was a relief which greatly assisted my recovery. Now I hope some day to gain her affections; and though I and you, and she, know I can not say she is the first object of my love, and I am some years older, perhaps she will not consider these as objections—perhaps I *may* succeed in time. Now after this, will you let her and Nest come to Lady Rupert's care?"

"I will talk to Maurice, and—and my husband!" her voice faltered.

"I have been, perhaps, abrupt, Mrs. Hepburn, but circumstances must be my excuse," added he.

"What will Lady Rupert say?"

"She is my kindest, best friend; she delights in your sister, and would receive her as if she really stood in that relationship to herself."

"You have my best wishes," said Hilary, holding out her hand with tears in her eyes.

He thanked her warmly.

"James behaved very ill," said he, presently; "though I hope to be the gainer, I can not excuse him. He was very, very wrong, one way or other. He was either too much or too little in earnest. Young as she was, she was not such a child as to excuse his devotion or his fickleness—and it has hurt his character too."

"Please don't. I would rather not talk of it now," said Hilary, gently.

"I beg your pardon; do you know we are almost at the terminus?"

"Yes;" she was looking very white, and seemed incapable of saying more.

In a minute the train stopped—in a very few more the two were in a fly, and driving hastily toward Southsea. She could not speak, she could hardly breathe, as she saw walls and houses fly past them; her heart seemed struggling to rush on faster, faster to that unknown spot in which her husband waited for her.

They reached the house, they stopped, the door opened, Maurice appeared; Hilary had hardly time to see his expression, as he hurried to lift her from the carriage and support her inside the house. He held her in his arms, her face was hidden on his shoulder, as she whispered, between gasping sobs: "Where is he?"

He gently opened the door, and disengaging herself, she sprang in.

"Hilary, my darling!" said Captain Hepburn; and in another moment she was on her knees, beside his couch, and her tears of joy and grief, of anxiety and gratitude, and love, were poured out in her husband's bosom.

CHAPTER XXIV.

"I'm wearing awa', Jean,
Like snow when it's thaw, Jean,
I'm wearing awa' to the land of the leal.

"There's no sorrow there, Jean,
There's neither cold nor care, Jean,
But days are all fair in the land of the leal.

"Then dry that tearful e'e, Jean,
My soul langs to be free, Jean,
And angels beckon me to the land of the leal.

"Then fare thee well, my ain Jean,
This world's care is vain, Jean,
We'll meet, and ay be fain, in the land of the leal."

The feelings which may be clothed in words of earth, and the love which can be depicted by mortal language, must be shallow, light, and transient at the best. Those to whom love is but a creature of the imagination, and sorrow a pleasant fiction, may delight in dressing their fancies in eloquent phrases, and in dwelling on scenes of ideal distress. But the heart which has felt the deep-stirrings of true, holy, devoted affection, and known all the sad and stern realities of grief, which ever in this world must flow from feeling, shrinks from portraying it as from sacrilege; and while it feels how vain and unreal are the most eloquent descriptions, yet holds it a profanation to lay such feelings bare to the public gaze. It was not the cry of the *true* mother in her grief, "Let it be neither mine nor thine, but divide it!"

A week passed away; it seemed as if skill and tenderness and rest might perchance prolong the precious life of the invalid officer. He was certainly better; stronger, with less pain and weariness, and there was no longer so much opposition on the part of the doctors to the general wish of himself and his family to transport him to Southampton.

Hilary longed to move him. The heat, the glare, the dust, the noise, the weariness of a town, to her eyes were indescribable; and she could not imagine the possibility of any one recovering their health without the fresh air, the sunshine and shadows, the soft breezes, the pleasant scents, and the soothing sounds of the country and the forest.

Was not the whisper of trees more soothing than the angry dash or mournful murmur of the waves? and yet this was their most agreeable music, and was sweet compared to the sharp crack of musketry on the common, the louder reports of the cannon from the shipping, the wearisome notes of the bugle giving signals to the parties of soldiers drilling or parading on the open ground, the wretched street organs which haunted the vicinity, the cries of itinerant venders of oysters and such like, the squabbling of children, or the rolling of carts and drays in the back street, which shook the house to its center.

For herself, she would have borne it all with indifference or patience— but for him, every jar thrilled through her frame, every discordant sound made her shrink, and every disgusting odor made her tremble for his comfort.

Oh! to have him but away in their quiet cottage, where the open windows would admit only pure air, and pleasant, shadowy sunshine, and refreshing scents, and songs of birds among the trees; where their eyes could rest on green grass, and young foliage on the waving boughs, and flowers unstained by smoke, unwithered by sea-breezes!

And by the end of the week it was done; Lord Dunsmore's yacht conveyed the whole party round to Southampton, and by his and Lady Rupert's care an invalid carriage was in waiting, which carried Captain Hepburn to the quiet, pretty home of his wife and her sisters.

The back sitting-room, whose French windows opened on the little flower-garden, was appropriated to his use, and had been previously arranged, through the zeal of Gwyneth and Nest, and the kind activity of their friends, in the way most suitable to his situation and infirmities.

And so May and June crept by, and the birds sang, and the flowers blossomed, and the bright tints of early spring deepened into the more unvaried hue of summer; and Hilary nursed her husband with unwearied care, and hoped still, and was patient and composed. There was nothing which friendship or affection could supply, wanting to their outward comfort; and nothing of cheerful resignation, trustful endurance, hopeful fortitude, and devoted affection, failing to their mental support.

Who could have guessed from Hilary's calm brow, and sweet smile, and steady voice, as she waited on, and read, or sung to her husband, that she had the smallest foresight of the inevitable end? She seemed so cheerful, so even happy while thus employed! and she was happy too.

Every day during which her precious charge was spared her, every hour that she was permitted to spend by his side, every sentence of hopeful aspiration, or gentle courage, which dropped from his lips, was received as a heaven-sent boon, a favor, as unexpected as it was precious.

"I almost think you like to have me ill," said he, smilingly, one day to her, "you take such delight in nursing me."

"Can I ever be thankful enough that you are *here*?" was her reply; "think what it would have been had your illness prevented you from leaving Halifax. Had you been lingering there in the hospital."

"Or buried under those walls, which I so narrowly escaped, Hilary."

She shuddered, and then added,

"Or had I not been your wife; oh, how thankful I am every time I think of that; how glad I am we married when we did."

"Are you Hilary? *I* ought to be, I know; but *you*! I sometimes think that it was a cruel and selfish precaution on my part; I reproach myself for having bound you to one, who, instead of being a protector and support, is but a useless clog, a heavy burden, a sad incumbrance upon you."

"Ah! don't talk so."

"And sometimes, when I have felt a little stronger, and thought that perhaps I might linger on for months or years, chained to this couch, and making you a prisoner too, wearing out the best portion of your life in this dull slavery, I have been tempted to repine, and wish the deed undone which united us; I have longed to give you liberty again! you might be happy but for me, Hilary!"

"What have I done, or said, or looked, or left undone, that you should speak so, dearest? Could I be happy otherwise? or is there any thing in this wide world which I could prefer to being near you, at least, while I can be of any comfort or use?"

"I know there is not, love," fondly stroking the head which was nestled on his shoulder; "I know it, and I thank you every hour of the day for the ineffable tenderness which makes me so happy. But, Hilary, you always make a pleasure of your duty, it is your nature to throw your whole soul into your pursuits, to do your very utmost in what you feel to be right. It is this which impels you now, which makes you my good angel, my too-devoted nurse. But were you not my wife, as I should have had no claim, so you would have felt less inclination for a task, whose charm to you is, I believe, that it is your duty."

She gazed at him with her soft, loving eyes; put back the black curls from his temples, and then answered, quietly,

"You know better than that; you know it is something more than duty which influences me. A hired nurse might be actuated by duty; *my* motive is beyond, above that."

"You do not know yourself, Hilary: you love me well, I know it; but you would not love me so much, were it not your duty. You would not have twined all those warm feelings round me, had you not been my wife; and you would not have had to suffer the grief which I feel it will cost you, when that day, not very far distant, comes, which will part us on earth."

"Are you worse?" said she, the whiteness of her cheeks speaking her sudden alarm.

"It is coming, Hilary; it came slowly, imperceptibly at first; now I can feel its advances from day to day. Can you bear it, love?—we must part!"

"For a time, only for a time," she murmured.

"For a time, dear love! yes, that is the comfort, we shall meet again; but you are young, my darling wife! you have perhaps a long life before you, and I shall not trouble you many days. Do not be too unhappy when I am gone; remember your promise long ago, to bear it bravely, and when time has softened your grief, Hilary, do not think that you will please me by remaining unprotected and forlorn. Do not let your respect for my memory, fetter your will or your actions. Ah! you do not like to hear me speak of it, but by-and-by, you will remember what I have said. There, do not sob so; did you not know from the very first, that we must part soon?"

"Ah, I thought—I hoped—a little, little longer—!"

"And I am glad I shall not linger to see your cheek grow pale with care and watching, to keep you from rest night and day, as I do now; ah, Hilary, you have made me happy, so happy! But would you wish the deed undone which laid me here? I do not."

"No, no," cried she, with energy, "do not be unhappy about me. God, who takes you from me, will give me strength to bear the loss. Do not think of it. While you *are* with me still, let me forget all but your dear presence; we will not anticipate sorrow. To-day is ours; to-morrow is in His hands, who will do all things right."

They all saw now, the end was drawing near; Maurice, Gwyneth, Lord Dunsmore, they all noticed the increasing weakness, the gradual change;

they left the sick chamber with anxiety, they returned with trembling; they feared any hour would end it all. Gwyneth especially was devoted to her sister; her unceasing cares and consideration could not be excelled by Hilary's attention to her patient; every household duty was fulfilled, every wish almost forestalled by the thoughtful girl; and yet she fancied she did nothing, and was surprised if fear was expressed lest she should be tired.

Lord Dunsmore sometimes expressed this concern, during those short intervals when Gwyneth allowed herself the relaxation of conversation with him, a conversation of which Hilary was usually the topic.

"What have I to tire me?" said she; "you should see Hilary; what a wife she is!"

"I admit as a wife she is unequaled," replied he; "but I know one woman who might compare with her."

"Do you? I could hardly believe it," said Gwyneth, innocently surprised.

"That is her sister Gwyneth. Miss Duncan, if you felt for me one tithe of the love I entertain for you, you would say yes, when I asked you to be mine."

"Should I?" replied she, wondering, and yet thoughtfully. "I do not know."

"Dearest, sweetest Gwyneth! will you not?"

"Oh, no, it would be too selfish, too cruel to think of such things now! Hilary wants my whole time and thoughts, and you would ask them for yourself!—I ought not—do not tempt me."

"No, I would not engross them, I would only ask to share your anxieties, and if I could, to lighten your sorrows and cares. I only wish to have a right to joy and grieve with you. Could you not love me, would you not be my wife, if all were well here!"

"All is not well," replied she, blushing crimson, and turning away, "why ask?"

But her manner was so little repulsive, that Lord Dunsmore persevered, and before long, won from her an admission that she would rather he should continue to frequent their society on the understanding that she would try and like him, than that he should go away altogether from the neighborhood.

"But I am so young," said she, "I can not promise—ask Maurice."

"I will!" said her suitor.

"I have still another guardian," continued Gwyneth, with a sigh.

"You have; shall I refer to him?"

She assented softly, and he went immediately to Captain Hepburn. Hilary, of course, was beside him; Maurice, too, was there.

"Dear Mrs. Hepburn," said Lord Dunsmore, "do you remember the wish I once ventured to express to you about your sister?"

"Gwyneth! oh, yes!" said Hilary, eagerly.

"And you do not retract?"

"No, no indeed!"

"And will you then plead my cause with these two?" looking from Maurice to his brother-in-law; the latter lay with his fine eyes fixed on him, listening, with the most lively interest, to the conversation, but evidently without surprise; while the former evinced considerable astonishment.

"Ask for yourself, Lord Dunsmore," said Hilary.

"I will. Will you two guardians trust your ward to me? Give me Gwyneth?"

"Ah, with pleasure!" said Maurice, "if she says *yes* herself."

"You have had my best wishes for these two months," replied Captain Hepburn; then turning to his wife, he added, "Do you think she would come here, Hilary? ask her."

"You would frighten her," said the lover, anxiously; but Hilary went to look for her at once.

"I am so glad," said Captain Hepburn, "I hoped to see this settled; it is my last concern on earth, and I shall leave her with confidence in your charge, my lord. Hilary told me."

It was an effort to him to speak, and his words were faint and slow.

Hilary found her gazing from the window, but her black eyes were dim with tears, and at the sight of her sister, she threw herself into her arms, with an entreaty that she would not think her cruel and selfish; much as she liked Lord Dunsmore, she cared more a hundred times for her.

Mrs. Hepburn smiled, and soothed and caressed her, and whispered her own joy and congratulations, and led her to the other room; and there the blushing and trembling Gwyneth had her hand placed in her suitor's by the feeble fingers of her brother-in-law, while in few, but affectionate words, he assured her of his satisfaction, his good wishes, and his fraternal regard for both.

Maurice too kissed and caressed her, but he said little; it was impossible to feel otherwise than deeply touched by the strong contrast between the look and the situation of those two sisters.

Gwyneth's black eyes were bent down and bright drops trembled on the long lashes; her color came and went like the flashes of the northern lights in the clear winter sky. She was excited, hoping, fearing, trembling between present pain and future joy; looking forward with a shy gladness into the prospect just opening, and then hurriedly calling back the glance, because to her dearest companions the hopeful view was closed; she could scarcely welcome the possible happiness which they might not share.

Hilary, on the contrary, stood by, with her calm, serene eyes fixed on her sister with a quiet but heartfelt pleasure; a satisfaction springing from the very depths of the soul, at the hope that Gwyneth might, perchance, have one long, plentiful draught of that cup of happiness of which her own short taste had been so sweet. She knew the full luxury of loving and being beloved, and what was denied to herself she rejoiced in anticipating for another. And when she had gone over in her mind all the bright visions which the future presented to Gwyneth, and joyed in her promised joy, she turned her eyes once more on her husband, and the thought flashed across her how great had been the blessings of her own lot, and how the privilege of having been his friend, companion, and solace during the last two months, was well worth the purchase, even though it were to be followed by a long life of solitary bereavement.

She was happy: not the happiness of this world, not the happiness which those of this world can understand; a happiness above all selfish joy, such as words could vainly endeavor to depict, unspeakable in its depth and purity: for in her earnest anticipation of peace and rest for him, she forgot herself; she saw him to her fancy encircled with the crown of martyrdom; and would she have robbed him of one ray of that future glory for her own selfish indulgence, or her transitory comfort? Oh no!

But to others, to the eyes of observers, her feelings were a mystery; and to outward view she stood there, another proof of the fading nature of all earthly happiness. Hers was the deepening gloom of twilight, Gwyneth's the rising of the glorious day-break. Life is full of such sharp contrasts, ever telling of change and decay to such thoughtful minds as can raise their eyes beyond their own footsteps.

Human feelings, indeed, afford but a quivering, changeful gleam, by which to view the edifice of life; as pleasantly deceptive, as unreal in their lights and shadows as moonbeams on a picturesque ruin; but there is a Light which does not mislead, which brings out each object in its true perspective, and decides the value of all earthly possessions; and it was by this pure Light that Hilary was now gazing on life; and so her heart failed not in that trying hour.

Gwyneth never forgot her sad betrothal; it was good for her to remember it; and afterward, in gayer hours, when surrounded by luxuries, and allured by the soul-engrossing littleness of rank and wealth, the recollection of the trembling fingers, faint accents, and calm, holy eyes, of her dying brother-in-law, hovered round her heart, and his memory, like her guardian angel, still came between her and temptations to cold selfishness and pride.

His approval spoken, and his blessing given, Captain Hepburn begged to be left alone with Hilary; so Lord Dunsmore led his young betrothed to the next room, and then there followed on his part, such an out-pouring of long-cherished feelings, suppressed and concealed from regard to his brother, as Gwyneth had little expected to hear; and which she now listened to in wonder, as she thought of the girlish infatuation which had made her blind to his merits, and had just missed making a wreck of her happiness for life.

They talked till twilight came down upon them, and then remembering the world beyond themselves, they wondered to hear no sound or movement in the next room; but fearing to intrude, they waited anxiously, till Maurice returning from a walk, ventured to enter that quiet chamber. All there was still, profoundly still; for Hilary, with her hand clasping the cold fingers of a stiffened corpse, was lying in a death-like swoon beside her husband's couch.

* * * * *

Three months passed away.

It was autumn again, a beautiful October morning, and the yellow sunshine which fell on the green-sward between the boles of the old trees, like bars of gold, streamed also gladly into the pretty chamber where Hilary, in her widow's dress, was attiring Gwyneth for her bridal. It was Mrs. Hepburn's earnest wish that it should not longer be delayed; it had been her husband's last act to join their hands, and till the union was accomplished, she felt his will was but half fulfilled. "Let it be then," she said, "that autumn;" and so it was to be; they could not have resisted her calm, sweet request, even had she demanded a sacrifice of them; and when she only bade them be happy, who could say no?

But it was really to be a very quiet wedding; Sybil and her husband came to them; and Lord and Lady Rupert joined the party; that was all; no pomp of gay bridesmaids, only little Nest—no grandeur, no display.

Hilary's weeds were too deep to grace a wedding, too recent to be laid aside even for a day; no one asked her to be present, no one thought of it; but her absence was a blank; it toned down gay spirits, it was the fennel-leaf in the cup, the skeleton at the feast, the thorn to the rose of love, which else had blossomed so sweetly for the married pair.

Maurice, anxious to remain with his sisters, had applied for an appointment to the Coast Guard; and through the interest of Lord Dunsmore and the Governor of Nova Scotia, just then in England, had obtained his request; and immediately after the marriage, they were to remove to his station, which was at a distance.

Mrs. Hepburn was very glad of the prospect of employment for him; he needed something to occupy his time, and engross his mind; and active as his duties would be, they would not take him from her, which was a blessing. The solitude of their future home was no evil to her; and as to Nest, when old enough to need society, she could go to her other sisters for a time.

So Gwyneth was married; and it was, perhaps, no small increase to Mrs. James Ufford's matrimonial discomforts, to learn as she did, about that time, how far her own manœuvers had contributed to place the late Vicar's daughter in the situation she now filled; for Mr. Ufford affirmed, that but for her intervention he should have made Gwyneth his wife. So he said, at least, and so he believed, whether truly or falsely, who can venture to tell, when we reflect on the inconsistency of human feelings.

It was a comfort to Lady Dunsmore's womanly feelings at last, when she heard from her husband's lips, that her brother-in-law, when appealed to on the subject by him, before the journey to Italy, had avowed an intention of proposing to her; since it proved that the feelings of girlish tenderness which she had wasted on him, had not been unsought, although undeserved.

Indignation at James's fickleness, and concern for Miss Duncan's feelings, heightened by very warm personal regard for herself, had hurried Lord Dunsmore straight home from Italy to Hurstdene, to find her; and the result was happy for both.

Mrs. James Ufford never forgave her brother-in-law for not having died in Italy; but she knew that family quarrels were ungraceful and unbecoming, so she abstained from them; and welcomed her dear Gwyneth with a cordiality and affection which deceived every one except their respective husbands.

In a house on the outskirts of a small town, on one of the most wildly picturesque shores of the kingdom, Captain Duncan and his two sisters soon settled themselves. There the days passed in the quiet but busy monotony, which makes time fly so fast. Affection and unreserved confidence were their solace; and Maurice, occupied daily, and often nightly, by his situation, soon recovered the cheerful tone of mind which, when springing from a right source, is one of life's best blessings.

As to Hilary, her resignation was calm, perfect, and even cheerful too; and strangers little guessed the history of her feelings from her face. They saw the surface only, and could not look into the depths of her heart; and yet, even that surface told as clearly of the peace of her mind as the waveless sea reflects the blue heaven which looks down upon it.

Nest was the glancing sunbeam of their house, and to make her happy was a sufficient object to excite the energy of both her affectionate guardians.

CHAPTER XXV.

"His long rambles by the shore
On winter evenings when the roar
Of the near waves came sadly grand
Through the dark, up the drowned sand.

Tristram and Iseult.

"And she is happy? does she see unmoved
The days in which she might have lived and loved
Slip without bringing bliss slowly away,
One after one, to-morrow like to-day?"

Iseult of Brittany.

"You heard from Gwyneth this morning, dear," said Captain Duncan to his sister one evening, as they sat together after tea. They had been in their new home about two years.

"Yes, here is the letter."

"Hurstdene Vicarage.

"Dear Hilary,

"You know how little I wished to come here, but George thought it right, and so we came; and the old place is so changed that it is not so very painful; only the date above looks like old times, and reminds me, more than any thing else, of the past. It is a fine large house, but I hope all future vicars will be rich, or I do not know what they will do. Isabel complains of it as cramped and small, however; it was too small to ask nurse and baby here, so my boy is at home. She considers it unhealthy too!

"The church is finished quite. It would not have been, but for 'my lord's' perseverance and purse; and as Isabel's extravagant plans were abandoned, it looks very nice. The graves at the east end are fresh and well-cared for; that dear old spot! You may guess how I went there first; and the seat under the lime-tree is carefully painted, and a date cut on it, of the day before we left Hurstdene. Why?

"I asked James who had done that? He did not know, but old Martin told me it was Mr. Huyton of 'the Ferns'—again I ask why? He is still abroad, poor man! and oh! poor, *poor* Dora! she is much the same, yet they fancy there are dawnings of intellect sometimes. I have seen her companion, Miss Lightfoot; I am not allowed to see her. Lady Margaret, you know, lives at the Abbey. Poor Mr. Barham is so changed; he looks humbled and heart-broken.

"After all, Hilary, real sorrow may be a great blessing; and can those who have never known grief—a grief they were not ashamed to feel and acknowledge, can they know how to feel for others? I think not.

"Lord D. went round with me, and visited all the old people; they seemed quite glad to see me again, and asked, oh! so many questions about you all. The curate is very good and attentive; I don't fancy they see much of the vicar; I wonder why I ever supposed him such a devoted clergyman; yet he seems always immersed in business, desperately occupied. I believe it is *system* he wants; I am sure our parish at Ufford is much better managed; but then with two such heads as 'my lord's,' and Mr. Barton's, no wonder.

"Things have certainly got wrong somehow. Isabel would have made a better wife to a peer than a priest, and there can not be a doubt but that George would have been a better clergyman than his brother; though to fill his own station better than Lord D. does would be quite impossible. I must not write any more, he is calling me to walk—"

Maurice listened in silence to this letter, and after some meditation, he observed,

"How happy Gwyneth is!"

Just then Nest entered the room.

"How it blows," she observed, as she sat down; "and it is so dark; I looked out just now, to try and catch a glimpse of the sea, but every thing was as black as pitch; and, oh, such a roar of waves!"

"Just the night for me to visit the South Point Station," observed Maurice, rising; "and it is time I was gone, too; but this pleasant fire and good tea make one lazy, Nest."

"Must you ride all along those cliffs to-night, Maurice?—it is such a storm!" observed Hilary.

She had not yet become accustomed to the night-work, so as to see him depart without anxiety.

"Oh, that's nothing!" said he, as he put on his great pilot coat; "and this is a fine night for smugglers: suppose I were to intercept a cargo to-night."

The horse was brought round, and his sisters both went to the door to see him mount. They stood within the shelter of the porch, shading a candle as well as they could from the draft, while its flickering streams of light fell on exterior objects, forming grotesque shadows and strange contrasts, and then losing themselves in the dark back-ground.

Maurice kissed them both, and bade them go to bed, then mounted and trotted off over the hill.

They listened till the horse-hoofs had died on the ear, then they turned together to the house.

"Let me stay with you to-night, Hilary—do," said Nest, coaxingly; "it will be so melancholy for you to sit here all alone, and listen to the great roar of the waves."

Hilary smiled an assent, and they sat down together.

It was not quite nine o'clock when Maurice left them; but as they could not expect him back for more than a couple of hours, Mrs. Hepburn did not intend that her younger sister, who was now growing into a tall girl of thirteen, somewhat delicate and fragile, should remain watching till nearly midnight. It was true that she herself felt unusually nervous and uncomfortable to-night, but these were foolish tremors, to which it would not do to give way; and Nest's health must not be sacrificed to her own idle fancies; she resolved that no persuasion should induce her to prolong their joint vigil.

The wildness of the night seemed to have affected even Nest's spirits; instead of chatting in her usual lively manner, she was almost silent, only now and then exclaiming as a louder burst of wind seemed to roll over the house, or a heavier wave dashed against the rocks below. Hilary had learned to love the deep roar, the hollow murmur, and the angry rush of the ocean-wave; they spoke to her of other times, in a strange language which was intelligible only to the finer feelings. What the connection was between their voices and the memory of the lost one, she could not have explained; but she never heard the one without musing on the other; and now her heart had traveled away to by-gone hours, as she sat by the fire, until roused by the clock striking ten, she begged Nest to go to bed.

But Nest still remonstrated, and entreated to stay; and to beguile the time, began asking questions of their old home, and leading Hilary to talk of her childhood; and so the minutes flew by, until it was really time to look for Maurice home; and Hilary again urged Nest to retire; Maurice would be vexed to find her up so late.

Still Nest said, no, he would not; he would not mind it for once; she must let her sit up, and when he came home they would have a little comfortable supper together.

While they were discussing this point, the younger, with a decided disinclination to leave her sister, and the elder almost equally unwilling to let her go, they heard, during a lull, the sound of a horse approaching at a rapid pace.

"It is Maurice!" said Hilary.

"No, that is not his riding; he went out on Acorn, and he never gallops him so hard," replied Nest, listening.

Hilary looked uneasy; ever since the one great shock she had received, her nerves were as easily agitated as a compass-needle, and though like it, too equally balanced to be moved from the center of rest, still they

"Turned at the touch of joy or woe,
And turning, trembled too."

"It is perhaps some messenger come to fetch Maurice," said the quick-witted Nest, who saw that her sister was uneasy; "for he is certainly coming here."

As she spoke the sounds approached quite close, and in another minute they had stopped at the gate. The sisters ran out, and threw open the door; a stranger was there, who advanced, and touched his cap to the ladies.

"Please, madam, I bring a note from the captain, and am to take back an answer."

"Nothing the matter?" asked Hilary, breathless, scanning the messenger's countenance, as she took the note.

"Nothing with the captain," was the answer.

And Hilary, retreating to the light, opened the twisted paper and read—

"Dear Hilary—
"Don't be frightened; I want some linen for a man who has been hurt here: some for *him*, some for his *bed*, he has nothing! the messenger can tell you about the facts. I must stay and take care of him to-night. I hope you will not mind.
"Yours, M. D."

"I will get what Captain Duncan wants, immediately," said Mrs. Hepburn; "come in and sit down while I do it." She put the note into Nest's hands, saying, "Ask for an explanation, dear," and hurried up stairs.

The man, while he gladly spread his hands to the parlor fire, and refused to sit down on the chairs, which looked too refined for his society, told Miss Duncan that a yacht had appeared off the coast in the morning, and that the preventive men, after watching it for some time, saw a boat put off for the shore, with only one person in her. As there was a heavy ground-swell, and the landing was extremely dangerous, although the sea at the time, a hundred yards from the shore, was like glass, they signaled the boat not to approach. Whether the signals were unseen or unintelligible, they could not tell; the boat made for the beach, immediately below the preventive station. As might be expected, no sooner did she come within the influence of the rolling sea, than she was caught on the crest of a wave, thrown violently on the shore, capsized, stove, and the gentleman, for such he was, was dashed into the surf, from which he was with difficulty rescued by the coast-guard men, half-drowned, with a broken arm, and other terrible injuries to his head and person. He had been carried into a small public-house hard by, and after some hours they had succeeded in obtaining a doctor to dress his wounds; the remote part of the coast making it a matter of great difficulty to procure help of any kind, until the fortunate arrival of the captain, who had told them what to do, and was now with the wounded man.

"And who is he?" exclaimed Nest.

"Nobody knows, miss; the yacht had been cruising about a while, but when the gale rose so heavily, she was obliged to stand off, and was out of sight before night-fall. The coast is so dangerous, you see, miss, she would be obliged to run for shelter to some better harbor, or keep out to sea for more room. It would never do to be knocking about here in these long dark nights."

"And you don't think they were smugglers, then?" said Nest, whose ideas of romance were all running in that line, and who was little interested in a matter-of-fact gentleman.

He assured her they had no suspicions of the sort; and Hilary coming down at the moment with the requisite articles, the man mounted, and rode off without delay. Nest had been both right and wrong; it was her brother's horse, though he was not the rider.

The sisters agreed now to go to bed at once, as Maurice was not coming home till morning; and when Nest had repeated the story she had heard, in every variety of way which her fancy could suggest, she allowed her sister to go to sleep.

As soon as breakfast was over, the next morning, as the day was fair, Hilary resolved to drive over to the station at South Point, and see whether any thing more was required for the sufferer there. Nest begged to go too; full of excitement and interest on the occasion.

It was a very lonely place; the small public house, into which the stranger had been carried, stood low down on the beach, beneath high, beetling rocks, above which was the preventive station, and it seemed only fit to be the resort of fishers, or men of the same class. Mrs. Hepburn and her sister, on entering found only the hostess below, and desiring Nest to remain with her, the elder made her way up the steep, ladder-like steps to a room above, where her brother was nursing the sick man.

The door and the window were both open, and the pleasant breeze streamed in with the morning sunbeams, which fell on Hilary as she stood contemplating the couple within the room. Her brother was sitting beside the bed, holding the hand of his patient, but his back was to the door.

Supported by pillows, and evidently laboring for breath, the sick man lay with his face toward her; but as his eyes were closed, he was not aware of her presence. The flush of fever was on his cheek, the contraction of pain on his brow; his countenance seemed the home of sad unquiet thoughts; a thick curled beard and moustache of dark auburn concealed the lower part of his face, while a bandage across his forehead gave a more ghastly expression to his sunken eyes. Yet even in those worn and pain-struck features, she thought she recognized a something familiar, a something which sent her memory back to her girlhood and her forest-home. He slowly opened his eyes, and said, in a low, feeble voice—

"Maurice, I should like to see—Hilary!" added he, in a tone of wild surprise, starting from his pillows, as his eyes fell on her. The effort was too much, he sank back, overpowered by weakness, while shadows of agony and terror seemed to cross his face.

"My mind wanders," said he, placing his hand over his brow; "Maurice, I thought I saw your sister—just as she was in the forest—the first time we met."

No wonder he was thus deluded; for as she stood there, with the glow on her cheek from the fresh morning air, with her brown hair smoothly parted on her forehead, her simple bonnet, and plain black dress, she looked so calm, so youthful, so like the Hilary of his happiest hours, he could hardly suppose her a reality; could years have made so little change in her, so much in himself?

She approached, and placed her fingers on the only hand he had at liberty; the other lay helpless by his side.

"It is I, myself," said she, in her low, gentle voice. "Do not be disturbed, Mr. Huyton."

She saw it all at once; it was the friend of his youth, the very man who had so deeply injured him, that Maurice had been nursing all night.

"Are *you* come too?" said he, in a broken voice, as he fixed his dark, glowing eyes on her; "are you come to see me die? Angel, whom I have so deeply injured; whose sad path in life I have made still sadder! Are you come to bless or to curse me with your presence? Can you forgive me now?"

"Forgive! ah yes—as I would be forgiven—long, long ago I forgave!"

"What a wretch I have been; yet I thought I loved you! and it *was* love, earnest, real love, till your rejection turned it into bitterness. Oh, if I had but listened to your pleading; yielded to your mild remonstrances. Maurice, tell her that I have repented."

"Hilary will believe it, I am sure, Charles," replied Maurice; "do not exhaust yourself by emotion."

"Let me talk, my end is near. Listen. I was wild, frantic with grief and remorse; horror-stricken at the wreck I had made of Dora's happiness, vainly repenting when too late—when—ah Hilary! forgive me—when, as you were once more free, I found myself fettered to her—poor thing! Miserable, I wandered from country to country—till I met with one who taught me better, a true minister of the Gospel, who taught me better, and sent me home to my duty—too long neglected. I intended to do right—I meant to try and remedy, so far as I could, the miserable past; my first step was to see Maurice, and ask his pardon. I came here, and now I am dying—it is the only thing which can really repair my crimes. To hear him speak forgiveness has been my best comfort. Now let me die!"

Hilary's tears fell fast over the hand she held in hers.

"Must he die, Maurice?" whispered she.

Captain Duncan shook his head sadly.

Charles again opened his eyes, which he had closed as sharp pains shot through him. The cold drops of agony which stood on his forehead his friend wiped gently away.

"Yes, I must die," whispered he again to Hilary; "I know it; this pain will only cease when mortification begins. I must die; and I am thankful for it. I do not deserve it; a long life of penitence and sorrow would have been my fitting fate; I have no right even to ask for a speedy release. But for you, for others, it is better I should go; if I could only repair my mad folly, my savage wickedness; if I could only, in giving Dora liberty, give her back the reason I frightened away; oh, I would suffer twenty times more pain, could I restore her to you, Maurice, as she was."

"God's will be done!" said Maurice, gravely; "He gave, He took away! Since she has been your wife, Charles, she has ceased to be the Dora of my fancy."

"You are weeping for me Hilary—how many tears I have made you shed. I do not deserve one gentle thought: it was in mercy, undeserved mercy, you were sent here, that I might hear you say you forgive me."

"I do, indeed, from my soul."

"And if *you* do, you, who might have felt resentment—a fellow mortal—I hope—I trust—I believe the Most High will hear my penitence—and for that dear love which died for us all—" his voice failed him again, in a fit of agonizing pain, terrible to see.

The injuries had been principally internal, and during the hours which had passed before medical aid was procured, inflammation had commenced, which it was now evident must end in death.

"Leave me," said he, when he again had power to speak; "leave me, Hilary, I do not deserve to give you pain; you suffer in seeing me suffer."

"No, let me stay," she said, calmly; "let me nurse you."

"Leave me; I once loved you better than life, than duty, than Heaven; but I have struggled with a passion, wrong in its excess, criminal in the husband of another. I have learned to govern it—to subdue it; but do not come between me and better thoughts, do not drag me back to earthly feelings. Let me voluntarily renounce the dearest, sweetest thing on earth; let me prove my sincerity to myself. Leave me!"

She rose, and though she longed to linger there, she passed from the bed-side, after one soft pressure of his feverish fingers.

"Farewell, till we meet above," said she, and went from the room. She did not, however, leave the house; but as soon as she went down stairs, she sent off Nest and the servant, who had driven them, over to the town to find the parish priest, and beg him to visit the dying man.

Whatever friendship could suggest to soothe his pain, or pastoral prayer and counsel could afford to support and guide him aright, was granted him. But it was not till toward the afternoon, that the fierce pain subsided, and he became calm. Then they knew that death was rapidly advancing.

In the gray twilight, Hilary and Maurice returned home together, leaving the friend and companion of their youth a quiet corpse. After years of disappointment, anger, remorse, and repentance, he slept in peace.

Hilary cried quietly nearly the whole drive home; she could not help it. It was not only painful regret, or sorrow for the dead; but old thoughts had been revived, old feelings, buried happiness, vanished hopes, the gay visions of youth, all seemed suddenly awakened at this painful meeting. And it is an awful thing to stand by the bed of one whose wild passions, ungoverned temper, and wasted youth, have brought on disappointment and death, even though we may hope they have ended in true penitence and faith. We may hope, but we must tremble too!

Mr. Barham was sitting one afternoon with his youngest daughter, who was amusing herself, with childish pleasure, over some brilliant flowers, when the second post came in, and brought him a letter from Maurice.

Captain Duncan wrote him for directions as to the corpse of his son-in-law. His yacht had come into harbor the day after the storm, and the captain suggested that they should carry the deceased owner round to Bristol, as to the nearest port to "the Ferns," from whence the corpse could be transferred, according to Mr. Barham's pleasure. They waited his orders, as the guardian of Charles Huyton's widow.

The letter contained the detail of his sad and yet hopeful end. It dropped from Mr. Barham's hands after he had read it, and crossing his arms on the desk before him, he laid down his head and groaned aloud. The manly, feeling tone of the letter, and all the sad thoughts it had called up, oppressed him deeply.

His daughter looking up and seeing his emotion, went close to his chair, and stroking his head as a child might do, she said, in a fondling voice:

"Poor papa! poor papa! what is the matter?"

This completely overpowered him, he sobbed like a boy.

"Don't cry, papa—yes, do—I wish I could, too: I never cry now—I have no tears left—if I could only cry, the great weight on my head might go."

Then, in her childish way, she took the letter he had dropped, and said: "I think I will read it too."

She did so, for her father was too much overwhelmed to think.

"Father," said she, "I think—I remember—did I dream it, or was it true, that I once married Charles Huyton—that I was called his wife?"

Her tone was altered, it was her own voice; her father raised his head in amazement, and looked at her. Strange gleams of thought flitted across her face, like lights and shadows on a still ocean; memory and mind were struggling with the dull torpor of disease. Her brain was awaking! she slowly read again the touching words of Maurice Duncan; she looked on his name at the conclusion of the letter. She thought—she felt—she remembered the past.

"He was my husband," said she.

"He was, dear child," replied her father, trembling.

"Why did he leave me?" said she, dreamily; he feared her intellect was fading again.

"You have been ill, my darling, we have been nursing you long," said he, drawing her down toward him.

"Stop, let me think;" she put her hand to her forehead; "he is dead they say—dead—poor Charles!—and did not see me first. I am his widow then—" again her mind appeared in her working countenance. "Ah, I remember all now; he did not love *me*, he loved Hilary Duncan, and there was Maurice who loved me—and we parted! poor Maurice—and he was with him when he died—oh, papa—"

She threw herself on the ground at his feet, and laying her head against his knee, she shed the first tears she had wept for years. Her father kissed and caressed her fondly, making her tears flow faster and faster, until she had wept away the mist from her mind, the torpor from her faculties, and was reasonable, rational, and quiet.

Extreme exhaustion ensued; but by incessant care, and the most skillful treatment, her strength slowly returned, and with her strength came perfect memory and command of her faculties.

Slowly she learned to appreciate her position, to interest herself in her property, to assume her station as the mistress of "the Ferns," the widow of Charles Huyton; and when a year had passed away there remained no traces of her illness, except the steadiness and gravity which now marked her manners, in striking contrast with her girlish habits.

* * * * *

"Hilary, dear," said Dora Duncan one day to her sister-in-law, as they strolled together under the old lime-trees at "the Ferns," while Nest, a tall, graceful young woman, was playing with her little nephew, Maurice, "Hilary, why are you not happy?"

"Happy! I am, content, peaceful, happy, as one can be in this world, dear Dora."

"But you have none to love you *best*," said Dora.

"I have enough: you, Maurice, my sisters, and the children; I am rich in love, and loving hearts."

"And do they satisfy you?"

"No, I should be sorry if they did. Nothing of this world can, in itself: it is only as it partakes of the nature of Heaven, that it can fill the soul. But, Dora, the one whom I loved best in this world is at peace, his longing for perfection is satisfied, his hunger for righteousness is filled now; no sorrow can touch him, no pain, no trouble more; and I shall join him, I trust, at last. What else have I to wish for now?"

"Still, Hilary, it seems sad."

"Who, going through the vale of misery, use it for a well, and the pools are filled with water," continued Hilary; "do you remember what follows, Dora? My best treasure is safe, and for the rest, though I can joy and weep with you all, I can not attach my heart to earth again. But does my gravity distress you?"

"Oh no, no, no! you are not sad to look at, you are all love, and peace, and sympathy; what should we do without you?"

"That is my happiness, so far as earth is concerned, to love and to serve here below, in the hope that in my home above I may serve and love forever."